DRYADIA

A LAND IN WAITING

ROBIN HAYFIELD

First published in 2014

Editorial and Design Services by The Write Factor
www.thewritefactor.co.uk

For those who mourn a world
They barely knew
But have the imagination
And courage
To create a lighter one

CONTENTS

PRELUDE

PRELUDE

There is an ancient tradition that is sometimes known as The Great Tradition.

Its philosophy is based on freedom and responsibility.

Many thoughtful people and teachers of spiritual wisdom are drawn to the tradition, often unconsciously; and are guided by this great rising of love and happiness from the heart that is always connected with the universal life force.

If we fall in love then we can only fall so far.

But if we rise in love we can rise forever.

The knowledge can be hidden in code form to protect it, but it surfaces in the silence of our hearts, in our unconscious thoughts and dreams, and in the mythologies of numerous civilisations. It may be wrapped up and possibly distorted by time and ignorance. But it is always there for those who want to know.

The Tradition is a philosophical system of behaviour, knowledge and spiritual awareness. Its mission is to lift the darkness of ignorance from the minds of Men. It gives knowledge where it is needed, raising the human state by combating cruelty, fear, greed, tyranny and mindless worship.

It encourages understanding, creativity and awareness in order to promote soul evolution around the earth, and eventually to make it so beautiful, light and refined that the vibrations of our planet are raised.

In the Tradition there is no creed or dogma, no rules enforced, no books to read, no leaders and it is not part of any organisation.

It terrifies those who crave structure, rules, leadership and power; because it teaches that all of us are totally responsible for ourselves and for our actions. Its adversaries often try to destroy it in whichever way it manifests. But they can only harm individuals – The Tradition goes on.

Few orthodox religions or intellectual establishments can grasp that this great energy and deep spirituality, completely individual and unstructured and based on total freedom, has survived, and will continue to survive, all obstacles.

PART ONE

ACROSS THE DRANGLE

It is as if we Dryadians and our precious knowledge, had been parachuted behind enemy lines and left to await our inevitable destiny.

We have long realised that our greatest truths are beautiful and good and very simple, and seldom found in the institutions.
The magic is in ourselves.

We know that in Love we can live; but without Love there is no world that will not eventually destroy itself.

– SOPHORA

CHAPTER ONE

A LAND APART

Dryadia. A small independent country situated in the extreme southwest of Britain. Most of the country is surrounded by sea, but all along its eastern border with England Dryadia is protected by a large uninhabited forest ten miles deep, which has long kept it safe from invaders.

Dryadia is a closed country: one that has for the most part turned its back on visitors and our Western civilisation. The countryside is well forested and broken up by a number of rivers flowing from the high central moors to the broad estuaries of the northern and southern coasts. It is believed that the landscape has changed little in hundreds if not thousands of years, and the few visitors report scenery of extraordinary and untouched natural beauty, as is now seldom seen in Europe. The land is rich in animal and bird life with a breathtaking array of wild flowers.

Dryadia's estimated population is around 250,000, with about 20,000 living in Cantillion the capital and only large town. There are twelve smaller towns in Dryadia, each the capital of one of the twelve lesser provinces of the country. Cantillion is not only the capital of Dryadia but is, with its rural surroundings, its thirteenth and largest province. There are no extremes of poverty or wealth. Most of the population live in the countryside, concentrated in the many villages. They live simply off the land and its related occupations practicing a high standard of husbandry and self-sufficiency. There are no big industries, or motor vehicles.

There is no democracy, or elections, as we would understand it. The Dryadians are ruled by a mysterious philosophical caste known as the Dryads or Elders. There is little crime and there is no army or police force. No written legal system exists. Justice is dispensed and disputes settled by the Dryads, who are held in great esteem. Fairness and common sense are at the root of the law. The people are generally reported to be friendly.

Yet Dryadia, from a western point of view is a seemingly intolerant country. No orthodox religions are allowed although people are encouraged to meet together at regular intervals and sit or meditate in silence. Political parties are forbidden and indeed deemed unnecessary. Most administrative matters are debated and settled at a local level, at the traditional village meeting hall.

Education is very different to that of the English classroom. The accent is on debate, discussion and play learning. Textbooks are avoided if possible. There is a strong emphasis on learning by heart.. The syllabus is flexible and is geared towards practical matters; like learning about the unique Dryadian way of doing things, and living harmoniously with nature. Every child has seven years of free schooling. English is taught at the higher levels. There is one university at Cantillion, which is open to only a selected few. The Dryads who run it are inclined to be very secretive about what is taught there.

There are strong musical and literary traditions. Libraries are well stocked and free to all. In the towns, local theatres are very popular. There is no television or cinemas but various companies of storytellers travel the countryside in the summer months, a custom that is now virtually extinct in the rest of Europe. The common language is Dryadian whose precise origin is un-known, but contains many Greek, Latin and English words. The script is unique and indecipherable to an outsider.

Most Westerners would consider Dryadian agriculture very primitive. It is very labour intensive and no chemicals are used. Most of the heavy work is still done by horses. Wind and water mills are seen everywhere. There is plenty of fertile land but no one is allowed to own it. Land though, is readily leased freely and indefinitely to those who wish to cultivate it, or to build their unusual hexagonal houses upon it. Every village has a communal walled garden, sheltered from the worst of the elements and all Dryadians are entitled to their personal plots. Fields tend to be small and held in common and are surrounded by thick hedges. Dryadians keep few cattle and hardly any pigs, but there are many sheep providing wool for clothing and insulation, as well as milk and cheese. Most of the population are vegetarian although some people eat fish.

Medicine is equally backward, although the Dryadians claim to be very healthy. Healing is mostly in the hands of a group of people known as the Therapeutae who after many years of training, profess to have a deep understanding of the human psyche as well as a wide knowledge of plants and locally grown herbs. Another branch of healers are known as the Bonesetters, who concentrate on manipulative therapies. Almost all Western chemically based drugs, including immunisations, and many procedures that we take for granted, are regarded as suppressive and invasive and therefore to be avoided.

On a day-to-day level there seems to be a reasonable amount of personal freedom. The Dryads apparently believe that their beliefs are superior to those of most of the rest of the world. They base their opinions on the grounds that their system works; that the people are happy; and they live according to their interpretation of the laws of nature. They say that this philosophy is spiritually motivated ensuring that their way of living does no harm to either themselves or to their environment. It also encourages people to look towards the ideals of self-responsibility, honesty, non-violence, equality and simplicity. The Dryads say that kindness should be at the root of all action.

Hardly any visitors have stayed long enough in the country to comment on their claims. There is very little literature on the subject. Dryadian history is shrouded in the mists of time, as are the reasons the Dryads think the way they do. They state that their way of life has remained un-changed for aeons

The Dryads are concerned that outsiders would corrupt their sacred values and unique life-style, if their borders were opened. Very few visitors therefore are allowed in. They say that the beast in man lies just below the surface of consciousness, and having kept theirs controlled for so long they do not wish to welcome in anybody else's!

Dryadia is strange anomaly of a country that has played barely any part in the course of Western civilisation. It seems to pretend that the west simply does not exist. The people are quirky at best, with their refusal to reject what are the now outmoded concepts of their neighbours. For example they consider their system of measure is sacred, although it is actually based on the British foot and pound. They also have a curious attachment to numbers like three and twelve, which are still used in the divisions of their measurements and currency.

In fact the Dryads follow in the footsteps of Pythagoras and believe that numbers have a specific vibration or energy field and are at the root of everything. They look at what they describe as these various realms of energy from a point of view that is un-known to western science. They even employ homoeopathy as a mainstream medicine judging it to work on a level of fine energy, and therefore superior to our bio-chemical approach. For daily work they prefer to use the energy of human labour wherever possible. They like to avoid machinery that is any more advanced than a water mill.

The Dryadians may sound very quaint but more worrying is their refusal to embrace the political maturity of a fully-fledged western style democracy and the trade and material benefits that it would bring. The people seem to be unable to stand up to or reject the dictates of their leaders the Dryads, however benign they appear. It is extraordinary that Dryadia has survived in its present form for so long. A very big question mark must lie against its ability to hold out much longer.

EXTRACTS FROM VARIOUS ARTICLES WRITTEN ABOUT DRYADIA

By Samuel Shinks aged 15
CROYDON – SUMMER 1996

Sam's Dryadian journal continued to grow over the next few years. Although facts were few on the ground, that had not stopped a minor fascination on the part of the British press to run mostly inaccurate and largely speculative articles on Dryadia whenever they were short of material. Sam recorded anything of the slightest interest, and he had become quite an expert on the subject. Sam's other passion was nature, and it was that which had drawn him to investigate Dryadia and its apparently un-explored and mysterious wilderness in the first place. His journal served a dual role, incorporating his nature notes amidst the Dryadian ones, but written up in different coloured inks. A couple of years previously, his parents had given him some binoculars and a basic bird identification book, with the view of getting him out of his room into the fresh air and away from what they considered an un-healthy bookworm life style.

The ploy worked, and soon Sam was exploring the fields, woods, hedgerows and ponds that were found within a few miles of his home. There was one particular piece of land in his local neighbourhood that he regarded as his patch. It was the large abandoned garden of an old Victorian house with an attached scrap of woodland. Owing to a long legal dispute it had somehow escaped the builders. This was the place to which he had escaped unseen for the last two years. A place where he could pretend that he was safe in Dryadia, and where he liked to think that nature was protected against the insensitive and greedy eye of man. But a large hoarding had recently been placed in front of the house against the road.

Two-acre plot for sale. Available for housing development.

To Sam this meant the destruction of the now windowless and rotting potting shed where robins and wrens found safe corners for their nests and where field mice took shelter from the winter frosts. Soon the overgrown meadow that was once a lawn, which had not been mowed for a generation, would give up its wild yarrow, marguerites and dandelions – plants that shone for Sam like beacons amongst the greenery. The destruction would not just be for a season but forever. His precious wilderness would vanish and be replaced by little boxes of brick, and smooth swards of monoculture pesticide-soaked grass where even a daisy, unloved and half-poisoned, would find it hard to survive.

Sam questioned the old people who lived nearby about their dying past and they muttered somewhat mournfully in reply. "We mustn't stand in the way of progress. It might have been beautiful once but we're much better off now than we were when we were your age." He hated their impotence and their acceptance of the destruction of what he felt was beautiful and true. He came to loathe those three terrible words: development, progress and growth, for in his view they meant exactly the opposite. They meant the destruction of what he cared about more than anything else he could imagine.

Sam was a solitary child, a dreamer, safe and happy in his imaginary world. A world that he did not want to share with anyone else. He was quite capable of lying on his back in a field for most of an afternoon watching the skylarks soaring above him, singing that unforgettable bubbling song. He dreamed of how much nicer the world would be if there were no people in it, just nature. The word progress should indicate only how high the skylarks flew; development would describe the state of their nest building; and growth would be confined to measuring the size of the young chicks.

Sam was often at loggerheads with his conventionally minded middle-class father.

"No drive" he used to say. "No self-discipline, dead lazy, that's the problem. How are you going to make any thing of yourself in this tough world?"

Sam's competitive school echoed his father's words in his termly reports but he had ceased to mind, for his heart was already decided on his future career. One day he would be the warden of a wildlife sanctuary – perhaps even in Dryadia.

Sam's love of nature had brought Dryadia to his attention, but it was his bird book that fuelled his addiction. At that time he was not so interested in Dryadia's philosophy, except for their obvious respect for nature. It was the British distribution maps for each species, and the accompanying text in his bird guide that particularly fascinated him.

They might read: *Common throughout the region;* or *summer visitor only;* or *Passage migrant to British coasts in spring and autumn.* But sometimes an extra note was added such as *Dryadian status unknown;* or *Breeding in Dryadia likely but not confirmed;* or more often *More Dryadian information needed.*

It was these little addendums that frustrated Sam and confirmed how little outsiders knew about the Dryadian fauna and flora. There was certainly no modern book in English available, although there was possibly something published in Dryadian. But hardly anyone could translate the language.

In fact very little of consequence had been published on Dryadia on any subject. A few Victorian and Edwardian 'explorers' had written their memoirs before the country broke off most of its contacts with the West after the 1914-1918 World War. Unbelievably, much of our knowledge of Dryadia had come from that period. Subsequently, a small number of investigative journalists had managed to slip illegally into the country over the years, before being quickly deported. They reported little change. After that first Great War, the Dryadians decided that they quite liked their isolation from worldly horrors and only granted visas to a very few empathetic applicants.

Sam slowly came to realise that his own sense of isolation mirrored that of Dryadia and consequently he started becoming drawn to their philosophy and culture. When the time was right, his hope was that he might be granted one of those rare visas and be allowed entry into this mysterious land.

Another strand to Sam's journal were his speculative musings on what rare birds and animals lived undiscovered lives in the depths of the Dryadian countryside. These consisted of many lists but with many crossings out. He incorporated numerous maps of the country in great detail, mostly drawn straight out of his imagination.

In these maps there was hardly a square inch of cliff that did not have breeding pairs of ravens, choughs or Peregrine falcons. On the moorlands, curlews, harriers and buzzards were abundant. A highly speculative eagle was inserted here and there, with an unbroken lineage stretching back to the end of the last ice age. Even more exciting were the animals. The enormous forest on the border with England, trackless and impassable and untouched by an axe for many thousands of years, especially excited his creative mind.

Sam possessed a much-cherished book *Extinct Animals of the British Isles*. It was evocatively illustrated with pictures of snarling bears and wolves; a lynx motionless on a tree branch waiting to drop on an unsuspecting baby deer below; a beaver building a dam on a river; and a wild boar snuffling its way through the acorn harvest. Even lions, sabre-toothed tigers and huge mammoths with their plough shear tusks made their appearance. Could any of these animals be still living in the vast, secret Dryadian forests, perhaps unknown even to the natives? Well, sabre toothed tigers and mammoths might be stretching it a bit, but surely beavers and a few wolves should be possible or perhaps the odd bear still living in his lonely cave in an isolated part of the woods. So Sam's Dryadian maps became engraved with wolves and bears and any other beast that seemed even faintly plausible.

Sam kept his journal private. Like many sensitive children or teen-agers he couldn't bear to be teased. His father never ceased to mock him.

"Imagination never got anyone a good job. The Dryadians are beyond the pale. They didn't support us in the war, because like Ireland, they were neutral. That wouldn't have saved them if the Germans had won. As for now, they are un-democratic. No one has a vote, they're atheists, isolationists, and everyone is downtrodden and poor. They are a primitive and backward people."

It was not an argument that Sam had any hope of winning so he kept his thoughts and his imagination to himself.

CHAPTER TWO

THE DELEGATION

In early 1999, there were rumours that some Dryadians were becoming restless over their enforced isolation from what they called paradoxically 'The East'. Although no one could complain of repression or grinding poverty the people were becomingly increasingly aware of the material prosperity of their neighbours, and some wondered why some of those benefits should not be available to them too. There was a great debate amongst the Elders as to how they should respond, and diffuse a potentially difficult situation.

Eventually they decided to have some informal chats with their great neighbour and after a lengthy discussion with the British government they rather reluctantly agreed to invite a delegation of civil servants from London to visit Dryadia. They wished to hear their opinion on what steps, if any that could be taken to bring Dryadia closer to the outside world without compromising their unique life-style and traditions.

Many of the Elders thought London moved far too quickly and eagerly in reply. Before the summer was out, a delegation was installed in Cantillion. They planned to stay six weeks. The weather was unusually wet and as the civil servants felt nervous at the thought of travelling by horse drawn buggy on Dryadia's bumpy roads, they decided to avoid looking at the villages and towns in the provinces and confine their stay to the capital. The delegation enjoyed their time there, although the quiet and serenity un-nerved some of them. They missed the hustle and excitement of London. The Dryadians took great pains to make sure that they were comfortable. They had a lot of pride in their country and took plenty of trouble to explain to their guests how Dryadia worked, or rather as they put it, how it ran itself, as it had been so well designed in the first place.

When the British finally left, it was clear that although they considered Dryadia was an anachronism, a throwback to a previous age and something they really did not understand, they did have a sneaking regard for their peaceful and stress free way of life. However, politely and firmly they made one thing chillingly clear, even though they much regretted saying so. Basically, Dryadia had two choices. Either they joined the industrial family of nations willingly, or internal pressures would force them to do so unwillingly. The Dryadians only had to look at what had happened after the break up of the U.S.S.R. some years previously to see that they were right. There was no middle way, no compromise.

Sam was deeply upset when he read the final report. He felt that his dream had ended. He had put so much of himself into Dryadia, even though he admitted it still was not much more than a fantasy. He summarised the delegation's conclusions in his journal in red ink.

Dryadia should join the west and open its borders for trading purposes. It should embrace a market economy and allow the free migration of people and money to and from Britain and therefore by extension the European Union, A proper banking system needs to be introduced plus of course a convertible currency.

Its natural resources of tin, copper and other minerals need to be fully developed. The fisheries are rich and also need to be exploited. The country's outstanding beauty and especially its unspoiled beaches should be developed as a tourist attraction.

The people of Dryadia will provide its biggest resource – cheap labour. To enable Dryadia to do these things as quickly as possible, partnerships with large commercial companies should be sought out. The British government naturally would be glad to assist in all these matters.

A traditional western democracy should be established with universal franchise and independent political parties. The present unelected rulers, the Dryad Elders, should confine themselves to cultural and spiritual matters.

The country needs to develop an infrastructure: – modern roads linking the towns, and specially one through the Eastern forest linking Dryadia with England; hospitals and an efficient modern medical system with appropriate drugs; schools and a properly structured education system; a parliament and government department buildings; a judiciary with prisons and a police force; a T.V. station; market places like shopping centres. None of these exist at the moment and need to be built or created.

The country's land tenure and agricultural methods need to be reformed. Land should be owned, and bought and sold like any other commodity. Dryadia's farms are labour intensive and far too small. They needed to be enlarged and mechanised using modern fertilisers and pesticides. The process will mean a flight from the country to the towns. New dormitory towns will have to be built to accommodate these migrants and these will be the workers for the new industries.

In effect the delegation considered Dryadia an economic and political basket case, which was not surprising, as Dryadia possessed neither economics nor politics. The only remedy that they could suggest was some sort of absorption into the U.K. A good model might be a partially self-governing province like the Isle of Man or Jersey. It was impossible for them to suggest anything else. They acted according to their lights and could do no other. Dryadia was beyond their understanding. They were right on one thing though. There was no middle way. Dryadia would have to choose between two extremes. East and West could not be happily married.

Yet the delegation had to admit that in its own quaint and old-fashioned way, Dryadia worked. They saw no poverty or civil unrest. There was virtually no crime or drunkenness despite the lack of a police force. Everyone appeared to be healthy and well fed. There was no shortage of the basic necessities of life, although the same could not be said of those luxuries that were commonplace across the border. The Therapeutae seemed to cope well with moderate diseases although the delegation did not know what they did in more serious conditions. The children were well behaved and seemingly decently educated at a basic level but most could not be questioned because of their poor English. Social cohesion was high and a strong sense of community meant that everyone seemed to be cared for.

The Elders appeared to rule lightly, acted justly and honourably, and were selected for their lack of ego. They were not feared. In their own rather strange way they seemed to be intelligent and wise and were obviously well trained and educated.

However these observations were regarded only as anecdotal evidence. What the delegation wanted were facts. The fact was, that at least on paper, the Dryadians' economy and general standard of living was amongst the lowest in the world. Its GDP simply could not be measured. Moreover the scientifically accepted measurements of religious and democratic freedom were also off the map. Unfortunately Dryadia could only be officially classified as a tyranny!

After the report was published the British press and most of the big industrial corporations were in a frenzy. It was described as *The Last Big European Gold Rush.* Executives, especially from the tourist, mining and construction industries were falling over themselves to apply for cherished visas and view the last undeveloped piece of real estate in the western world. They dreamed of unspoiled beaches and pristine seams of tin and virgin forests. Dryadia would be for sale at last!

Yet the Dryadians wanted time to think. All the Elders of the country needed to be consulted. The British newspapers noted with glee that they didn't say anything about asking the common people. The British government was told to wait patiently for their decision. It might take a while.

Sam wrote all this down in his journal with a heavy heart. Dryadia had become his *Shangri La*, the paradise of his imagination and of his heart. He had noticed how in his own country so many of the woods and fields he had known and loved during his short life, had disappeared under building sites. He already knew how greedy men were, when there was easy money around. He knew exactly what would happen if they let the big corporations in. Could the Dryadians hold fast to their principles? Could he hold onto his faith in the best qualities of human nature, let alone his own sanity, if they didn't? The Dryadians kept quiet for many months. Sam liked to imagine their conferences and debates as they considered the report, willing them to come to the correct, and as far as he was concerned, the only acceptable decision.

Eventually the Dryadians sent a short letter to London. They thanked the delegation politely for their report and for their hard work. They had given due consideration to it. But they had to say that they were completely horrified. The ways of the East were not for them. They could not allow thousands of years of their unique history, their natural way of life, their spiritual traditions and their beautiful country to be destroyed in the name of greed and ignorance, and receive in return some materialistic benefits of which they had little need. They felt that they owed it to the world and themselves to preserve their precious knowledge, and carry this bright light safely into the future.

The British were appalled at what they called the Dryadians' stupidity, not to mention their arrogance. Sam though was over the moon. For some time there were no further comments from the Dryadians. Yet something was stirring in the country. The Dryadians had decided that they would after all like to engage with their neighbours, but on their own terms. They wanted to share a bit of their wisdom, which they believed to be both beautiful and true.

As a first step, they decided to allow a small number of like-minded people into their country to work in the villages and study at the university in Cantillion. They would be carefully selected to ensure that their hearts and minds were in tune with the Dryadian philosophy. A basic guide to

Dryadia would be published in English and sent to anyone who asked for it. Moreover, an application form for the new visa would be included inside.

On the day of his nineteenth birthday Sam wrote rather dramatically in his journal in green ink, the following –

I, Samuel Shinks, being out of love with my country and in despair at its continuing descent into ugliness and materialism, and wishing to follow only my heart in the future, have if accepted, decided to travel to Dryadia as soon as possible.

16th May 2000.

It was an easy decision. He had left school. No particular career or university interested him. His conventional parents found it hard to understand what motivated him. They were prepared to let him go. "He needs to get it out of his system. Then he will come back with his head cleared of all this nonsense."

So Sam filled in his application form to the Dryadian consulate and after a few weeks (they had been inundated by applications) received back an *Application for an Interview* form. It contained five questions for him to answer and rather strangely they also requested him to ask five questions of them. Based on the strength of his reply, an interview would then be arranged.

The five questions were simple and direct, although some were a bit quirky.

Q.1 Why do you want to visit Dryadia.

Sam's answer – To understand more about the Dryadian philosophy and way of life. I have kept a journal about it for the last six years. I am also interested in the natural history of your countryside.

Q. 2 Would you be willing to learn Dryadian.

A. Very willing

Q.3 Could you live in a country with no television, cars or telephone contact with the outside world and be happy with a much slower pace of life.

A. It sounds like heaven.

Q.4 Would you be able to live in a country where the silence is so deep and the night so dark that you believe that it is part of you.

A. More heaven.

Q.5 Would you be willing, when you are not studying at the university, to live and work hard in a small village, helping with the household and garden chores, the reaping and ploughing, and looking after the horses. In return you will have a comfortable warm bed, good wholesome food and plenty of time to dream and think.

A. Can heaven get better.

Sam hoped he had not been too flippant or brief in his replies but he guessed that the Dryadians were not looking for an intellectual approach. He decided that he would ask his own questions in a similar vein. Dryadia must be a very unusual country in that they wanted him to interview them.

1. What do we learn at the university.

2. Where did the Dryadians get their philosophy.

3. How have the Dryadians survived in their present state for so long.

4. Could outsiders ever rise to be Dryad Elders.

5. Are there wolves in the Great Forest.

It was six weeks before Sam had a reply from a member of the Dryadian consulate in Britain. He apologised for the delay in replying but they had had thousands of applications and it had taken a long time for him and his few staff to sort through them all. But he would be delighted to meet Sam as soon as convenient and would he phone to make an appointment?

The consulate was unfortunately a long way out of London but he would be met off the train. Accommodation would be arranged if he needed it. Sam did not remember such consideration when he applied for visas for other countries. But after all this was Dryadia, and it seemed more like a cottage industry than a normal country

CHAPTER THREE

THE STING

"Come in." The young man entered.

The room was densely panelled in dark oak giving it a solemn, intimidating feel. A high ornate ceiling only added to the formality of its gloomy atmosphere. The large Victorian windows bedecked in heavy drapes, looked down on the busy London streets clogged with the evening rush-hour traffic.

"So good of you to come and see me again." A middle-aged man immaculately dressed in a dark suit held out his hand. His demeanour, like his office, oozed authority. It was not to be questioned. He pointed towards the leather sofa.

"Please sit down. Coffee? Cigarette?"

"Both, thanks," said the young man.

"I hear that you have been accepted at the university. Without an interview. Amazing. Your fame travels before you."

"Well you asked me to apply at our last meeting. I was all set to be seen by the head of the consulate. But then he went on a long visit back to Dryadia. My application went through on the nod for some reason. I was born in Dryadia, so I suppose that helped."

"I am sure it did. But you have been only accepted for a year, I hear. On probation."

"You know a lot."

"That's my job. Now I need to explain some things to you. This is a private matter between her Majesty's government and yourself. You will have to sign the Official Secrets Act. Agreed?"

"Agreed." The older man leaned over to shake hands. "We have a deal. I have explained your remuneration. Two thousand pounds now. Straight to your bank. Another two thousand, when you report back to me. That's three months after you have started the course, subject to the information that you give me being useful. There will be a final two thousand pounds payable in one year at the end of the contract. If there are any leaks about your involvement then the whole thing is null and void. So you had better keep very close counsel indeed. Understand?"

"Understood. But what exactly is the information that you want?"

"What's going on in Dryadia? I'm not interested in their naïve philosophy or their traditions or their strange ways of healing or their poetry. Nor even in their agriculture or cottage industries. I am interested in their politics and what the people are saying in the streets. Is it true that there is some dis-satisfaction with their leaders, or perhaps a whiff of revolution in the air? What I particularly want to know as well, is more about their science. Is it just schoolboy stuff, as I am sure they would like us to believe? Or is it more sophisticated than that? What are they experimenting with? What are their boffins talking about? We suspect that a lot of them work and teach at the university. Get to know the professors and the older students. Talk to the girls. You're a good-looking young man. I'm sure you know how to get into a woman's heart if you find that she can be useful to you."

The phone rang quietly on the desk. The 'Boss Man' as the young man had dubbed him, or Mr B as he had asked to be called, picked it up, listened intently and merely answered, "I'll be there". He looked up and said. "I'm afraid you'll have to excuse me for ten minutes. Don't wander around. There are cameras everywhere."

Stephano Anders sunk back into the sofa and ruminated about his first visit a few months earlier. He was a moody young man and few would claim that they knew him well. When he was relaxed he could be charming and funny, turning every sentence into some kind of joke. But there was a dark perverse side to his character, which showed up particularly when he was unsure of his ground. Then those whom he crossed, found themselves looking into cold unprincipled eyes, and the humour that they once enjoyed changed into a cool passive aggression.

He had in fact only visited Dryadia occasionally in recent years although his mother had been born and raised in Cantillion. She had left the country early in her life after she met Stephano's father, who unknown to her had already been recruited in to the British secret service. After they married it was quite an easy transition for Charlie Anders to switch from spying on communist sympathisers in Britain to doing a bit of sleuthing in Dryadia, courtesy of his wife's passport. Gradually the work petered out for it seemed that nothing ever happened in Dryadia. The recent visit of the British delegation and its subsequent report had changed all that and the British authorities had contacted him again. He felt that he was too old to go 'active' again so he proposed Stephano, who was currently doing a little office work by day and a great deal of gambling at the cards at night, an occupation that he enjoyed immensely.

Stephano's father had accompanied him on that first visit.

"So nice to meet your father again," Mr B commented to his son. "He's done invaluable work for us over the years. Maybe you will emulate him one day."

Mr.B spent much of the time questioning Stephano about his life in England before gently switching the subject to Dryadia.

"You mean work for you." Stephano grinned awkwardly when he had finished.

"You would like to?"

"Yes." Stephano had been well briefed by his father that Mr B liked directness.

Mr B had moved his chair closer. "Then we may be able to come to an arrangement. I happen to need an agent in Dryadia, someone discrete, and someone who can play his cards close to his chest, as you do every night I understand. Above all it has to be someone whose loyalty is to us and not to any friends you might make there. We would pay you well of course. But no gambling. The Dryadians are rather puritanical about such things. And no getting drunk on Saturday nights. Could you live without that for a while?"

"Don't they have any fun?" A small frown played on Stephano's lips. "What shall I do for fun?"

"Do what the Dryadians do. Visit them in their homes. Go out with the girls. Lots of bracing walks. No cars as you know. Melt into the surroundings. Be as them. That is what a good agent does. You will be accepted and then of course no one will question who you truly are."

"So you want me to be a spy."

"I would never put it so crudely, but basically if you must be so direct – yes."

Mr B sighed deeply. Stephano asked too many questions.

"I would like the job", replied Stephano.

"You can have a trial. But there is a condition. Apply for the new university course at Cantillion starting in September. It's for non-Dryadians. Their new idea. Get accepted and you will probably have a job. My secretary will sort out the details."

Mr B rose and held out a rigid hand to both father and son.

"I hope that we will meet again soon."

Mr B's brisk business-like manner didn't upset Stephano. Sensitivity was not his middle name and he had a job he hoped, an exciting job. With a bit of luck the money might even pay off his gambling debts. Stephano held his head high with self-importance. He awoke from his reveries as Mr B opened the door and returned to his chair. Stephano was impressed when he realised that without pausing for breath, Mr B restarted the conversation exactly where he had left off ten minutes earlier.

"When we communicate we will use different names. I will be your uncle B. I will call you my boy. My boy in the country, Stephano in town. He smiled wanly. But then I don't suppose you understand the reference to *The Importance of being Ernest* do you. Education is not what it was."

"I was born in Cantillion. So, no." He smiled at his self-assurance.

"Ah, that would explain it. I assume you are still fluent in Dryadian."

"Brilliant. It's my mother tongue. I still have relations there. My brother used to go out with a Dryadian girl and I sometimes visited him."

"Indeed." Her Majesty's representative spoke with no emotion. Years of devoted duty had separated his head from his heart

"So the bottom line is that you want me to find out if the Dryadians are any threat to us. That is why you want me to go to Cantillion."

"Exactly. You may discover nothing and we may all sleep more peacefully in our beds if that happens to be true. Or you may find something interesting and we will deal with it in our own way."

He stood up. "Well, good luck my boy. I look forward to our next meeting. By the way, when you have a bit of time, see if you can locate Anaxamander the Consul to Britain. His Dryadian home is in Ceradoc in the north of the country. Go there too and have a root around. Though without drawing any suspicion on yourself of course."

CHAPTER FOUR

THE DRYADIAN CONSULATE

Anaxamander of Ceradoc, the Dryadian consul in Britain, generally led a quiet life in a comfortable old Georgian house, which had been a gift from the British after the Peace Treaty of 1792. In return the British had gained a nice house in Cantillion for their consulate, and both countries had agreed that they would leave each other alone and not give shelter to one another's enemies.

Since he had started on his tour of duty five years previously, Anaxamander had built up a good relationship with his opposite number in Cantillion. They both agreed, that because there was so little communication between their countries and therefore not much to do, and their deputies and their respective spouses did most of that, with a little stamp licking for their children, they could devote plenty of time to their other interests. In fact for Anaxamander, it was only a part time posting for he spent half of every year back in Dryadia, which he much preferred.

What work the consulate did do, was largely confined to keeping an eye on the English newspapers and issuing visas – mostly six hourly ones (the time spent in port) to the passengers on the twice-weekly boat to Trigonia, the small docks adjacent to Cantillion. Since the boat was basically a cargo one and only carried twelve passengers, the time spent on this duty was not demanding. The rest of the time was spent sending out a standard letter to other applicants saying that the boat was full. Since very few people qualified for longer visits the consulate was not particularly taxed by that duty either. His only other job was to care for a very small number of Dryadian exiles, many of who seemed to drop in for Sunday lunch.

Now everything had changed. Since the publication of the delegation's report and its subsequent rejection, the consulate had dealt with more than twenty thousand applications to visit the country. Almost all of these had been unwelcome, especially those in the category that included car dealerships, mining concessions and beach developments. Rejection letters were also sent out in large numbers to those who simply were interested in a quiet life and had no interest in the Dryadian philosophy or making a contribution to its culture.

In Anaxamander's eyes, only a very small number of applicants were deemed suitable for the three year Cantillion university course, where he had long been one of the principle teachers. It had been decided that that no more than about two dozen prospective students (Dryadians liked to count in twelves) would be interviewed. After studying a shortlist of the questionnaires, he eventually accumulated a neat pile of those he would like to see. Amongst them was the name of Samuel Shinks.

Sam had not been a great traveller todate apart from the odd overseas holiday with his parents and visits to his grandparents' smallholding. But he had often roamed the English countryside with his binoculars around his neck, and occasionally slept rough when he wanted to experience the dawn chorus or get a glimpse of badgers. Although he was not always confident with strangers, he was so with adventures.

His parents had agreed to fund his journey to the consulate, but he had made all the arrangements himself and would travel alone from Paddington to the west of England where the Dryadian consulate was. He had been told that a large hairy man with a blue cloak, a big laugh and a hat with a raven inscribed upon it, would meet him at the station at the other end.

"Quite unmistakeable" was the comment on the phone.

He was indeed quite unmistakable and soon after he had left the train Sam was having his hand shaken with great warmth and verve by Anaxamander himself.

"Now we must find the other two." He explained to Sam that if all went according to plan they would be his companions on the trip to Dryadia. They looked around and were quickly spotted by a striking willowy girl with long red hair dressed in a flowing multi-coloured caftan.

"Mary" she announced in a Welsh accent. She was a vivacious woman, perhaps a few years older than Sam. She was inclined to sing her sentences rather than to speak them, and those at almost twice the speed of anyone else's. For this, Sam was truly grateful as it more than made up for his own temporary shyness. In her wake was a tall serious man in his mid twenties, a bit overwhelmed as he waited for this female whirlwind to pause to take breath.

"And this is Pushkin," Mary informed them, "We met on the train amazingly."

Pushkin reached forward to shake hands, eager to assert his authority over his identity and deny that he was from Wales.

"I caught the train at Bristol, lovely journey, time to read, until I met Mary."

He looked at her intently, with a twinkle of resigned amusement.

Anaxamander twiddled with his car keys. "About an hour's drive to the consulate. The British were too mean to give us a place in town! Still we are all friends now, though there used to be a few battles in times past." He laughed loudly, but kindly. "Not that I would like to live in this noisy city. The best thing about it is the view that you get from the stern of the boat as it leaves from the port here to Dryadia. Here's the plan for today. Lunch first. I expect you are all famished. We can get to know each other during the drive there. I suppose that's a part of the interview. Then I will interview you all separately. Then tea. Then home. I'll make sure you'll all be on the last train back as none of you asked to stay."

The consulate stood in a large garden that looked more like an old vicarage than a diplomatic outpost. Anaxamander had shepherded them into the comfortable kitchen dominated by a well-used twelve-foot long pine table.

"I'm afraid my wife Ruth is away this week. Could you bear beans on toast?"

Sam was the first to be called for his interview. Anaxamander scanned his questionnaire and said he was impressed by both his answers and his questions.

"I've had to check on the wild animals though. We've definitely got wild boar in the Great Forest of Dreagle. That's the big one that borders your country. There are beaver on some of the rivers, and plenty of otter too. I've often seen those on the estuary where I live. We protect our animals well. No guns or poisons, so we live and let live. I don't think we've had bears for a thousand years, though it would be good to think there could be still a few holed up in some remote cave. The last wolf was seen in the 18th century, killed off before the treaty

I'm sorry to say that us Dryadians were not always as peaceful as we are today. That only happened when we felt safe from outsiders. Then we destroyed all our weapons."

His voice was suddenly drowned by the sound of a strimmer next door, buzzing like a thousand angry wasps.

"That's one bit of torture that you won't hear in Dryadia, nor overhead planes or pneumatic drills for that matter." He got up to close the window. "Should only last a few minutes. The guy's probably just seen a dandelion! Too lazy to bend down and pull it up by hand."

"You told us in the car that you would explain who the Dryads were," questioned Sam.

"Well, there are many groupings, but the ones we are interested in right now are called the Traditional Elders. They are sometimes known as Cantillion Dryads. These Elders are all spiritually minded and have trained at the university with the responsibility for maintaining our traditions. They ensure that there is justice for all.

Our university, as you will find out, is completely different from the ones in the East. We are not interested in training you for the job market. In fact there is no job market. It is partly an academy of natural philosophy, both for science and the imagination; partly about learning how very powerful us humans are, and discovering how to use that power wisely; and partly a de-mystifying school where we learn to let go of our prejudices. We have a saying that in order to find out who you truly are you first of all have to discover who you are not. We search for the truth that lies hidden between the great pillars of observation and imagination. Life will not be the same again after three years at Cantillion, I promise you."

Sam's eyes glowed with attention. He did not dare ask any more natural history questions, in case Anaxamander thought he had a one-track mind. But Anaxamander had the gift of making people feel comfortable and Sam soon found his shyness quickly melting away. Anaxamander drew the conversation back into his derelict Victorian nature garden in Croydon and shared his anger at its destruction in the name of development and progress. He agreed strongly with Sam's opinion that the words meant just the opposite.

"What a way to run a country. Like the dark ages. Too much greed and too many people. How can you buy and sell land? It belongs to itself, like air and water. Typical of the ways of the East. They are going to attract big trouble one day if they don't mend their ways and harmonise themselves with nature.

I will tell you a story, Sam. It happened last year in this village, next door to the man with the strimmer, so only a stone's throw from the consulate here. There is a small patch of open land, about an acre in area. It's beautiful, though much of it is scrub. The villagers go blackberrying on its edges every year in late summer. It's an impenetrable place and I have been told that it has been like this for at least seventy years. I hear many birds singing there in the spring including blackcaps and whitethroats. My cat goes hunting inside this prickly sanctuary, though obviously not with the approval of the blackcaps and whitethroats.

It has always been considered to be common ground belonging to everyone. The trouble was that in this case, unbeknown to all of us, the land did belong to someone. In fact, to a very famous and extremely rich person who was responsible to no one but himself. His company decided to sell the land to a developer by the name of Charlie Anders, a local man. We had no idea that this had happened until we were sent a notice from the local planning authority informing us that Mr Anders had applied to clear the land that we had enjoyed for generations and that he wanted to build a small block there containing an office and a few workshops. The plans showed it to be ugly and functional, and it was obvious that it would do nothing for the village.

A petition was drawn up. Virtually everyone in the village signed it. The parish council opposed the plans. So did the Council for the Protection of Rural England and the local Wildlife Trust. A date was set for the hearing at a town about thirty miles away. Far too far away for the planners who were sitting in judgement to have any local knowledge. Our petitions were forwarded. Mr Anders for his part promised jobs and made a plea for the small struggling businessman. He was amongst friends. On a show of hands the plans were passed by a group of people who like him, almost all had a business background themselves. They were people who had barely heard of the village and who had no knowledge or care for nature. It was dispiriting and extremely disempowering for the people who live here. And the East dares to lecture us about democracy!

What was even more galling was that I already knew Mr Anders, though our paths did not cross often. I knew him because his wife Ena is a Dryadian. She often used to come to the consulate Sunday lunches though she has not had the nerve to show her face recently. Mr Anders is very unpleasant man who is not welcome in Dryadia.

Ena of course, we cannot stop for she was born there. Nor can we stop their equally unpleasant sons who were also born there and occasionally cross the border, and whom we believe stir up trouble in Cantillion. Sadly, we are likely to hear a lot more about those two young men especially the younger brother whose name is Stephano."

"The enemy within," exclaimed Sam. "But what happened to the land?"

"Well, they cleared it as soon as they got consent, breaking all our hearts as they did so. It has left a big hole in the middle of the village. But nothing was built. Then Mr Anders put in another application, this time for a mobile phone mast. We got fresh petitions together, submitted them and were once more ignored. He can build his mast. For a week or so there was a lot of scurrying around by officials measuring things up.

When Ruth and I were away, they knocked on our door and asked to do some soundings from the upstairs windows. Unfortunately they were let in. Ruth thinks they have put in bugs. I suppose that's possible, now that we Dryadians have drawn attention to ourselves and put our heads above the parapet. We had a good search but nothing was found. We even asked the police. They sent in Special Branch, who gave us the all clear. Then the men in suits went away. That was four months ago. There is still no sign of the mast going up and what is more, no sign of Mr Anders either. It's all very puzzling. We have a suspicion that the British government has a finger in this particular pie but we can't prove anything. There are rumours that Anders has run out of money. Let's hope so. None of this could ever happen in Dryadia, I assure you. All decisions are taken at a local level and the protection of nature is always a priority.

Sam was thoroughly enjoying his interview with Anaxamander and his avuncular manner. For almost the first time in his life he felt understood and that he had met a kindred spirit. He was so relaxed that he even asked Anaxamander a little about himself. He had such a perfect English accent that he wondered whether he was really a Dryadian.

"I'm a mongrel", was the reply. "My father is Dryadian, my mother is English. My wife is English too, but she is Dryadian in spirit, which is all that matters. I've spent many years living in England and still partly do of course. It is the best qualification to spy on you all. I am saved by diplomatic immunity. Just joking of course.

My home is in Ceradoc, a village in the north of Dryadia on an estuary not far from the sea. It's wild and beautiful. You'd love it there, Sam. The estuary is crowded with waders and ducks. Ravens and buzzards breed there, almost in my garden. I don't like to be away very long. We would all go mad if we didn't spend at least half the year there."

He looked at the clock ticking peacefully on the wall. "Sam, we must stop. I have to talk to Mary and Pushkin. You've passed your interview, though. Welcome to Dryadia. Be patient. There are lots of arrangements to be made. The wheels of Dryadia turn slowly."

Pushkin went in next, leaving Mary and Sam to talk in the consulate's slightly overgrown garden. A black cat examined Sam sleepily from the back of one of the chairs, with Mary's extended hand stroking it absent-mindedly. She examined his collar and said. "You know he's your namesake, Sam. Meet Sam, Sam."

"I thought he looked familiar." Sam felt at a loss to say anything more intelligent, and wondered if it was the same cat that used to hunt in the patch of land that Anaxamander had just been describing.

"Or your familiar?' But her meaning flew past him. Mary stared intently at him and then found it hard to contain herself any longer. "Well, how did you get on? Was he as friendly as at lunchtime?"Sam grinned happily back. "Yes he was very friendly. We talked a lot about nature and lots else. He grilled me about my life, but it wasn't really and interrogation, more like a nice chat. Then he said I've passed. I've been invited to go to Dryadia."

Mary squealed, threw up her hands and kissed Sam hard. Sam blushed hard in return. He wasn't used to these displays of exuberance! "He hasn't set a date though. The wheels of Dryadia turn slowly, apparently. But I've waited for this for the last seven years, so suppose I can wait a little longer." Mary became serious again. "I'm going to pray very, very hard that Anaxamander gives me a visa as well. I have been waiting a long time too. Sam, I must tell you my story. It's a very romantic one. I've been dreaming of going to Dryadia all my life. Look, you are not going to believe this but my Welsh great grandfather was a fisherman and there was this terrible storm and his boat was shipwrecked on the north coast of Dryadia. It's like a Shakespeare play. It was't a mermaid that rescued him exactly, but a young lady from a local village most certainly had a hand in it. She took him in, fed him up, married him and the result was my grandfather.

Then the First World War started, and the family returned to Wales. He died in the trenches and then my great grandmother died of grief. My grandfather was too young to return to Dryadia. He spoke a little Dryadian though and a few words have travelled down the generations to me."

Mary smiled and cradled the cat and sang softly in a language that seemed to be slightly familiar now and then but didn't really fit into any tongue that Sam had ever come across. "There, my mother used to sing it to me. It's a lullaby as you might have guessed. I think Dryadia is in my blood, though I've never been there. Sometimes I dream vividly about it as if I was actually there, several times a month if I am lucky."

Sam became increasingly amazed at Mary's ephemeral chatter delivered at extraordinary speed. He longed to tell her about Anaxamander and Mr Anders but it was hard to fit it in. On the one hand he was entranced by this human Catherine wheel, warm and enchanting as if she had just stepped out of *The Sound of Music*. But her conversation about Druids and dreams and healing by touching people, words that tripped so readily off her tongue, left him bemused. These subjects were so far out of his experience, let alone his reading, that he decided to mentally create a very large pending tray called 'stuff to be considered later.' Mary was filling this at great speed and although he understood only a little of what she said, he basked under the torrent of kindness emanating from this elfin sprite and what he fervently hoped was 'real wisdom'. Two kindred spirits in one day! Why had he not come across these people before in Croydon?

Pushkin moved quietly into the garden and sat beside them. There was no time for Mary to question him for Anaxamander was beckoning her in from the window. Pushkin and Mary were polar opposites. He talked slowly, each word measured as if he was savouring a precious wine. He told Sam that he was accepted. Sam told him that he was too, and Pushkin unleashed a hand from his long frame and they solemnly shook hands. Formalities over, Pushkin started, with genuine interest, to ask Sam about his life although to a casual listener it sounded a bit like that he was ticking the boxes on a questionnaire. Responding as best he could, Sam tried hard to describe the world of nature as he saw it, but felt increasingly inadequate as, apart from a basic knowledge of Dryadia, that seemed to be all that he knew.

Pushkin on the other hand knew a lot. He had a degree in philosophy and sociology and had been a researcher for a prestigious journal. Unlike Sam though, he did not know the difference between a starling and a blackbird or how to locate Sirius in the winter sky. His gifts were intellectual and although he appeared a bit emotionally distant at times he was a kind man, open to new ideas, with an extremely dry sense of humour. Pushkin had studied many types of societies during the course of his career and that had inevitably led him to the borders of Dryadia. To him Dryadia was an extraordinary phenomenon and would have seemed implausible if he did not know that it already existed. But it did exist, and he needed to know how.

As he and Sam spent their time together in the garden exchanging their theoretical Dryadian knowledge and wondering what delights might be in store for them, Mary bounded out, squeezed both their arms, crying excitedly.

"I'm in, I've been accepted. I can't believe it. And Anaxamander wants us all inside immediately for tea and crumpets before the children arrive home from school and eat them first."

Anaxamander was beaming.

"Three year visas agreed all round then, assuming you survive the five hour voyage to Trigonia in our little Dryadian leaky bucket of a boat first. We sail in about a month. That should give you enough time to prepare."

"The boat's quite safe?" asked Pushkin, his face looking paler than usual.

Mary, the sea still in her genes, looked at him comfortingly.

"Oh, don't worry, Pushkin, Sam can steer by the stars, if we get lost."

"And by the curlews' call if we go too close to the shore", added Sam, trying his best to impress."

CHAPTER FIVE

CANTILLION

Anaxamander was as good as his word. Instructions were sent in good time, and once more he had agreed to meet them off the train. It was early April. Spring was in the air but the weather was grey and wet. A forceful westerly that could only have been nurtured in the Atlantic possessed a vigour that could not be ignored.

Anaxamander wrapped his enormous arms around them with a huge smile and his usual exuberance. "We'll catch the bus to the docks. It will only take ten minutes and that's where we will find *The Leaky Bucket* waiting for us. It's the pride of the Dryadian navy, and indeed its only ship. Don't worry, its unsinkable. We have a pact with Poseidon. We ancient Greek philosophers are privileged in these matters. Pushkin understands. He has an unusual name too. But he's assured me that he is not going to emulate the sticky end of his illustrious Russian namesake. I'm coming with you by the way. My family have already gone ahead."

"What happened to your namesake, Pushkin," questioned Mary.

"He was killed in a duel when he was only thirty nine. My father loved his poetry. Pushkin was Russia's national poet and I'm named after him"

"My neighbour had a cat called Pushkin. He came to a sticky end too, but I don't think he was poetically inclined." Mary looked at Pushkin's strained face and wished she hadn't said it. She resolved to be more serious with him in the future.

All Dryadians knew the boat affectionately as *The Leaky Bucket*. It really wasn't as bad as Anaxamander's dark humour had portrayed. *The Three wise seekers from the East* as he now collectively described them, found themselves on a sturdy converted fishing boat. It was not modern, but it was well maintained and freshly painted. It also had, its passengers noted happily, plenty of lifebelts.

Apart from the three-man crew, the only other passengers were a warmly wrapped Dryadian family returning home. Mary listened intently to their chatter to see if she could make some sense out of it. Her smattering of the language needed quite a bit of work, she decided. What they all noticed, was the respect that everyone seemed to have for Anaxamander. There was no doubt that he was quite an authority figure.

They chugged slowly out of the gloom of the sound with the wind in their faces. Behind them were the great docks and the moored warships of the British navy and further back still, the faceless blocks of the city. As they turned starboard towards the open sea, the lights of England were swallowed up in the mists and were exchanged for the darker mysteries of the Dryadian shoreline. No buildings beckoned them as they crossed the mouth of the estuary of the thirty-mile river Drangle whose length marked most of the border between Dryadia and Britain. A little later the outline of the Forest of Dreagle loomed across the sea, only a mile away on the right hand side. They sailed past leagues of steep cliffs, on top of which was a skin of the faint greenish brown tracery of the winter trees, barely touched by spring. The forest looked dark and forbidding over the grey swell of the sea.

"Dreagle and Drangle". Anaxamander explained. "Many of our poets have used those two beautiful words when they have described the woods and the river. Humans have barely touched the forest for five thousand years. It protected us from the peoples of the East. That's why it was never logged. Now we regard it as a nature sanctuary, the biggest natural forest in Europe I believe. It is largely pathless and virtually impenetrable except to a few trackers who know how to reach the old sacred places that are contained within it.

In the old days our enemies tried to cut through it but they never succeeded, for the Dryadians had scouts everywhere and were masters of the ambush. Other invaders tried to come by sea to land in one of the many coves. Then we had other ways of dealing with them"

"Like how?" Sam's imagination was on fire but he asked his question respectively for he was also sensing that Anaxamander was not just the big cuddly bear that he sometimes pretended to be.

"That's a story in itself," was the reply. "Nature did most of the managing. We'll teach you more in our history lessons. You will be amazed by Dryadia's history. It's an extra-ordinary story."

Mary was quietly thinking of her great grandfather. He must have been lucky to survive.

After more than an hour's sailing on what was quite a choppy sea, the line of forest started to thin although the trees never completely disappeared. Anaxamander had already explained that a lot more than half of Dryadia was covered in woodland and moors and left to nature. The gaunt cliffs were now not so high and sandy coves and rocky inlets were beginning to appear. The occasional village came into view but they were too far away to make out any details, though they noted flashes of colour – yellow, red and orange and other bright hues. The boat stayed well out to sea, avoiding the dangerous rocks submerged just off the shoreline. These rocks were particularly treacherous during a sudden storm, and they had saved Dryadia from invasion many a time. So many disasters had happened to the English ships in the distant past that eventually they came to believe that the country was the abode of witches, a delusion the Dryadians were in no hurry to dispel.

The wind and rain were now abating and a watery sun was growing stronger in an apricot sky. They were alone in the sea, for foreign boats were not allowed in Dryadian coastal waters without special permission, and the small Dryadian vessels, most of them sailing craft, stayed safely in port in rough weather. The skies over Dryadia were also empty. There was no noise or even vapour trails, for all the planes of the East had to make detours around Dryadian airspace.

As the sea calmed, Sam had his binoculars at the ready, his spirits raised at the sight of cormorants and groups of oystercatchers flying close by. A little later he almost gasped with delight as a gannet, its six-foot wingspan furled over its back, dived like an arrow towards its unsuspecting prey beneath the sea. He was also keeping an eye out for dolphins but Anaxamander had explained they were usually seen in calmer weather. Huge Basking sharks were seen off the north coast in the summer although Anaxamander assured them that they were plankton eaters and that they spat you out quickly if you fell into their jaws!

The Leaky Bucket was primarily a cargo boat. On this voyage it was carrying a consignment of second hand washing machines, bought for next to nothing in England. Anaxamander raised his voice above the wind. "We are a low tech country, but we do like our creature comforts. We take no pleasure in backbreaking work but nor do we want to pollute our land with heavy industry. So we import these old machines from England and do them up. They would only go into landfill in your country, so your authorities are only too glad to find a home for them. They may not be the latest models, but they are highly serviceable once our engineers have taken them to pieces, made a few new parts, polished them up and re-assembled them. You would think them as good as new. The result is that every family in the land is spared as much drudgery as possible. Most of the washing machines are placed in the community building, which every village has. There will often be some deep freezers there too, as well as large baking ovens, for bread making is usually a social activity. We are a very resourceful and friendly people and no one is a lonely slave to the kitchen if they don't want to be."

Eventually the sun broke fully out in the south western sky, and the swell turned from grey to green in the ever-increasing light. More than three hours had passed since they had left England and the pilot now changed tack to the north towards the mouth of a great estuary. Grey streaks of land began to appear on both sides of the boat. Its passengers, wrapped warmly in their thick coats, stood transfixed at the prow. Occasionally they moved from one side to the other and back again in order to absorb every new sight as the streaks gained definition, Their excitement grew increasingly palpable, as the realisation dawned in them that they were not only entering a new country but crossing the threshold of a new world. They were about to encounter a way of life that existed nowhere else on the planet.

Sam had one eye on the exposed sandbanks where shelduck and curlew were resting, until the rising tide forced them to fly to fresh feeding grounds. Mary strained her eyes, when she hadn't managed to prise Sam's binoculars out of his hands, trying to obtain glimpses of the locals in their cottage gardens and wondering what kind of clothes they were wearing. Pushkin stood trance-like and open mouthed as his greatest dream was turning into reality.

Then they noticed Anaxamander's pointing finger, directed at a small group of buildings right ahead of them.

"Trigonia. Our journey's end. It means the port of the three berths" he announced. "That's where we will dock, and unload the cargo. We can walk to Cantillion from there. It's virtually next-door. We can stay in the university hostel. The students are on vacation at the moment, so there's plenty of room for us all."

As they stepped ashore, it seemed that every gull was crying its welcome and every Dryadian child's curiosity was directed at the strange attire and language of these visitors from the East. Dryadians loved colour. It showed not only in their houses but also in their clothes, which looked back to a previous age with voluminous layers and flowing shawls for the women, and tunics and trousers for the men. But as Mary remarked. "No silly top hats or bonnets, or anything to trip over."

As they already knew, the houses were normally two storied and hexagonal. They seemed almost round. The windows and doors also were unusually shaped, round or arched, often with coloured glass. A cupola, looking like a tiny lighthouse, crowned most of the rooftops. Because of the risk of fire, almost all the houses in the narrow streets were built in stone although the opposite was true in the countryside, where wood was generally preferred. The whole effect was like a colourful overgrown village and rather charming. As Anaxamander pointed out, every thing was built to human scale. Even the public buildings were no higher than three stories. Equality was paramount in Dryadian thinking and therefore no house was allowed to dominate any other, although in the details no holds were barred. Only in the meeting halls and in public buildings was there a little grandeur, but even that was always displayed with grace and a lightness of touch.

As they walked the few hundred yards into Cantillion proper they saw that many houses were grouped around tiny open squares which usually included a fountain or a well and a tree or two in the middle. Large terracotta pots stood before each home with spring daffodils rising up amidst the lavender, rosemary and fuchsia whose blooms were still to come. The whole town glowed care and friendliness. There were no extremes of rich or poor, or signs of the throwaway society that the three of them had left behind. It was so quiet. There were no cars or lorries or tarmaced roads, although the streets were neatly paved. Horses and wagons were plentiful but animals were not allowed to foul the streets. A bag was tied under the tail of every horse before it was allowed to enter town!

Mary in particular was relieved to discover some shops, although there were no high streets as such. Shops were scattered amongst the houses. They were usually of a practical nature, selling food and hardware or doing repairs. Tins or packaged goods were rare. It was of course clothes shops that she was really on the look out for. There were not many though, for as she learned later most garments were made at home where every family had a loom in the back parlour.

However there were plenty of places to eat. Anaxamander said he would take them out for supper once they had settled into their rooms at the hostel.

"It's called *The Crazy Duck*, if you translate from the Dryadian. They won't serve duck or any other meat for that matter, for almost all of us are near vegetarians. But as you will see, the walls are covered with pictures and cartoons of ducks, even in the most unlikely places. Guaranteed to put you off ducks for life!"

After coffee they settled down to chat. ("You mean you can get coffee in Dryadia," exclaimed Mary, rolling her eyes in mock surprise).

Anaxamander laughed. "Of course. We take our homegrown herbal teas to England and barter them for tea and coffee or whatever we need. All our food is exceptionally pure for it is grown in unpolluted soils without any chemicals or poisons. There's quite a market for it in England, where the emphasis is usually on quantity not quality."

Pushkin had not spoken much during the meal although he had listened intently to every word that had been discussed.

"I have a burning question," he finally announced. "I can see that Dryadia works in Dryadia. We're already very impressed and I know that we still have a lot to see. I realise that you might like us one day to export your knowledge back to the East. I don't want you to think me rude but I don't think it will work there. We are too far-gone in materialism. Our most important values are generally based on getting and spending."

"Ah!" Anaxamander sighed contentedly "Getting and spending, we lay waste our powers. Wordsworth! I do love the English Romantic poets. Our university students are asked to memorise all the best lines. In English too. But do go on."

Pushkin continued. "Perhaps one day if our civilisation collapses, which is more than likely as it is un-sustainable, some of us may be attracted to the Dryadian way of doing things. That is if we don't all kill each other first. So, us being here, what's in it for you, if you forgive me for being so blunt? The delegation called Dryadia a basket case in their very narrowly defined terms but had to reluctantly admit that it worked from your point of view. I'm sure that you would consider in return that the East is a fruit and nut case, and all three of us would largely agree with you, or we wouldn't be here. Most people in the East would say that that their countries worked too."

"It is a good question," replied Anaxamander. "I agree with you that the East will not change unless they are forced to. That sadly will mean that you will almost certainly have to have some form of catastrophe first. It's our belief that there are a small number of Easterners like you, who are very aware and who have a good understanding of the important things in life. They will be attracted to living simply and naturally, like us. When the time comes, we hope we will be able to help them to salvage something valuable from the wreckage and to rise from the ashes of their world. I want to tell you a story that might help you.

As you know, I grew up and still live in a village called Ceradoc. When I turned eighteen, and needed a bigger jungle to roam in, but was not old enough to go to the university, my father suggested that I renovate a derelict cabin next to the family home and cultivate the land around it. It was not very big; perhaps half an acre, and it had all gone to waste. In fact no one alive could remember when either cabin or land were last used.

During the winter a group of friends and I refurbished that cabin, all six sides of it. It looked like a mini version of our house. It is a Dryadian tradition that all able bodied persons in the community help in the building of each other's homes. We insulated and panelled it within, painted it and put on a new slate roof. I furnished it simply. I just had a bed, a table and a couple of chairs. A wood burning stove with a cooking ring on top kept me both snug and warm and helped fill my belly with good food. I got my water from the rain barrel under the eaves. With so many hands the cabin was finished in a week.

Then I borrowed one of the village horses and a plough and cleared the whole area in a day. I had more cultivated land than I needed so I planted only half of it, the west side. I sowed potatoes, carrots and onions. I had a cabbage patch and a row of beans. I grew herbs around the cabin door, which faced south. Herbs that enjoyed the full sun like thyme and parsley, lavender and rosemary, mint and marigolds, most of which I could use in my cooking. There were two old apple trees, an eating one and an ancient sour one. I pruned the old stems back and they rewarded me nine months later with a wonderful crop.

Then there was the east side of the garden. I left this alone. I didn't need any more food. The west side did well over the following year and I had plenty of fresh fruit and vegetables. But the east side, the wild part, my little nature sanctuary completely astonished me. For although the expected thistles, nettles and dandelions appeared in profusion, the greater part turned into a poppy field. Not just great swathes of our common red ones. Their glory was miracle enough. But amongst them were the oriental poppies, the lilac ones with a black splash at the base of the petals, which can provide opium when grown in hot countries. These were much bigger than the red ones and dominated them, for some of them were five or six feet tall.

All summer I lived amongst the poppies. Except when they invaded my crops, I left them to grow as they pleased. I blessed them every hour of the day. Now, poppies like to grow on disturbed land so that their tiny seeds are brought as close to the sun as possible, in order for them to germinate. I did not sow those seeds. They had waited in the darkness of the earth biding their time for at least half a century. That was the last time the seeds had been exposed to the sun. Waiting for someone like me to clear the wilderness and bring them into the light. Amazing isn't it. From out of the battlefield of the plough comes this incredible beauty."

Anaxamander paused, almost over come by the emotion of his own story and the memories it engendered. At last Sam broke the silence. "So you think we are like those poppy seeds."

"Exactly," replied Anaxamander. "It's as if we are all biding our time, watching and waiting for you to blossom and spread your light. You can't fail for it's your destiny."

The next day Anaxamander left them on their own and told them to wander around Cantillion as they choose. "Whenever you are hungry pop into *The Crazy Duck*. They have instructions to fatten you up. In two days we will travel to Ceradoc together."

Cantillion was endlessly fascinating to Sam, Pushkin and Mary and the people of Cantillion found them equally so. Word had got around that they were the forerunners of what was becoming known as *The Great Experiment*, the Dryadian initiative to share and promote their knowledge. The three of them had in part been selected for their easygoing nature and their ability to adapt to such a different culture. The Cantillions for their part, having lived peacefully in a non threatening environment for over two hundred years and being fully at ease with themselves, found no difficulty in embracing them wholeheartedly whenever their paths met.

The town's children took particular delight in tagging along behind them as if they were a collective *Pied Piper of Hamelin*. Mary especially delighted in playing grandmother's footsteps with them, stopping and starting suddenly and pointing in mock excitement at any children she discovered moving before they had time to freeze themselves to the spot. Soon the children were running ahead trying to herd them into their houses. Even Sam forgot his diffidence and became a willing victim of the children's games.

Cantillion did not seem to have much of a ground plan other than the great main square and the four arterial roads that divided the town into quarters. Within the quarters it was possible to get lost, but not for too long as the town was not that big. Given time they would soon find themselves back in the main square or at their hostel on one of the main streets. Anyway, time not being important, they were quite content to follow the children wherever they led them. The adults too were friendly, but understandably had to force themselves to stop pointing and staring. However many Cantillions, at least those who had enjoyed a higher education, spoke some English and the three of them often found themselves gently ambushed and questioned continually about their life in the East.

Every house was a gem, almost always built in the familiar hexagonal shape and painted in strong bright colours. Yet no house was quite like another. They were invited inside several times. Homes were usually panelled in pinewood throughout and so always looked and felt warm and cosy. A central spiral staircase connected the two floors. The rooms on the upper floor opened out onto an internal circular balcony that looked down over the largely open plan area below, and upwards to the glass cupola. Dryadian homes were not only warm but also extremely light. Their walls were triple insulated, usually with straw bales or sheep's wool. Great attention was paid also to draught proofing, using triple glazed windows.

A small factory in Cantillion produced these essential units in assorted shapes and sizes. Hot water was pumped under ground through pipes from a localised power source that served each neighbourhood. Electricity was wired in as well from the same local micro-power station, but as it was not always plentiful it was used with great care mainly for lighting and cooking. As kitchens were simply equipped and televisions, computers and other electronic equipment, (the baubles of the East as Anaxamander called them), were absent, a low powered life was not a great hardship. The prime power sources were derived from sun, wind and water as well as wood and charcoal. Dryadians had given a great deal of thought to sustainable energy, using water and windmills, heat exchange pumps and extremely efficient wood burning boilers. Another small factory was beginning to make photoelectric cells from natural resources and these were being attached to the roofs to harness the light of the sun. Anaxamander often said that Dryadia was no *Shangri-La* and life could be hard sometimes. However their aim was to use technology lightly and well, in order to make life gentler and more enjoyable. But that was not to be at the expense of the environment or indeed their mental or physical health.

Every neighbourhood in both Cantillion and indeed throughout Dryadia had a meeting hall. A neighbourhood was the smallest political and cultural unit in the country, and consisted of no more than about five hundred people. The meeting hall was the nerve centre of the community and amongst other things ensured that nobody felt isolated or uncared for. These halls were often octagonal in shape and usually three stories high. They housed the local school, the library, and included a large area set aside for music and story telling and the regular Dryadian festivals and celebrations. High in the cupola a room was set aside for quiet and meditation. Basements were utilised for the communal bakery and laundry room and doubled up as gossip centres!

The halls were non-exclusive and open to all. They were considered the small-scale community palaces of Dryadia. They were simple inside, though exquisitely decorated and always beautifully proportioned. The material wealth of Dryadia was channelled not into private homes but into these halls, where all could enjoy it. The halls had no obvious religious significance, for in Dryadia little distinction was made between the secular and the spiritual. They were two sides of the same coin. Both were equally beautiful.

There was only one large building in Cantillion, and indeed in the whole of Dryadia. The Great Moot was a five- storied, octagonal, sixty-foot high edifice and dominated much of one end of the central square, known as Fontaluna. The view from the top of its magnificent cupola took in the whole of the capital and some of the landscape of three of the surrounding provinces. The national parliaments took place here, as well as important concerts, plays and debates for the large circular amphitheatre could seat over one thousand people. Here lay the beating heart of both Cantillion and the whole country. Fontaluna was the home of many cafes and theatres and what were known as the Houses of the Storytellers. There were no cinemas. All entertainment was created within Dryadia. In the evenings, Fontaluna buzzed like a honey hive, but there was never any drunkenness or violence, just people having a good time. The population of Cantillion was spread evenly throughout the town, and work places were always within walking distance. In fact you easily could walk across the whole of Cantillion in an hour, and as there were no suburbs you would be immediately surrounded by fields and wooded countryside.

Most front doors were left open when the sun shone, for crime was rare and in fact most people had little to steal. The Cantillions were almost a street people when the weather was warm, and often sat out on the benches amidst the large pots of flowers and shrubs that adorned the front of every house, Mary was pleased to find more shops than she first thought, including clothes shops. Dryadian women were just like any other women in the world in that they liked to be well dressed. Although they were not such slaves to fashion as in the East they took pride in smart and well-cut clothes. The accent was on grace and simple refinement rather than frippery and impracticality. Rolls of cloth and yarn were also sold in great quantities for almost every person could weave, including the men. Dryadians were also famed for their wood- carving and pottery and some shops served as outlets for their work.

"It seems just too good to be true. The people seem happy and friendly. We've seen no slums or poverty or any form of exploitation. The Dryadians seem to have got their politics just right." Pushkin beamed his approval at the others as they ate their last supper at *The Crazy Duck*. Tomorrow they would be leaving for Ceradoc. Mary nodded her head thoughtfully in agreement. "I can see that we have a philosopher amongst us."

"What are you then?" said Pushkin trying hard not to sound ill mannered.

"Just an ordinary Welsh witch, but with a good heart."

CHAPTER SIX

CERADOC

"A good day's journey, all being well." Anaxamander greeted them outside their hostel early the next morning. "I think you will enjoy it though. We could ride there but none of you are safe on horseback yet, so we'll travel in the traditional wagon. To Viribus first, the provincial capital, and then by boat down the estuary."

The road to Viribus was not as bad as they feared. True, it was not tarmaced or even paved except where it was liable to get boggy, but Dryadian roads were well made and maintained by the traditional road menders so it was reasonably smooth and level. The two horses drawing the open wagon were strong and steady and made the thirty-mile journey a pleasure. Five hours later they were in Viribus and in time for a late lunch at the town's rest house, which like the others scattered all over Dryadia, was obliged to provide food and lodging for all passing travellers.

The countryside was very different from what they had been used to in Britain, mainly because of the lack of ugliness and clutter. Nature was the ruler here and as the human population was modest and contained in the villages, there was no sprawl of derelict buildings, caravan sites, pylons, advertising hoardings, and the general detritus of a people who find it hard to keep their nest clean. Their speed being slow, there was plenty of time to absorb the beauty of the journey.

There was a huge variety of scenery. A mile or two out of Cantillion the cultivated fields petered out and were replaced by woods, although small well-kept villages appeared now and then. Fields were small and thickly hedged, suitable for ploughing by horses, for machinery was used only rarely. The meadows were lush and full of wild flowers, grazed by numerous sheep and horses. The lower slopes tended to be marshy for they contained the many streams that found their way down from the hills above where the trees were left to grow in dense profusion.

The road gently meandered through the forest. On lower ground it sunk into deep clefts, where hundreds of years of feet and wheels had carved narrow fissures into the earth. This made the trees that towered above them appear to be as twice as high as they really were. These deep cuttings, hidden from the light of the sun, tended to be damp and were the home of ferns and the early spirals of bracken that greened the faded browns of the rocky walls of the road.

Then the road rose higher and opened itself to the warmth of the spring sunshine. It passed between banks of yellow primroses and white jewels of stitchwort. Red campion and wild garlic mingled amongst them and below them the green tufts of bluebell leaves jostled towards the sky, protecting the hidden flowers that were yet to bloom. In their turn the banks, meadows and woods gave way as the road climbed yet higher towards the wild granite moors, which ran down the spine of Dryadia towards the remote west where they met the sea. So long as the sun shone, and the wind and rain held off, the moors rose above any sense of desolation.

The moors hummed with the murmur of foraging bees, as they searched out the rich nectar from the blooms of the yellow gorse and the brilliant white flowers of the spring blackthorn. Overhead, buzzards mewed and wheeled, their course directed by the slightest almost imperceptible flicker of their wingtips. Ravens tumbled and croaked with that memorable sound that seemed to have been forged deep in the bowels of the earth. From the estuaries curlew had come up to the high moors to breed, calling that unforgettable bubbling cry, a fitting tribute to the loneliness of wild places.

As they began their descent, much of the landscape of North Dryadia lay visible before them. Anaxamander pointed out the estuary of the Tamara River and the open sea at its mouth. Ceradoc was hidden from view in an inlet about two miles from the ocean although they caught a glimpse of Viribus, their immediate destination, some six miles up stream. "Not long," he said. "It's now all down hill. Easier for the horses."

Viribus, a town of some five thousand people, was a lot smaller than Cantillion, but its layout and construction were similar. In its centre was the traditional square with a fountain and cafes and the outsize potted plants. After lunch at the promised rest house, Anaxamander led them down to the river where a small fishing boat was heaving gently up and down at the small pier. It boasted a full set of sails with a conventional engine in reserve, which they probably would not need to use today. They would take advantage of a gentle breeze behind them and a tide beneath them that was in full flow towards the sea. Soon the four of them and the ferryman were enjoying a modest speed and the rhythmic peace of the tidal road that led to Ceradoc.

"There it is," announced Anaxamander just after they had rounded a brooding hill, which he had already informed them went by the name of Kantala or Sanctuary Hill. The estuary was still almost a mile across at this point, so Ceradoc (pronounced softly as if it was Seradoc) had a seaside feel to it. A clutch of colourful houses surrounded the tiny dock. Behind them was a lane mostly hidden amongst trees, which meandered up through a tiny hillside valley to the centre of the village. They wondered what it was like to be there in a great Atlantic storm with the waves crashing against the sea walls.

As if reading their thoughts, Anaxamander commented - "Not as exposed as you might think. We're sheltered from the worst that the ocean could deal us and most of the houses are out of the main force of the winds. We have constructed some very good stone walls and have encouraged trees that don't mind the salty winds too much. Anyway, welcome to my home village." And he jumped ashore, followed by Sam, Pushkin and Mary, aided by the firm hand of the ferryman.

Ceradoc consisted of about a hundred houses, mostly hidden at the top of the valley in sheltered hollows protected from the prevailing winds by belts of huge Holm Oak hedges. Amongst the trees was a flat piece of land, perhaps an acre square, high walled in stone against the forces of nature. This was the village's community garden. Some plots were individual, others were shared by agreement. Greenhouses and potting sheds huddled against the northern wall to catch the sun. Where there was space, espaliers of many fruit trees were carefully trained. Most of the ground was cultivated with newly planted potatoes, carrots, onions and many other vegetables, growing well out of the wind. At the junctions of the various pathways, ponds and wells overflowed with the winter rains. Further up the valley were the community owned fields. All were tiny, walled or hedged, with a gate or two, just wide enough to allow a pair of horses to enter. Higher up still, was the wood, which seemingly separated Ceradoc from the world as the estuary did at the opposite end of the village. Much of this was ancient forest that was never felled but there were also patches of hazel, willow and sweet chestnut, which were coppiced at regular intervals for their wood and as a source of charcoal.

The houses of Ceradoc were constructed in the familiar six sided, doubled storied Dryadian design, looking like so many multi-coloured beehives. In fact the local word for beehive and house were very similar. Houses were arranged in small friendly groups – Dryadians disliked the rigidity and remoteness of streets. The upstairs windows peered from out of the wooden shingles of the steeply pitched roofs. They were crowned by glazed cupolas, ensuring the maximum use of daylight within. Most houses were made of wood except right by the estuary where they needed the extra protection of stone and a very well laid slate roof.

The Three Wise Seekers from the East were billeted separately. Great care had been taken to find them suitable companions. Sam, to his great delight was lodged with Zephyr and his family. Zephyr lived close to the waterside with a telescope permanently focused on the estuary and was the local expert on all things feathered, furred or finned. Pushkin was given a room in Parmenides' family home. Parmenides was Anaxamander's brother and like Pushkin, and as befitted his magnificent name, was highly philosophical in his thinking. His house naturally boasted the biggest library in town and being situated at the top end of the village looked down airily on the rest of it.

"A commanding view helps a man think," he claimed.

Mary too was equally happy. She was going to live with Tara, a woman only a little older than herself who lived alone with her widowed mother who was as quiet as Tara was vociferous. An old and much used grand piano took up much of the living space. A number of friendly cats completed the household. Tara was a trainee bard, and already knew a large number of stories, which she could relate or sing from memory. Like Mary she could heal by touch and was as comfortable with her gift of healing as with her way with words. Unsurprisingly, both found it equally difficult to pause for breath when they were in each other's company!

Anaxamander's home lay further round the cove and a little set back from the estuary. Like most houses in Ceradoc it was set in a large garden where its many plants and shrubs were protected from the winds by the usual stone walls and evergreen Holm Oak hedges. It lay almost on the western edge of the village although not quite. Just beyond it, was the most westerly house in Ceradoc. It was a bit different from the others. From his eyrie, Pushkin had already noticed, that unlike the normal beehives, this house appeared almost circular, though it was in fact octagonal. He already knew that eight sides were normally reserved for public buildings, such as meetinghouses or schools, places that were set aside for the community or for learning. The cupola of this particular house was wider and higher than most. It appeared like a little lighthouse where someone might sit and send out a beam of light or transmit messages to the outside world.

"Sophora's house," answered Parmenides to Pushkin's question. "Her house has eight sides because she is different, not quite like the rest of us. Sophora is a very wise woman. Anaxamander will tell you more. He's very close to her."

Anaxamander had in fact invited the three of them to lunch the day after their arrival. Sam felt very much in awe of him. He seemed to know so much. Add to the fact that Pushkin appeared to be all brain and Mary all warmth and heart, he felt a bit of a minnow swimming amongst much bigger fish. He comforted himself with the thought that he was younger than the others and had time to catch up.

Lunch at Anaxamander's was very much on the informal side. As in all Dryadian homes the ground floor was largely open plan and given over to a large combined living and dining room, dominated at the kitchen end by an ancient cooker in a vivid shade of blue. The furniture was well worn for he and his English wife Ruth had raised two children here. That is, whenever they had managed to escape from Anaxamander's consular duties in England. Melissa was the eldest of the two, about a year younger than Sam. Her raven hair framed a friendly warm face and her eyes were bright and determined. Her younger brother Zach was a lot less serious, and shared the dry humour of his father. A shaggy dog of doubtful pedigree dozed and periodically scratched in his basket by the cooker while two cats surveyed the scene from the top of an old dresser. A black one reminded Sam of his namesake which he had met previously at the Dryadian consulate in England.

Ruth was a highly sensitive earth-mother type of a woman who cheerfully bossed the rest of the family about. She immediately took Sam under her not un-ample wing, insisting that he sit between her and Melissa. She explained that she was one of the Therapeutae and that Melissa was in training and later she was going to show him the herb garden. He also must identify a few bird songs that puzzled her. She introduced him to all the animals and yes, the black cat was indeed his old friend Sam. Within an hour, Sam's self-belief had been raised to stratospheric levels and he felt that at last he could take his rightful place at the discussion table.

Anaxamander had decided that their Dryadian education should start right away, in fact after lunch. He took them to a large wooden cabin at the top of the garden, overlooking the estuary and the small fishing community on the other side. This was the back door to Dryadia and a small number of cargo boats from England, Wales and Ireland, and even occasionally France and Spain, docked there to trade. The cabin was the very one that Anaxamander had built with his friends more than twenty years previously. Later, helped by many of the villagers, as was their custom, he extended the old family house, basically by adding a 'beehive' into which he and Ruth could move in to raise their family.

Ruth's great creation was the herb garden. His was the cabin, where he came to write and think and where he could find peace away from the phone and the children, especially when they were younger. It was also a place for serious discussion, known to all the family as 'cabin talk'. The cabin had plenty of room for the four of them to sit comfortably. Anaxamander had explained that this was initially to be a question and answer session.

"Fire away," he exclaimed. "Anything you like."

Pushkin was first off. "Who really rules Dryadia? Who polices it? How does it stay together? I can't see any signs of a Dryad dictatorship, or a priestly hierarchy. And it can't be simply that you're all just lovely people who never rebel and live happily according to the laws of your ancestors and the laws of nature."

Anaxamander laughed. "Ah. I see you know all the British propaganda and you are discovering that it's not true and that we are all a lot freer than you thought. In fact we would consider that we actually have a lot more freedom than you have, at least the fundamental ones, Let me explain a few things.

There is no hierarchy as such. We are all equals and that fact is completely respected and recognised by all. We do though have a system of Elders who uphold our ancient traditions. These laws are in essence very simple ones, highly practical, and not ones that any good-hearted or reasonable person would want to oppose anyway. They are not dis-similar to those of the Quakers in your country or those of the Amish in America but without their religiosity. So there is no need of a dictatorship, however benign. We all run our lives in the way that we want to, within those basic parameters. We know it works because we have had a stable and contented society for hundreds of years. We have proved that we are able to live harmoniously with each other and share the land we need. At the same time we have every opportunity to lead happy and fulfilling lives for ourselves.

Yes it's true that we don't have votes or elections as you do, and we don't have political parties either. We don't need to. It would be divisive. It would set neighbour against neighbour and community against community. It creates unnecessary class divisions and secrecy. You only do these things because you don't trust each other, probably with good reason. Here, our politics if you can call them that, are consensual and we work within a framework of kindness, always seeking out a harmonious conclusion. No one should feel that they have been treated dishonourably. We like to trust each other. There are no losers in our country and minimal grievances.

Let me explain how our system of government works. Like all good things it's very simple. One of our most important guidelines is that all decisions are made at the lowest possible level. For the family unit, the home is their castle. No outsider would dream of interfering, unless obvious harm was being done to a family member, like a drunken husband abusing his wife or children. An unusual event in Dryadia, I am glad to say. That would be the law of Britain too of course. But we would take it further. As you know, Dryadia is full of hundreds of little communities about the size of this one. Even our towns are broken down into these self-governing neighbourhood units. The size is manageable and people have a sense of belonging to something intimate. As in the family home, no other community would interfere in an internal dispute unless it spilled over its border, or there was a grave breach of the law of kindness and fairness. I must say that hardly ever happens. If it did, then we would turn to the referees to ensure fair play. We call them the Traditional Elders, who are well trained in these matters.

Neighbourhood councils usually meet monthly to ensure the smooth running of the community. They are run on the same principles that a household is run, except of course on a bigger scale. But always on a human scale, to which all of us can relate easily. All are free to attend and make their opinions known, in an orderly way of course. Decisions are made by agreement, not by a vote, which would be bound to leave someone unhappy. If agreement cannot be reached then they would sleep on it and try again another day, or perhaps call in an Elder in to arbitrate. There is never a question of consulting rules and regulations hidden in old books. There aren't any. It's the spirit that counts. Before any changes are made or disputes settled, three questions are asked.

'Is it kind? Is it true and fair? Is it necessary?' When these questions are answered thoughtfully and satisfactorily then every one can go home happy.

Further up the line there are provincial and town meetings, usually held quarterly, to discuss and debate anything appropriate that cannot be dealt with at a local level. Each neighbourhood community sends a representative or two, preferably an Elder. They may be different people each time. They are not paid. It's an honour as well as a responsibility to attend. It's bottom down government where everybody counts, not a top down centralised one like yours, where people feel disempowered.

There is only one level left. The national parliament. We call it 'The Great Moot', which is of course held in the building of the same name. The one that you explored when you were in Cantillion. Representatives are elected from the provincial meetings plus anyone else who has something useful to say. It's very informal but a clerk is appointed to keep us in order. We meet for a few days once a year and occasionally more often if there is an emergency, though this is seldom. For the most part we carry on with our daily lives in our happily organised way. It's very simple, very efficient and it works.

There is one extremely important thing left to say. We keep our numbers steady. Efficient birth control and small families. That means there is no excess population in the countryside flooding into the towns because there is a shortage of land or work. That means our towns don't become bloated and over crowded. You are in trouble in the East and over stressed, because you cannot regulate your numbers. We do.

Our population has remained constant at a quarter of a million, for hundreds of years. We have equilibrium. There is stability in our lives. No need to rush like lemmings into the sea or invade a neighbouring country when you can't feed yourselves or find work. We have more than enough land for our necessities. We have self-sufficiency in food, clothing, housing and fuel, and plenty of land left for nature as well, because we are not overcrowded and don't have too many people to support. But we do have enough people to make Dryadia a vibrant and creative society.

The pressure is off us. We live simply. We do not exploit or fight each other or outsiders. We live in harmony on the land, which sustains us so wonderfully. We co-operate with nature. We do not seek to conquer or exploit it or it will eventually destroy us, as it will surely do to you in the

East." Anaxamander leaned back in his chair, stretched out his arms and grinned. "Quite a speech, eh," he finished.

Pushkin could not stop himself. "But there are basic freedoms that you don't have, like religious freedom, or freedom to travel or even to enjoy a good film. And I don't understand the system of the Traditional Elders. They are obviously held in great respect, but I wonder who appoints them and what if someone disagrees with them. I'm only playing devil's advocate to get good answers. I have a philosopher's training, as you know, probably a very un-Dryadian one by your standards but I need to understand."

"That's a lot of questions, Pushkin. I will try my best to answer them." He turned to Mary and Sam who had been sitting very quietly during his lecture. "I hope this monopoly doesn't make you feel left out."

They assured him that they were as interested as Pushkin, though Sam felt a little disconcerted that Anaxamander had spotted him with half an eye on an enormous buzzard that had just glided silently through the garden.

"Nesting in that tree over there," he exclaimed. "They do every year. Amazing birds, lots of rabbits for them around here. Ruth is pleased too. They help keep those hungry creatures out of the vegetable garden.

Yes, I suppose you could say that we don't have the freedoms you describe. We are mindful though that one man's freedom might be another man's restriction. Freedom is a funny thing. All of us now would agree that we no longer want the freedom to own slaves, restrict women's rights or be cruel to animals. One day hopefully we will all agree that it's not a good idea to pollute the earth or drop bombs on people we don't approve of. With freedom comes responsibility. They are two sides of the same coin. All freedoms result in consequences. We need to be aware enough to see the outcomes, and make the correct decisions accordingly. As for the specific freedoms that you mention like travel, religion and cinemas, and of course television and computers. Well there is another way of looking at this. We take the view that here in Dryadia we have created a way of life that is unique in the world. It has taken many centuries to reach this point and it does seem extraordinary that Dryadia has survived amidst the present chaotic materialism of the rest of the earth.

We believe that it's important not only to us but to the whole planet that we continue as we do, in the hope that one day we will become a beacon of light to the rest of you. We would like to demonstrate to you that it's possible to be happy and fulfilled without draining the earth of its finite resources and then polluting it, perhaps to the point where it will take thousands of years to recover. We can all choose to live in peace and harmony with the earth and each other if we really want to.

I would also say that we do this without continually living like peasants on the edge of poverty. As you see we live simply and fairly comfortably here in Dryadia on a material level. But as you will discover that we have great riches in our intellectual and cultural life: in philosophy, healing, the arts and science, which bring great pleasure and fulfilment to many. We don't want to loose what we've got, but we are willing to share our knowledge with those outsiders who honour us and don't wish to destroy us or even dilute what we believe to be true

Our society would almost certainly disappear if we opened our doors to hordes of tourists from the East who had no empathy with our ideas. Almost certainly our young people would be seduced by their show of wealth in the same way that hundreds of years ago, the South Sea islanders were decimated by diseases to which they had not been previously exposed. That would be the end of Dryadia. For as everywhere, the young are our future.

Our religion, if that is the right word, is about our feeling a strong sense of belonging to a caring community and in knowing justice is always available to us. We need no outside religion. Although it can be comforting at best, it can also be divisive, causing strife and wars at worst. We don't need or want to let conventional religion in. We are already a spiritually aware society. Our spirituality lies within us. Likewise television and the cinema. It would corrupt. We would start craving those things that we couldn't afford and don't need. We would learn about violence and dishonesty, and it would eventually cause our downfall."

There was a knock at the door and Ruth' s smiling face edged round it.

"Haven't you finished yet? I promised Sam, and Mary and Pushkin of course, that I would show them the herb garden. What have you been talking about all this time?"

"Dryadian politics," replied Anaxamander with a grin. "I've been boring them silly," brushing aside Pushkin's protestations.

"I didn't know we had any politics," replied his wife.

"That was precisely the point I was trying to make. But I'm not sure that I've convinced them that there isn't some Mr Big behind the scenes pulling the strings. In some foreign embassies I'm told, it's the third in command that's really in charge."

Melissa pushed her head round the door in the wake of her mother's. "Then in this house it must be a Miss Big. I am the third eldest in the family."

Anaxamander laughed. "Maybe I was wrong. It must have been the fifth secretary."

"Then it's the dog," responded Melissa.

"That figures, he gets the best food. But that's enough work for one day. Come round tomorrow afternoon and we will reveal our secret dictator!"

Ruth and Melissa led them out into the fresh air and they cut through a little gap in a hawthorn hedge. It was fresh with green leaf but its buds of May were still curled shut, waiting for another week of warming sunshine to tease them out. Beyond the hedge, deep in a hollow and sheltered from winds of any direction was an amphitheatre, the size of a small tennis court with the southern side lowered to allow in as much sun as possible. Its centre was paved in stone with a fountain playing gently in its midst. It was fed by a constant stream of water that rose from a natural spring below it. Beside the fountain were a number of wooden outdoor chairs arranged around a table on which had been set a large teapot and piles of what seemed to be oatcakes, still warm from the oven.

Ruth beckoned them to sit down. "The cakes are a Dryadian delicacy. Full of fruit and honey and spices, you didn't know existed. You could walk back to England on these if you wanted to. Every family has a slightly different recipe. These are actually barley cakes. There are competitions every summer for the tastiest ones of the year. Serious stuff, and I've won it twice, I'm proud to tell you. Have as many as you like. Don't worry about Anaxamander, he will sniff them out very quickly. I will explain about the herbs and the Therapeutae another day. Meantime, enjoy the peace here. We think it's the most sacred part of the garden especially when there is a warm sun and the bees are humming happily amongst the flowers."

Anaxamander arrived and heaved his large frame into one of the chairs.

"Many a time on a warm summer afternoon, Ruth and I have spent an hour here drinking in the peace and doing a little weeding."

Ruth opened her mouth wide in mock derision"What you mean to say is that you drink in a lot of peace and I do a lot of weeding!"

At the next day's meeting Mary burst out;"We think that you are Mr Big and you are just being modest."

Anaxamander roared with laughter."You must have been visiting my sumptuous palace in Cantillion! I must tell Ruth. Perhaps she will give me those extra titbits that she currently gives the fifth secretary, I mean the dog."

"We mean to be serious, Anaxamander," added Pushkin."No beehive can exist without a Queen Bee, and you all live in beehives linguistically speaking."

"Well, you have a point. Ruth could certainly be described as the Queen Bee in this establishment, for example. And at least when they are young, children need to be guided and cared for by their parents. There always has to be order. It's the same in the councils at every level. We'll always make sure though that those people who have wisdom, compassion and energy are particularly listened to, and if appropriate, guide the rest of us. These people are usually Elders. But everyone has a voice.

You think that I am being disingenuous when I say that we are all the same. I still say we are but that there many kinds of groupings. You might want to call them guilds. Some of them are very hands on, like the carpenters, the engineers or the stonemasons. The most able of them, chosen by their fellows, eventually become Elders and are known as the Practical Elders. They may or may not be spiritually aware but they get things done and Dryadia would be a pretty chaotic place without them.

Then there is the second kind of Dryadian Elders, the Traditional ones, all of whom at one time or another have completed the Cantillion university course. They are not superior, just different. Some of them are very wise indeed. Because they are guardians of the ancient laws they could overrule the Practical Elders if the spirit of the law was being broken. This is very rare, and hardly ever happens.

The Traditional Elders can be further sub-divided as well. Their roles would be barely recognised in the East. They wouldn't be taken seriously there and no doubt would be ridiculed. Here they are highly respected, for they have been taught, and later will share, the ancient wisdom with others. For example there are the Seers, those who can see or be aware of what lies beyond the five senses. A few of them have the gift of prophecy. You would call them psychics. The wisest of them are particularly revered. One of the greatest of them actually lives next door. Her name is Sophora and you'll meet her soon.

Then there are the Therapeutae, the healers. Ruth of course is one of them. Medicine in Dryadia is very different from yours. We barely use any drugs and we primarily treat any energy imbalance in the mind and body that can be identified. Balance within is vital to good health. Great attention is paid to the cause of the disease. We have little interest in bacteria and chemicals. We consider that the signs and symptoms of a disease are merely a reflection of disorder within. The inner environment of the body is the important thing. We harness the great forces of nature in our healing, especially the minute doses of homoeopathic medicines which work on the sub-atomic level of energy. We believe that herbs and a nutritious diet are essential for good health. Another branch of the Therapeutae are called the Bonesetters who are also skilled in manipulation and massage, and can even do simple operations like remove an appendix or do an emergency Caesarean section. Very occasionally we consult our tame surgeons and dentists in England in exchange for a Dryadian holiday!

Yet another important branch of the Traditional Elders are the Natural Philosophers. They study the laws of nature and learn to apply them wisely for the benefit of all. They protect our heritage amongst other things. Any technological advances have to be approved by them before being put to use.

The Bards next. You will know about them Mary, for there is a strong tradition in Wales. Ours are more than just poets and musicians, worthy as they are. They are storytellers and historians too. One of their duties is to make sure that our sacred traditions are never forgotten and that we do not veer away from that which is true. They will tell you that truth is always beautiful, and beauty is always true, just as your poet Keats wrote. The Bards would never allow an ugly building to be erected or a beautiful piece of art to be destroyed.

Then there are a few of our people, whom we call The Wise Ones. They have a deep awareness of the spiritual side of life, and are able to inspire us, preventing us from sinking too heavily into materialism, or beastliness as we often call it. Like all Traditional Elders they would have studied for three years at Cantillion and waited quite a time before they were considered wise and mature enough to become Elders. They will have learned to control their little egos and become what we call 'soul wise' before they become part of this informal but greatly respected group.

These then, are the people that the East considers to be our rulers. They are wrong though. The laws of nature and our soul knowledge are our true rulers. The Traditional Elders do their best to make this happen. They guide. They don't give orders. Every community has at least three of them, with official duties – a chief, a deputy and an assistant. The last two move up a place if there is a vacancy. At least one of them will represent the village at the quarterly provincial meeting.

Everyone has his or her say at one level or another. We have a vibrant system and it means that there is plenty of wisdom around where it matters. Major disagreements are rare. A consensus of voices is our aim and no one should feel left out or ignored. If they do feel that way then we try hard to get understanding. To be honest we think your form of government is crazy. There's no stability. Unlike you, we avoid dis-empowerment so we do not have losers. We really do have a true democracy. There is the lightest touch on the tiller. We try not to do 'heavy.' We seek contentment for all. Are you happy now Pushkin?"

Pushkin nodded. "I didn't mean to be rude by being so direct."

"You weren't. It is a rule in Dryadia that all teachers must allow their students to challenge them. A good student should ask searching questions. After all we may get it wrong sometimes, though not too often I hope. We need to be kept on our toes. Our system is very different. I often wonder how the East's professions would regard us. Their lawyers would look down on us because we have no written laws. The accountants would have to ignore us because we have very little money. The doctors would throw up their hands because we are not interested in their drugs. The pharmaceutical and oil companies would find no sales here. The military would find no soldiers to recruit. The estate agents would not be interested in us because we don't buy or sell land. Your priests would find our un-written spirituality difficult and your scientists are too materialistic to be at home with our science. You can see how impossible it would be for our two worlds to get into bed with each other."

"My turn now," said Mary. "Tell us about Sophora. None of us have met her yet. I was told that she is one of the Wise Ones."

Anaxamander nodded. "She's certainly very wise. She's the senior Traditional Elder in the country at the moment and has been so for some years. She is also the chief Dryad, if we have to use that word, of Ceradoc. Zephyr is her deputy here and I complete the triad. As I said we always work in threes."

Sam felt proud that Zephyr was so important. He was obviously rather more than just an exceptional naturalist. As if reading his mind, Anaxamander looked at him and added.

"It is important that we all follow our vocations, our inner calling. Zephyr follows his. He is a Natural Philosopher, one who studies how the earth works. His passion for wildlife is part of that learning. Being an Elder as well and a wise man he is also one of the guardians and protectors of the Dryadian way of life. Sophora is not only a very wise human being but is a Seer and Healer of great power. I am also trained as a Natural Philosopher, and have a special interest in the sacred places of Dryadia, the places where the power of the earth is particularly strong."

"I have never felt so alive as here in this cabin," responded Mary. "I know this place is special. Is one of those power points here?"

"There is an energy connection with the earth here. We call them gateways. It feels vibrant because it vibrates. Dryadia is full of them. You may be drawn to them, Mary, because there is the sensitive in you, the makings of a Seer."

"But I want to be a Bard when I grow up," grinned Mary.

"Well there is nothing stopping you doing both. Plenty of people do more than one thing if they have an aptitude for it. Ruth is a Natural Philosopher as well as a Therapeutae. Pushkin will always be drawn to philosophy, no doubt. And Sam, we deliberately lodged you with Zephyr to learn Natural Philosophy with an emphasis on nature. But you could do other things with your sensitivity. Ruth thinks you could do well as a Therapeutae and maybe other things too. There is no rush to specialise. Everyone does the same university course first. Then you decide."

Anaxamander rose to his feet. "I've just remembered. Ruth told me earlier that she was making crumpets, Dryadian style. So please ask her for the recipe. Why don't we go down to the kitchen?"

Anaxamander was absent from the village for the next few days. They were told to make the most of his time away and prepare questions for their next lesson.

"Do talk to anybody who has the time to talk to you which will be almost everybody since we are equally nosey about the ways of The East," he said. "Possibly for the same reason that some people are attracted by horror movies!"

Pushkin spent much of his time with Parmenides who was not, as he might have feared, a watered down version of Anaxamander but a very knowledgeable man in his own right. Parmenides was a Bard but one of the historical ones.

"I can't sing or write poetry, but you can ask me anything about Dryadian history, or even world history for that matter, for we must see everything in context."

Parmenides had just written the definitive history of his country. *Dryadia. From the earliest times to the present day.* Recently he had translated it into English and it was now at the printers. Pushkin had been promised a signed copy.

Mary danced her way through the streets of Ceradoc, often in the company of the equally extraverted Tara, talking to everyone, struggling with the language and writing down the words and music to whatever local songs and stories she heard. She refused to be daunted by Tara telling her: "It can take seven years to be a good Bard. And that's just the beginning. There are at least two hundred stories to memorise and an equal number of songs, accumulated over five thousand years of history. And that's all before the nervous breakdown!"

One night Mary woke in dreadful pain and was horrified to learn that she had not brought her usual painkillers with her. Tara dispatched her in the morning to see Ruth. She was sure that she could help. Ruth's healing room looked nothing like her doctor's surgery back in Wales. There were no certificates or notices on the wall. There were no receptionists hovering around or stethoscopes or other instruments of examination, or government health warnings.

The room was simply and comfortably furnished with a bunch of daffodils on the table. Boxes of little white pills and bottles of dried herbs were on the shelves that lined the walls of the room.

"Frontline medicine, Dryadian style, which means very simple," she smiled. "All drugs and invasive instruments banned here. You don't have to even take any of your clothes off! We just have to talk, and I have to understand." After half an hour, Ruth exclaimed: "This time we will just try and get on top of the pain. Suck one of these little pills every hour for the rest of the day. They are quite harmless with no side effects. And come again next week and we will deal with the cause of the problem. It is a question of balancing your hormones. Well, as I know Anaxamander has already told you, all health is about balance, come to that."

It was only when Mary went to bed that night that she realised that she had only remembered to take three of those tiny white homoeopathic pills and that she had been virtually without pain since the last of them.

Sam' s time with Zephyr was going equally well. In England he largely led a solitary life, at his happiest in the countryside with his binoculars and his bird book. Here in Dryadia he found Zephyr such good company and he and his family were so kind to him that he started to blossom in a way that he had never managed before. Zephyr was a much quieter man than Anaxamander. Being less imposing, Sam felt easy with him particularly on their almost daily bird watching walks along the estuary. He was as equally fascinated at Zephyr's tales about Dryadia as with Anaxamander's stories, especially when little jewels of natural history were often dropped into the conversation, such as his description of the family of foxes that regularly scavenged for crabs at the water's edge or the five species of orchid that grew in his beautiful garden.

Sam and Zephyr shared a great love of the wilderness that existed in those places where humans had made little impression on the landscape. Outside the towns and villages and their immediate vicinity, almost all Dryadia was wild. Zephyr told Sam that he could hardly bear to cross the Drangle now because the ugliness, noise and over-domestication of the English countryside grieved him so much.

"The cars take the mystery out of life", he told Sam on one of their walks along the Tamara estuary. "There's too much instant gratification and no proper adventures. It may be comfortable in the car looking out but hell if you live by a busy road. No hidden corners or interesting people to talk to at a rest house. It's the same with the internet. Too much information that you don't really want. No time for debate. No need to use your imagination in a constructive and thoughtful way. All too fast and noisy. The key to finding the peaceful heart that is at the centre of all things including ourselves is just like what we do while we're bird watching. Sam. We're quiet but alert. We move slowly but with purpose. We open our hearts to all possibilities. And it gives us great joy, doesn't it Sam, that we find ourselves at one with all things."

Sam quoted in reply Gerard Manley Hopkins's beautiful lines.

What would the world be once bereft

Of wet and wildness? Let them be left,

O let them be left, wildness and wet;

Long live the weeds and the wilderness yet.

Zephyr smiled. "Spoken like a true Dryadian."

CHAPTER SEVEN

SANCTUARY HILL

Near Ceradoc, and just out sight of it, was an imposing hill, rounded seductively, and cropped short and green by the local sheep. It hung low over the estuary like Janus, straining to look in both directions at once. In the Dryadian language it was known as Kantala which meant 'Sanctuary Hill' and being the highest point for a mile or so and within easy walking distance of Ceradoc, it was a popular place for the villagers to visit, picnic and enjoy the amazing views. Mary had suggested that the three of them should follow the custom of the local people and have their supper up there. As the evening was still and clear it seemed the perfect place to watch the sun going down.

The path to the top of Kantala was a well- trodden one and threaded its way through the usual gorse and thorn. As they walked Mary recited softly –

For us once more the birds will sing

The songs they used to sing last spring

For us once more the rose will bloom

The summer rose that hid the tomb

And when the world is wintry white

Love's warmth shall keep our hearts alight

"That's beautiful," said Sam. "Where does it come from?"

"My mother used to say it to me. She said it came from *The Sleeping Beauty* when the good fairy undid the curse of the bitter frost after a hundred years of sleep. It's a bit like us coming to Dryadia."

"And Dryadia waking to the rest of the world," added Pushkin. The path did not go straight up, but wound very gently completing a full circuit before reaching the summit. Mary noted that it spiralled up in a clockwise in a clockwise direction, or sunwise.

"Not widdershins, thank goodness. That's the way of the 'bad witch'."

The easy gradient allowed them to reach the top without pausing for breath. The view was very heaven. The panorama over the estuary and the hills beyond stretched almost to Viribus in the east and to the Atlantic Ocean in the west. There was barely any breeze and the water below them shimmered like liquid crystal. Skylarks soared high above them dropping their notes in blessing. Beneath their feet in the shadow of the thorns grew rosy pink campion scattered between the numerous buttercups and daises.

There was a surprise at the summit. Just below its top, in a sheltered hollow overlooking the estuary as if it was guarding it, was an octagonal stone building constructed in the style of the familiar Dryadian meetinghouse. Its cupola though was wider than normal and unusually, a miniature wooden spire had been placed on top. The eight windows of the sanctuary were each stained in different colours; blue, mauve, pink, red, yellow, green, silver and gold. Within each window various diagrams such as a pentagram or Solomon's seal had been carefully traced. The oak door was not locked and they found the interior bare except for an old table and a few cane chairs. Light streamed down on them from the cupola, piercing the gloom. A delicate spiral staircase beckoned them upwards from ground level to an open and large trap door that was a part of the cupola floor.

Well-worn cushions lay around the perimeter of the cupola beneath the large windows that were barred for safety reasons. It was obvious that the place was used a lot. Once the trapdoor had been closed it became a bright and cosy room. Some of the cupola's glass walls could be moved sideways to let out the stultifying heat of this greenhouse on high and allow in the fresh and cooling estuarine air.

Guiltily at first, for they had asked no one's permission to be there, and then with much abandon they tucked into their picnic. Apart from the skylarks and the occasional cry of gulls, silence reigned outside. When they managed to be quiet and allow the spirit of the place to flow where it willed, they had a strange feeling that they were lifting off in a great spaceship and were severing their connection with the earth. The time passed swiftly as they discussed their stay and wondered what they would study at Cantillion in the autumn, and why they never wanted to leave.

As the evening sun grew cooler and dipped slowly towards the hills across the estuary, they were ready to go. Mary though persuaded them to stay until sunset and see if they could spot the famous green flash around the sun that Sam had been talking about earlier. It didn't happen and it was getting quite dark but Sam said the spiral path home was quite easy to follow and there would be no problem in finding their back to Ceradoc.

Final moments grew into even more final moments, as they basked in the peace of the sanctuary. At last they stood up to leave, but suddenly froze for they became aware of a distant murmur that they hadn't heard before. The sound was very faint and seemed to be coming from the north, from the direction of the ocean. They listened in silence, totally mesmerised. The murmur grew in intensity and turned, as it grew louder, into a penetrating drone. It was not a natural sound, more a mechanical one and rather sinister, never ceasing and growing steadily nearer. Then they saw a small star in the northern sky glowing in the half-light. As they gazed at it, another light made its presence known, and then a third. Three small blobs of buzzing light were heading straight towards the sanctuary. Within moments it became quite obvious what they were. The noise and the bright lights were intense as three huge shapes flew low over them in triangular formation and then over the estuary towards the granite moors of central Dryadia. As the sound died away, Sam, Mary and Pushkin turned towards each other in amazement and said almost as one;

"But there are no helicopters in Dryadia!"

The event was so shocking and so unexpected that they sat down again in the shelter of the cupola while the deep peace of the Dryadian countryside surged gently back.

"I think we should wait a while, they may come back," said Pushkin in a whisper. "I don't think that they were ordinary helicopters. They were large military machines, Black Hawks or something."

"Perhaps they were just R.A.F. helicopters taking a short cut home between Wales and England, but that would be highly illegal." Mary tried to look positive. "I remember Anaxamander saying that no foreign aircraft, which means all aircraft since Dryadia doesn't have any, are allowed in Dryadian airspace. It had been agreed with the British government and other countries as well. All pilots know this or they would not get their licence. The same applies to foreign ships too. Nobody has violated those agreements since the war."

"The moon will be up soon and it's quite full." Sam's voice seemed surprisingly calm. "We're getting a bit jittery so we might be grateful for its light. Then we'd all better go and explain everything to Zephyr, as Anaxamander is away. I'm sure he will know what is going on."

"How do you know when the moon will rise?" asked Pushkin.

"That's easy. Firstly, you need to know that the full moon rises at sunset and the new moon rises at sunrise. Secondly that its phase and rising and setting times change gradually at a rate of roughly one hour a day between those two positions and then back again, over the month, like the tides. You can make a rough guess as to its state of play at any time, if you keep an eye on things. In fact I think I can see it rising now." Sam pointed his finger to low in the eastern sky, as he lapped up Mary and Pushkin's admiring glances.

An hour or more had passed since they had seen the helicopters. The moon now was just high enough to help guide them safely back to Ceradoc. However just as they were about to open the trap door and make their descent, they heard once more the menacing drone of the helicopters returning from the moors across the estuary. Within minutes the deafening noise and blinding lights were above them as they returned towards the sea. But this time there was a difference. Only two of the helicopters had come back.

In the near darkness they climbed carefully down the spiral staircase to the bottom of the sanctuary, grasping the walls and even each other as they sought the door out of what now seemed a prison. The moon that illuminated the spiral path around the hill of Kantala made it appear like a silver ribbon but they went slowly trying hard not to stumble. Fear was affecting their concentration. Gone was the cheerful chatter of their ascent. Now they walked in silence. When they reached the bottom, almost in sight of Ceradoc, they stopped short, for again they heard the drone of a helicopter. It must have been the third one for it flew from the south, but this time was following the estuary. Flying very low, it banked in a tight circle right around Ceradoc before heading out to sea. The noise was terrifying, made worse by its suddenness and the fact that no such event had ever been experienced in Dryadia before.

There was no one asleep at Zephyr's house. Most Dryadians prepared for bed when it got dark to save on electricity and for the same reason were also up and about before dawn. The door was open. Twenty or thirty chattering people had spilled out of the house into the garden, looking shocked and scared. Sam, Pushkin and Mary were not the only people who had heard the helicopters. Sam edged his way inside looking for Zephyr. A big sigh of relief etched both their faces. Sam could usually be relied upon to arrive home before dark. "There's been a terrible commotion, Sam. We have been invaded at least three times and we may have just been bombed. They must be planes. We have not seen any of them, just heard the awful noise and now these lights. We have never, ever come across anything like this before."

"They weren't planes. They were helicopters, three of them. Enormous military machines. They flew over us when we were on top of Sanctuary Hill. They've gone now, out to sea."

"Where were they heading, in the first place?"

"South, over the estuary towards the moors. We don't know if they landed."

Zephyr looked pale. "They must have gone over to The Beacons." He was almost whispering, overcome with shock.

"Look Sam, all three of you, stay here. I want the full story. I will try and calm these people down and ask them to go home. I don't think anything else will happen tonight. Go to the kitchen and maybe Amarinta will make you all some cocoa."

A little later Zephyr joined them. Amarinta, his wife stayed with them. She too was a Traditional Elder. Zephyr made them relate every single detail of their experiences of the evening. And if they were not quite clear, then he would make them repeat the story, especially on the precise directions that the helicopters took and the time taken on both their outgoing and return journeys. Eventually he took out a notepad and a map of the district and made some calculations. Zephyr turned to them and repeated. "Yes it was The Beacons. This is very serious."

"Why?" asked Sam in what seemed to him a rather over eager sounding voice.

"I can't say now. I need to do some investigations. I also have to talk to Sophora and Anaxamander. They are both due back here tomorrow. Look, there is nothing more we can do tonight. Pushkin and Mary, you had better go home and get some sleep. Parmenides and Tara will be getting very anxious. Come here at noon tomorrow. Hopefully we'll have some news."

Zephyr sent word later that the noon meeting was cancelled. Anaxamander had not returned, but Sophora had, and would everybody meet at her house in the afternoon. Sophora was a tall slim woman about fifty years old with a strong aquiline face and the darkest penetrating brown eyes imaginable. She exuded warmth and rose and hugged all three of them as well as Zephyr. Sophora was not a person for small talk and after the briefest of pleasantries she asked them to tell their stories once again, gazing intently at each one in turn as they spoke. She didn't interrupt once and when they had all finished she got up and started walking restlessly around the room, seemingly oblivious of them. Then she left, and they watched her from the window as she paced around the garden.

When she returned, Sophora sat down and looked at them gravely.

"I talked to Zephyr earlier and I think the three of you need some sort of explanation. I know only a part of the story, but what I tell you I will trust you to keep to yourselves for the time being. I would also ask you not to leave Dryadia for the moment that being in your own interests as much as ours. I hope you don't have anything pressing in the East and that your families are in no hurry to have a visit. As you have already been told I am what is known as a Seer. There are not many of us and we are scattered here and there throughout the world. Hundreds of years ago if we lived in the East we were feared for our knowledge, ridiculed and persecuted, and if discovered often as not burned. Here in Dryadia they have always been respected for their ability to see beyond the physical world. It seems a strange gift to possess if you aren't familiar with it. Even some Seers find it difficult to manage this extra layer of energy, which is something that you are born with, a gift from the soul if you like. In Dryadia, and specially here in Ceradoc, there are more on the ground than in most places, and as with most faculties there is always a big range of abilities. It is an ability that can enhance whatever you do, be it in healing, storytelling or counselling. Less commonly, there is the skill to see into the past or the future and into peoples' minds and hearts. I am that sort of seer. But don't worry. The Dryadian way always works towards the good. That is partly why you are here, to be amongst like- minded people, who are attracted towards the lighter side of being."

Sophora spoke with no sense of ego. When she spoke of herself she could have been speaking of anybody. She talked though with such authority and certainty that no one wanted to question her. It wasn't that anyone was afraid of her. Awe might have been a better word. Sophora just seemed to 'know'.

"This is my opinion on what I have seen or can sense at the moment. When you saw the helicopters last night you saw something remarkable. As you know, they had no right to be here. Again as you guessed, they were military machines. Each contained a lot of soldiers, heavily armed with guns. I don't think they were British. We have a reasonable relationship with your government at the moment, which doesn't mean I trust them. They have already put out a denial that the invasion had anything to do with them. No, I am reasonably sure that they were Americans, and that they flew in from a large ship, moored well out to sea, perhaps an aircraft carrier. They were on a mission, which I can't explain at the moment. It was only partly successful, and hopefully will in due course, fail.

They flew to and landed at the place that we call The Beacons. They stayed awhile and flew out again. They thought they knew what they were looking for, although there was little for them to find. However there were a few Dryadians there, including you will be surprised to learn, Anaxamander and myself. When we heard the aircraft coming we all ran and hid, though we had little time. The lights and the noise were absolutely terrifying. Two of the helicopters landed. The third hovered around the hill, using its searchlight. They found three of us, including Anaxamander. They were bundled into one of the helicopters and that one and one of the others flew off. The third helicopter switched off its engine and remained quietly hidden in the darkness, hoping no doubt that more of us would reveal ourselves. We didn't, and eventually that one flew off too."

Sam, Mary and Pushkin looked totally amazed. "Anaxamander kidnapped! Why him? Why anyone? Why there? What brought the helicopters in?" The questions tumbled out.

"We're on the case", replied Sophora. "Lots of questions still need to be answered. We'll get Anaxamander and the others back. He's not stupid and nor are we. I'm afraid that's all I can tell you at the moment. Now I want you to enjoy your stay. Talk to any one, especially the families whose guests you are. Go anywhere but obviously no one is going to show you the way to The Beacons at the moment. Learn as much as you can about Dryadia and our way of life. It's a truly remarkable place. And study Dryadian. It will be essential and it's a beautiful language with a rich literature. I know almost everyone knows some English, at least in Ceradoc, but try and speak Dryadian with your families and you will soon pick it up. And Sam, I am told that some little egrets have been seen on the estuary."

With Zephyr's help Sam soon spotted the small flock of egrets, but could get very little more out of him on what the three of them had begun to call 'The Mystery'. Zephyr was particularly concerned about Anaxamander.

"My best friend, you know Sam. We grew up together and are distant cousins. Anaxamander knows a lot. I hope the Americans don't do anything horrible to him."

Pushkin didn't get much out of Parmenides either.

"The Beacons! An old place in our history. There was a battle there four hundred years ago. There are more sheep than people there most of the time though we go there for picnics occasionally and we have our mid-summer celebrations nearby too."

Mary did much better with Tara who was far less discreet.

"We know who the other missing men were. They are shepherds from here in Ceradoc. We know them well. I think Sophora and Anaxamander used them as guides. They know the land backwards. They are lovely but just ordinary people. The Americans won't want to keep them. There is another story too. Empedocles was also there that night. He is Anaxamander and Parmenides' brother. Their father loved Greek philosophy, hence their crazy names. Empedocles is another Natural Philosopher, but different. He's a boffin and always doing experiments. He's always joking too. The last time I asked what he was up to, he told me that he was working on a perpetual energy machine powered by the purr of Anaxamander's cats! As for The Beacons, we have known it well since we were children. We used to sail upstream and land on the other side of the estuary, and then walk. Only the highest tip of one of the three hills there is visible from Kantala if you use binoculars. Everything else is hidden in a dip. There are a lot of standing stones there and a stone circle and an oak grove not very far away, hidden in the woods. We used to pretend that we could fly from stone to stone. That's what the old myths used to tell us. Perhaps Anaxamander and the others were investigating those old stories, but it was a very strange thing to do at night."

There was no news from Anaxamander's house, and Sophora had gone away again.

"Be patient," Zephyr kept saying. "There's plenty going on behind the scenes."

"Is there any real reason why we shouldn't visit The Beacons?" asked Sam after a few days. "Sophora didn't really forbid us as if it were a commandment. Tara told us that it was a nice place for a picnic and that she would go with us."

"You won't find anything new at The Beacons. But I hear half of Dryadia has been sight seeing up there so I don't expect a few more visitors will make any difference. Tara has a boat. She can sail you there. But please go in daylight and be back well before dark. I don't think the helicopters will return, but you never know."

The Beacons was a curious place, which strangely had no Dryadian name or if it did, no one used it. Nor was there an actual beacon or any memory of one. The highest of the three hills did not seem to be the most important. Most of it was covered in prickly scrub although a small footpath led to its summit where you could wave a flag at Kantala if you wanted to. Tara always had the feeling that its function was to stand guard over the two lower hills that lay concealed from prying eyes until you were almost on top of them. The three hills were exactly aligned, seemingly the same distance apart.

The ground between the two lower ones was remarkably flat, a smooth plain about the size of a couple of football pitches. A large stone circle fashioned from undressed granite stood almost drunkenly in the middle of it between the two lower hills. More granite standing stones, green with lichen and age, lay seemingly haphazardly around the perimeter. Beyond them, the scrub and trees offered some protection from the casual rambler coming across the stones by chance. The main impression was that this was a secret place and not meant to be easily found. But its makers had seemingly not considered the view from the air.

Tara led the three of them to the stone circle. The whole area between the two hills was simply known as 'The Field'. Its sward had been cropped short by sheep enjoying the fresh spring grass.

"Now we'll all have to walk around the circle touching each stone as we pass. We must all go round clockwise or we will instantly be turned into goblins. That's what we were all told as children anyway. Then we can have our picnic but not in the circle, otherwise it's more goblins I'm afraid. We'll go to one of the perimeter stones."

A number of other groups of people were doing the same. Zephyr had been right. Their curiosity had overcome their fear.

When they were settled into munching Tara's version of the Dryadian barley cakes the talk and questions began, most of them directed at Tara.

"What was it used for? We have stone circles in England but people don't agree as to their purpose." Pushkin kicked off in his emphatic way.

"You know I have lived in this area for twenty seven years. That's all my life. I have to say I still don't really know. Anaxamander has said one of the gateways is here. That's where the earth energy comes up out of the ground, but he has never explained any further. I do think there are people in our community who know more than they say. That must mean that they consider the knowledge could be mis-used if it got into the wrong hands. There are old legends about serpents slithering around between the stones but only when the sun or moon is right. There have always been lots of silly stories like the goblin ones and that if you come here on the wrong day you will be banished to England forever! Which of course meant that we never came here without our parents' blessing.

There have always been celebrations here, like our midsummer one to which I am sure you will all be invited. That takes place in the Oak Grove amongst those trees over there, and not in the stone circle. Our rituals are not secret though they can be spectacular. They are open to all Dryadians. There is usually one at every full moon and they are often sweet and fun, not something that you would send out a helicopter to spy on or worse."

"So who knows more than they will say?" asked Mary mischievously.

"The scientific knowledge, which is the only knowledge that people are likely to be careful about, would only be known by a few of the Traditional Elders, the ones who have been trained in Natural Philosophy. In Ceradoc, that would include Sophora and Anaxamander, Parmenides, Empedocles and Zephyr and probably their wives who are all Traditional Elders too and therefore of course much wiser than their husbands, as we witches know. They will never tell. My father once told me that the Elders with the most secret knowledge were completely without ego and therefore incorruptible."

She grinned at Mary. "That's all I know. We Bards just tell the stories."

"You know I can see where the helicopters landed." Sam's sharp eyes directed them to some deep indentations in the ground twenty yards away. "Well one of them any. The others must have been on the other side trying to stop people getting away."

"Poor Anaxamander has a bit of a bad leg and can't run very fast," commented Tara. "It's said that the two shepherds were caught trying to help him."

Sam got back onto the original subject. "So we think we now know that Anaxamander and the others had some special knowledge and that this place is a gateway with energy flowing around like serpents. They must have been conducting some secret experiments. Then the Americans wanted the secret too, which means that whatever experiment they were doing that night must have been very important."

They all nodded in agreement. There was no other alternative.

"So how could the Americans possibly have found out?" Mary looked incredulous.

"Spy satellites," answered Pushkin. "They've got the whole earth covered, every inch of it. Though that does not explain why they were looking at this tiny little bit of Dryadia, a country that is not exactly a threat to anybody."

"Some one must have tipped them off," said Sam. "I can't believe it was anyone in Dryadia as the information was known to such a few. There are no mobile phones where messages could be traced. Oh, I've just thought of something. At our interview Anaxamander was telling me a story about a plan to put up a mobile phone mast near his house and that the engineers had got into his house on a pretext when he was away. He joked that he thought that he had been bugged, even though a later search revealed nothing. Possibly he and Ruth had mentioned the experiments and it got picked up and the satellites were trained in on this area. The experiments must have seemed inexplicable on their screens. Perhaps the Americans thought there was some military potential and flew in for a closer look to try and find some evidence."

"Meantime," said Mary, "Anaxamander and those poor shepherds are rotting in some awful jail having their arms twisted to reveal secrets that may be nothing, or everything. And nobody here is going to say anything, especially not to the three humble students from the East."

"Wise seekers, Mary, wise," commented Tara. "Anaxamander called you wise. And Sophora accepted you, even insisted that you stay here in Ceradoc, which is a great honour. No other Eastern students will be staying in this village. She also said that you were like-minded. You are much more respected and trusted than you think."

"Any news?" asked Sam when he arrived back at Zephyr's that evening.

"A little Sam. We have had some word from the British government. They have been in touch with the Americans who have confirmed that they are holding Anaxamander and the others. They have been arrested as spies believe it or not. We have been informed that they consider that they have been working for a foreign power whose interests are in conflict with those of the American people. Crazy world, eh!"

"So what happens now?"

"Negotiations via the British. We are pleading that it's an invasion of an un-armed sovereign country. No authorization from the United Nations, not that we are a member. That sort of thing. American governments do not obey the rules unfortunately. They will release them in their own good time."

CHAPTER EIGHT

DRYDADOGENES

Parmenides was beaming as he handed Pushkin his book.

"Received from the printers this morning. I've already left copies with Sam and Mary. Prescribed reading in advance for the Cantillion course. All the Dryadian students have read it in their own language. This is the first English edition."

FROM GODS TO PHILOSOPHERS THE STORY OF DRYADIA

FROM THE EARLIEST TIMES TO THE PRESENT DAY

By PARMENIDES OF CERADOC

Below the grand title on the cover was an even grander picture of a raven. Its wings were half outstretched, its beak open and raised defiantly towards the sky. It was seemingly calling of freedom and independence from its perch at the top of a large oak tree. The oak, itself on the summit of an isolated hill, towered high above the surrounding countryside of woods, fields and villages which nestled in the river valleys winding down from the moors that lay in the distance. Beyond the moors was the faint ribbon of the open sea. In a vivid blue sky, streaked in the west with the pink of the recently set sun, was the thin silver crescent of the new moon cradling within its arms the evening star, the planet Venus. This picture was one that was familiar to all Dryadians. It hung in all their public places, in their schools and meeting houses, and it had long been their national emblem.

In three houses in Ceradoc that day: in Zephyr's at the water's edge; at Parmenides' on its higher slopes; and at Tara's in the small street of the Bards; Sam, Pushkin and Mary began to read.

CHAPTER ONE IN THE BEGINNING

Many histories are dry as dust, with voluminous footnotes and references. They tell of the deeds of kings, driven by their desire to maintain and expand their power, and their resulting wars against their neighbours and their own people, They are about greed, robbery and violence and man's bestial triumphs over nature and each other. What Dryadians call 'fouling your own nest.' In the East these histories are usually written by academics who spend their lives wading through other dusty books, letters and diaries. They probably wouldn't know a raven from a blackbird, an oak from a hawthorn or the planet Venus from Sirius. They would have little interest in the world of the Bards, and their stories and orations, which tell of events millennia ago, for they would not understand the poetry of myth and legend and its rich layers of meaning. They would have no knowledge of, and would have no interest if they did, of the world of the Seers and their ability to see and make sense of those matters that cannot be seen with physical eyes. They wouldn't realise that nothing is ever completely forgotten and that memories and events, faint as they maybe, still live on as echoes in the auras of wood and stone, in our imaginations, and in the realms of the energy field of the earth itself. They would think it ridiculous to consider that long before their written histories began, there lived on this planet, extraordinary races of highly cultivated human beings, who had technological expertise superior to that of today, and who were capable of engineering achievements of which we know nothing. Just like today, human morality and wisdom ranged between the bestial and the high-minded.

There were those who created terrible weapons that were used in wars that nearly destroyed our planet. And there were others whose knowledge of both the realms of spirit and the physical world of nature was so deep that they were known as 'The Wise Ones'. Some of those amazing people were the founders of this country, and their descendants, continuing with their tradition of knowledge, still live on in Dryadia today.

Twelve thousand years ago much of the Northern Hemisphere shivered in an ice age. Thick sheets of ice covered most of the British Isles stopping just north of Dryadia. It was far too inhospitable for anyone to live here. Only the hardiest of lichens and mosses could survive the intense cold. Sea levels were three hundred feet lower than today and Dryadia was connected by a land bridge to Wales, and through what is now England to continental Europe. The land of Dryadia would have looked desolate and unrecognisable compared with that of today. The ice had already lasted at least ten thousand years. There had been a complete break with what had gone before. Almost all life; humans, animals, birds, insects and plants had long migrated to the warmer south to wait out the great frost.

Finally the cycle of cold began to end and the ice to melt. Sea levels rose again and Dryadia gained the shape that it has today. Birds began to visit and breed in the summer months bringing many seeds of plants and trees with them. The wind blew in the rest, with insects following in their wake. There was a great greening of the northern lands. Within a few thousand years Dryadia, in common with the rest of Britain and Europe, was covered in a rich range of tree cover; from birch, rowan and pine in the hills to oak, ash and elm in the richer soils of the river valleys. The animals followed next: lynx and wildcat; wolf and bear; boar and beaver; wild ponies and cattle and many others. Only some of them still survive here today. The woods and open spaces were alive with the singing of birds in spring and the rivers sparkled with salmon and trout. Humans then were few in number and would have made little impression on this natural paradise.

Not all men behave in the same way. The first settlers were simple uneducated people who built their primitive huts in sheltered valleys and cut small fields out of the woods. The population was small because most migrants had settled much further east in England where the soils were more fertile and the living easier. But they were not the only people who were attracted to this country. The ancestors of the present Dryadians had also discovered it and had noted that there were particular conditions here that suited their purpose over other lands. There was its remoteness of course and the secret hidden places that lay in the oak woods and amongst the heather on the high moors. They were aware that this new country was a strange and unusual place. It felt different to the lands that lay across the Drangle. There seemed to be a different vibration, a strange power of nature that pulsated invisibly and silently through the ground. Not that many people would notice it. Perhaps it was just a kind of wildness, something encouraging an independence of thought; a sense that any people who lived here would be unable to happily conform to the accepted norms of other lands. It was a different 'spirit of place'. People would be drawn to it or repelled by it according to their nature. They probably would not understand why.

But actually there were a group of people who were sensitive enough to understand. They were known as the Seers, or the people who could see. Their ancestors had long carried the ancient knowledge in their hearts and souls, and had passed down what they knew. For thousands of years right up to the present day, the best of them had been renowned for their wisdom. Many of them were part of the old Druid movement, who were latterly associated with the Celtic race. In fact the Druids were much older than the Celts and originally were spread across Europe and even beyond. There is an obvious connection between the words Dryad and Druid and both were linked with the ancient wisdom. Some of the original Dryads settled in our country and unlike the ancient Druids were not destroyed by the Romans.

These Dryads were both knowledgeable and wise. They were not interested in war or violence or in exploiting the earth or its people. They preferred to keep to themselves, which was one of the reasons that they decided to settle in the remote wilderness that came to be known as Dryadia. However the increasing ignorance of other races persuaded them to mingle amongst them and share at least some of their wisdom. These old Dryads were a remarkable people who possessed a now lost technology. They used it moderately and wisely. They were kind and compassionate and loved the earth that was their home. They had been the bearers of the ancient wisdom since time immemorial. Most of their neighbours looked upon them in awe and simply referred to them as 'The Gods'. One of these tribes of so-called 'Gods' came to Dryadia many thousands of years ago. The leader of this tribe and the founder of our nation was known as Dryadogenes.

When Sam had finished the first chapter he set off for a long walk down the estuary, following the water's edge until he reached the open sea a mile or two later. His brain was alive with the new ideas that he had just read and re-read. It was so different from anything that he had come across before that he virtually ignored the cormorants, curlews and oystercatchers that were sitting the tide out on the sandbanks. These would normally always excite his attention. Gods, Wise men and women who knew more than we do today? Seers like Sophora who could see the past and the future, and who could access knowledge as if she had the key to some exclusive library? And their direct descendants, with at least some of that old knowledge still imprinted in them, still around today? Where did he fit in, here in Dryadia? He certainly had not belonged in Croydon. He only knew that he was different. His God was nature. But was he that different? Yet Sophora had implied that she had virtually invited him, along with Mary and Pushkin, to be Dryadia's special guests in Ceradoc. He sat on a large rock and stared out to sea. Like the sea birds, he too would sit out the tide.

Sophora's house was the first one you passed on returning from the sea. Like Zephyr's and Anaxamander's it overlooked the estuary. It snuggled down in a little hollow that kept the worst of the winds out. Sophora was out in her garden, admiring and picking the last of the fallen daffodils. She saw him walking hesitatingly by.

"Hello, Sam. Come to tea?"

"Um, um. Are you sure?"

"Sure, I'm sure. It would be nice to have a good chat. Your head seems to be bursting with questions."

"How did she know?" Sam almost thought aloud. He melted into Sophora's big warm hug, not a habit that he was accustomed to in Croydon. He suddenly felt very strong, almost powerful. She led him into the kitchen and put the flowers into a vase on the windowsill. The late afternoon sun turned them into gold.

"I've been reading the history book that Parmenides wrote."

"Enjoying it?"

"Very much. I've just finished the first chapter. The cover picture, the raven is amazing. I keep loosing myself in it. It transports me."

Sophora laughed. "Perfect for a bird watcher like you. It's our symbol, as you know. It's a design that goes back a few hundred years though artists often re-draw it. The raven though has always been our national bird. Tara drew this one specially for the book."

"Why the new moon and Venus?"

"The new moon because it is fresh and full of potential. Venus, not just because it is an icon of love as you Easterners say, but because it represents the ancient wisdom as we Dryadians say."

"Did wise people come from Venus, then?"

"It's a dead planet now. Too hot for life. But long ago, people lived there. There was a lot of wisdom around then, according to our traditions. We are talking of a time that was millions of years ago, although you may find it hard to believe"

Sam gasped inwardly. Was she being serious or was she just being a romantic? How could any one possibly know? Yet Tara had told him that Sophora seldom joked. She was always serious and sincere. She only spoke of what she believed to be true. One of her favourite sayings was that it was fine to have your head in the clouds so long as you had your feet on the ground. Sam thought that he would change the subject.

"Is there any news of Anaxamander?"

"Yes. He and his friends are having a grilling. But at least they are safe."

Sam wondered how she knew but didn't feel brave enough to challenge her on the subject. "Will they come back soon?"

"As soon as the Americans understand that they are of little use to them."

"What are the Americans after?"

"The one thing that all fearful and greedy people with big egos are after. Information that will make them powerful and rich and give them an edge over their enemies, whether imagined or real."

"They think that Anaxamander has that information?"

"Anaxamander thankfully is one of the most technologically impracticable people in Dryadia. He can build a nice cabin with a bit of help but not much more than that. He was on The Beacons mainly as an observer. The shepherds are good but simple people. They were only there to act as guides and keep their sheep away. It might be best if we don't talk any more of this at the moment. Don't worry about it Sam. You will learn more at the right time. There are lots more important things for you to do."

"Like what?"

"What we talked about before. Learning Dryadian. Reading Parmenides' history book. Thinking about the university course. It's only about four months away."

"I'm doing all those things. I love it here and want to stay here as long as I can. Do you want me to do anything else?"

"I never tell anyone what to do. I just point out to them their choices, and perhaps tell them of the likely outcome. I answer questions and encourage people to take responsibility for their lives."

"I want to stay here and discover what I'm really good at."

"I think we could help you along that path. Did you go to university in the East?"

"No I deferred it. Nothing appealed. My father wanted me to study accountancy and make lots of money."

"You won't make much money from the Cantillion course, but then you don't need much money to live on in Dryadia. Nor do you need much to study at the university. Our course is completely unlike anything you have in the East. It's learning about life, spiritual awareness, the laws of nature and how energy works in all its wonderful manifestations. You will learn about science, real science that is, not just narrow specialities that don't seem to have any connection with each other. We call it Natural Philosophy and we learn about the nature and power of numbers and their vibrations. We learn about colour and music and sound. We study geometry and the nature of the earth and the patterns that are generated from it. We look at the stars and the planets. We study history so we understand ourselves better and don't make the same mistakes again. We read our ancient poems and stories, and the literature and history of other countries as well, so that we don't become insular. We ask ourselves why we are here, where did we come from and where are we going? We get some surprising answers.

We learn about how to best live our lives and how to heal ourselves when things go wrong, always remembering that the first thing is to honour ourselves and everyone else. Only after each student has completed the three years and widened their minds would anyone make a decision about following their vocation. It's a true universal education open to anyone with the aptitude and the passion to know. Does that interest you, Sam?"

"Completely and utterly, though I'm absolutely overwhelmed by all you say."

"I'm not surprised. Even our Dryadian students will find that much of the syllabus will be new to them too. The course is a great leveller."

Sam had never been so happy. Sophora liked him. He didn't know why, but it was important to him. He knew from the depths of his being that he was doing the right thing. He couldn't wait to tell Pushkin and Mary of his conversation. The three of them had grown very close since their voyage to Dryadia on *The Leaky Bucket*. Sophora wanted to have similar chats with them as well.

As he walked home to Zephyr's he thought that the curlew's call had never been so haunting. The evening light was fading and the sun had left its echoes of pink in the western sky. A bright star shone there with a crescent moon nearby. A pair of ravens cronked high above him, tumbling downwards in their free fall way, not for any particular reason, but just for the sheer love of being alive.

Mary had settled herself in the window seat of Tara's home, stretched her legs out to brown in the morning sun, and tried to ignore the sound of what seemed to be a Bardic choir practice taking place in a house across the lane. She began to read.

CHAPTER TWO THE DESCENT OF THE GODS

The Gods were not supernatural beings. They were men and women of flesh, blood and bones just as we are today. They appeared as Gods to more primitive peoples because they were wiser, and their technology was much the superior. Indeed they must have seemed incomprehensible to the first inhabitants of Dryadia who lived simply in their wooden huts at the edge of the forest.

No one knew how the Dryadian Gods obtained their knowledge, and when and from where they got it. Presumably they brought it with them when they moved north into the country as the climate warmed. As with so many ancient peoples their stories hinted that originally they came from the stars. Venus and Sirius were often mentioned. They claimed that they could move rapidly over great distances both on earth and in the heavens. They undoubtedly had great mathematical and astronomical knowledge as careful measurements of their standing stones and circles have demonstrated. We believe that some of these ancient monuments are six thousand years old and were probably constructed not long after the arrival of these first Dryadian Gods.

A famous story that has been passed down for countless generations describes the creation of the planet and the arrival of our extraordinary ancestors. It is one that every modern Bard has to learn by heart.

Dryadogenes had grown weary of his journey amongst the stars. For millions of years he had travelled through the universe and found that it had no beginning or end. His chariot shone with golden fire and left silver sparks in its wake that spiralled to every part of space. Its wheels were made from serpents whose mouths issued forth drops of knowledge that sparkled like diamonds. Whenever Dryadogenes passed by a star the serpents spat and life sprang forth from where the spittle landed.

Eventually Dryadogenes discovered the planet Erith. It had been green once but it was now brown and barren. Its air that had once been as transparent as crystal was now choked with the fumes of Sulphur. The sea and rivers that had once flowed pure and clear were now stagnant and stinking. The sun and moon no longer had the strength to shine through the foggy stench and Erith had grown sad and cold. Nothing could live there. No flowers or trees, no crawling things whether with six legs or eight. No birds in the air or fish in the sea. No animals on four legs or men on two. Hardly any signs of life at all. Only ancient bones were left lying deep in the earth. It was a reminder of terrible bygone wars of destruction where men were pitted against men, and men against the four elements of earth, air, fire and water, until even the sun turned its back, unable to look upon such appalling evil. Death was now the ruler of Erith. Only in the darkest, muddy pools did some sparks of potential life still exist, and they were so tiny that even Dryadogenes could barely see them.

The serpents spat on every square inch of the globe. From their venom grew ferns and mosses, grasses and flowers and trees great and small. Insects appeared and pollinated the plants so that they could reproduce. The water, air and earth became pure again. The light of the sun and the moon reached the most hidden corners of Erith and it was no longer barren and brown. The land sparkled like glittering emeralds and the sea glistened like polished sapphires.

Dryadogenes looked at his creation and blessed it. He gazed at the evening star in the west and exclaimed:

You now have a sister and she shall be as wise as you.

He looked at the Dog Star in the south and said:

Be proud of your child, one day she shall inherit your wisdom.

Then he departed in his golden chariot in a shower of silver sparks with the sound of the hissing of serpents.

A thousand years later Dryadogenes returned. Erith was as beautiful as he had imagined. There was no finer planet in the universe, no greater place for life to flourish in all its manifestations. He promised himself that he would do everything in his power to make sure that it would never be destroyed again. The only thing that might be stronger than him would be the stupidity and ignorance of men. The serpents spat again and from their venom came not poison but the eggs of lizards and toads and other cold creatures. Other eggs created the fishes in the sea and colourful birds of the air. The serpents spat once more and the animals appeared – cats and dogs, bears and elephants, horses and monkeys and many more. Some creatures Dryadogenes had brought with him. Carefully he let dolphins and whales into the oceans. But there were no humans. Dryadogenes blessed his creation again and said he would return.

Ten thousand years passed and Dryadogenes returned once more to Erith. His eyes were moved to tears as he saw that it was more beautiful than even he could imagine. Dryadogenes then divided himself into two parts and tussled with himself. He recalled that he had once been a humble man that crept along the ground. He remembered that it was aeons before he had grown wise enough and strong enough to reach the stars and become whom he truly is. He knew that humankind was capable of doing amazing things as he had, but was also capable of terrible destructive acts, as they had done previously on Erith. Only humans were able to both reach the heights and plumb the depths. Within them was contained the pinnacle of creation and the engine of its destruction.

If there were humans on Erith it could become even lighter and more beautiful. But humans could also do the opposite. He could not control them, only guide them. Without humankind it was true that there could be no wars, fear or greed. But there could also be no laughter, love, wisdom or adventure. There could be no striving to embrace the spirit and know your true self.

Dryadogenes felt his two selves merging. He was of one mind again. He decided that he would allow humans to walk on Erith once more. So the serpents spat and the first men appeared on the planet. But this time, he thought, I will do everything possible to prevent them becoming too heavy and not being able to feel the light. We the Gods will walk amongst them until they rise to become Gods themselves and reach for the stars in wisdom and peace.

Dryadogenes blew on his trumpet and its golden sound echoed throughout the universe. As it died away, it left a gentle hum, as sweet as the murmur of bees, which vibrated in every corner of space. All his kindred heard his call and he selected some of the wisest of them to accompany him on his journey to live on Erith and guide the affairs of men.

The planet prospered for a long time under the firm but gentle hand of these benign Gods and word spread amongst the stars of its magnificence. But not all Gods are kind and selfless and there were some of the darker kind who wanted Erith for themselves. They were no better than pirates. They travelled from *many star systems until they found us. They sought out the gold and diamonds that Erith was rich in and lusted after its beautiful women. Gradually many of the inhabitants of Erith became corrupted and no longer looked to be guided by the wisdom of Dryadogenes and his friends. Once more fear, ignorance and greed invaded their hearts and war raged both in their minds and on Erith. Some of Dryadogenes' friends said that they could no longer live in the growing impure vibrations of Erith and left for the stars. Dryadogenes wept but he knew that he could not leave Erith and humankind to its fate. A few of his companions agreed to stay with him and keep a light glowing, so that those who still sought out the truth could find some hope in the increasing darkness. Dryadogenes broke down at the thought of what he had to do. At last he flew to the top of a high mountain and surveyed the wonder of the planet. Most of it is still beautiful, he thought. How can I let it be destroyed again? As he pondered he saw a black speck in the sky coming towards him from the cooler lands of the north where the ice had now melted.*

The raven drew along side him its huge black wings beating slowly and firmly, every feather shining in the sun with a magnetic intensity. It landed right in front of him and began to speak.

"Oh, Dryadogenes, there are still many places on Erith where the light is bright and the energy of truth still vibrates strongly. I come from such a place. Only a few simple people live there. We ravens are mighty there and have sowed thoughts of enchantment in the minds of those that wish Erith harm. To them we are invisible. They cannot find us. In our land there is a great forest of oaks and we are protected on three sides by a stormy ocean. There the veil between the earth and the heavens is thin, the air and water pure and the energy of the serpents winds purposefully through the ground. Come and join us in the secret places amongst the oaks, where we have our nests and where the power of the earth is at its strongest. There you could make your home."

So Dryadogenes called his companions and together with the ravens they flew to the great forests of the north. There in secret they built their homes and sowed their crops and fished the rivers. The ravens watched over them for they nested in the highest trees and mountain tops. Dryadogenes and his kin approached the simple people who already lived there and taught them knowledge of the basic sciences and arts, how to plough and weave and make simple tools. When they were ready they learned the wisdom of the spirit and the way to the stars. And that is how the land of Dryadogenes became to be known as Dryadia.

CHAPTER NINE

THE PILLARS OF WISDOM

Mary put the book down and simply said, 'wow' to herself about four times. Well, she thought, as creation stories go that's a lot more dramatic than Adam and Eve. Now I can understand why the raven is Dryadia's national emblem. But I do know that most legends are encoded so I expect I'm going to need a little help as to what the story really means. Sam had already told her about his visit to Sophora, and as she had been invited to tea herself that same afternoon, some of the agenda had now been settled in her mind.

"I am glad you're enjoying Parmenides' history. Very important background reading for all three of you before you start the university course."

"I've got lots of questions about Dryadogenes and all those Gods. I hope they're just myths and don't need any worshipping," said Mary anxiously. She hoped there wasn't any element of cultism in the Dryadian philosophy.

Sophora reassured her. "I'm sure I've already mentioned that we steer clear of all un-necessary groupings that lead to separation, like hierarchies or party politics. They would push us towards disintegration. We're also wary of fashions and new inventions from the East for the same reason. We vet all major new ideas to prevent social or environmental disharmony. You can read the Dryadogenes stories in many ways, always remembering that like your King Arthur legends, there will have been more than one Dryadogenes, operating at different times in our history. They merge into one another. Obviously the first one is a kind of poetic myth trying to make sense of eternity and the sacred knowledge that has always guided us, and guides us still. The word Dryadogenes actually means sacred knowledge, the kind that needs to be kept safe by those people who would use that knowledge wisely. That tradition has operated through a historically unbroken line for thousands of years. There is also an association with oak trees, partly because of the power of the tree itself and also because the Elders once liked to meet in hidden oak groves.

The final Dryadogenes, the one you read about at the end of the creation story, and the one that led his tribe to this land of Dryadia was a very wise man. The ravens were symbols of that wisdom, and of course they make the story a bit more entertaining. That Dryadogenes was a great man, a God if you like, to those who stared up at him in awe. But in a way he is no more important than you or me. We all carry our light within. We all have the potential to reach the stars, both spiritually and physically. It was not Dryadogenes who was important, it was what he did. Same as us.

There are many tales about various peoples who in the earliest days were called the Gods. Parmenides has retold some of them in his book. Some are profound stories with deep messages for the listener, for originally they were not written down. Some are more historically accurate than others and a great mine of information for Parmenides. Others are just good stories, sad, funny, entertaining. Similar to your traditions in the East. You have heard of our Storytellers, the Bards who travel from village to village in the summer acting out these tales, often with music. It's our main source of entertainment. An experienced Storyteller has a huge repertoire all committed to memory. But I expect Tara has explained all this to you already.

I know you have the aptitude to become a good Bard and Storyteller. That's why of course we lodged you with Tara. The Bards play a very important role in our society. Because of them we cannot escape our past, nor would we want to. Dryadia has made many mistakes in its thousands of years of existence, mistakes that we would not wish to make again.

The Bards help us to remember and evolve. It's a great responsibility. But it's good fun too. Music, poetry, art, history, stories, meeting people, bringing joy into their lives. When you go to Cantillion to study you will discover a lot about yourself, and what you really want to do. But I would be surprised if you stray far away from the poetry that's already in you."

Pushkin had his turn with Sophora the following day. It was beginning to look like a repeat of the 'Anaxamander' interviews at the consulate but Sophora was more probing, like 'having my brain decoded' as he described later. Pushkin was the eternal student. He had read 'everything' and had had several careers in the East but had never settled. He was more reserved than the others even though he was the eldest. He did have a particular secret though and as he conversed (Pushkin didn't quite 'do chat') with Sophora he wondered if she would 'sense it out,' as she put it.

The fact was, that he had become rather smitten with Mary. It was creeping up on him, like rising dough, and he had to admit to himself that he rather liked the sensation. Had she noticed? He didn't think so. But he thought Sophora had. As they said their goodbyes, she gave him a huge wink and said enigmatically:

"I don't think Mary will prove to be particularly contrary, do you?"

A week had now passed since the helicopter incident and Anaxamander's disappearance. Although their paths crossed every day they had decided that they would have another picnic reunion at the sanctuary on the top of Kantala hill. Mary and Tara had become good friends and Tara had asked if she could accompany them.

"You will need a guide this time, and Sophora has especially asked me to help the three of you in your education."

The visit to the sanctuary took place on one of those beautiful late April days when a warming sun and a cooling breeze were in perfect combination. When they were inside Tara quickly pointed out something that they had barely noticed before.

"Look closely at the walls at the back. Are they as smooth as they look?"

"Pillars," observed Mary. "But not proper ones as their backs are embedded in the walls. We can just see the front of them. They are tall though, must be ten feet high. They reach half way up to the cupola floor. I never really noticed them before. I thought that they were just part of the wall, a sort of curvy wall."

"They must be very old." Sam was peering closely at them. "They are scratched all over, as if visitors have been carving their names on them."

"Scratched! Scratched! Tara looked appalled as if she had just witnessed a particularly gruesome murder. "On these pillars are carefully inscribed much of the wisdom of Dryadia, not to mention the universe and everything, and all the knowledge that lies buried inside you and which you don't even realise exists. It's in fact an Oracle. Like the one at Delphi in ancient Greece, but without the fumes and the wailing women, apart from me just now of course! Look how hard the stone is. You can't carve deeply into it. That's why it looks scratched. But once cut, the marks remain forever. Sun won't fade them. Water won't soften them. You're right Sam. They're very old. Some of the inscriptions are as ancient as the Sanctuary itself. And it was built at least four or five hundred years ago at the time of our great Dryadian civil war which you will be soon be reading about in Parmenides' history book. But this is a living book. Inscriptions have been added throughout the centuries. Even today, if someone can think of something memorable enough and wise enough and the Traditional Elders agree to it. Now look around you. Notice that most of the sanctuary is lit from above, mostly from the windows of the cupola. How tall those windows are, like a lighthouse.

We need that light down here. If the sun doesn't shine, then it can be quite gloomy down below and the pillars can't be read. And because of the design of the cupola one particularly bright shaft of sunlight can be concentrated on a bit of a pillar at a time. That sunbeam continually alters its position with the time of day and with the seasons. We can also direct the beam from above with various contraptions, which I will show you later. Now let's follow the sunbeam of the moment and see what it tells us. It's shining here isn't it." Tara stroked a small section of one of the pillars, conveniently at head height. They peered at the illuminated area.

"It's unintelligible," said Pushkin.

"Unless you know Dryadian. Generally our writing, and probably the spoken language too, have not changed much in thousands of years. This particular script though, which we call sanctuary script, is different to our everyday writing. So only the Traditional Elders can read it, which of course includes us Bards. I'll translate it for you before the sun moves round. It's a poem, quite a well known one.

If you listen to the songs of the birds

Really listen

Then you will always have a song in your heart.

If you listen to the sound of the tide as it ebbs and flows

Really listen

Then you will understand the pulse of life that lies within you.

If you listen to the murmur of bees on a sunny morning

Really listen

Then you will know that you can never be really alone.

fgk

If you listen to the laughter of children playing

Really listen

Then there will always be a smile on your face.

"That's beautiful," said Mary. "I'm already smiling."

"It's even more beautiful in Dryadian and it's been set to music too."

Tara sung the words gently as if they blew out of the wind itself, and as many generations of Dryadians had sung before her.

"Look," said Sam after a long silence, "the sun's moving on. Another inscription is beginning to show."

"You'll like this one," said Tara.

If you are not green and growing

Then you must be ripe and rotting

"Which we'll all be, if we don't have our picnic soon. I'm starving. Let's go up to the cupola and eat there."

"Did you go to the university and will you become an Elder one day?" asked Pushkin as they munched on their barley cakes."

"Of course I did. Everybody who truly wants to understand what it is to be a Dryadian and why we do the things we do, needs to go. At Cantillion we study wisdom for its own sake. It's essential if you later want to play a part in fostering our traditions, learning to be truly creative, and nourishing the spirit of being not only a good Dryadian, but a good human being as well. For the Traditional Elders, Cantillion is part of their training.

To become one of the Practical Elders who are equally important in other ways it's simply necessary to be highly respected in your community or in your guild. As to whether I will become a Traditional Elder one-day, well you have to be invited first. You are judged on whether you will put Dryadia's interests before your own. The worst thing that anyone can say about a Dryadian is they have an ego the size of Mount Cynthos. That's our highest mountain, all two thousand feet of it. Did you know that you are virtually the first foreigners, apart from Ruth, to go to the university here? You are our great experiment."

"I hope the experiment succeeds then. Are there others like us in Dryadia at the moment? Anaxamander did say that he was interviewing a number of prospective students."

"I believe there are," replied Tara. "The idea is that you will be in a first year class of around a dozen. So I guess that there will be three more similar groups to yours somewhere else in Dryadia. In fact I already know of one of the students involved. He is the brother of an ex-boyfriend of mine. Their father is English and the mother is Dryadian. Your classmate's name is Stephano. If he is anything like his brother, then he will be smart, charming and not entirely to be trusted. Anaxamander didn't want him to do the course but Sophora somehow persuaded him otherwise. He will probably only be allowed to do a year, and we'll have to keep a careful eye on him. Sophora asked me to tell you that but to keep the information to yourselves."

She looked down through one of the little portals set in the cupola floor, which let light into the chamber below.

"The sun is sinking. See how gloomy it's getting beneath us. It doesn't have to remain like that though. It's amazing what you can do with mirrors."

Tara stood up and carefully drew back some curtains that concealed a number of adjustable mirrors that were arranged around the sides of the cupola. By altering the angles of some of them, after first capturing the rays of the sun with one and then deflecting light downwards with the aid of others, she managed to cast a sunbeam directly at a small portion of one of the pillars below.

"The Oracle is about to communicate", she said solemnly. "Follow me."

She opened the trap door and led them down the spiral staircase to the place where the shaft of light had settled.

"Ugh, it's horrible!" gasped Mary. A great snake with piercing eyes and flickering tongue glared menacingly from out of the pillar.

"Only at first sight. Look more closely. What else do you see?"

"Another snake. Intertwined with the first one," said Sam a bit nervously.

"It's like a caduceus, an age old symbol of healing I think, or a piece of DNA," said Pushkin not to be outdone.

"You are all correct. We know this symbol too. It's a universal one. It's thousands of years old. And if you look again at the serpents' coils you will see some writing, though it does look like scratches, as Sam put it."

"Sorry Tara." Sam took the gentle admonishment in good part. "Could you translate it to us please?"

Tara spoke the words firstly in Dryadian, gently almost beguilingly as if the words were trying to penetrate their brains through the back door. She saw their quizzical looks and explained.

"There was a time in the early history of the world when great importance was paid to the actual sounds in a language. It seemed almost possible to understand a word's meaning even if you didn't know the language at all. The idea is still present in modern languages if you listen.

For example in English it's hard to make the word love sound angry, while hate most certainly does. Hush has a calming effect while if I change it a little and hiss like a snake then you're going to back off fairly quickly. You didn't hear any hissing just now when I spoke the serpents' words. You heard something completely different."

"When you spoke its words, I felt the serpent was trying to teach me something but trying to by-pass my brain. It seemed like something important and very old," exclaimed Mary in some astonishment.

"Well done, that's right. All the Dryadian language is like that. There is meaning behind the sounds. We never lost that principle. Indeed we perfected it. That's why we insist that you learn our language and speak it precisely without an accent. There is power behind the words too, especially if you truly understand them and get the resonance right. We study this at Cantillion. Now I'll translate the serpents' message into English for you."

Acknowledge the serpent's power within you, and in all living things

Within its sinuous coils there is great wisdom

Know the serpent's power outside you

For where it is strong there is great power in the land

What is still, can be moved

What is broken, can be healed

Greatness lies in the mouth of the serpent

But beware. Do not approach in ignorance, or in fear

Nor in desire for something that does not belong to you

The serpent acts only for itself

"What's that all about?" asked Mary looking slightly stunned.

"Cantillion. Third year when you are ready to be trusted. Then you can meet the serpent face to face, in a manner of speaking. The Oracle apparently wanted you to know of the serpents' existence so that's fine by me but I can't tell you any more for the time being. You're getting a flavour of what you are letting yourselves in for. Dryadia is not just a lot of happy yokels living in harmony with each other and rejecting much of the modern world. It is that of course but it is much, much more. We are not mystics and we don't wish to be thought of as being particularly mysterious. We seek out the meaning of everything except the oneness of bliss of which we are apart and from which we originate. We like to understand the processes of life. Sometimes we need science. On many occasions we need our imagination. Mostly we use both. Never underestimate the power of our minds. If necessary, we have to protect our knowledge so it doesn't get into the wrong hands. That would make the world even more unsafe than it is at the moment."

"Getting too close to the serpent's mouth. Like the helicopters and Anaxamander."

"I think you understand, Pushkin," added Tara with some satisfaction.

"Are there other sanctuaries like this," asked Sam?

"Yes, dozens. I've visited quite a few of them. There is one at The Beacons but it's hidden away in the woods, so we missed it. They are all in special places."

"Where the serpents are strong and where there are gateways."

"You're learning, Sam."

"Some sanctuaries are high on the moors, some by the sea, others deep in the forest. There's a lovely one at Cantillion. It's special to the university.

One of our ceremonies, an event that happens every year in the summer, is an endurance competition open to everyone but especially for our younger Dryadians. There is a race around the country with the sanctuaries acting as finishing posts. It's an initiative test too as many of the sanctuaries are hidden away and are very hard to find. The route is also changed each year. The course takes about a week to complete. It is not all running. There is riding, rowing and swimming too. It mops up the excess testosterone of our wilder boys and it stops them thinking of war games and ravishing the women! Not that I am adverse to the odd ravishment." Tara winked at Mary. "It's just that I much prefer to choose my admirers my self."

Pushkin gave Mary a sidelong glance and quietly looked away. Sam made his escape by looking down at his shoes.

CHAPTER TEN

DRYADIA'S EARLIEST DAYS

Sam had created a hideout on the estuary's shoreline where he knew no one would disturb him. It lay just off a little path, probably made by a badger, which linked the estuary with the low cliffs above. Here, hidden amongst the scrub, was a small cave hardly any bigger than a round version of Anaxamander's cabin. It almost completely enveloped him like a shell. Here obscured from prying eyes, he had an almost perfect panoramic view of the water and sands below. Here he came to watch the birds and think and read. Today, he had brought Parmenides' history and settled down to read another chapter.

CHAPTER THREE EMERGING FROM THE MISTS

When Dryadogenes and his companions first settled in Dryadia more than six thousand years ago they found a completely unspoiled land. The few people that were there before them were quickly absorbed into the Dryadian culture through the sharing of knowledge and inter-marriage.

Amongst their memories the early Dryadians carried one in particular. This was the story of a great catastrophe that had been visited upon the earth in relatively recent times and in which a great flood or tsunami had washed over a greater part of the earth, including Dryadia. The devastation had been terrible and the Dryadogenes of the time and the other 'wise ones' in the world, many of whose friends had perished, took note as to how easily their precious wisdom could be completely lost and how the whole earth's population could fall back into beastliness. The 'wise ones' resolved that they would conceal the knowledge in various secluded areas of the earth in the event of any future calamity. Dryadia was of course one of these places. It is still probably the only major place in the world today where the ancient wisdom has not been diluted or corrupted.

Many of the world's cultures have a flood story. This is our version, as told by the Dryadian Bards today.

Dryadogenes, from whose loins the forefathers of the Dryadians sprang, was amongst the wisest of men. He was skilled in all the sciences including the movements of the stars and the lights of heaven. One night the Keeper of the Great Circle, whose abode lay in one of the highest mountains of Erith, came to Dryadogenes and said; 'We have seen a new star, one that has never been observed in the heavens before. We have watched it for many months now and it is gaining in brightness. What does this mean?'

Dryadogenes summoned all the wisest men and women in the world and they set forth east and west and north and south and flew amongst the stars in their golden chariots. When they returned they said that they had never seen such a star before for it had a head like the largest serpent and a tail so long that it could wind itself hundreds of times around our world. Dryadogenes was afraid because he knew that the serpent would soon consume the earth.

He ordered that all his tribe should scatter across the world so that there was at least a possibility that some of them would be saved .He built great lodges high in the mountains and his chariots flew constantly above the clouds. Soon the starry serpent struck the earth and the prophecy proved correct for much of the world was in fact destroyed. The waters boiled and great winds turned the earth to fire. For a whole year the sun did not shine. Most of the peoples of the earth perished.

But Dryadogenes and many of his tribe survived in the high places in the mountains .He managed to save many animals that he had collected and carried to safety, and the seeds of countless plants. When the waters receded and the sun shone again, Dryadogenes left his mountaintop and flew many times around the earth consoling those who were still alive. He shared his knowledge of the secrets of the arts and sciences and gave away the seeds of the plants that he had collected, so that the survivors could begin their lives anew. After seven generations the planet Erith became as it was.

The descendants of Dryadogenes multiplied and settled all over Dryadia. At first they communicated with all the like-minded peoples of the planet, the ones that were known as 'The Gods' because of their superior knowledge, both technological and spiritual. But most mated with the ordinary people of the earth and forgetting their old traditions, descended into beastliness. Many tribes had by now migrated to the islands of Britain. The majority were warlike who did not respect each other's rights and saw the earth as a place to exploit rather than to protect. So long as their numbers remained small it may not have mattered very much, but the population of the East was expanding greatly and the Dryadians became aware of covetous eyes sizing up their beautiful country.

About three thousand years ago when the dawn of what we call the 'The Iron Age' was approaching and when iron was entering the soul of many of the inhabitants of the earth, the Dryadians looked into the future and saw that if they did not take precautions to protect themselves, then their existence would be in peril. They realised that they would now have to take physical action using minimum force to dissuade potential invaders. With great sadness the Elders gave permission for all families to arm themselves and learn a kind of mobile warfare, *for there were no forts or large towns to defend and their villages were largely concealed in the forests. Dryadia, then as now, was heavily wooded.*

The Great Forest of Dreagle had already been preserved as a protection against invasion from across the River Drangle. Trackers walked there regularly and no tree was ever felled. A system of coastguards was set up to patrol our shores on a daily basis as they still do today. Spies were sent to the East to seek out information that might warn them of any possible attack. They also took a lot of trouble to spread dis-information that Dryadia was an enchanted land under the spell of a mighty sorceress. Her band of goblins and ghosts lurked in the Forest of Dreagle and along our shores. They were certain to devour anyone who set foot uninvited on our sacred land. Dryadia was well guarded.

For the most part the Dryadians were not attacked and lived peacefully and even traded with their neighbours. There were occasional incursions usually up the estuaries of the south coast but the combination of stormy weather, treacherous rocks and the vigilance of the coastguards invariably meant a satisfactory conclusion in favour of the Dryadians. By 500 B.C. in the Eastern manner of counting the years, Dryadia was a strong, and, in its own terms, a prosperous country.

The early Dryadians did not isolate themselves completely. We know from pottery remains, and from some annals still recited by the Bards that they had regular contacts in the Mediterranean area and probably beyond, even as far as Sumeria and India. They traded in knowledge as much as in artefacts like wool and ingots of tin and copper. Their philosophers certainly visited Egypt and Greece.

In fact when the Greeks spoke of the Hyperboreans (literally the people that lived beyond the North Wind) we like to think that they were referring to the Dryadians. We know that there were strong links between the Pythagoreans and the Dryadian Philosophers and refuge was often given to the Pythagorean brotherhood and similar seekers after truth when they were persecuted. There are many stories of this trade in philosophers and ideas and we are tempted to think that the Greeks obtained many of their best ideas from us as opposed to the traditional belief that the reverse was true.

Plato was one of the Pythagorean heirs and the founder of the famous academy in Athens. There its pupils studied the quadrivium, the four related sciences of numbers, geometry, music and astronomy or in other words, the study of the life force in all its subtle manifestations. Most of this precious knowledge was lost a thousand years ago in the East, but in Dryadia it never died and it is still taught in the university at Cantillion to this day.

Kings and Emperors, war and peace, prosperity and poverty, all waxed and waned in the East. In Dryadia, although no doubt there were plenty of internal disputes, we lived in a state of stability and peacefulness that must have been almost unknown in Europe over two thousand years ago. Then the Romans arrived in Britain having already conquered most of the known world over the previous few hundred years. Their values were brutal and materialistic and they imposed them on all their subject peoples. But the Romans did not conquer Dryadia. The Dryadians had a policy that they would only fight in self-defence and only on their own soil. As the Dryadians were no threat to the Romans, and with their terrain and weather being on the wild side, the Romans somehow, having more than enough to do in keeping their existing empire together, never got around to a full- scale invasion of our country. True, a few small reconnaissance expeditions were mounted but they had little effect. The Roman Empire eventually fell, but Dryadia remained as it always had been.

Sam paused in his reading. Anaxamander had been right. Dryadia definitely had had a 'history.' He wondered how they had kept their traditions alive with those 'barbarians' continually knocking at their borders. Or did they have to re-invent themselves at a future date? He trained his binoculars on a small party of redshanks drawing attention to themselves with their piping calls as they flew in tight formation low over the estuary. Some things never change, he thought. Some one like him might have been sitting here two thousand years ago watching those redshanks' ancestors, wondering if the Romans would destroy his future just as the modern Romans, the materialistic and greedy culture of the East, were threatening his. Had he fled the East to the security of Dryadia, where everything that he valued flourished, simply for it all to be taken away from him again? Then he rued his selfishness and thought of the Dryadians and their beautiful country. It must survive and become a shining light for the world. Well if the Dryadians had survived before, then they could survive again. He read on.

CHAPTER FOUR A THOUSAND YEARS OF TWILIGHT

Rome had collapsed under its own enormous weight. The Dryadians no longer needed to watch out for the galleys and their fierce warriors landing in their secluded coves. For a long time they felt free from invasion. Nature though always fills a vacuum and Britain soon became a home for peoples of the Germanic races, the Angles, Saxons and Jutes. The existing Celtic tribes were pushed westwards, some of them towards the Dryadian border. We do not know a great deal about Dryadia in those years. If there were books, they must have long perished. It is likely that some sanctuaries were in use at the time and it is just possible that some of the earliest pillar scripts may date from those days.

There are a few indications that there were some skirmishes on our shores with the Celts and the Anglo-Saxons, and the odd raid from a Viking longship, but no foreigners managed to settle. Dryadia remained vigilant and as far as practical kept itself to itself. Our archaeologists (another section of the Bards) have discovered that the villages of the time were small and scattered and mostly inland. If invaders did manage to get past the sharp eyes of the coastguards and approach the settlements the inhabitants could have melted away into the woods. Then they would have returned to set up lethal ambushes. Generally, the five or six centuries after the Romans left Britain, was a peaceful era but an uneasy one. Dryadia always had to be alert, and never felt entirely secure.

As every British child knows, 1066 is the date of the Battle of Hastings and the Norman Conquest. We of course have a different calendar and started counting our years from the time when we believe Dryadogenes first came to Dryadia. A new threat had reached our borders, perhaps one that was not very different to the Romans. For like them it was materialistic, militaristic and strong, and bent on conquest. The Normans introduced new concepts, ones that were totally alien to Dryadia. One was the feudal system where the king ruled by divine right. All were subservient to him through a hierarchy of nobles descending down to the poorest serfs who were treated little better than slaves. Power was centralised at the cost of individual freedom. A 'winner take all mentality' became the norm and kept Britain in its grip for centuries. That idea is still prevalent in Britain even today. Dryadia felt alarmed. They stayed aloof from the Normans and kept their defence and espionage systems primed. For a long time the Normans busied themselves with their new English vassals and their other borders, those of the Scots, the Welsh and the Irish. Nevertheless there came a time when they started casting envious eyes on Dryadia. They tried to invade several times. Fortune though was always on our side and storms often broke up the English fleet. The fear of our 'witches and goblins' caused panic and mutiny amongst their soldiers. Then England became preoccupied with expensive and prolonged wars with France and Spain and the 'little problem of Dryadia' got sidelined.

By some miracle Dryadia remained free, sometimes through force of arms, occasionally through diplomacy but generally through some large helpings of good fortune. We are a common sense nation but sometimes we like to say that the spirit of Dryadogenes and the ravens must be still watching over us. Nearly six thousand years had then passed since our ancestors had first arrived here. Meanwhile in England, Queen Elizabeth the First had not been many years on her throne.

For more than two thousand years Dryadia had been in a constant state of watchfulness for invaders and had almost entirely thwarted them. But there was a price to pay. The country had spent so much energy watching the enemy without, that it had become gradually exhausted by the endless effort. This state of being was not what Dryadia's founders had intended. The original philosophy was that the country should largely remain hidden and virtually unknown. It would therefore feel secure and be able to evolve peacefully according to its lights .It would communicate with the outside world only when necessary. That basically meant only when the East was getting too heavy, to use the Dryadian term, and it needed more light, in both senses of the word. However expanding populations in the East resulted in a move away from sustainability and an almost inevitable greed for land. That could only mean unwelcome pressure on Dryadia from across the River Drangle.

Far more difficult to deal with, was the pressure and discord within. The Elders managed to keep faith with their age-old philosophy and traditions but were unable to cope with the increasingly more worldly and competitive behaviour of the ordinary people of the country. As a result the Elders had largely left the villages and withdrawn to the seclusion of the sanctuaries.

The Elders were of the opinion that it was now necessary for them to live a more monastic life and leave the rest of the population to live their lives without their guidance. Dryadia began to crumble from within. Households no longer co-operated as willingly as they once did. Village communities looked at one another with suspicion. The Elders were still revered, if only for their healing skills and powers of seership, but they no longer entered into the lives and hearts of their more worldly and practically minded countrymen. They became a tribe apart.

A few of the more aware Elders felt that this state of affairs should not be allowed to continue. If they were not one nation then they would be destroyed from inside. The inner enemy was far more dangerous than their external adversaries. They resolved to do two things. The first was obviously to encourage as many Elders as possible to see their point of view and return to the villages. Some took up the call but many felt unable, as they had lost the common touch. Indeed some arrogantly argued that if they had to live with ordinary people, then they would loose their spirituality and refinement and become heavy and beastly like them!

A second course of action was to seek some sort of diplomatic treaty with the English. If they no longer had to live in a twilight zone between war and peace, then the Elders would be better placed to solve their country's problems. They realised that Spain had replaced France as England's major enemy, and with that in mind the Dryadians dispatched emissaries, under the leadership of an Elder called Sastamoro, to the English court. A proposal was made to the Queen. The Dryadians would guarantee that they would give no support or refuge to Spain or France or any of the Queen's enemies, if she in return would respect Dryadia's independence. Much to their surprise, the Queen agreed. A peace treaty was agreed between the two countries. In fact the Dryadians had no intention of getting into bed with the Spanish or anyone else for that matter, but they took the view that in desperate times, needs must. Although they really did not trust the English they were desperate for a measure of security. The Queen and the Dryadian emissaries signed the treaty, but what was agreed in public was not quite the deal done behind the scenes.

Unknown to the Elders back in Dryadia, Sastamoro had accepted a considerable amount of gold bullion from the Queen. This was gold that previously had been looted off a Spanish galleon, which in turn had been stolen from the Incas of South America. For his part Sastamoro agreed to convert to Christianity, and in particular and more importantly to the Protestant faith of England. Moreover he swore that he would do his utmost to persuade his fellow Elders to do the same and allow English priests to enter the country to facilitate the process. By this subterfuge the Queen considered that Dryadia would truly be immune from any Spanish Catholic intrigue. Sastamoro stayed a year at Elizabeth's court, his treachery concealed from his peers. When he finally returned with his gold and two priests, whom he had to conceal in his house, he pondered exactly how he might carry out Elizabeth's request. He had managed to persuade a few of his fellow Elders to come to his side, helped no doubt by a share of the gold and the promise of refuge in England if things went wrong. Not that the Queen would look kindly on any of them if it did.

It was not long before Sastamoro's treachery became known. The majority of the Elders were appalled. They refused to endorse his plans in any way, knowing how it would split the country. They realised institutionalised religion was alien to their own philosophy, which espoused self-responsibility rather than the idea of some Being rescuing you if you followed the rules. Two of the

Elders in particular, Sastamoro's own brother and sister, were adamantly opposed to him. Alanda and Isola were considered to be the wisest Elders for many generations. It was they who had given the lead to persuading the Elders to leave their Ivory Towers and return to the communities where they could do most good.

The country split into two. Sastamoro and his supporters fuelled by English gold waxed strong in the south of the country. The true Dryadian philosophy now under the protection of Alanda and Isola remained strong in the north. Their headquarters were at The Beacons, though little now remains of the original buildings. The Elders of the north were determined that this was a fight that they could not afford to loose.

CHAPTER ELEVEN

ANAXAMANDER'S RETURN

Sam was greeted by Zephyr with the words "Anaxamander's back. He's been released at last, along with the two shepherds. He's with his family at home resting, and doesn't want to see anyone else at the moment."

For almost a week, there was no sign of Anaxamander. There were rumours that he had been tortured; that he was near death and Ruth and Sophora were trying to save him; that he knew terrible secrets that had nearly destroyed him. Parmenides, whose brother of course he was, reassured Pushkin that none of these were true and that Anaxamander, and the shepherds too for that matter, were reasonably well considering their ordeal. He added that we should all be grateful that there was no Dryadian tabloid press camping out on his doorstep trying to buy his story. "He asked me to tell you something."

Better to light a small candle than curse the darkness.

Then the invitation came. Would the three of them plus Tara come to lunch the next day? They were relieved to find that Anaxamander didn't look too dreadful though he had lost a lot of weight and much of his normal jolly manner. His 'Eat up, Ruth has really surpassed herself this time' smile was wan and forced. He still clearly was in some state of shock. "We'll have some cabin talk afterwards and I will tell you the story of my adventures."

It was such a lovely afternoon that they took the comfy cabin chairs to the herb garden and settled down to tea with the fountain playing soothingly in the pond. There the tadpoles, born of the great migration of toads two months previously, were wriggling in masses under the lily pads.

"The peace of all this has helped me no end," mused Anaxamander. "I often think of this strong spring of water. It rises from deep under ground and never fails. It bubbles away, always in motion, always pure. It has so much vitality quite unlike your moribund chemically treated water in the East. We pipe it into the house. We would never drink anything else. Now, I expect you have got some questions."

"One question," replied Tara. "What happened?"

"I want to explain as much as I can. I know you were witnesses to the helicopters. Sophora has explained a bit more and I hear that you have even been to The Beacons to do a little detective work of your own." Anaxamander's voice was tired as he smiled benignly at them and they realised appreciatively that he trusted them. "Sophora has already told you that The Beacons is one of the most sacred places in Dryadia and you must have read by now that it was also the headquarters of Alanda and Isola, two of the most important people in our history. The sanctuary at Kantala where you saw the invasion, is also an important place, especially so to the people of Ceradoc. As you all know the earth energy, or as we call it serpent energy, is strong in these places. These are the places of power in the earth, like electric sockets into the mains. Dryadia has more of them than anywhere else in the world so far as I'm aware. That, as you know was one of the main attractions to Dryadogenes, when he brought our ancestors here long ago. It's very interesting that the serpents revealed their presence to you at the Sanctuary. That couldn't have happened by accident. There is a strange intelligence behind the oracle. Knowledge is only revealed to those who can be trusted with it and have a real need to know. That's one reason why I feel that I should tell you about my adventures.

These lairs of the serpent are the places where time seems to stand still; where mass can become weightless; where the boundaries between earth and spirit are thin; where we can have visions of past and future more easily than at other places; where there can be profound healing to those who seek it; where things move when they shouldn't; where the physical laws of nature can be suspended and we appear to enter another dimension; where the impossible becomes possible. Are you getting the idea? Is it not an alchemist's dream? The energy is stronger at some places and not always on tap at others. The serpent responds to the cycles of nature both in the earth, in the sky and in ourselves. The energy waxes and wanes like the tides. At the time that we were at The Beacons the power was exceptionally strong. You may have noticed that it was a full moon. Now I won't tell you what we were doing that night, though you can guess the sort of things we were interested in. But what I will say, is that what seemed initially beautiful and fun and absolutely fascinating, now appears to be dangerous and ugly. Instead of bees we attracted some horrible flies.

The people who directed the helicopters to fly to The Beacons that night were not interested in the welfare of Erith or its people. They were after something else that they thought would make them powerful and feared. Like you, we heard them coming. We were mesmerised. It was entirely out of our experience. Only when we saw them landing did we start to run and hide. We took our equipment and instruments with us and when we were at a safe distance threw them down rabbit holes or into the gorse. Luckily they weren't found and they wouldn't have made any sense to our assailants even if they had been. They have since been retrieved and well hidden. The helicopter people landed. They had guns and flares. One of the helicopters hovered above with its great searchlight trying to illuminate us. It managed to pick me out along with my two companions and they must have radioed to the soldiers below who started chasing us. I can't run fast because of my leg and my two gallant friends sadly got caught too as they were trying to hurry me along.

We were flown to an aircraft carrier well outside coastal waters. It was an American one. I found that out later but I had already guessed it from the soldiers' accents. We were put in separate cells and shackled. No one was allowed to talk to us. The next day we were transferred to another helicopter and flown off the carrier. The flight couldn't have taken more than about an hour and I suspect that we were taken to an American base in England. I don't think the three of us had ever been so frightened in all our lives.

The shepherds were just our guides in case we got lost in the dark and most of the time that we were on The Beacons they were moving their sheep to new pastures. They had just returned, and we were packing up, when the helicopters arrived. The shepherds knew nothing of the experiments. I obviously did though, but I only understood about a third of what was going on, and that bit was largely theoretical.

We have long had a policy in Dryadia that we share any scientific information, which has the potential to be used destructively between three Elders, none of whom really understands what the others know. The experiment can only be activated when all three mix their unique ingredients. That's our safeguard against any corruption, however unlikely it may seem. It goes without saying that our intentions were completely honourable. The other two Elders escaped, one of course being Sophora. Without them, any information that I may have held would have been completely useless.

My captors were convinced that we were making weapons of mass destruction, to use their phrase. They wouldn't explain how they had arrived at that conclusion. If we were not making them for ourselves than it must be for the Chinese or the Arabs or anyone else who took their fancy. What were they paying us, as if we had any use for their wretched money? They had decided that as we were an isolated and remote country then we had plenty of places to hide those weapons.

Our Dryadian way of life was completely beyond their comprehension, as mine was of theirs with their fixation on fear, violence, duplicity and greed. Those are their mantras. I find the ways of the British government hard enough to understand but those of the American military machine defy description. We were questioned for what seemed weeks. Sometimes we were bullied, even roughed up a bit, poked and slapped and deprived of sleep. The lights were never turned off, the continual discordant music never turned down. And the American food! That was a torture in itself. We told them very little. The shepherds knew virtually nothing anyway and English was not their strongest subject. I was forced to translate for them, for none of the Americans knew any Dryadian, which seemed a major oversight on their part. I played the role of a naïve yet inquisitive schoolboy who was totally out of his depth with his first building set.

Eventually they had to give up. The British were putting them under pressure to release us. Our Elders were in turn exerting pressure on the British government, who were probably implicit any way. So we were released, flown to the Dryadian consulate in England by yet another helicopter, and told to find our own way back home. All so-called charges have been dropped. Their evil eye is still searching though. They are convinced that we have something of military value. In practical terms we don't. At least no more than the equivalent of the giant magnifying glass the old Greeks used to redirect the rays of the sun and set fire to the sails of the Persian ships. Dryadia is now in their radar. I'm sure that they will try to find other means of discovering what they think we know, and we do know some interesting things. For the moment they will be kept well buried. We must be on our guard. Sophora and I think that they will infiltrate spies into Dryadia and get to know some of the Elders. Perhaps not here in Ceradoc. It would be too obvious. The university at Cantillion seems a more likely place and a lot of the Elders go there to teach. So keep your eyes and ears open when you are there and let us know if you become aware of anything suspicious. So I'm home. I'll tell you one thing. I'll never make fun of *The Leaky Bucket* again. The voyage back here was the sweetest journey of my life."

"What's going to happen now?" asked Pushkin after a short silence. "And does this affect your plans for us?" The others looked on anxiously.

"For you there should be very little change. We may revise the Cantillion university syllabus a bit just to make sure that we're not being too open in sensitive areas. For myself, I'm going to rest up a bit and regain my strength. I'm not going back to the consulate. Too dangerous for one thing. I couldn't face being kidnapped again! Someone else will run it. In Dryadia we'll shortly hold an emergency moot at Cantillion, and Elders from all over the country will meet to discuss the whole sorry adventure. We are no longer a country that has an option about ignoring the East, much as most of us would like to. I suspect that at the moot we'll confirm what many of us have already agreed. We will be positive and try and carry our values to them rather than us be swamped by theirs."

A rather chastened quartet settled down to supper at one of Ceradoc's pair of inns down on the quay. There was much to discuss and much that still puzzled. They felt afraid. Anaxamander was obviously not letting on as much as he knew and he had lost his great zest for life.

"*Sweet are the uses of adversity*," he called after them in his best Shakespearian manner as they left, but he didn't sound entirely convincing. Tara tried hard to rally them. "Dryadia's mirror has been cracked many times before. Alanda and Isola had a rougher time than us. We know we're right. We won't let those unspeakable politicians and soldiers get us down."

"What on earth were Anaxamander and Sophora really doing there?" they kept saying to each other.

"Well, we know the name of the third Elder. Empedocles, the boffin man." Pushkin put on a satisfied look. "That's a bit of the jigsaw solved."

Tara blushed. "Oh, I shouldn't have let his name slip. I didn't realise at the time how big a secret it was."

"Don't worry." Mary put her arm round her reassuringly. "The secret is safe with us. Isn't it interesting what Anaxamander said about the oracle, that it was no accident that the serpents searched us out."

"I can't get my head round it," replied Pushkin. "No British scientist could possibly accept either that or the serpent energy idea."

"Aren't your scientists supposed to say, 'Absence of evidence is not evidence of absence.'? Don't you remember Anaxamander saying that where the serpent energy is strong the impossible becomes possible," said Tara forcefully.

"Most of them take a very narrow view of science. It's all statistics. They can't see the whole picture. They find it hard to bring the pieces together."

"Then they lack imagination," retorted Mary. "And speaking of the oracle, haven't they heard of the 'Library Angel' who comes into being when the book that you are looking for suddenly stares you in the face. Then it opens up at the very page where the answer to the question that has been driving you mad for the previous week is there before you. That's happened to me several times. Sam's experienced it too. We were talking about it a few days ago."

"You'd be told it was just a coincidence, Mary." Pushkin wanted to back away from this subject. He didn't want to be thought of as an apologist for something that he had quite a few doubts about. He realised that on examination the science of statistics was not as watertight as its proponents wanted the public to believe.

"We have a saying that science, or Natural Philosophy as we normally call it, and imagination are like husband and wife," said Tara. "The two serpents can be looked at like that. In a creative sense one serpent is powerless by itself. We believe that if you combine the imaginative power and the wisdom of the human heart with the power that is locked up in nature, then as Anaxamander said, 'The impossible becomes possible'.

I don't really know what they were doing up at The Beacons that night, and it's probably best that we don't find out, but I wouldn't mind betting that they had managed to bring those two serpents together and the results were quite spectacular. When you come along to our mid-summer celebrations next month you'll get a hint of what I mean. It's quite an event. Don't ask me what is going to happen because I want it to be a big surprise for you. We will meet up at The Beacons and many of us will participate in the celebrations."

Sophora was giving them lessons in what she called 'Spiritual awareness.' They were wide ranging talks and were uniquely Dryadian. They didn't seem to follow any tradition that even Pushkin was aware of. He trawled his mind and could see some links with India, Egypt, Greece, early Celtic Christianity and the Cathars. He wondered if all the old teachers had drunk at the same pool of knowledge. Sophora's tale was all her own though. She added that the tradition had changed little in six thousand years of Dryadian history.

"All the greatest truths are very simple. It's our brains that complicate things. Everything is connected to energy, the universal life force. Our basest acts and our negative thoughts are heavy and will always fall back to earth when we manage to shed them. Our essence, our spirit in fact, is light and eternal and made of very fine energy. It likes to fly and be free. That's our destiny. But remember it's not your opinions or your beliefs that are important, but how you live your life and use the power that lies in your heart."

"I love Sophora's teaching," said Sam later. He had brought them to his secret cave on the estuary. "Zephyr is telling me the same thing. He says that life is very simple and that you don't need volumes of books to understand it. In fact, did you know that there are no Dryadian spiritual books, only the pillar scripts and we now know that they often have to find you, rather than the other way round. Zephyr made me laugh. He said truth is like a zip fastener. You can see that it's very simple. You can see that it works. But try as you might you cannot quite see why it should."

"Imagine that in the bible," laughed Pushkin.

"In the beginning was the zip," said Mary in a solemn tone. "God saw that it was good as it would be very useful for keeping up your trousers."

"What about buttons," said Sam mischievously?

"Now you're being silly, Sam," replied Mary wagging her finger at him. "Buttons obviously come from another planet. Different God, see."

"Of course," smiled Pushkin. "It's obvious."

"Next time we must have some of our conversations in Dryadian. Don't forget we are supposed to be fluent in it before we go to the university. We start in three months."

Mary pretended to be strict. Thanks to Tara and her stories and songs her Dryadian was coming on well. Sam's was too, as Zephyr and the family always insisted on speaking Dryadian at table. Pushkin was the weakest for as he put it:

"How can you have a deep conversation on philosophy in a language that you only half understand?"

"Then I'll have to give you private lessons, if you would like me too."

Was Mary being flirtatious? He rather hoped so. Pushkin's face reddened as he stammered out a grateful reply in the affirmative and quickly changed the subject.

"Isn't it nice to see Anaxamander looking so well at last."

CHAPTER TWELVE

BECOMING DRYADIAN

Spring had merged imperceptibly into summer. For Sam, Mary and Pushkin their time in Ceradoc seemed like one glorious holiday. The trauma of the helicopters had faded. Anaxamander was well again, and he and Sophora and some of the other Elders were giving them regular lessons. The aim was that by the time they started at Cantillion, they would be reasonably fluent in all things Dryadian and be nearly as knowledgeable as the native-born students. They were encouraged to talk to everybody and work in the walled garden, weeding and digging. They learned to ride and care for the horses. Sometimes they were taken fishing in search of the local mackerel. They were lent bicycles when they were not on horseback and explored many of the local villages. These were all small (the average population of a village was around five hundred), and as self sufficient as possible. Most communities had their own unique character. Some specialised in certain crafts like woodworking, obtaining the raw material from the local forest and coppicing the under-storey. One local village had made a niche for itself making parts for the many wind and water mills of Dryadia. These mills played a part in generating electricity. Although the supply was not always reliable it was sufficient over all. When it was cold the Dryadians made the most of their well insulated and tightly shuttered houses and their lagged hot water tanks.

Pushkin was the group's scribe writing down the lecture notes and distributing them to the others, although they were encouraged to learn every thing by heart. He had arranged that they should try and meet every day for discussion and to read out aloud Parmenides' history, in the best Bardic tradition.

CHAPTER FIVE A NEW DAWN

Dryadia had split into two. In the south, Sastamoro's greed and his attempt to convert the villagers to the religion of Queen Elizabeth was gaining strength. Many of the southern Elders remained aloof in their sanctuaries. They had forgotten that their countrymen needed their guidance and wisdom, and that without it they lacked direction. They didn't realise that the villagers would be vulnerable to any leader who promised to best satisfy those animal and materialistic instincts that lie in us all. Consequently the south became a ship without a rudder.

In the north, Alanda and Isola were also on a crusade. They knew that they could not save Dryadia without the help of their fellow Elders. Already, some of them were returning to their villages to remind the people of the Dryadian message about living kindly, simply and honestly and that all of us were equal. These were the time-honoured values that had made Dryadia a contented and stable society. From their headquarters at The Beacons, Alanda and Isola and many others, travelled tirelessly around the country, cajoling the Elders to forsake their isolation and trying to persuade the villagers to return to the old traditions. It seemed that the very soul of Dryadia was at stake. It took quite a while but almost all the Elders of the North eventually answered the call. The great mission of Alanda and Isola had half succeeded as the north became united and remained at peace.

Alanda and Isola now turned their attention to the southern provinces. They knew that the people of the region, like them, were also descendants of Dryadogenes and were steeped in the same traditions and spoke the same language. There was no good reason why the country should be separated into two halves. The Dryadian spirit lay deep in everyone's heart. Gold was a new concept. An external religion seemed a strange idea to a people who had lived in harmony with themselves and their land until relatively recently. Why give up on a tradition that had brought peace and prosperity to the country for thousands of years? The Elders of the North had rejected violence in their attempt to unite the country. They knew that such action would only sow perennial seeds of bitterness that would take generations to weed out. They would use only powers of persuasion that were based on reason. They hoped that their words would speak to the hearts of Elders and villagers alike so that the communities could draw together again. It took about three years, but they succeeded. All but Cantillion, then a smaller place than it is now, joined Alanda and Isola in their quest to unite and rejuvenate Dryadia.

In Cantillion, Sastamoro fumed. He had no intention of giving in but he realised that he only had two options. Either he could retreat to England, to the country mansion that Queen Elizabeth had promised him, assuming that she didn't cut off his head first. Or he could stand and fight. Not with bows and arrows or the new fangled muskets. It was too late for that. He would play to his strengths and use treachery and guile, attributes that were of course totally alien to a true Elder of Dryadia. Indeed Alanda and Isola, with the agreement of almost all their fellow Elders, had already stripped him of that title.

Sastamoro decided to negotiate. He put it about that he would like to surrender and discuss terms. He invited Alanda and Isola to a great feast in Cantillion stating that he was sure that they could come to a satisfactory arrangement. Isola had been ill and was too tired to go. Alanda did not really want to attend without her but since he wanted to conclude the matter as soon as possible, and as Sastamoro seemed so conciliatory, he decided to go by himself. Sastamoro had lain on a great party. Jugglers, dancers and musicians mingled amongst the guests. Most of them had been imported from England, their wages paid in stolen gold. The food was rich and not to Alanda's taste. Nor was he accustomed to the wine with which Sastamoro plied him and especially not to the sleeping potions with which it was laced. By the end of the evening his brain swam in that twilight world between sleep and intoxication. He was barely aware as he was carried off into the night by Sastamoro's cronies.

Isola was distraught when Alanda failed to return home. Sastamoro sent word that he had safely left the feast of his own accord. Perhaps he had an accident on his way home? Isola sent out search parties and found his dismembered body in a ditch. Alanda had been murdered. His killing had been brutal. Isola was inconsolable. Her brother had been her whole life. They had sustained each other. They had worked so hard to return Dryadia to its former harmony. Now, on the brink of success, one of its architects had been struck down. Alanda's body parts were located and they were cremated on a great fire at The Beacons. It was with great difficulty that Isola's friends restrained her from throwing herself on the pyre.

Isola never totally recovered. But her work was done. Shocked by the murder Sastamoro was abandoned by most of his followers, and he fled to England never to be heard of again. Isola lived on a few more years, spending most of her time wandering between the villages, ensuring that the Dryadian spirit burned brightly where ever she went.

Isola created the order of the Practical Elders so that no one would feel excluded if they had the ability and desire to serve their country in a less philosophical or spiritual way than the Traditional Elders. She founded the great university at Cantillion where the greatest wisdom is taught and ensured that all future Traditional Elders were not only educated to the highest degree but were compassionate people dedicated to the path of truth. After her day, Dryadia never left its traditional path, and it was a very rare event if an Elder became corrupt. When Isola died, her body was cremated at The Beacons in exactly the same spot as Alanda's had been and her ashes were scattered to the winds.

By the end of the summer Sam, Mary and Pushkin had visited the majority of the forty or so communities of the Northern Province, including the capital Viribus. They were always made welcome and often stayed at the local rest house if the journey home was too long. Travelling though was very enjoyable when the weather was fine. Noisy machinery was very rare in Dryadia and as the narrow lanes that meandered through forest, meadow and moor linking the villages were bereft of cars, the peace and silence of the countryside and the richness of its wildlife brought the whole country close to paradise. The East has not known a state of equanimity such as Dryadia's for two hundred years. The industrial revolution had put paid to that.

At Parmenides' request Pushkin had spent his spare time writing something that had as its working title *An Englishman's travels in Dryadia* which if acceptable would be incorporated into the next edition of *The History.*

Their roads and tracks are far from lonely. No village is more than five or six miles distant from another and during the daytime they are often busy with travellers, usually journeying on foot but for the more pressed, there are bicycles, horses and wagons. Most highways are narrow, squeezed between the hedgerows with regular passing places. There is usually just enough room for a horse and cart to inch past a group of pedestrians going the other way. Friendly greetings are always exchanged, and most people know each other. This sense of community has long been lost in the speedy, dangerous roads of the East. Every mile along every lane there is a shelter, where travellers can take refuge from the rain or enjoy their lunch out of a cold wind. Ever burning lanterns are placed beside each shelter like welcoming beacons, and it is the duty of any passing traveller to replenish the oil or re-ignite the wick if they find it has gone out or is burning low. The Dryadian children have a delightful custom of placing fresh flowers or berries by the flame in honour of 'the spirit of the light'.

Each village is responsible for the upkeep of the roads in their neighbourhood. Throughout Dryadia it is the custom for every able-bodied man and woman to give up a day a week of their time to work on such tasks for the benefit of everyone. This in effect is the Dryadian way of taxation. Only some of the Elders, like the Therapeutae and the teachers who already work full time helping others, are exempt from such work. If the Elders have little time to support themselves, the community makes sure that they do not lack any of the basic necessities of life. The same help is of course available to the old and sick if their families are unable to look after them. A lot of trade is done through bartering although there is a Dryadian currency in use, the chola, which is based on the work a man or woman can do in a day. All Dryadians are entitled to be paid a chola a day whatever type of work they do, for all work is valued equally and no one earns more or less than their daily due. However, everyone is allowed to add extras to cover the costs of say their tools, materials and travelling expenses.

Training in nearly all crafts and professions is managed through apprenticeship schemes, and is funded by agreement through the communities and the provincial government. Any disputes are referred to the Elders. Health, education and public libraries are free to all, and the community pays or supports the people involved. There are a few factories, mostly small and mainly confined to the towns, especially in Cantillion, where they assemble things like heat exchange pumps and freezers. The raw materials are often imported cheaply from England. Some smelting of tin and copper is also carried out there, but in a small way, for although Dryadia is rich in minerals there is a rule that any mining in the countryside should be as good as invisible. Another interesting factory in Cantillion is one that makes contraceptives – diaphragms impregnated with honey, a natural spermicide and anti-septic. Combined with other natural methods, the honey cap has enabled the Dryadians to keep their population steady for a long time.

A few of the communities are known as the story telling villages. Every summer troupes of these actors, musicians, poets and weavers of tales leave their homes, often in whole family groups. They travel through the villages and towns entertaining and instructing their countrymen, in return for accommodation, food and small gifts. For once their bellies are full, their bodies well clothed and they have a comfortable home to live in, most Dryadians have need of little else, at least on a material level. It has been calculated that eighty per cent of the Dryadian economy is devoted to providing necessities, and twenty per cent to joyful pleasures that do not drain the earth's resources. In the East, the percentages are thought to be the other way round and their more dubious and wasteful pleasures in the Dryadians' opinion will in time make the earth uninhabitable.

Like everyone else in the world, the Dryadians need security, love and a sense of purpose in their lives. Much of this is provided by a strong sense of community and the support that it gives. The villages tend to be compact so that no home is isolated from another. There is no class structure or rich or poor. Everyone is given the power and the opportunity to achieve whatever they feel is best for them, providing it is not at the expense of anyone else's freedom.

Of all the villages of the Northern Province Ceradoc was the most unusual. It was a place that felt quite different from the other communities, perhaps because it had a higher proportion of Traditional Elders than anywhere else. Many of them had been born there like Anaxamander and his brothers. Others had settled there as Sophora had. To encourage her to stay, the villagers had built her a beautiful house on a knoll above the water's edge, sheltered by trees from the worst of the winds.

Amarinta was a seer, like Sophora and had come specifically to Ceradoc to study with her. Finding Zephyr was an additional bonus. They had two small children who very quickly had come to dote on Sam. Amarinta was also a Bard, the artistic kind, and was currently involved in two projects. The first, almost inevitably, was in illustrating Zephyr's *Natural History of Dryadia,* a book that he often told people he had been working on since he had been five years old! Her other project was in using her powers of seership often in collaboration with Sophora to 'see' into the past and garner pictures of important events which she could then bring alive through her drawings. Parmenides planned to use these intuitive illustrations in yet another edition of *The History.*

Sophora's presence in Ceradoc was a magnet for many of the more thoughtful Elders of Dryadia. They travelled from all over the country to learn from her and sometimes stay. In return for her wisdom they were encouraged to travel like simple pilgrims around Dryadia in the summer months, teaching the traditional knowledge. Many of them taught at the university at Cantillion.

Tara was not only a constant mentor and companion to Mary but had extended that role in an informal sort of way, to Sam and Pushkin. She often joined them in their discussion times and filled them in on anything they hadn't understood from Sophora and the other Elders' teachings. It was helpful that she was much closer in age to them and had a more recent memory of what it was like to be a student.

The four of them often went up to Sanctuary Hill to have their 'meetings' and to 'read' the pillars, although it was only Tara, with her skill in using the blinds and mirrors and her knowledge of the old Dryadian script that was able translate them. They usually consulted the oracle at the beginning of each discussion and the same reading had so far never appeared twice.

"Here it is," called Tara peering at the ancient script. "It's about courage. Listen."

If you do not have the courage to listen to your own heart, then you are in danger of becoming a slave to someone else's.

Underneath the words had been scratched the name *Isola.*

"It must have been one of her sayings," said Tara, "Not one I've heard before. You know her story of course. We consider she and her brother Alanda were the founders of modern Dryadia even though they lived more than four hundred years ago."

"We've read about them in Parmenides' history", replied Mary. "It's such a sad story".

"It is. But if they had not existed, I doubt if Dryadia would be here today. We owe them a huge debt. Now lets tuck into those cakes I brought."

Mary munched happily. "These are other worldly. I never saw you make them. What do you put in them, Tara?"

"It's a state secret. My mother made them. It's her speciality. Rumour has it that it has something to do with wild strawberries and honeycomb."

Pushkin brought out his file. All Sophora's recent talks on spiritual awareness had been typed out neatly. "Would you like me to read them out and then Tara can explain anything we don't understand." For twenty minutes Pushkin read aloud. This was a world that he barely recognised from his study of religion and philosophy in the East. He would have been ridiculed if he had discussed Sophora's ideas with his academic friends at his university. Perhaps she was not even right. After all she usually ended each talk with the words 'in my opinion,' although she never seemed to have any doubts at all about what she was saying. The words streamed out so fluently. Pushkin had underlined some of Sophora's more memorable sayings.

Every thing consists of energy from the grossest to the finest. Energy is simply a vibration or resonance.

It all begins with number. One to nine. The greatest truths are very simple.

Man is a three tiered being, soul, spirit and physical.

Our soul, our higher self, never comes to Erith. Soul energy spirals in bands around the earth. The soul is our personal God – the captain of our ship.

We always have an energy connection to our soul and spirit. The spirit is a facet of the soul and is connected to our physical body.

Our spirit joins our body at conception and leaves it at death.

We are spiritual beings having a human existence.

Many of us are so beastly we do not yet deserve to be called human.

We all have thousands of life times, and we evolve spiritually through them.

Our earthly lifetimes are very short compared with the fullness of our existence. We barely need to pack a toothbrush! It's like having a weekend away from home.

When we die our spirit, because it is so light and pure, floats up to our higher self, our soul, and becomes part of it once again.

Our physical body, along with any negativity it has acquired during its life, has a much grosser energy and falls back into the earth at death and is reabsorbed by it.

There is no purpose to life; it's just the way it is. It is a life sentence, and as we don't know the parole date, we might just as well learn to live well, and enjoy the experience.

We must take responsibility for our actions. Nobody out there is going to save us.

Do not take away anyone else's freedom. Do not steal is one of the greatest ideas for living well and harmoniously on the earth.

There are no divine instructions for living. There is no heaven or hell, reward or punishment, right or wrong. Only what is acceptable or unacceptable. We just are.

Yet it makes sense to live peaceful and kind lives treating others as you would yourself like to be treated . If we live lightly in this way then we will we raise our consciousness and that of our planet, and wonderful things will happen.

It is a great honour to have a life on this planet. It is even sweeter to have one in Dryadia especially at this time.

"Where does Sophora get this amazing knowledge from? We know so little about her," asked Mary, in some bewilderment.

Tara replied. "Some of it's no secret. She was born and brought up in Cantillion in just an ordinary family. There were no Elders in it. She went to the university there, like the rest of us. People at the time said that she already knew more than her teachers. We think that she was born wise. Sophora often says that she doesn't know what she knows, until you ask her. Then her eyes gleam, as I'm sure you have noticed, and the answers come flowing out like an oracle. She doesn't seem to think. Her brain seems to be by-passed in some way. I've heard her say that she has a key to the library, a sort of celestial library, I suppose. She seems to be plugged into the mains. That's the way of the seer. We have quite a few in Dryadia, but there's no one else to compare with her. Some people even say that she is a re-incarnation of Isola. She certainly speaks with real authority. We all listen intently when she talks. And she is so kind. She always has time for me when I am in trouble.

Yet Sophora can be very human too. We all know that she has a boy friend in Cantillion even though she is past fifty! She can swear like a pirate too, though it sounds much sweeter in Dryadian as we don't have your harsh Anglo-Saxon sounds. We accept her for whom she is and are very grateful to her, especially after the invasion of the helicopters. She has steadied us though the chaos, and I know she is very concerned about it. But I have to say that in many ways she is a bit of a mystery."

Now I want to talk to you about something else," exclaimed Tara dramatically.

"Mid-summer rituals. I've mentioned them before. It's a very special one this year as the summer solstice and the full moon are on the same day. So the energy will be powerful. You know that we have some kind of ceremony at every full moon?"

"We know about them," responded Mary. "But we haven't been invited to any yet. I had assumed that you all had orgies in the woods, at least in the summer months, and you didn't want to embarrass Pushkin until he was older!"

Mary nudged him in the ribs. "Only kidding, Pushkin," looking at his alarmed face. "I'm sure you will be ready for them next year."

Tara laughed. "Well you are all invited to this one and I promise you, everyone keeps their clothes on. Our mid-summer celebration is the most important one of the year. The Oak ceremony is a mega-extravaganza and is particularly important to us. It's celebrated in different places all over Dryadia. Ours is held in the Oak Grove in the woods close to The Beacons. It's quite dramatic and shows you an aspect of Dryadia that you haven't seen before. I won't tell you any more because I don't want to spoil it for you. But I think you will be amazed."

Sam was extremely happy living with Zephyr and Amarinta and their children. The house looked out over the estuary and the long back garden, half cultivated, half wilderness, climbed up the hill towards the woods. Here Zephyr had his vegetable garden, and Sam used to dream and watch the birds in the tumbled down potting shed between the cabbage patch and a small stream that trickled down from the woods to the estuary. It suited him perfectly. He could loose himself in the way he always had, through being aware of the world and enjoying its natural state, but avoiding being too much part of it. Sam's oversensitivity to ugliness or violence would have been regarded as extreme amongst most people in the East. In Dryadia he at last felt safe from the so-called development and progress of his former country. Here the earth and every green living thing was loved for itself and a piece of land could never be destroyed, or bought or sold for a miserable bit of profit. No one would lightly put an axe to a tree or clear a piece of rough ground without considering the outcome. The custom was always to ask three questions first.

'Are you doing any harm? Are you creating ugliness? Is it necessary?' As a safeguard, the Bards were consulted if people couldn't agree on any major or controversial project. For them beauty and harmony, and the well-being and peace of the people who lived close by, was the most important thing

He could never go back to his old country. Never! He would remain in Dryadia for the rest of his days, if he were allowed.

Another of Sam's favourite places was in Ruth's herb garden. He was welcome there and in her large homely kitchen, any time he chose. Ruth felt that he might one day be a good Therapeutae and she herself would teach him if he wished. Meantime she taught him the names of all her plants in Dryadian, English and Latin and what they were used for. It was a lot of work but Sam took to the task effortlessly in the same way that he had previously taught himself the names of birds and trees when he had lived in England.

Melissa also helped in his botanical education. Unofficially apprenticed to her mother her knowledge was already substantial. She introduced Sam to the joys of weeding and her sharp and expert eye brought a precision to the work that filled him with admiration. Melissa was a little younger than Sam and would not be going to Cantillion for another year. They shyly found out that they rather enjoyed each other's company and Melissa was already wondering how she would manage without seeing him regularly when he went to university. She did not worry too much though. Sam was good fantasy material in an innocent way and she could leave it at that for the time being. For his part Sam was far too shy to make any overtures.

Here in the herb garden he learned about the healing powers of nature. Amidst the vast array of plants that were lovingly cultivated in this amphitheatre of green harmony cascading between rocks and pools and sun and shade, Sam had found peace.

CHAPTER THIRTEEN

AMONGST THE OAK TREES

A dome of high pressure encircled Dryadia. There were no clouds and only the gentlest breeze. It was going to be a beautiful day. It was no surprise.

"It's always fine on Oak-Summer day", everyone said. "Dryadogenes must have done a deal with the Weather God."

Sam, Mary and Pushkin had noticed how quiet Ceradoc had become over the last two days. Its inhabitants, loaded with tightly sealed cases were slipping out by boat and obviously heading towards The Beacons. Mary guessed that at least some of them contained costumes, for she had spied Tara surreptitiously packing away some exotic and brightly coloured materials. No one was telling them anything, except to say that the three of them should go to Anaxamander's for breakfast on the day of the celebration. But Anaxamander and Ruth were not at home. They had left the previous evening. Melissa and Zach greeted them after an eerie walk amongst empty homes.

"We're the last people left in town," grinned Zach. "Without us you are lost."

"Oh do shut up, Zach. We're here to look after them, not terrify them. Just how un-Dryadian can you get?" Melissa explained. "Every one has gone on ahead to prepare. We know the way and can sail the boat, so Mum and Dad have asked us to feed and water you and when we're all ready we can start on the big adventure."

"Have you been before", asked Sam.

"Many times. I think the first time was when I was three months old. We couldn't be left alone in Ceradoc obviously, so our parents took us with them. We had a big crèche nearby for the younger ones. This time we will be with you a lot of the day. During the rituals we'll have to leave you but you'll be safe, I promise you. You'll probably be pleased to get rid of Zach anyway." Melissa deftly dodged the piece of bread that her younger brother aimed at her. "So eat up your porridge and toast and we'll be off."

The boat was tied up at the little quay not far from Zephyr's house. Melissa and Zach were responsible sailors, and their mock enmity was forgotten as they expertly guided their craft into the main channel and allowed the tide and wind to sweep them gently between the sandbanks and around Sanctuary Hill, and then across the estuary towards The Beacons where the fabled Oak Circle lay.

"Now, you're going to have to be all very focused," ordered Melissa as they walked across the green sward of the field of the stone circles. They remembered it as the place where they had had their picnic two months earlier when they were trying to fathom out exactly where the helicopters had landed.

"What an outrage," said Mary indignantly to Pushkin. "Didn't they know that this is hallowed ground?"

After twenty minutes they entered a scrubby area and Melissa led them through what seemed to be a kind of maze. The path criss-crossed, dipped and rose, and sometimes doubled back unexpectedly through tracks deeply lost in overgrown hawthorn amidst the sweet scent of wild roses and honeysuckle.

"The helicopters couldn't see the tracks in this area from the air, thank goodness," said Melissa. "See, that's where we're going," and she pointed to a dense belt of trees, just visible from the path as it rose for the final time. In a few minutes they had reached it, a great wall of green.

"But there's no way in," said Sam puzzled.

Melissa's face lit up with one of her solar powered smiles.

"Follow me." She turned to her right and dropped quickly through what appeared to be a gigantic rabbit hole. For a few yards it descended into darkness. When the path opened up they found themselves walking along a deep tunnel, just about open to the sky through a tracery of green, and sunken by centuries of scrambling feet. The towering trees above them became sentinels to their journey, shutting out the sun and shrinking them to the size of midgets. Then after about a hundred yards the track climbed abruptly and they were now walking on the brooding bracken floor of the forest.

"Keep going," said Melissa quietly. "The path is obvious now. It's been used by hundreds of us over the last few days. There's a very large oak ahead. We'll halt there. Don't go round it even though it looks a bit gloomy when you stop."

When they reached it, Zach grinned at them all rather mischievously and said:

"Now you all must shut your eyes and hold onto your neighbour's hand and we will lead you to the Promised Land."

Melissa led the way, daringly taking Sam's hand lightly in her own, and guided him and the chain of his fellow seekers slowly around the circumference of the enormous oak. "Now open your eyes," said Melissa. "We call it the Egg."

"Oh my God." Sam, Pushkin and Mary spoke almost in one voice as they stared into another world.

Before them was a large green space of about an acre. It was completely flat and as beautifully groomed as any suburban back lawn. It was not really a circle. The area was oval shaped like an egg or an acorn. The dark gloom of the last part of their journey was gone and a lighter shade of green drifted through the canopy of branches of the fourteen immense oaks that were spaced around the Egg's perimeter. The branches of each tree were so entangled with those of their neighbours that a deft squirrel could have circumnavigated the whole Egg without touching the ground or having to leap more than a few feet. The two largest oaks grew at each end of the Egg. These two immense and magnificent trees were at least five hundred years old – standing like ancient gladiators, the grandmother and grandfather of all oak trees, battered and hollowed through age, but still green and growing. They stood like a king and queen ruling over the twelve other oaks that stood like disciples around them.

In the middle of the Egg there was what seemed an altar, a huge twenty foot square slab of granite raised high in the air and cracked and weathered by rain and time. Upon it was heaped a carefully arranged mound of dead branches and twigs as if prepared for a great bonfire. Pushkin remembered his researches into the ancient oak rituals of Europe and their hint of bloody sacrifices, and hoped that what he saw before him was not a funeral pyre. Surely it was not possible that Dryadia had its dark side? A quick look at Melissa's innocent angelic face largely re-assured him.

There seemed to be no one else around. A deep hush lay amidst the trees. It reminded them of a great outdoor cathedral. The trunks of the oaks provided the supporting columns and the greenery of the canopy above their heads, the roof. Time and space no longer seemed important. Zach had already melted away and now Melissa too was preparing to leave them.

"Now I just want you to stay here, exactly where you are, next to this oak. I have to prepare for my role. Take off your shoes. We all have to connect with mother earth. Enjoy the peace and when it ends, don't be afraid. Watch and listen. You'll be perfectly safe, but you may be very surprised in a moment." With that Melissa slipped behind the oak and was gone. The silence came floating back broken only from time to time by the wistful song of a robin or the explosive chatter of a wren.

It seemed that there was something in the air though. A feeling of expectancy perhaps? There was a flash of green behind one of the oaks on the far side of the Egg. Traces of movement could be observed or heard from behind every tree, including a persistent rustle from the back of the one they were sitting under. Eventually a hidden voice said gently.

"Make yourselves comfortable. It's particularly soft amongst the roots where the moss is, but the cushions that you brought with you may help even more. The show is about to begin." The voice sounded friendly and didn't ask for a reply but it reminded them very much of Ruth's.

The green flashes soon manifested into figures, both large and small, adults and children, clad in green cloaks and hats, like so many Robin Hoods from Sherwood Forest. Groups of about twelve surrounded and embraced each oak like bats on a wall. They remained stationery for a minute, still and silent. Then emerging out of the twilight of quiet came the faintest of sounds, like the murmur of insects far away. The sound grew louder, the hum of a hundred whisperers, swelling and ebbing around every oak. It grew in resonance and the Egg became alive with the noise. Even the branches seemed to vibrate. Seemingly the green people were up there as well. Then the wood appeared to move. The green figures, mostly holding small branches of leaves, had unclasped and lowered themselves from the walls and roofs of their oaken homes, and had begun to move away in unison. They had aligned themselves in the form of a great serpent and barefooted closely followed each other clockwise in and around the great perimeter trees of the Egg. As they moved, very slowly at first and then speeding up to a trot, they danced and swayed in time to the strong pulse and hypnotic tune that by now was on everybody's lips.

Then the three heard Tara's voice. She had appeared from behind the oak clad in the same green costume as the others. At close range they could see that it was lined in white, and that her hat had three green feathers stuck in it, the mark of the Storyteller.

"Why not come and join us? We want you to feel apart of everything."

She helped Sam to his feet followed by Mary and Pushkin. Then a space was made in the serpent chain to accommodate them, before they all went dancing on. The pace quickened as the music grew louder, and the excitement and passion of the participants increased as if they had been mesmerised. Half way round and at at the completion of every circuit, in the shadows of the grandfather and grandmother oaks, they stopped and bunched up, and sang a different tune, a slow haunting refrain in a minor key. It was so moving and compelling in its heart stopping effect that once heard it was never to be forgotten.

Then without any obvious signal the serpent was off again, cloaks flapping against the oak trunks as they once more snaked around the trees until they had completed seven circuits of the Egg. As they danced, they gradually became more oblivious to their surroundings. Their minds appeared to be intoxicated by their passage out of the material world towards the ethereal.

The humming stopped and the serpent spoke in the Dryadian language of gateways to other worlds and the oneness that lay beyond. The movement of the serpent, which seemed initially like the contractions of labour, had now turned into the cries and wild spasms of birth. Then suddenly without any warning there was a huge climatic shout, an orgasm of sound, followed by a deep sigh and a sensation of deep peace and quiet like being held in a lover's arms. They had done their work. The Egg had been charged up once more. Completely exhausted, every green man, woman and child disengaged themselves from the body of the serpent, and sat or lay motionless. They quietly rested between the mossy roots of the oaks, tuning into the massive energy reserves that were now stored within the Egg.

For perhaps twenty minutes they waited inside the oaken shell of the Egg. No one spoke. Then quietly walking in from the shelter of the trees, almost drifting in, fourteen cloaked figures settled themselves in the middle of the clearing. Their cloaks were not green this time but dark sapphire blue lined with creamy white, the colour of hawthorn blossom. Their heads were covered with their cowls giving them the appearance of medieval monks. Their demeanour was solemn, even stately. Gone were the almost Dionysian rhythmic movements of the green dancers. These people were some of the senior Elders from Ceradoc. Sophora's tall slim figure was as obvious as Anaxamanders's rounder one. Sam was sure he got a glimpse of Zephyr's beard. Amarinta, Ruth and Parmenides were also there and others whom he didn't know so well.

The Elders approached the great altar stone and sat down about thirty yards from it. Twelve of them placed themselves in a horseshoe shape around it, six on the left and six on the right. Sophora and Anaxamander sat as a pair completing the central part of the horseshoe, but had distanced themselves from the others. They faced the altar, with their backs to the Grandfather Oak. All the Elders remained completely still in their allotted positions, their heads bowed a little under their hoods. They were concentrating intently. The Egg was as silent as a country graveyard. It was remarkably still. No cloud blotted the sky. The green dancers had recovered and were sitting up, staring into the centre of the Egg, also rapt in concentration. It seemed that something was going to happen.

And it did. Nothing had prepared Sam, Mary and Pushkin for the drama that followed. The shock was the most unexpected of their lives. Out of that cloudless and windless sky from right above them came a crash that sounded like ten thousand cymbals striking at once. It was as if a great meteorite or comet had violated the middle of the Egg. But nothing physical had landed. There was a fire though. The great mound of dry wood on top of the altar was aflame. Not simply alight, but blazing so bright and high that every oak in the Egg had added a red and orange sheen to its coat of greenery. The shock had been so great that the Elders had been forced to move well back from the pyre towards the oaks. Some of them had their heads between their knees almost comatose. Under every tree there was a huddle of green-cloaked figures holding each other for comfort or pressing themselves against the rough bark of the trunks for support.

Absolute stillness reigned in the Egg after the thunderbolt. The only sound was the crackling of the oak logs on the altar. Eventually the Elders, once they had recovered their strength, rose to their feet and one by one walked towards one of the fourteen oaks. Each stood with their back towards the trunk as if guarding it. They mingled with the other Dryadians who by now had also risen to their feet. Blue merged with green. No one had been hurt. Most had been prepared, and for those who were not, the comfort of their friends was helping to ease the shock of their baptism of fire. Smiles were creeping back onto faces and turned to delight as they looked up to see scores of orange, red and yellow banners unfurling from the branches above. Each was inscribed in Dryadian and emblazoned with the national emblem of the undefeated raven. From seemingly out of nowhere, another group of people emerged, dressed in yellow, red and orange cloaks, in fact the same colours as the banners. They had just a few minutes previously, pulled the cords that released those banners into the Egg. Many were singing but others were playing musical instruments. It was quite a band with its accordions and drums, cymbals and trumpets and flutes and recorders. The tunes were unfamiliar to those brought up in the East. They alternated between songs of almost unbearable sweetness followed by wilder rhythms and harmonies, nature's own sounds that could have only emerged from the untamed places of the earth. All began to dance to these seductive rhythms. Cloaks of many colours mingled around the fire and were then thrown off because of the heat.

As the Dryadians danced it seemed that their spirits were as vibrant as the fire and their bodies as orgiastic as in the great rituals of Dionysius. But they were always in control, always in line, spirit always in harmony with the body. For this great celebration of summer, fertility and love of the earth, was acknowledging the purity and lightness that lies at the heart of creation. And so they danced around the fire until the embers burned low, and finally exhausted, they returned to the shelter of the oaks. Their souls were filled with the feelings of consummation, not of the body, but of the very oneness of being. The marriage of heaven and earth, between the forces of lightning and the serpent energy that lay under their feet, had been completed. The oak trees and the unlimited power of the human imagination and spirit had acted as a catalyst. In return all had been blessed and renewed once more.

Day was subsumed by twilight and twilight faded into night. A full moon sailed across a clear sky and illuminated the oak grove of The Beacons through ghostly shadows. Hampers were unpacked and young children retrieved from the nearby crèche. The Dryadians of Ceradoc began to eat and drink their midsummer feast. All over Dryadia, in other groves, similar celebrations had also just taken place. Then all would find their sleeping bags and rest under the stars in one gigantic sleepover. The night passed. At dawn two magnificent ravens flew over The Egg croaking loudly. No one heard them though, and they flew on towards the sea to greet a new day.

Zephyr's remark that the great altar also marked the spot where Isola and Alanda had been cremated, probably on those very same stones five hundred years ago, drew Sam back on the following day to Parmenides' history in search of greater understanding

CHAPTER SIX THE LEGACY

Following the death of Alanda and Isola, neither outside forces nor internal rebellion ever again seriously threatened Dryadia. It certainly helped that the country was poor in material wealth, had no cities or roads and was encircled by stormy seas, high cliffs and the dense forest of Dreagle. It was also fortunate that the English had other fish to fry. Their traditional enemies: Scotland, Ireland, France and Spain and their own civil war kept them busy. Later the British became pre-occupied with creating a global empire. Exploiting the peoples and natural resources of America, Asia and Africa seemed to be much more rewarding than invading the desolate moors and forests of Dryadia. Moreover the Dryadians never totally isolated themselves again from the outside world. Small embassies were exchanged, treaties were regularly signed, and a small amount of trade was agreed. But generally Dryadia still remained a land apart, reasonably secure in its newly found external security and in the renewed mutual respect that had been forged between the Elders and the villagers.

Everyone was honoured for who they were. Anyone could become an Elder if they were wise enough and sufficiently ego-less in the case of the Traditional Elders; or respected enough for the Practical Elders. Nor was any one disadvantaged by not being an Elder, for there were no material rewards. The desire to serve was enough. There was little wealth to squabble over and there was plenty of land available for those who needed it. In any case, land was not a commodity to be traded. It belonged only to itself. The population was optimum and remained stable. Our lifestyles and the Therapeutae kept us healthy and no one was allowed to live in poverty or want.

Alanda and Isola's great legacy was that through their own knowledge and the breadth of their teaching, they had ensured that the Dryadian Elders had become wise again. The philosophy was light and spiritually minded. It was based on common sense and what worked in practice. Everyone needed to feel included. So long as the country did not stray from the traditional and universal values which belonged to everyone anyway, Dryadia would remain a well run and contented society. The Elders settled any disputes with these concepts in mind, and no laws needed to be written down. Dryadia was, and still is, a land without lawyers. Nor for that matter have we ever felt the need for accountants, bankers and estate agents or even conventional doctors – some of the major professions of the East.

It is often asked where Alanda and Isola, usually regarded as Dryadia's greatest teachers, obtained their remarkable wisdom. Had their own teachers passed down the knowledge or was it inbred in them? The answer was probably both. Dryadians have always accepted the principle of re-incarnation and we believe that many wise souls decide to experience a lifetime in our country. This is partly to protect and enhance our wisdom but also to experience the joy of living amongst like-minded people. In the East such people are thinly spread, and they are as a result often frustrated for lack of understanding and lonely for their own kind.

For thousands of years, since Dryadogenes and the original wise ones had arrived in the country, Dryadia had been evolving both spiritually and in the practical art of civilised living. They had not entirely lived in isolation, but had maintained connections with most of the major spiritual and cultural societies that had risen and fallen in Europe over that time. There always had been a cross fertilisation of ideas between Dryadia and civilisations such as the Greeks, the Druids and later the Italian renaissance. One of the most interesting was the Dryadian connection with the Cathars of the Languedoc in Southern France. Their remarkable spirituality reached its zenith in the twelfth and thirteenth centuries, before they were destroyed by a papal crusade at the Siege of Montsegur in 1243.

Many Dryadian Elders visited the Cathars to share their knowledge and likewise many Cathars came here. As may be apparent from the name, some settled in the village of Ceradoc in Northern Dryadia. Ceradoc literally means the place that says 'Yes to Peace'. Legend tells us that Alanda and Isola were born in Ceradoc and spent their childhood there. Unlike the Dryadians the Cathars considered themselves Christians, but their form of Christianity was very different to that of the orthodox Catholic Church. In fact they called themselves 'The Good Christians' to distinguish their religion from that of the papal church of the time, which they considered satanic. Their elders were known as 'The Parfait' and led a particularly ascetic life style.

After the final massacre, a number of the wisest of their elders and some of their followers escaped to Dryadia, where existed a tolerance that was unknown in the rest of Europe. In fact the two philosophies were so similar that many of the 'Parfait' were able to become Dryadian Elders. We might add here that there is a belief that the Cathar refugees, who came to Dryadia, carried away with them a great treasure. There are many theories as to what that treasure might be but it has not been knowingly found. One abiding story taught to all Dryadian children at an early age, was that it was buried deep under Mt Cynthos and that it will be rediscovered at a time of Dryadia's greatest need.

Like the Dryadians, and the old Druids of Britain and the Pythagoreans of ancient Greece 1500 years earlier, the Cathars believed in the Immortality of the Soul; that we experience many lifetimes on earth; that all men and women are equal; and that our highest aim is to live simple, upright and truthful lives, in peace with one another. Although nominally Christian, the Cathars did not accept the divinity of Jesus.

Their ideal was to try to lead a good life. They had very little dogma apart from what they called dualism, namely that there were two Gods at war with each other. One God ruled the spiritual world and the other the material. Even that idea was not properly understood and much of it could be comfortably incorporated into the Dryadian philosophy, which already accepted that there were many dimensions of existence, none of them truly separate from the others. Our main concern has always been to provide an environment where our spiritual natures can flourish, and the ignorant beastly side in man be kept well in check. To Alanda and Isola these great and simple truths were self evident and universal. It does not matter whether they obtained the wisdom from within their own hearts or from others. This perennial philosophy, whatever its origins, has been known as The Great Tradition since time immemorial.

Every so often in the great stream of human evolution, there is born in the minds of men a pulse that raises them above the common place. New directions are taken in art and science. Where the soil is fertile and the conditions right, old thoughts are discarded and boundaries cracked open. Fresh ideas can germinate. Sometimes a spiritual impulse is released as well and people start behaving in a more compassionate way. It is not so much that new ideas are discovered but that the timeless wisdom is rediscovered. The knowledge that has been lost has been found again many times in the world's history. Where people of one mind are concentrated in one place then the pulse is strengthened by their combined thoughts and energy. In other places at its worst it can degenerate into the horrors of the rule of the mob. We like to think that in Dryadia we see this energy at its best for we are fortunate in having here many wise, well- educated and sensitive souls.

We believe that there was a major impetus towards a lighter way of being in the time of Alanda and Isola, a time when the wise were losing their direction. Elizabethan England was stirring too about the same time, at least in a cultural way. In Dryadia the spiritual path was found once more, and we feel that we have not lost it since. We also like to think that at the present time the pulse is strengthening once again all over the world. A great debate is now under way in Dryadia to determine how we can play our part in supporting this striving towards the light.

A few days after the oak rituals, Sam was ambling by the waterside near the quay reading his mother's latest letter when he met Melissa on her way to Zephyr's house.

"I was hoping to bump into you, Sam. Mum and dad have invited you to lunch tomorrow. Just the four of us, as Zach is going to visit his friend in Viribus. The meal is special. We call it our oak celebration lunch though I promise you acorns won't be on the menu." She looked at his forlorn face. "Why are you looking so sad, Sam? I thought you might be glad to see me."

"Oh I am," replied Sam reddening a little." It's my mum's letter. They've chopped down all the oak trees on my patch. There were six of them. I've measured them and they are all over one hundred years old. They're going to build an executive housing estate there and my mum has written to say that the developer has told her that the new inhabitants can't be expected to be clear up all the acorns in the autumn or clean the messy bird droppings off their shiny new cars. They want boring low maintenance gardens where nature doesn't give any trouble."

"Well I'm so glad you're here and you don't have to watch it," said Melissa consolingly. "What barbarians some of your countrymen are. I'm so very sorry. We'd never axe a mature oak unless it was dangerous and might fall on someone's head. The only oaks we fell are the young ones in the plantation, which are planted very close together so they grow quickly towards the sky to find the light. In any case they would crowd each other out if we didn't thin them and we do put the wood to good use.

Our wild oaks are sacred and very precious to us. Mum and dad always call them the king of all the trees. Their energy is very powerful. We'll give you an oak lesson tomorrow so that you'll feel better. My parents are experts."

"Absolutely outrageous. Quite appalling," exclaimed Anaxamander over the lunch table that had been freshly decorated with acorns and oak leaves in honour, as he put it, of the Oak God. "Did you know," he said, addressing his remarks to Sam, "it wasn't always like that in your country or in the rest of Europe for that matter.

Once upon a time oaks were revered. Kings were crowned under them, sick people healed under them, and the seers prophesised under them. As you have seen, oaks attract lightening more than any other tree. Your Saint Columba, who was an ex-Druid before he became a Christian, supposedly aligned his church north and south, rather than the usual east and west, to avoid cutting down an oak grove. The world started losing its respect for nature in the Iron Age nearly three thousand years ago and the old wisdom and spirituality was gradually lost. Except in Dryadia of course."

"What exactly was the point of the oak rituals at The Egg?" asked Sam. "I can see it was a wonderful communal gathering and you've already told me that you were firing up what you call the battery, but what will you do with all that stored energy. Could it be anything to do with what you were doing on 'Helicopter Night'?"

Anaxamander smiled. "Everything and nothing. The energy we experienced is not just physical but ethereal as well but they were not joined up properly at the solstice rituals. That's not to say that wasn't the case many hundreds of years ago and that it won't be again when the time is right. Our experiments at The Beacons were also ethereal but unfortunately premature as we painfully discovered. I will tell you one thing though. Never underestimate the strength of the heartfelt emotion that you saw in The Egg. The energy of brainpower alone is miniscule by contrast. Our deepest emotions have the power to move things on a physical level as the word indicates. There is, in other words, nothing greater than the power of love as my American friends never found out."

"I want to tell you about the healing that oaks can do," said Ruth.

"Like your oak tree therapy," said Melissa excitedly. "When you tell your depressed patients to sit with their backs to an oak tree for twenty minutes daily to raise their spirits. It really works too. I've tried it many times when I'm sad. You need to tell Sam too about your oak compresses for wounds, so that they dry up and any poison is sucked out."

"It seems you've told Sam yourself," replied her mother patiently. "But I will add that the oak, like all trees and healing plants, has a kind of essential energy that makes it different. The oak heals the emotions and gives you strength of purpose. You can use it homoeopathically for emotions, herbally for more physical problems and of course, as Melissa says, obtain the power directly from the tree itself. I believe that it has energy more akin with human beings, especially in the heart area, than any other tree. Just as we saw at The Egg it charges you up, especially when you are feeling a bit down.

The East are a funny lot in their attitude to healing. They don't think like us at all. They believe that they need those enormous buildings, hospitals that look like factories, which scare you to bits as soon as you enter them. They love their high-tech machinery and can't wait for you to be to hooked up. Then they try to diagnose you and give a posh name to your disease. Finally, you are prescribed some rather toxic chemicals, which seldom really cure and at best may palliate, but at worst make you sicker. I must admit that some of their surgery and emergency work is impressive. We, on the other hand, believe that the power is within us and in nature and not in the buildings or the technology. Nature cures us from within, and the most important thing is to have loving and knowledgeable people nursing you using non-invasive natural remedies. Not to mention having a lovely big comforting oak tree outside your window! What more could a sick person want?"

"Mum and dad said I should take you to Mount Quercus," said Melissa after a pause. "Well, that's dad's name for it."

"Quercus is the Latin for oak tree," commented Sam."

"Precisely. Mum says my father mixes his languages unashamedly."

"I only mean it's an oak covered hill," replied Anaxamander. "It's about three miles away with some amazingly big deciduous oaks. We call them the summer oaks as opposed to the evergreen winter Holm oaks that grow here and shelter us from the winds. The summer oaks grow much better away from the sea. Now if you walk fast you'll be there in an hour."

Sam and Melissa left Ceradoc through the woods at the top of the village. Eventually the road would arrive in Viribus. Not many people were using it that afternoon. On the way Melissa showed Sam the plantation where they coppiced the hazel and chestnut and the few small oaks that were felled from time to time.

"We always tell the trees what we are going to do in advance so they are not in shock. We don't really need to plant more acorns either as the jays and squirrels mostly do it for us. We're definitely not short of oaks of any ages and we honour them all."

The road climbed and then levelled following a ridge through more woods until it dipped into a small valley. It then rose again winding itself around a small flattened hill covered with some of the largest oaks Sam had ever seen.

"Dad thinks there used to be an oracle here until it was moved to Kantala. How old do you think some of these are? You said you could measure them."

"I was told that they grow in circumference by about an inch a year. So if my outstretched arms measure five feet and I can encircle the whole tree then it's about sixty years old. My trees in Croydon were two stretches round so they were about one hundred and twenty years old."

"Sam, why don't we measure some of the ones here starting with some of the smaller ones here? I'd guess that the jays were busy here a good century ago."

Melissa walked up to the nearest tree and put her arms around it.

"About half way. You stretch out on the other side."

Their fingers just touched and Sam felt a little frisson of unexpected excitement as they lingered a few seconds more than was strictly necessary. He hoped that the next tree would be slightly smaller! Melissa however chose a much bigger tree and said she would stay still with her arms clasping its trunk while Sam worked his way around like a caterpillar. He was a good three feet short after four turns and then greatly daring put his arms round Melissa's shoulders as he completed a fifth. She turned around and laughed and they couldn't help themselves as they hugged each other again.

"Nearly three hundred years old," stammered Sam.

"Now let's try the biggest one – that huge knobbly hollow one over there. We call it the marriage oak because couples used to get married under it in the old days. There's a soft hollow between its roots. Zach and I used to sit there and put the world to rights when we were younger."

A few minutes later, Sam pronounced;

"Nearly nine stretches – that's over five hundred years old."

"Wow. It must have been here before Isola and Alanda's time. We'd better sit down so we can recover."

"Then we can have our very own oak tree therapy," said Sam as they settled themselves between the mossy roots and pushed their backs against the tree's mighty trunk.

"Now you must tell me a story Sam, just as Zach and I used to."

"What sort of story?"

"Why your story of course. Start at the beginning."

Sam thought for a while and then smiled.

"Once upon a time a cuckoo deposited her solitary egg in an ordinary suburban house in Croydon! This was surprising because the cuckoo wasn't meant to be in Croydon at all. Its flight plans had been muddled up in Africa where it had been spending the winter and its final destination was supposed to have been Dryadia."

Melissa laughed. "What a silly mistake. I hope the mother cuckoo speaks to the African authorities when she goes back."

"Unfortunately we will never know if she did for the cuckoo took no further interest in her child and the baby cuckoo was left to fend for itself. It grew up lonely and isolated and had so little in common with everyone else that it decided it must have been adopted by aliens which of course in a way he had."

"What happened then?" asked Melissa eagerly. "Did he escape?"

"By the skin of his wing tips. He heard of a land where he believed he might be understood for it was rumoured that the people thought like him. After a lot of adventures he crossed over a great river and entered a most remarkable country that had been hidden for a long time. And that's where as they say the story really begins."

For two hours Sam and Melissa talked out their innermost thoughts snuggled up in the oak tree's roots until the moon came up and they walked and ran back to Ceradoc hand in hand laughing and giggling as they went.

CHAPTER FOURTEEN

THE UNIVERSITY OF CANTILLION

The university stood on high ground at the edge of the city, not far from the tidal river that flowed to the southern sea. It consisted of about a hundred of the typical Dryadian triple storied structures although some were octagonally shaped rather than built in the traditional hexagonal style. Eight, to the Dryadians, was the number that was associated with the teaching and preservation of the higher learning, and it was in these eight-sided buildings that most of the teaching took place. All of these ancient university lodges were sublimely elegant and beautiful. Built in wood or stone, the eaves, doors and window frames were usually exquisitely carved with flowers and foliage or with bucolic scenes of Dryadian life. Each group of lodges had a large garden attached with views of the sea in the far distance. Four of these buildings had been set aside for the first intake of the 'Students from the East.'

In all, there were twelve students from across the Drangle, including Sam, Mary and Pushkin. One of their lodges was the teaching building, with traditional desks on the ground floor, a more informal room above, and a quiet meditation area in the cupola. The students lived in the other three lodges, each under the supervision of a mentor. Antheus was a quiet serious man from western Dryadia with a firm mouth and gentle eyes. Rosa was a brisk older woman, who everyone was startled to learn, had once been the captain of *The Leaky Bucket.* Much to Mary's delight, she had discovered that Tara was the third of the supervisors, a secret she amazingly had kept to herself. This was the first time she had been a mentor. All three had been graduates of the university previously and would live and work with them over the next year.

The morning after their arrival the students had been asked to assemble in the teaching lodge. A grey-headed man with long hair and a beard to match rose to address them. Beside him sat an elfin woman with a chunky necklace, darting eyes and a yellow flower in her hair.

"My name is Nestor," he began. "I and my dear friend Silene here are the principals of the University of Cantillion, indeed the only university in Dryadia. I bid you all welcome, 'Students from the East', virtually the first ones that we have ever taught from your country. This is the first day of the Bramble month. I hope by now you are familiar with our lunar tree calendar. Our solar year is 6,250, for it is that number of years ago that Dryadogenes first came to this country and founded our nation. He brought with him a philosophical tradition that in its essence has changed very little from that day to this. This is unique in the history of the world. We have now decided to share our knowledge with our friends from across the Drangle.

You, my dear friends are guinea pigs in this extraordinary experiment, which if successful, will lead to further intakes from Britain. We hope that you will achieve a happiness here that you have not experienced before, and learn about things that you had no idea existed. Cantillion is like no university on earth. We share our knowledge of life, both material and spiritual, though we usually use the word ethereal, and learn how to live well on both levels. We have no exams, few books, and certainly no electronic aids. You don't have to write anything down unless you want to.

For the best effect, wisdom should be sipped and absorbed slowly. Then it can simmer in the heart for the remainder of your life. Much of what we teach here may not be really new to you. It is just a reminder of what you have forgotten. The greatest truths are already part of our souls, and part of our DNA if you like. In fact we consider that what we teach here is more food for the heart than for the brain. There are no career openings at the end of the course, as I believe you say in the East. I do feel though that a deep part of you will be profoundly satisfied, long before you finally leave the university in three years time."

Stephano smirked to himself.

'Not quite my thing', he thought. 'It looks as if I am going to have a dull time. Some of the girls are a bit of all right though.' He glanced at Mary's flaming red hair, and at a petite dark haired girl with a lively manner called Nell. Nell, he later learned, was a Londoner like himself. 'But I don't suppose they will know anything about the science labs. The mentors would be a better bet, or some of the native students from the second and third years. But as Mr B said, I have to settle in first before I ask too many questions.'

At last Nestor sat down and Silene rose to her feet.

"We have a curriculum that is unlike that of any other university in the world. Here we all learn the same things. There is no specialisation in the subjects that we study. You will notice there is a lot of music and poetry. We all learn how to tell a good story even if you don't want to train to be a Storyteller. We learn how nature works – what grows from the earth and what moves in the sky. We study a lot of maths and geometry, but it's is not like the stuff they tortured you with at school. We study the science and meaning of numbers, and the resonance and vibration that is associated with them. It is from the energy of numbers that all life springs. We learn about healing and wholeness whether or not you want to be a Therapeutae one day. Our medicine has little in common with that of the East. And we learn about the true nature of Man, both in the physical world on Erith as we call our planet, and on the ethereal planes."

When she had finished, Silene and Nestor walked around the room and hugged every one in greeting. It was such a lovely day they were going to have their first lesson on the riverbank and watch dragonflies and water birds and learn how to relax and become aware of life around them.

"And please would you bring your best voices", pleaded Silene. "We are going to sing and try and charm the water rats out of their holes."

Stephano hoped that she was joking.

Their accommodation was simple. Their three residential lodges were part of a group of twelve arranged in a large circle, the other nine being used by the native Dryadian first year students. In the middle were the teaching lodges, a meetinghouse, a cookhouse and a laundry/storeroom. All university students lived in these simple communes where they could both mix or seek privacy as they wished. Sam, Mary and Pushkin were separated into different houses. Sam was in Tara's lodge with three other students. Tara had specifically requested that Stephano was not to be lodged with her because of her rather unhappy relationship with his brother. He was placed in Rosa's house along with Mary and Nell, the girl Stephano had been eying up.

There were two hours to spare before supper so Sam, who always felt uncomfortable with people he didn't know, left his lodge and walked back to the Dragonfly River where they had been earlier. He drank in the peace and dreamed of Melissa. Moorhens clucked in the reeds, shepherding their young. He listened to the plopping sounds as they dipped below the water in search of evening snacks.

Sam drew out the timetable, which Silene had given him earlier He would have been bemused by it if he hadn't been living in Ceradoc for the last four months and become completely immersed in the Dryadian way of thinking. Firstly of course, they used their lunar tree calendar for short-term reckoning. Moreover each tree month had a particular meaning. As Nestor had pointed out, this was the first day of the Bramble month, which had some association, Sam thought, with resilience and making connections. In the Eastern calendar, the present date was probably at the end of August or in early September. Then there was no Monday, Tuesday or Wednesday or any other familiar day. This month, like all months, was divided into two halves or fortnights. The first half was simply known as Bramble Swelling, with the days delineated one to fourteen from the time of the new moon. The second half of the month, beginning at the full moon, was called Bramble Shrinking and its days, also numbered one to fourteen or fifteen, ended at the following new moon, which in this case was that of the Ivy month. Then the counting began once more. The calendar was significant in the university year in that the students only worked for the twenty-one days after each new moon. Then they had a seven or eight day break until the next new moon and could even leave the grounds and go back to their homes if they wished. The university year stretched over about nine or ten months ending in comfortable time for the mid-summer oak festivals. This devotion to the lunar calendar and its associated trees was to ensure that the relationship between man and nature was never forgotten. Sam looked at his timetable again. The days were simply divided into morning and afternoon sessions. It was all written in Dryadian but the twelve foreigners had spent the summer in Dryadia and they were all now passably fluent. Everyone was pleased however that much of the first year at least, was to be taught in English.

BRAMBLE SWELLING

	MORNING	AFTERNOON
1	*Introduction*	*The Whole Picture*
2	*Numbers*	*Geometry*
3	*Music*	*Astronomy*
4	*Nature*	*Storytelling*
5	*Cooking*	*Pattern-graphs*
6	*Life*	*Death*
7	*Free Day*	
8	*History*	*Peacefulness*
9	*The Elders*	*A system of non-goverment*
10	*Equality*	*The Pulse of Life- Energy of Two*
11	*Simplicity*	*The Pattern of Creation-Energy of Three*

12	*Truth and Beauty*	*The Physical World-Energy of Four*
13	*Kindness*	*The Ether-Energy of Five*
14	*Free Day*	

BRAMBLE SHRINKING

	MORNING	AFTERNOON
15	*The Therapeutae*	*Relating- Energy of Six*
16	*First do no harm*	*Cycles- Energy of Seven*
17	*Less is more*	*The Higher Wisdom- Energy of Eight*
18	*Silence*	*Completion-Energy of Nine*
19	*Re-incarnation*	*The Seers*
20	*Freedom and responsibility*	*Let the universe take the Strain*
21	*Free to enjoy yourselves*	

That was the first month in Dryadian reckoning and each class was considered no more than an introduction to its subject. The next few months went on in similar vein. Subjects often repeated themselves but Sam noted with some relief that death only appeared once! Sam was so grateful that Zephyr and Amarinta and the other Ceradoc Elders had already taught him so much, including understanding Dryadian. He already knew about pattern-graphs for Anaxamander possessed one of these extraordinary instruments that could trace out patterns by altering the length of its swinging pendulums, or through projecting on it the energy of sound or colour or even human feelings. It was fascinating to observe how harmonious energy produced such beautiful patterns and discordant energy caused such disturbed ones.

Sam felt reasonably hidden on the riverbank and didn't want to be discovered. He was happy in his dream world. But he heard voices approaching. There were two of them, male and female. It was too late. He had been seen.

"Hi mate. How are you doing?" It was Stephano and he had Nell with him.

"Mind if we sit with you." Without waiting for a reply, they dropped down beside him.

"Enjoying yourself?"

Sam tried to be polite, but inside he was irritated. Next time he realised that he must find a better hiding place.

"Oh, you've got your time-table, Sam," added Nell enthusiastically. "I thought cooking looked good. Then I discovered that it meant that our group was to spend the whole morning preparing lunch for the rest of the school."

"No meat." Stephano grunted. "I'm a chicken and chips man myself."

"You must have known that the Dryadians are mostly vegetarian," replied Sam.

"Yes I know, but it still hurts. Well at least I can go to England once a month for a steak and a beer."

Sam felt annoyed. He wondered what on earth Stephano was doing in Dryadia.

Nell butted in. "Stephano's a joker. Don't take any notice of him."

"You will, if I share my tin of steak and kidney pie with you".

"Where were you staying before you came here Sam?" asked Nell changing tack.

"In Ceradoc, in the north. Mary and Pushkin were there too. And Tara."

"Isn't that where Anaxamander comes from?" Stephano tried to sound nonchalant.

"Yes, we know him quite well. But you must too. He must have interviewed you."

"No. Apparently I didn't need to be since I was born here. And my brother did a term at the university a few years ago. My family is well thought of, I suppose. We are descended from Sastamoro. My mother says he was one of the great Dryadian kings."

A shudder went down Sam's spine. That was not how Parmenides described him in his history. Stephano had been away some time and must have been indoctrinated or had developed a very selective view of Dryadian history.

Stephano continued. "I heard Anaxamander had been kidnapped by the American army in the helicopter invasion. Someone told me that it happened not far from Ceradoc. Were you there at the time?"

Sam nodded coyly for Anaxamander had requested that he didn't want the subject talked about outside Ceradoc.

Nell's jaw dropped. "He was such a lovely man. I only met him at the interview and he was so kind. I hope he's all right."

"Oh he was later released unharmed." Stephano tried to impress Nell with his inside knowledge. "Isn't that right, Sam?"

"Yes. It's all over now. I don't really know much about it." Sam hoped that his lie was convincing. He badly wanted to change the subject.

Stephano persisted. "I've heard that Ceradoc is one of the most beautiful villages in Dryadia. Did the helicopters fly close?"

"It all happened at night. We only heard them flying over. I don't like to talk about it."

Stephano felt satisfied. He felt that his first foray into espionage had been a success. And if Sam was a bit reticent, then he concluded that Mary probably knew just as much. Unlike Sam, she liked to chatter. Stephano climbed to his feet. "I'll think I'll go back. Supper will be ready in an hour."

Nell also rose. "Coming Sam?" She smiled warmly at him.

"I think I'll stay a little longer."

"Bit of a meditator are you, Sam," grinned Stephano. "Try not to get bitten by those pesky dragonflies."

Sam sighed with relief when they had gone. He had not enjoyed the intrusion. He couldn't get the measure of Stephano. He appeared to be friendly on the surface but somehow Sam didn't quite trust him and he didn't feel comfortable with his crudity and brashness. He knew only too well how awkward and shy he could be with strangers. Stephano had had him at a disadvantage and he felt irritated at his gaucheness. Nell seemed easier. He quite liked her. Maybe he could get to know her better, but not in the presence of Stephano and his chicken and chips culture.

Sam loved the timelessness of Dryadia. The deep peace of it all. The river not only symbolised eternity, it was eternity. Maybe Alanda and Isola had sat here, perhaps even Dryadogenes. No doubt nature had altered its banks from time to time, and different types of vegetation would have arrived and departed. But humans made little difference. Here in Dryadia they respected and cherished the wild sacred places. The river would be little changed in a hundred years time, long after he was dead. No deep diggers or gigantic tractors ripping the guts out of the earth. Nothing threatening the birds and the wild flowers, or the water rats in their holes.

The next morning Nestor started the first lecture of the year.

"Everything starts with numbers. Pythagoras said that long ago and because he was referring to the eternal laws of nature, what he said then, is just as true today. A little later in Plato's academy in Athens, the subject was called Arithmetic but it bears little resemblance to modern arithmetic, which is basically no more than calculating and counting, multiplying and dividing, making profits, making losses."

Nestor sounded quite disparaging about the debasement of what he regarded as one of the greatest studies in the world. Our numbers relate to resonance, vibration and energy. Every number has a meaning. You can make them work for you, if you really understand them, for each has a unique energy. They move things. They can make things happen. They are the building blocks of life. To start with, there are really only nine basic numbers. One to nine. All others are created from them. All life springs from the first nine. There is no zero. That is an invention of the East, not of nature. Nothing comes of nothing. Zero is an empty place. Any numbers after nine have to be reduced to a single digit by adding their components together. So eleven is a two. It's really one and one. And 135?" He looked around at the class questioningly.

"Nine" shouted Nick, an enthusiastic young man who used to be a journalist until he became sickened by the cynicism of it all.

"Correct. And 1043?"

"Eight" yelled Nell. Nestor kept throwing numbers at them until he was happy that they fully understood.

"Now let's look at them individually. What do you think is the inner meaning of the first number which we know as One?"

Pushkin was the first to speak. "Bliss. Oneness. Peace. Stillness. Wholeness. Eternity. Perfection. Completeness."

"Excellent. Parmenides has been teaching you well."

Pushkin reddened a little. How did he know? Nestor was no different from the other teachers though. It was obvious that they had all been thoroughly briefed on their students' backgrounds beforehand.

"Oh, don't take offence. Parmenides is a wise man. Use him mercilessly. Believe me he likes it! Good teachers should be challenged and pushed into debate. They may even be wrong. In my case of course, very unlikely."

He looked around at the class impishly and roared with laughter.

"Yes, Pushkin. One is One and all alone and ever more shall be so. The old song sums it up about right, doesn't it. And remember that all other numbers are contained in the One for there can be nothing outside unity."

Nestor carried on in the same vein throughout the morning teaching the essences of the other eight numbers. In the afternoon he taught them the basics of Geometry and how numbers were at their root.

"Literally true", he said." Why do you think we talk of square and cube roots?" It was quite a demanding day. "Don't worry if you don't get it all straight away. We will have plenty more lessons on all these subjects. And don't groan at the thought. There is an extraordinary beauty in numbers."

Every evening before supper, if he wasn't on cooking duty and the weather was fine, Sam took himself off to his hidden place above the river. He had 'moved house' since Stephano had discovered him and now felt undetectable, with his back against an enormous oak and a clear view of the water below. Here in the peace of the river he felt the Oneness of existence that Nestor had been talking about. As always he thanked the spirit of Dryadia, whatever that meant, for preserving these wondrous places where he could find refuge from the busyness of other people. Sam moved seamlessly between worlds: from daydreams to musing over what he had learned in class to acute observation of the natural world around him. Below him he watched the brown head of an otter drifting downstream in search of his supper, disturbing on its way a solitary kingfisher from his perch.

Sam brought out his notebook. Although students were encouraged to trust their memories, Sam like everyone else took copious notes, as there were no textbooks. The world of Numbers and its related subject Geometry, the blueprint of life as Nestor described it, fascinated him. He had entered the magical dimension of the Golden Section and the Fibonacci series, spirals and gnomons and magic squares. He struggled with the meaning of the Platonic Solids and squaring the circle, with the shapes of sounds and the dimensions of the pyramids. His imagination soared in the ethereal regions of the Quintessence, the mystical fifth element that was not confined within the boundaries of the physical world. He learned how numbers worked in space, as taught in the Dryadian version of Astronomy, and how important the dimensions and cycles of earth, moon, sun and the planets were, and how they were all in such precise and exquisite proportion to one another. There was absolute order in space.

He noted that the Dryadians used the ancient and sacred metrology of miles, feet and inches, not out of sentiment, but because they related to, and encodified so perfectly the cosmic dimensions of the earth including its diameter, circumference and speed of rotation. Which begged the question – how had our ancestors measured the earth and the moon so accurately (and it must have been many thousands of years ago) in the first place?

Music was taught not just for enjoyment, but also to study the construction of the sounds that lay behind it. He learned how the science of numbers was behind every vibration and every note. He discovered how numbers and geometry worked in nature, in the growth of plants and in the dance of insects. He learned about the energy that pulsated within the earth. They were called leylines in the East. The resonance of numbers existed in everything, from inside the atom to the furthest stars, in movement and in stillness, and even in areas that existed beyond our conventional ideas of space and time.

Each student had been lent a pattern graph, a strange but simple contraption, which looked like a four-legged stool with adjustable pendulums hanging down from its base. Exquisite tracings could be obtained from the vibrations of the moving pendulums by way of the attached pencil and drawing paper. The pendulums could be tuned to every imaginable musical note and harmony, and even colours. Students were asked to meditate on the pattern that an octave made, on the sound of a grasshopper or the extraordinary throbbing and subtle warbling design that happened when two similar but not quite exact notes were played together. This was known as 'the near miss,' a vibration of great power and beauty that was considered to be the energy that was behind the healing power used in homoeopathy. Discordant harmonies produced far less pleasing patterns. Human emotions could also be fed into the pattern graph. It was fascinating to see what exquisite and harmonious patterns were formed from happiness, good humour and loving thoughts and how ugly and chaotic they looked when the equipment was exposed to such negative emotions as sadness, jealousy and anger. A favourite experiment was to hook up of one of the university's cats to the machine and gently stroke it. Its purrs of satisfaction produced an unusual yet pleasing pattern that reminded Sam of a smile with perhaps just a hint of whiskers!

"Now you know why thoughts and emotions are so important," said Nestor. "If they affect the pattern graph they can also affect the human body and mind, and indeed the earth itself. 'Good vibrations' is not just the name of a song, but they keep us in good health as well. Dis-harmonious ones do the opposite. The pattern graph proves it in my opinion." Nestor beamed at his class. "Those who truly understand the power and nature of numbers and the geometry, music and astronomy that flows from them can make a real difference to the world, for good or for ill. In Dryadia of course we are only interested in the former. There is a saying that when we understand someone, we claim that we have got their number. We therefore had better make sure that our intentions are honourable and kind. But we don't intend to move mountains until at least the end of your second year!" He spoke these words benignly before looking directly at Stephano who turned away from his gaze, uncomfortable with the power that shone out of Nestor's eyes. It seemed that he had Stephano's number at any rate.

This curious mix of science and imagination, as it was never taught in the East, combined with the art of storytelling and healing and the observation of how the energies of nature and spirit underpinned the whole of existence, lay at the heart of what was taught at the university. The teachers appreciated the discomfort that most of the students felt at being overwhelmed by so many seemingly strange subjects. If they seemed despondent, Nestor and Silene never stopped encouraging them.

"This is a truly classical and sacred education. Nobody else in the world at this time, so far as we know, can teach a course like ours anymore. Sacred means that which lies at the root of things, like the sacral bone that is at the bottom of your spine. In essence it is all very simple, even though you probably think at the moment that your brains aren't big enough to absorb it all. When the knowledge moves to your heart and it becomes natural and self-evident to you, then believe it or not, you will find it easier. It does though take quite a long time to learn to be truly simple. We hope you will be getting there at the end of your three years at Cantillion."

THE UNIVERSITY OF CANTILLION

CHAPTER FIFTEEN

GETTING HEAVY

Sam spent many evenings wrestling with what he had been taught, trying hard to learn every thing by heart, in the Dryadian manner. Silene used to say, "Learn deep so that it becomes a part of you, then it is yours for ever."

He felt settled in his hidden nook on the Dragonfly River. The branches of the oak tree were thick and kept most of the rain out and the natural seats that had been formed amongst its roots were reasonably comfortable. He sometimes invited Mary and Pushkin to join him and they continued with the debates that they had begun at Ceradoc. So often the talk turned to gossip and especially to one topic, Stephano.

"What on earth is he doing here," remarked Pushkin indignantly. "He's so cynical. I heard him say the other day that only a fraction of what we learn here has any value in the modern world. Only if we are truly intelligent, by which I think he means mainly himself, could we identify what particular fraction is the important one."

"He's always disappearing," added Mary. "Presumably for a cigarette. He must have smuggled them in from England. There's a rumour too that he's got a lap-top at his Gran's so that he can play card games with himself. I'm quite sure that Nell is after him. She's always gazing at him, but I don't think he's much interested in her."

"That's because he's interested in you," countered Pushkin unsmilingly with the air and keen observation of a hopeful lover in waiting.

"Don't be silly, Pushkin. Though he can be very charming and he makes me laugh."

"Well, that's all right then," replied a miffed Pushkin.

Tara had joined them that day. She leaned forward conspiratorially. "I'm not really supposed to say this, as I'm a mentor, so keep it to yourselves. Stephano is like his brother except worse. Don't trust him. What you're seeing is not real. I'm concerned that there is a hidden agenda somewhere. I'm still not clear how he avoided the interview. Anaxamander would have seen through him. Sophora was here a few days ago so I asked her. She said that she was aware of the backgrounds and aspirations of all the students, including Stephano. She told me that I was not to worry but to keep her informed. We might even learn from him. She says she's on the case."

Nell was indeed breaking her heart over Stephano and it was beginning to upset the class. He tended to ignore her in a group situation but was more attentive on their days off, when as he put it he was afflicted by 'Saturday night fever', a disease Mary assured Pushkin that she was not going to catch, at least not from Stephano. Nevertheless Stephano constantly harassed her.

"What's life like in Ceradoc? Who was Sophora and was it true that she knew everything and lived in Ceradoc? What's Anaxamander like? How could he meet him?"

His persistence started wearing Mary down and she, like Sam before her and with Tara's encouragement, started to clam up."

"Never tell him anything about the Oak Midsummer rituals," ordered Tara. "If he hears anything about the lightning then we could be in trouble. He hasn't earned the right to know. We mustn't let him anywhere near The Beacons."

"He knows the helicopters landed there," said Sam. "He's horribly curious."

"Be careful all of you. Sophora said tell him nothing and watch him for everything."

"Talking of the lightning flash." Sam cocked his head on one side. "I think I understand how the Elders did it."

"Tell us Wise Master Sam," smiled Mary.

"I think they used the power of numbers. They were using a particular type of resonance and chanting it under their breath as well as concentrating very hard. Nestor did say that you could move mountains if you knew the right combination."

He looked to Tara for confirmation. Tara grinned but looked enigmatic.

"You might be on the right track, Sam."

There were no classes in the last quarter of a moon and as the Bramble month was waning or, as the Dryadians said shrinking, the three of them plus Tara decided that they would spend the time in Ceradoc. In particular Sam was looking forward to seeing Melissa again. When he finally learned of their plans, Stephano begged to be included.

"It's a bit of a bore at my Nan's," he explained. "Ceradoc sounds a lot more fun."

Tara was firm. "We're going to be very busy. We've no time to look after you."

She dismissed his pleas that he didn't need looking after, and that he would stay at the local resthouse, simple accommodation that almost every village provided for the homeless traveller. Having shaken off

Stephano, there was another surprise. On the night of their departure, Nell appeared. She was crying uncontrollably, pleading with them to be taken to Ceradoc. She had only arrived in Dryadia three months before school started, so her Dryadian was lagging behind the others. Moreover she didn't feel at home in her adopted village. And she ' just had to get away from Stephano.'

Tara was suspicious. "Had Stephano put her up to this – to be his surrogate informer?" There was no doubt though that her heart-rending sobs were genuine. Tara phoned Sophora for advice. The answer was in the affirmative. Two reasons, Sophora explained.

"One was kindness." The other was more pragmatic. "Pump her all you can, for any information that she might have concerning Stephano."

In Ceradoc, Tara agreed a little reluctantly that Nell could stay with her and Mary. Tara of course knew something of Stephano's background because of her previous relationship with his brother, but the more she reflected on it she realised in fact how very little she knew about either of them. Both brothers seemed to enjoy creating smoke screens.

"I just don't understand him," Nell kept saying. She was only too eager to talk about Stephano. Indeed she wanted to talk about nothing else. "I don't know what he does in England. He says he has a first class degree in Economics and was once head hunted for a big job in the City. He turned it down because he hoped for something better, and he's still waiting. He has a love/hate relationship with Dryadia. He says it is run by a bunch of old fogies, and that he would change things a lot if he were made an Elder. I don't feel I know him. He's always asking me questions, but he doesn't like giving answers. He never seems grateful for anything I do for him, and he won't apologise when he's upset me. I know we've only known each other three weeks but I think he's wonderful. I really do love him. That's when I'm not hating him. Why can't he see?"

They could get very little more out of Nell. She was a lovesick puppy. Tara finally became convinced that she was not Stephano's stooge. Unlike him she appeared guileless, at least on the surface. She didn't seem to have anything to hide. Her horizons apparently ended with Stephano.

Two days later there was a loud knocking at Tara's door. It was Stephano. He was carrying a large bunch of chrysanthemums that Tara thought looked suspiciously like the ones that her neighbour grew in his front garden.

"I've come to see Nell," he said defiantly.

"How do you know she wants to see you? We brought her here so that she could get some peace and quiet," said a shocked Tara. But it was too late. A sobbing Nell brushed past her and hurled herself into Stephano's arms, crushing the stolen flowers as she did so. He glared at Tara over Nell's bowed head with an air of barely concealed triumph.

"I don't believe it, I don't believe it." Tara kept repeating the same refrain to the others after Stephano and Nell had gone off to the resthouse to stay. "And did you hear what he said as he was going. 'I've also come to see Anaxamander. I think that I need some higher teaching, something that I'm not getting at Cantillion.' I'll give him Anaxamander. He won't get near him. Stephano is a hundred times worse than his brother. What a creep! I'm going straight to Sophora."

Sophora seldom raised her voice in anger and very little ruffled her calm exterior. But Tara's visit raised her to an intensity of feeling that Tara had never seen before.

"Stephano is a man on a mission. Nell was a pretext. His interest in Anaxamander is not what he says it is. I can't see him being interested in any higher learning as you describe it. No, Stephano is after something else."

"Why was he allowed into the university?"

"You know the saying about holding your friends close and your enemies closer. Stephano is our enemy. Not so much him perhaps but the people he works for, those who sent him here. My hope is that he leads us to them and we find out what they're really after. I'm afraid that Dryadia has drawn far too much attention to its self. The helicopters were a start, but our enemies learned next to nothing. Stephano is the forerunner of the second wave."

"Can you sense what they are after?"

"What all politicians, the military and commercial interests are after. Power, money, land, raw materials, cheap labour – that sort of thing. In our own case some of these things are not of immediate interest, but they are not off the agenda. In the short term it is quite obvious to me that they are after scientific knowledge, stuff that they think might be useful to their military forces."

"But we don't have anything like that."

"Until recently, I would have agreed with you. And if we had, then it's concealed deep in the brains of a small number of Elders. And even then, any knowledge we possess is mostly of theoretical interest. Nevertheless, our tentative experiments at The Beacons have been observed and have attracted trouble. I'm worrying a bit about drawing down lightning again at the Oak-Festival. I appreciate that the celebrations are hidden under the trees and that lightning can be considered a natural phenomena, but we do need to be very careful in the future." Sophora paused. "This is not the first time that Dryadia has been under attack for its knowledge. This time it's from outsiders. But as you know the enemy within can be even more dangerous. I'll tell you a story." She got up and started pacing the floor, her eyes barely aware of the room around her.

It was during the time of Alanda and Isola. Many of the Elders had abandoned the villages and lived apart. They no longer wanted to share their knowledge. Some had just chosen a more contemplative path, not really wise in the context of the times, but not worrying. Others wanted power for themselves and unfortunately were not concerned about the greater good. That way is dark and heavy.

These Elders started doing scientific experiments, not in a small and innocent way as we were, but bending the laws of nature to their own advantage. They were utilising the power of the sun, lightning and the energy of the earth. They were playing with forces that they didn't really understand and some best forgotten. At first, things were manageable. As time went on, their greed and selfishness grew enormously and their egos blinded them to what they really were doing. It became dangerous, and they became completely out of their depth in dealing with the energies they were releasing. The most dangerous of these wayward Elders were based at Dracola, a place up on the moors not far from Mount Cynthos, and about twelve miles from The Beacons where Isola and Alanda had their centre.

The Elders at Dracola possessed a great treasure. Nobody knew where they had found it or how long they had held it. There was a rumour that it once belonged to the Cathars, and they had buried it under Mount Cynthos when they fled here after the great massacre in their country. It was believed that it had enormous potential to either create or destroy. The Dryadian tradition is that if certain scientific knowledge has the power to harm it's kept secret, its use known to only six people. That really means three but each has a deputy in case of death. And those three pairs only have a third of the secret each so that they could only act in combination. In the time of which we are telling, four of the six Elders involved were at Dracola. The other two were Alanda and Isola at The Beacons. The Elders at Dracola had tried many times to persuade Alanda and Isola to join them. They had always refused, not least because they knew that the Dracola Elders' intentions regarding the treasure were not at all honourable.

Sophora carried on with her pacing. Half relating the story, which she obviously knew well and half seeing it again with her inner eye, she mesmerised Tara who remained transfixed as she sat gazing intently at her, drawn into her vision, not daring to interrupt.

Alanda and Isola decided to trick the Dracola Elders and steal the treasure from them, not for themselves but for the common good. Then they could put it beyond harm's way. It was Oak Summer's eve, the night before the Oak Festival, when they visited the Elders at Dracola and they gave them the impression that they were on the verge of capitulating. They were ready to join forces in unlocking the supposed secret power of the treasure. Alanda asked to be shown its hiding place and the two other keepers of the secret walked him to a ravine where it was kept in a concealed cave. Alanda gazed at it, and confirmed that after much thought he would join them and pool his knowledge. The Dracola Elders were overjoyed, and at nightfall after much backslapping and toasting their agreement in the local Dryadian wine, (Alanda being careful to spill most of his) they parted and agreed to meet tomorrow in the afternoon. Alanda however did not intend to honour the agreement. Not far away, Isola was waiting for him with a strong mule. They quietly made their way back to the cave. The treasure was heavy and it was with great difficulty that they loaded it onto the mule's back and secured it safely. They travelled straight to The Beacons just as the dawn sky was beginning to lighten. Leading the mule into the centre of the Egg they unloaded the treasure, still wrapped in its sacking, and hoisted it up onto the altar stone. They sat down exhausted, too nervous to sleep, in case the Dracola Elders recovered their befuddled minds, and discovering their loss, set off in pursuit. They waited, eyes alert to any movement in the trees on the perimeter of The Egg. After a few hours they heard rustling. Cloaked figures emerged from the undergrowth, two or three at a time until there were twelve of them sitting cross-legged around the altar stone with Alanda and Isola.

They were not from Dracola but were Alanda and Isola's own kind and the meeting had been pre-arranged the previous day. Alanda stood up and walked towards the altar stone. Carefully he removed the sacking to reveal the treasure.

There gleaming in the morning light was a huge black crystal, more than two feet long. It looked menacingly powerful and did not seem to be comfortable in the light. All the Elders who looked at it felt that it did not quite belong to this world and if it had to be here, then it would be better that it be kept underground, like in the dark cave from which it had just been removed. The Elders waited knowingly, staring straight ahead in intense concentration. Then as one, they lifted their eyes skywards. Without warning the altar was on fire, crackling in conjugal agony as the lightning flash and the thunderclap struck. The crystal was smashed to fragments, its shards scattered in the grass.

The Elders stood up and looked at the pieces of black crystal around them, still hot from the fire. As they cooled they picked up the visible fragments like gleaners in a cornfield. There was no ceremony or conversation. They walked away in silence out of The Great Egg, through the forest of oaks and along the shady paths that led them to their homes. The crystal had been destroyed and their mission was over.

Sophora sat down. "You understand the power of the crystal?"

Tara nodded, shaken by what she had heard.

"We can use that power again if we need to. But not while the East is on our backs." Sophora's voice was grim. "First of all, I want you to send Stephano to me. For your part keep him off the scent. You are quite rightly keeping him away from Anaxamander and The Beacons. Try and get him back to Cantillion as soon as possible. Use your influence as a mentor. Don't trust him."

"And Nell?" Tara was wistful.

"Nell, I fear has a stormy path to follow. She won't be getting any peace until she can shed Stephano. I fear she may then attach herself to someone who deserves better. Nell also is someone who is not what she appears to be. She is a minx and I think a little un-hinged. Trouble ahead, Tara, I'm sorry to say."

Stephano discovered little in Ceradoc and was soon back in Cantillion. In fact Sophora had ordered him to return and informed him that Anaxamander now spent most of his time away from Ceradoc. She gleaned little more from him. In her heart she felt increasingly certain that Stephano was no friend of Dryadia and was an agent of the British government.

After he arrived back in Cantillion, Stephano found a letter waiting for him at his grandmother's house where he usually stayed when he wasn't at the university. It was postmarked London.

My Dear boy,

I hope you are enjoying your stay. Things are not as well with me as they ought and I would greatly appreciate a visit from you as soon as you can. Sometime in the next two weeks would suit.

Your Uncle B

Within a week Stephano was on *The Leaky Bucket* bound for England. Despite his protests, Nell went with him, excited by the thought of a trip to the bright city. Like Stephano she missed the busy streets and the nightlife. She had come to realise that the peace of Dryadia was just a little bit too peaceful, and that the university course at Cantillion was a lot more exciting on paper than in reality. Dryadia was idyllic in a way but she thought to herself 'a girl can't live well without proper shops.'

Stephano decided not to explain to Nell the purpose of his visit to London. He left her at a nearby café and walked the short distance to B's office. B didn't smile and seemed tense and hurried. This time he didn't waste time on preliminaries.

"Well, what have you found out?"

Stephano was taken aback by his brusqueness although he thought he was well prepared for the encounter.

"I've managed to get into Ceradoc. I'm sure it's an important place. I was given the impression that I was not welcome there, and I had to leave after two days. I was told Anaxamander was away and no longer spends much time in Ceradoc."

B barked at him again. "Where do they do their science? Their laboratories? Have you scoured Cantillion?"

"Yes, but nothing to report. The labs may be outside the town. I've been told that much of the science is taught in the second and third years. The science that we learn in the first year is merely number theory, geometry, music and astronomy."

"The Quadrivium. Like the Platonic Academy." B seemed interested.

"Yes, we were told that. But it's all rather boring. Far too abstract and we're not given any practical reasons why we're studying it. It's not real science. Dryadia, I'm sorry to say, lives in a time warp."

"What else have you found out?"

"Not much else at the moment. But I'm working hard at it," said Stephano firmly.

"Not hard enough obviously. I see you have time for a girlfriend though. Where did you find her?" B's tone was becoming even unfriendlier.

"At Cantillion. She's one of my classmates."

"Have you told her about your visits here?"

"Of course not. You told me not to. And how do you know I have a girlfriend?"

"She's waiting for you at the café across the road. I was watching you from the window. Not very bright of you. What does she think of Dryadia?"

"Like me, a bit bored." Stephano was feeling out of his depth.

."Any questions?"

"Yes. What is the truth behind the helicopter incident?"

"What do you know?"

"Only what I have read in the papers. It was obviously kept low key. All I know is that three American helicopters invaded Dryadia and kidnapped three men."

"Who were later released. Mistaken identity I believe. If you get any more information then I would be glad to hear about it. The matter is not quite closed. Remember that Great Powers have to protect their interests. We all need to be wary." B looked intently at him. "I must say that I'm very disappointed in you. I expected a lot more information than you have given me. Do the Dryadians trust you?"

"Yes, of course. Why shouldn't they?"

"No reason. And the girlfriend?"

Stephano nodded in the affirmative.

"You're on probation until the end of the school year. What are the chances that you will be accepted into the second year?"

"I'm told almost everyone is if they want to. So presumably, yes."

"Do you want to?"

"If you pay me."

"I'll pay you if you deliver. I want you to find their science labs, and the names of the people who run them. I'll give you two months, then come and see me."

B got up from his chair. "And, there's one more thing. Measles! I want you to find out all you can about measles in Dryadia. How many people get it? What's the death rate? How do their doctors treat it? I know that they don't immunise."

"Why do you want to know about measles?" Stephano asked in some puzzlement.

"Let's get two things straight. I ask the questions. You provide the answers. You get information and I'll pay for it. Now if you'll excuse me. I think you know the way out."

CHAPTER SIXTEEN

STORM CLOUDS

Sam's brain was exploding with what he was learning at the university. This was real knowledge, where there was no conflict between science and spirituality. It all seemed to make perfect sense. Using just a compass and a ruler he was uncovering nature's blueprints. True, he only understood a small proportion of what he had learned so far, but he was getting there. With some of the more sophisticated patterning machines that could tune into the resonances of flowers and leaves, he was able to discover the quintessence or 'greenprint' of any plant. Sounds and colours could also be fed through other machines so that their vibrations could be translated onto graph paper, and their patterns revealed. All forms of life and energy had a distinctive vibration. That applied to animals and people as well. Moreover when they were unwell the patterns changed, even if there were no obvious physical symptoms. Match the pattern of a sick person to that of a plant, then you might well find that you have found a cure to their disease. He spent many hours discussing and enlarging on what he had discovered about these resonances with Ruth, who was the most experienced of the Therapeutae in Ceradoc. He started to realise that along with Melissa he had a real gift for healing alongside his passion for natural philosophy. Anaxamander and Zephyr provided extra coaching in this subject where Pushkin, and sometimes Mary, often joined him although Mary enjoyed her storytelling sessions with Tara and her friends more. The greatest story though was Dryadia's own, made accessible to everyone through Parmenides' history, now at last translated into English.

CHAPTER SEVEN AN UNEXPECTED THREAT

Alanda and Isola had not only rescued Dryadia from a road that it should not have taken, but had cemented new foundations for its future. For a long time Dryadia sailed on at peace with itself, and more or less at ease with its neighbours .Now there was a new threat that would not have remotely concerned Alanda or Isola, for in their time it had not been born. That great beast rose in the East about three hundred years ago and for good or ill made an enormous impact on the world and its inhabitants - more than anything that had ever gone before. It was called The Industrial Revolution.

The Dryadians are not averse to change if it harmonises with our principles. The new technology in the East was something that we had at least to consider. We had become aware of the challenge around 1700, in the Eastern style of reckoning. About that time there already had been some very useful inventions like the telescope, the microscope and the pendulum, which had led to a more accurate mechanical clock. We had no problems with such things for they were both useful and fascinating and they deepened our knowledge of the world. Many of our meetinghouses possess grandfather clocks, often ancient, and all made in Dryadia. They not only tell the time, which in Dryadia is aligned with the sun and correspondingly twenty minutes ahead of Greenwich Mean Time, but often incorporate mechanisms that show the phases of the moon, sunrise and sunset, the state of the tides, and even the cycles of the planets.

It was the invention of the steam engine that challenged us most. We watched closely its development in the East. The first ones were used to pump water out of mines so that seams of coal, iron and tin, previously out of reach, could be brought to the surface. Others were used to drain low-lying land so that new pasture was drawn out from the wetlands. Later of course they revolutionised transport with the invention of steam trains and ships, and steam engines were used for threshing grain on the farms.

None of these things were wrong if used in a small and thoughtful way, but once the genie was out of the bottle there was no stopping the urge to speed faster and further. We saw the blight on nature, the enslavement of the poor in the 'dark satanic mills' and the enormous wealth that accrued to a few. We also saw the assault on the imagination and the crushing of the human spirit when man became subservient to the machine. So we decided to reject the steam engine on the grounds that it would not improve the quality of life of all Dryadians.

Dryadia is of course a land rich in minerals – tin, copper, granite and china clay and many others. But we knew that the beauty of our landscape would be destroyed if we were able to mine deep. The forests would be denuded for pit props and fuel. The fumes from burning the coal and wood needed to power the engines would pollute the air. The spoil heaps would create barren wastes in the countryside. The health of the miners would be destroyed in the darkness of the pits and later in the monotonous and dangerous work in the factories. That would be no way for men to live. So the Bards who were on the side of beauty and harmony, and the Therapeutae who believed in health and wholeness for all, and the Natural Philosophers who had undertaken to protect the laws of nature, sustainability and equality for everyone, agreed – that in the interests of common sense (or uncommon sense as we often call it) we would not travel the path of heavy industry.

We have always extracted minerals from the earth in a small way, but only where they were close to the surface. We filled in the holes and grassed over the scars so that no one would guess later that we had done what we did. We took trees from the forest and coppiced the understorey but we planted more than we took and a few years later the woods looked no different. It has always been our axiom that we should travel lightly upon the earth. We have never opposed change if it removed drudgery. For example, we have made many improvements to our ploughs and wagons over the years and selectively bred some of our animals and food plants, but always thoughtfully and kindly

A hundred years after it was invented, the East put the steam engine on wheels and on ships, and for a while we considered whether we should introduce a light railway system to our country. By then we were fully aware of the horrors of the industrialisation of the East – the smoking factories; the destruction of the landscape; the great migrations of people driven from their homes in the countryside to seek work in the cities, where conditions were so squalid that no human being should be even allowed to visit, let alone live there. The railways could only speed up the process, and cherished and stable communities would be broken up forever. So again we said no. The journey across Dryadia from East to West can be made in two days on horse back, and the North to South crossing by horse or bicycle in well under a day. There are wagons for the infirm and elderly, and plenty of comfortable resthouses along the way. So what was the point? We have plenty of time and our legs are strong and our roads well kept. We kept the steam railways at bay.

Throughout the nineteenth century Dryadia remained strong in its self-belief. The fear of invasion had long gone .The Traditional Elders were loved and respected for their knowledge and kindness, and fairness in their dealings. Our ideals were sculptured in their hearts. The Practical Elders were also respected and looked after the day to day running of the country. Every citizen had their say in anything that concerned them. We took what ideas and trade we needed from the East and perhaps gave fair measure back. The industrial age passed us safely by and we continued to live in reasonable prosperity. Our population remained stable and the natural migration of people manageable. Most Dryadians were content.

By the beginning of the last century, the speed of change in the outside world was extraordinary. The internal combustion engine had been invented. Terrible wars were fought. The carnage could not have been imagined even fifty years earlier. Populations expanded exponentially and mass tourism began in the gap between two world wars. The East could no longer be pushed aside and it was no longer ignoring Dryadia. Outsiders looked at our beautiful countryside and our empty beaches, our mineral resources, our green forests and our large shoals of fish. Having soiled their own nests they gazed enviously at ours. We knew that if we allowed these cultural aliens to enter the country in any numbers our country would be brought down to the level of our neighbours. Our people would become corrupted by the material pleasures of the East. We did the only thing possible and cut ourselves off from the world. In fact we had always largely done this, the degree varying according to how threatened we felt. We could afford to be lax about visitors when the population of the East and their interest in us was low. But the oil-fuelled prosperity of their rising numbers could not be ignored.

After the 1914-1918 World War, we became a closed country. Our only connection with England was by small boat that sailed a few times a week carrying essential supplies and a few passengers. Within Dryadia, development remained slow. We still have no cars and only a few small tractors for really heavy work. We take the view that if we have heavy machinery we will only be tempted to carry out big projects that we really do not need. We plough and reap with horses as we always have. We did however like the idea of the telegraph and later the telephone for they were non-invasive and brought communities together. It is only recently that a landline link has been set up with England. We have resisted television and the cinema, which might have been a wrench for some, although educational films are shown in the schools and in the university. Our storytellers provide much of our entertainment. We have a small radio station that broadcasts regularly, especially during winter evenings. Our only newspaper is a weekly one that is published in Cantillion. We have mostly turned our back on the electronic revolution so we do not have mobile phones, satellite communications or computers although we have recently introduced some simple laptops to replace our old cumbersome typewriters. There is innovation in other areas such as simple technology that helps us keep our homes warm in winter so we can cut down on our already minimal fuel costs. We are looking at micro power plants like solar cells, more efficient windmills and electrical applications for watermills. We use simple technology efficiently and well. Our purpose is to make life easier for ourselves and to enhance our happiness. It is not to make gadgets and toys, which drain the earth of its natural resources and ruin its beauty. That is the way of the East and it cannot be sustained for much longer.

"It's so hard to believe that we've nearly finished our first year," exclaimed Mary as they squeezed into Sam's secret den on the bank of the Dragonfly River at Cantillion. In fact it had grown considerably over the last nine months for Sam had gradually built a small six- sided Dryadian cabin around the trunk of its supporting oak tree. Only the two walls overlooking the river were incomplete. They had been replaced by canvas, which could be rolled back when the weather was fine. An old bit of sailcloth, lashed tightly to the oak and the wooden wall posts, did for a roof. The only furniture was a chest where cushions were stored and with some blankets for colder days. The cabin was snug and waterproof and it was here as Pushkin put it, the three of them held their 'Ceradoc Parliament in exile.' Only Tara knew their secret, apart from a small black and white cat that often followed them to what he obviously regarded as exceptionally comfortable snoozing quarters.

They met there at least twice a week and Sam went there more often, if it wasn't too cold. Sometimes, when Sam wasn't using it, Pushkin and Mary visited the cabin on their own, for they were becoming very close and the university campus was not a very private place.

Sam was now twenty-one and Croydon had now faded well into the background of his brain. He had not visited his parents there since he had come to Dryadia a year before. He went to Croydon only in his nightmares.

"I know you'll be invited to join the second year," consoled Mary. "Tara told me that there is a question mark over two of us but not us three Ceradocians. I asked her and she confirmed it with Sophora. The school is her baby even if she doesn't teach us very much, at least not until next year."

Pushkin stroked his chin thoughtfully. "Let me guess who the two are. I think Stephano and probably Nell."

"Probably right, though Tara wouldn't say."

"I don't trust Stephano. Dryadia is not in his heart. He slopes off to London at every opportunity." It was obvious that Pushkin didn't like Stephano.

"I expect he has to call in on his bookmaker," Sam added impishly. "Nell still seems besotted. If he goes, I expect she'll follow."

"Tara won't miss them," said Mary. "She calls them the enemy."

In fact as they were speaking Stephano and Nell were preparing for yet another trip away. *The Leaky Bucket* was to leave for England on the early morning tide. Stephano always dreaded his regular visits to see B who was exasperated at his slow progress and had withheld much of his promised fees. Last time he thought he had done well on his measles report but B seemed very disappointed that it wasn't considered a particularly serious problem for the Dryadians.

"What do you mean that there has been only one death recorded in the last twenty years," he spluttered.

"And that was a very sickly child," added Stephano, apparently unhelpfully. He thought that he had been very diligent in obtaining the information.

"Epidemics every few years like mumps and chicken-pox. It's almost always a mild disease though with a high fever that they hardly interfere with so it burns up properly. A week in bed and lots of nursing from the mother and it's all over. Every child gets it. Afterwards they have life-long immunity. The Dryadians are not scared of it. They say it's a midge-like fear if treated properly They even have 'kissing parties' at the beginning of an epidemic to make sure that any child that hasn't had it before, gets it this time. The kids are so healthy anyway, they don't expect problems."

B was not impressed. "If what you say is true then why do the authorities here call it a killer disease? Why are we told that a lot of children will die or be maimed permanently? Why do the medical people scare us half to death about an epidemic hitting the country? Indeed the Chief Medical Officer has described measles as a disease of 'mass destruction.' Are they all lying? No, it's the Dryadians who are lying. Go back and get some better statistics. More deaths, brain damage, lives wrecked, that sort of thing. Understand?"

"Yes," said Stephano lamely. But he knew he wouldn't succeed.

At the present meeting, Stephano felt more pleased with himself. True, he couldn't get any more information on the measles. The Dryadians just considered it a rite of passage. B was not happy with this, but when Stephano presented his next bit of information he became rapt with attention.

"I think I've discovered where the labs are, the ones you asked about, where they do their experiments. They won't let us first year students into them. We're told we're not ready. We're not even told what they do there, though someone explained to me that's where we learn the secrets of energy, how life works. It's the practical side of the course. One evening when there was no one about, I went to look at one of them. They are easy to spot as they are in a group of four and they are all octagonal in shape. The teachers had forgotten to lock the one I went into and the place was unguarded. There was a humming sound coming from a machine. It was a strange looking contraption, not very big, just sitting on the table blinking at me with various coloured lights. I think it was an advanced version of what they call a patterning machine, which prints out tracings of energy. There were lots of plants there too, buds flowers and leaves, perhaps for decoration but perhaps raw material for the machines. There were lots of tracings and designs lying around too. I could see microscopes and long tubes, through which I think they transmit light and sound. I looked through the windows of the three other labs too. They had even bigger machines but no plants."

"I've brought a map. The four labs are on the south side of the university near the estuary, so it's tidal. You can get a boat up to the jetty there. I could almost smuggle a machine away for you but I would probably be caught and then expelled for sure."

Stephano laid the map on the table. He had marked out the labs in red and the jetty in blue, half guessing what B had in mind.

B carefully traced his fingers over the map. "How far is it between the labs and the jetty? And the jetty – is it strong?"

"About a hundred yards and the jetty's well built."

"What about perspective? How does your plan fit into the bigger picture?"

Stephano brought out another map, showing Cantillion and its port, and the estuary flowing down to the sea.

"I'll keep these if I may. B's face had relaxed considerably. "I would like to say that you've done well but the proof of the pudding is in the eating."

"What are you going to do?"

"As I've told you, I ask the questions. When are you going back to Dryadia?"

"In a few days. I'll only stay three weeks, as it's the end of the year. I want to spend the summer holidays in London. I'll go back in the autumn if they'll have me."

"And the girl friend?"

"She'll try and follow me. But she' s too clingy. Cramps my style. I need a break."

"I like your plan. Spend the holidays here. I won't need you in Dryadia for a while." B smiled. Something that Stephano hadn't seen him do for a long time.

In fact Stephano's visit to the university was his last one. Nestor and Silene summoned him soon after his return and informed him that he hadn't qualified for the second year. They considered he was better suited for life in the East. They spoke to him kindly but were emphatic. Stephano protested a little, but only a little. He was secretly relieved and without telling anyone, not even Nell, booked his passage on *The Leaky Bucket.* Within a few days he had contentedly returned to his old way of living in London. What he didn't know was that the Dryadians had on his last visit sent someone to trail him to B's office in London. B didn't know it either.

Not for the first time, Nell was hysterical when she heard the news. She kicked and screamed, ranting about what she would do to Stephano if she found him, and more frighteningly, what she would do to herself if she were left alone. If she had been in England she would have been given strong tranquilising drugs or even sectioned.

That however was not the Dryadian way and so a number of the Therapeutae took turns to watch over her and used soothing herbs to calm her down. By the next day, Nell's sobs and writhing had subsided and she finally fell asleep. Most of her fellow students and teachers visited her daily until one by one they fell away, bored by her repetitive stories and the blame she heaped on anyone but herself. Sam kept on seeing her longer than most, and at her insistence did not abandon her when she was finally discharged from her healers' care.

On one of their walks by the Dragonfly River with Sam gamely pointing out the local wild life to an increasingly disinterested companion, Nell suddenly stopped, took his hands in hers and looked him directly in the eyes. He felt penetrated to his very being as she said, "Sam, you would never treat a woman like that, would you?"

Her eyes never left his as she waited for his answer. Sam could only think of escape – his den, the reassurance of his friends and teachers, Melissa's gentle voice. But his knees went weak, and his emotions flattered by the attention, were cast loose from their moorings. Finally he stammered.

"Of course not. I'm not like Stephano."

Nell loosened her grip. "I thought not, Sam. I wish there were more men like you. You understand how a woman should be treated."

Sam raised his eyes and noticed perhaps for the first time how pretty she was, that there was some softness behind her smile. He smiled back.

"Dear Sam," Mary commented much later. "What a honey pot she was. You didn't stand a chance. You were well and truly nobbled.

CHAPTER SEVENTEEN

MADNESS AND BETRAYAL

While Nell was spinning her web, another intrigue was unravelling out at sea unseen by the people of Cantillion, under cover of a moonless night. A small warship lay at anchor and was unloading four motorised dinghies, each containing a number of armed soldiers in camouflage gear. The flotilla then made their way up the centre of the estuary at low speed, towards the jetty that Stephano had so carefully marked on his map. Two Cantillion citizens walking on the quay were quickly coshed, bound and gagged and left comatose where they fell, like sacks of vegetables. The soldiers soon located the laboratories and smashed in the doors with their shoulders. As Stephano had indicated the buildings were not guarded. The invasion lasted no more than ten minutes. All four labs were cleared of their contents, and the machines that Stephano had described were carefully lowered into padded boxes and transported back to the boats. Three more passers-by were coshed and a silent bullet put through the night watchman who stumbled across them as they were leaving. Mission accomplished, the soldiers clambered into their waiting boats with the Cantillion secrets. There was no attempt at silence now. The boats roared off towards the mother ship. Stephano's betrayal was complete.

This second act of violence against Dryadia was not hushed up – either in Dryadia or in England. With the death of the night watchman it couldn't be avoided. The Dryadian Elders not only protested to London but also quickly leaked the episode to the British press. Loving a mystery, the newspapers ran the story for weeks. It was fuelled by something the Dryadians hardly ever did. They allowed a small number of reporters into Cantillion to inspect the scene of the crime.

At first the British government denied that the invasion had ever happened. 'It was an internal matter. Dryadia wasn't completely crime free. Or maybe it was a bit of Dryadian propaganda.' Later they put out that it might be 'rogue secret service elements from another country acting without authority.' It was several weeks before they admitted responsibility, and said that 'the episode had been pursued at the instigation of the Ministry of Health with the collaboration of The Ministry of Defence.' This was hard to swallow but the government insisted that they had concrete information that the Dryadians were experimenting secretly with various dangerous diseases. The British in their own interests had to confiscate the contents of their laboratories. Asked what the diseases were, it was declared that 'they included measles, rabies, foot and mouth and probably others.'

The British government put out a statement. 'We have to protect our citizens from these terrible diseases. All countries should support us in this war for a healthy world. We are sorry for the absolute minimum of violence that was committed on Dryadian soil but they only have themselves to blame. If only they had obeyed The World Health Organization protocols instead of using the amateur methods of their native healers. They should have allowed our inspectors in to look over their facilities instead of conducting dangerous experiments in secrecy. Then all this could have been avoided.' The Dryadians naturally protested, but the British public got bored with the story as their government hoped they would, and the front pages moved on.

The Great Moot of Cantillion is by far Dryadia's largest building and is where many of the country's major conferences and cultural events are held. It was originally built in Alanda and Isola's time and rebuilt two hundred years ago after a disastrous fire. The Moot contains within it a magnificent amphitheatre in the Grecian style, which can comfortably seat more than a thousand people.

The acoustics are so fine that a whisper can easily carry from the pit to the rafters. In the wake of the second invasion, Sophora, as the most senior of the Traditional Elders, summoned her fellow Elders to the Moot to discuss the matter and decide how they should respond. The Dryadians were unsettled and confidence needed to be restored. The invasion was the chief topic of conversation. The first attack with the helicopters might be looked on as an aberration. The second one couldn't be brushed aside and couldn't be forgotten. All were saddened at the murder of one of their countrymen. Nestor as the joint head of the university was the first to speak and everyone was fascinated by his explanation of what had happened.

"It's no great loss," he began. "They have stolen four of our patterning machines. The Traditional Elders amongst you who have completed the university course will be familiar with them. Indeed some of the Therapeutae and the Natural Philosophers may well possess them. The Practical Elders and the reporters from the Dryadian Weekly and the Radio Station will not be so knowledgeable, so I will explain. A patterning machine is simply a device that can trace out the patterns of life. These normally look like abstract swirling designs to the uninitiated. These patterns demonstrate the underlying energy or subtle vibrations of all living things, whether they are of plants, sounds or people, both sick and well. They are fascinating to those of us who are interested in such things and probably quite boring and meaningless to those who are not. The healers may find them the most useful. The machines are quite simple to make when you know how, and in any case there are plenty more around the country in all shapes and sizes, and made for different purposes. Our only loss is the death of one of our countrymen and the injuries to several of our citizens who are thankfully getting better. Our puzzle is why the British wanted to steal these instruments. The pretext that we were carrying out dangerous biological experiments is simply rubbish, as no doubt they are now finding out. The machines are of little use to anyone in the East unless they have sufficient imagination to appreciate the wonders of the energy of life. I doubt whether the soldiers or doctors involved have those qualities. If any one in the East was genuinely interested, then we would have gladly given them the machines and shared this simple knowledge. The patterning machines in our laboratories were of theoretical interest only and were used mainly to create a sense of wonder and a deeper understanding of the life force for our students. There was no dark or heavy side. We are therefore drawn to the conclusion that the British were misinformed and were after something quite different."

When he had finished Sophora rose to her feet, speaking slowly and deliberately.

"Nestor has summed up the situation well. We are more than willing to share much of our knowledge, although whether the majority of Easterners are interested is debatable. There is no need to steal when people are willing to share. I am sure that Nestor is right in thinking that the East wouldn't be interested in the patterning machines if they had known what they were used for. I suspect that they will be shocked and surprised when they find out, and probably very angry at their mistake. We now know why they came. One of our English students, who happened to have a Dryadian mother and who was actually born here in Cantillion, was in the pay of the British secret services. He located the laboratories, without really understanding their purpose, and informed the British. This, as you know, was the second time that Dryadia has been invaded.

The other was of course the helicopter incident last year, when Anaxamander and his two friends were kidnapped and held prisoner on an American warship. There can be no doubt that the two events are connected. We are now aware why the helicopters visited the place that we call The Beacons on that fateful day. American spy satellites had spotted movements on the ground that they were unable to make any sense of.

Their action was initiated from information that they had obtained via the British after they had bugged our consulate. They flew in to investigate. As in the latest invasion they discovered nothing of significance. Their efforts were hugely mistaken. I strongly suspect that they will try again unless we can convince them that we have nothing to hide. We will have to persuade them that we are not harbouring dangerous diseases, which in any case was probably a pretext. We would have to convince them that our experiments in teleportation, (that is the power to move things using only the forces of nature) on The Beacons were relatively playful and had no military worth. In any case we have stopped those experiments and there is nothing to be found, apart some from interesting ideas locked up safely in a few of our heads. Even then no one knows the whole story. We know nothing that could help them in their wars. That is what they are looking for. We only want to help human kind. If we discover anything that has the potential to cause harm then we will close that road immediately. Rest assured, that although we do not welcome the East poking around in our country since we cannot trust them, we need them to believe us when we say we are absolutely no threat to their security. There is now no enemy within, apart from fear. We cannot fight the enemy without, except with diplomacy and reason. So we must connect. I propose that we send a delegation to London headed by Anaxamander, who of course knows the British well, and seek mutual understanding."

Then Sophora invited anyone else who had anything helpful to say to address the moot. Anaxamander was the first up and gave a detailed account of the helicopter invasion and his treatment at the hands of the Americans. Dozens of people spoke after him and almost all were sympathetic to Sophora's idea of sending Anaxamander to London. He would try and seek out those fair and reasonably minded people that must be lurking in their government somewhere, and try and get them to listen. Sophora proposed that all the Elders present should join in meditation and launch two 'bubbles' – one protective one over Dryadia and a calming one over London. She added that she was not alone in sensing war clouds ahead. Although war might distract the British and Americans from Dryadia for a while, it did not bode well for countries in the Middle East. When all had had their say, Sophora asked everyone to enter 'The Great Silence.' After an hour they stirred and she stood up and said.

"If any one wants to add anything or disagree, then stand and speak your truth."

No one did, and a sense of great purpose hung over the thousand Elders at the moot. The setting sun shone benignly through the great west window. Sophora rose a final time and exclaimed in a loud clear voice.

"Then are we agreed?"

"We are all agreed," came the reply in unison.

"Then return to your villages and tell your friends and families what you have witnessed here today. This is the way of Dryadia."

Tara had been present at the moot that day and wasted no time in letting Sam, Mary and Pushkin know what had happened. When she had finished they chorused,

"What's a bubble?"

Tara grinned knowingly. "They are like thought forms – bubbles of concentrated energy, created by a number of people all with the same idea. We call the process the power of intention.

The three of you can add to the bubbles, if you like, with the power of your thoughts. We have created a nice protective one over Dryadia that will hopefully draw attention away from our country. And a soothing one has been launched over London to stop them going to war.

Apparently the British and the Americans want to invade Iraq. People are marching through the streets there, to try and stop it. We're adding our bit too. We obviously can't guarantee success but our combined thoughts can help."

The school year had ended and all the foreign students apart from Stephano, who had already left, were invited into the second year. There was a question mark over Nell, and she had been given a month to make a commitment to the school. They were encouraged to live on in their adopted villages through the summer apart from visits to their families in England if they wished. Mary and Pushkin had more or less paired off and were content. But a shadow lay over Sam, a shadow that brought in conflict to his otherwise bright spirit. That shadow was called Nell.

Nell continued to fume over Stephano but even she was beginning to accept that he was physically and emotionally out of reach. She had now decided not to return for the second year, and was secretly relieved, for her bitterness over Stephano overshadowed any other emotion. Almost all her university friends had grown tired of her histrionics and looked forward to her imminent departure. The exception of course was Sam whom she latched onto like a rudderless boat. No woman had ever been so needy of him before and he was flattered by her attention. Soon he was hopelessly and dangerously besotted. In vain did Mary and Pushkin warn him about her shallow, manipulative ways. Melissa faded from his mind. He could think of nothing but Nell and even the Dryadian philosophy took second place in his heart. Never was the saying 'falling in love' more appropriate. It was a long time before he wondered why people didn't describe the state as 'rising in love'. In fact the Dryadians had long realised the difference between the two and the Elders sometimes mediated in the 'fallen' state if it became too disruptive to the people concerned.

Eventually he told her about his den overlooking the Dragonfly River, a secret known only to his Ceradocian friends.

"Oh Sam," she drooled. "What fun. It sounds like heaven. Can we go there now?"

Nell took his hand and it wasn't long before they were sitting on cushions while Sam was excitedly pointing out the moorhens and water rats. But Nell wasn't listening. She was gradually sinking against Sam's body, her face nuzzling his neck and very soon Sam's thoughts were no longer on waterfowl. He had entered an unstable world where nothing else mattered.

Nell delayed her departure for several weeks, long after almost all the other students had left for the long summer break. Then came the news that Sam was dreading.

"I have to leave next week, beautiful Sam. Nestor and Silene are pressurising me. But I can't live without you. You can come with me if you love me enough."

Sam felt his heart thump. "I suppose I could stay with you some of the holidays instead of going to Ceradoc. But it would be very sad for me not to live with Zephyr and his family. It's my home now."

Nell stared at him. "Your home could be with me. You've had your Dryadian experience. Lovely while it lasted. But Dryadia's a backwater – not the real world. That's in England, Sam. That's where it happens. And I have something to tell you. I haven't told anyone else. But after the first shock, well I'm so excited. I'm pregnant."

Sam's draw dropped. "Well, you did say you were a little worried when Stephano left. Then you went all quiet, so I assumed that all was well."

Nell gave him another of her hard stares. "It's not Stephano's. It's yours!"

Sam went pale. "Are you sure? You said I didn't need to worry. You had taken one of those things."

"Accidents happen. Aren't you to pleased to be a father? You can look after us."

Sam stuttered. "You could consider an ab----------."

"Don't even dream about it." Nell's voice was harsh. "You really have to take some responsibility, Sam. Unlike Stephano – that bastard."

Sam didn't dare tell Mary and Pushkin who in any case had returned to Ceradoc. He knew what they would say. He would leave Dryadia with Nell in secret and would send explanatory letters to all concerned. He comforted himself with the thought that once they had been away for a month or two Nell would miss Dryadia as much as he did, and then they would come back together. He knew that she wouldn't be welcome back at the university but he would, and maybe they could find a little house nearby and raise their family together. Mary and Pushkin alas couldn't see Nell in the way he did. She was just very insecure. Once Nell felt safe then all would be well.

So Sam took a similar risk when he left Dryadia with Nell, as when he came into the country alone. Except that this time he managed to suppress his fear that he was not following what the Dryadians describe as 'your soul's calling'. Neither he nor Nell had any money so they went to stay with Nell's parents, by strange chance not very far from his own parent's house in Croydon. He had arrived backwhere he had started. As the weeks passed Sam had to finally admit to himself that he was not happy. He missed Dryadia dreadfully and what's more he missed Melissa and he was unlikely to see her again. Nell's behaviour became increasingly volatile and unpredictable, fuelled by Sam's gradual protective retreat into himself and his increasing inability to communicate with her.

Once he asked her: "Would she mind if he went back to Dryadia for a week, absolutely no longer, and to go for less wouldn't be worth it?"

He asked only the once. Her sobs and tantrums over 'his abandonment of her and their baby' were so violent that he quickly withdrew his request.

In her madness she had even threatened to report him for abuse if he visited Dryadia again. Sam sunk into depression. His love for Nell had evaporated like boiled over milk. He now could only dream of escaping to Dryadia. He was trapped and he had no understanding friends to talk to in England. Nell had brainwashed him into believing that he was some abusive fiend. There was no way out.

Nell had left no forwarding address. The only address that Mary and Pushkin possessed was that of Sam's parents. Mary wrote weekly there in the hope that Sam would pick up his mail. The letters were chatty with all the little bits of gossip that travellers yearn for when they are far from home. Initially there were no replies. Then after about six weeks Mary received a grief stricken letter of absolute despair. It concluded with the words. 'I am no longer fit to live in this world. I can please no one. I don't know how much longer I can go on. I no longer understand the workings of my own mind. I miss Dryadia and you all so much.' The letter disturbed Mary such a lot that she and Pushkin took it straight to Sophora for advice. Could anything be done?

Mary had known a number of 'sensitives' in the East but Sophora was unlike any of them. There was nothing flaky about her. She didn't talk in funny voices or bring messages from departed spirits. Apart from her extraordinary deep brown eyes and air of authority she was in appearance just like anyone else. Yet the respect that everyone had for her had meant that she had remained the chief Traditional Elder and leader of all the Dryads for very many years. Sophora never imposed or commanded, only suggested. But her words contained such good sense and certainty that it was hard to ignore her.

She read Sam's letter twice and listened intently as Mary and Pushkin related the story of his relationship with Nell. Sophora was concerned. "I am very fond of Sam. I believe that his place is here in Dryadia and at the university. Nell has disturbed his mind and I would rather he never saw her again.

Their relationship was not based on friendship, as all good relationships should be. There was no rising in love – the lightest, most lasting way. There's something else. The baby. I'm not at all sure that it is Sam's. I think it's Stephano's, and I suspect that Nell knows that too. I think that DNA tests can be done in the East. That would confirm it. If I'm right, then Sam has no reason but to leave her immediately. She will create merry hell but if we can get him back here than he will be beyond her reach. Now, in two days Anaxamander will be leaving for London at the head of the delegation visiting the British authorities, as we agreed at the Moot. He is sure to have Nell's parent's address and phone number in his file from his interview with her. Travel with Anaxamander, both of you and find Sam. Bring him back. Don't take no for an answer. He'll go mad otherwise. He will have learned something from his experience with Nell, but he will learn far, far more here. His only failing was that he was too kind. Kindness is the greatest of virtues but it needs to be tempered with common sense and strength of character. Otherwise people like Nell will take advantage. I'll send some positive energy to him as is the custom of our kind, and you go and find him. Believe me, Sam is worth rescuing."

Mary and Pushkin first visited Sam's parents, who were naturally alarmed to hear the full story. 'Yes, they could phone him and try and entice him over, though he seldom visited them now.' They believed that he didn't really want to leave Nell's side. Sam had told them that Nell had been rather ill and had been in and out of hospital. It might be something to do with the baby but they weren't sure.

His mother called Sam immediately, dreading that Nell would pick up the phone, for she was intensely possessive of him. Luckily Sam did answer, sounding very frightened. He was just off to the hospital again. Nell was haemorrhaging and her blood pressure was all over the place. 'Yes he would drop in on his way back to see his concerned Mum.' No mention was made of Pushkin and Mary.

At the sight of his two old friends, Sam broke down. He had not cried like that since he left Dryadia. The floodgates opened, and Mary and a rather bemused Pushkin sat on either side of him on the sofa while his even more bemused parents sat looking at them from the other side of the room.

"We'll make some tea," his mother said dragging her rather relieved husband behind her.

Sam released a torrent of emotion. Again and again he referred to Nell's violent ways. How she screamed at him for hours on end, though only if her parents were out. How she constantly threatened him if he ever mentioned Dryadia. How once she had had a knife at his throat and once at her's, saying she would kill herself if he left her. He was trapped, trapped, trapped! She had convinced him that he was an evil monster far, far worse than Saddam Hussein. His mind was so unsettled at this constant abuse that he now believed that her words were true. He hated her now. He sometimes wished that she would die and then felt guilty when he saw her looking so soft and vulnerable in her hospital bed.

Mary explained at length what Sophora had told them, and a flicker of hope crossed Sam's face as he realised that he was not forgotten. When he heard that it was Sophora's opinion that the baby was probably not his but Stephano's, his eyes changed from the habitual hopelessness to complete confusion.

"You'll have to get DNA tests after the child is born," said Pushkin.

"That's six months way. I'll be dead by then." The despair returned to Sam's face.

"How can I prove its Stephano's. Nell said that there was a month between us."

Pushkin leaned forward. "I bet she wasn't telling you the truth. You know that Nell was making up to other students too. That baby could be anybody's!"

At last Sam said,"Well what do we do now?"

Mary felt relieved that at least he realised that he had some options. "Sophora wants you to come back with us. She agrees with you that you will go insane if you stay."

"How can I leave her now, so sick in hospital? And I can't see Nell allowing a DNA test even in six months."

Mary thought for a while. "We're not going back to Dryadia for a week or two. We want to visit parents and friends meantime and we are waiting for Anaxamander to finish his negotiations. You have time to think. Nell may be OK by then. Don't forget that she has parents to look after her here."

Nell did get better and was out of hospital within a week, but by then events had overtaken them. The day after Mary and Pushkin's visit, Nell haemorrhaged again so heavily that the doctors pronounced a miscarriage. The father was never known for sure. Nell's rages continued, perhaps even more so, as she had lost her main weapon. Sam was glad that her behaviour remained so appalling. He had made up his mind. He was going to leave her and soft words might make him waver. He waited until she had an appointment with the consultant and pleading that he had a migraine, persuaded her parents to take her to the hospital. He then phoned his parents, left a note for her's, and wrote a savage letter of anger to Nell. Two hours later he had linked up with Mary, Pushkin, Anaxamander and his delegation at Paddington station. Soon they were travelling on a westbound train to honour an appointment with *The Leaky Bucket.* The weather forecast spoke of sunshine and calm seas to Dryadia.

Zephyr called it 'The Great Escape.' Amarinta fussed over him with never ending brews of calming teas to repair his ravaged nervous system. He often visited Sanctuary Hill to consult the oracle, usually in the company of Pushkin and Mary. Tara often came with them, as she was a better translator, although the others were catching up fast. Sam wanted to do a reading for himself. Delicately he directed a beam of light down onto the pillars below using the familiar blinds and mirrors. With Tara's assistance he read the old Dryadian script.

If you do not allow your light to shine, then you lay yourself open to destruction. If you do, then you could ignite a thousand stars.

Sam thought of Nell and smiled ruefully. He reckoned he could now at least glow.

Sophora had asked Sam, along with Pushkin and Mary, to come and visit her. She couldn't hide her pleasure at seeing Sam again.

"You've survived a 'Nell'. Well done. Now consider a thousand Nells or a thousand Stephanos and be grateful that they live in the East and not here. Their lights do not shine as we would wish them to, or as we like ours to. It's hard to shine when the heavy 'wants' of the East weigh on your shoulders or if you are mentally or physically ill. We've all appreciated that idea more after your recent adventures. Anaxamander and his crew have also come back with good news. They have done a deal with the East. He's convinced them that we have nothing hidden: that there's nothing in Dryadia that could help their military. As I feared, the East now has bigger fish to fry. They have sent their armies into Iraq, looking so they say for weapons of mass destruction. Almost certainly imaginary, or it's all a pretext. The war will be terrible. At least their attention will be diverted from Dryadia and our diseases of little or no destruction.

Summer cast its warmth long that year, and Sam gradually regained his emotional strength. He spent a happy month amongst his friends in Ceradoc before they all had to return to Cantillion for their second year at the university. There was one thing that saddened him, and that was Melissa.

At first she avoided him. Then like the others, she was glad to see him back. Her father Anaxamander had given her a somewhat edited version of Sam's adventures in order not to upset her. Not entirely satisfied by his tale of events and being a woman who needed to get the whole story straight, she persuaded Sam to give her the complete picture.

They both bitterly regretted it. Melissa felt angry and betrayed, although any understanding between them was more assumed than spoken. A seething frost bubbled between them and they once again avoided each other. Sam hung his head in shame and was overwhelmed by sadness for the loss of a friendship that he discovered was much more important than he realised. He no longer felt able to visit Ruth in her herb garden for her teaching, and that too was a great loss. Ruth tried hard to reconcile them, but both Sam and Melissa had walled themselves off in their respective griefs.

Melissa was about to start her first year at Cantillion. Thinking that she had already gone on ahead Sam went to the herb garden for one last time before he too travelled to the university. He was surprised to find Melissa sobbing by the fountain. She was holding a piece of paper in her hands. Sam sat quietly beside her while she tried hard to ignore him. Eventually through her tears and without a smile she said.

"I've just come back from the sanctuary. I thought the oracle might give me some words of advice about starting at Cantillion. Here read it." She handed him the paper.

Of all the flowers in the garden of our heart, none shine more brightly than loving kindness freely given.

"And I thought. Have you and I been that kind to each other?" She raised her head to look at him directly for the first time.

"I'm so very sorry for my part," replied Sam.

There was a long pause before she said at last, "And I'm sorry for mine. You've been a complete cuckoo but I'm glad the cuckoo found his way home again." She struggled with her words for a moment and then almost in a whisper she added "You've no idea how much I missed you."

They fell into each other's arms, half laughing and half crying and saw no good reason why they should part again.

CHAPTER EIGHTEEN

RUTH AND THE THERAPEUTIC JOURNEY

A year had passed and Sam had finished his second year at Cantillion, and Melissa her first. He had been captivated by many of the subjects taught there, including Natural Philosophy in which he had been particularly encouraged by Anaxamander and Zephyr. He had also risen in love with the Dryadian way of healing. Ruth had agreed to teach him and he would join Melissa in learning all the knowledge that was needed to be a successful Therapeutae. They both had learned a lot already about the plants that grew in Ruth's herb garden but as Anaxamander had so often told them:

"It's the philosophy, the wisdom of applying the healing that's just as important and there's no one that knows more about it than Ruth. I'm going to be away for a few days and leave you in peace so Ruth has agreed to start teaching you the rules."

Like Anaxamander's, but higher up and further away from the house, Ruth also had a cabin by the herb garden. Called the 'cabinette' by Anaxamander it was reached by an impressive row of steps from the north side of the garden and was perched on a mound overlooking the estuary. It was here that the lessons were to begin.

"I've had a word with Dad," said Melissa. "He wondered whether you would tell us about both sorts of Therapeutae. He says that means it is explained in the story of the early part of your life with him and your journey to India. You've only told me bits of it before but Dad says it's very exciting and that Sam should hear it too."

"Anaxamander was encouraging me to do the very same thing yesterday so I will, but without the gesticulations and the roars of laughter."

"You'll do it just as well," said Sam. "But I've never heard of any other sort of Therapeutae before."

"That's because they're not so much healers as magicians. Anaxamander got the idea when he was trying to find out what happened in the ancient mystery schools of ancient Greece and Egypt. He discussed it with Sophora and she felt that the rituals that he was talking about were valid, and that thousands of years ago they had experimented with them here in Dryadia. Then the secrets were lost and Sophora felt that it might be just as well. There was a dark side to them, and the magicians' activities might not fit in with the Dryadia that exists today."

"It's lovely when Dad and Sophora get debating, Sam," said Melissa. "He's told me about their conversations many times."

"Yes," replied Ruth. "Anaxamander has read everything, talked to everybody, and been everywhere. He takes his thoughts to Sophora. She puts her Seer's hat on and between them they reach a conclusion as to how accurate they are. Anaxamander hasn't always been the larger than life figure that he is now. Like all of us he had to grow into his own wisdom and find his voice, so that he could express himself properly. When I first met him over twenty years ago he was quieter and less sure of himself although his big sense of curiosity and awareness was already well developed. He was a bit like Sam as he is today and very thoughtful, though still a lot noisier."

"How did you meet him?" asked Sam, flattered by the comparison.

"As you know I was born in England, the only child in a very good Quaker family with beliefs not all that different from those of Dryadia. I lived only about ten miles from the Dryadian consulate where Anaxamander also spent some of his childhood.

At that time of course Anaxamander was not the consul. He was too young. But his father Pericles was. You can see why the three boys got their crazy names. Parmenides was the first. Then came Empedocles. And last of course was Dad. Their mother, Clarissa was also English like me but rather fragile, and when sadly Pericles was killed in a car accident in England about ten years ago she died shortly afterwards, from it is said, a broken heart. There's just one other important character in the story. And that is Clara, Pericles mother, and therefore Anaxamander's paternal grandmother. It's strange that both his mother and grandmother from both sides of the border had similar names. Clara was an old but strong-minded lady when I met her, but she still had all her wits about her. She was a Therapeutae and when I eventually moved to Dryadia and had made up my mind that I wanted to be a Dryadian healer, it was she who taught me."

Melissa sighed. "You haven't told us anything new yet. Dad told me that the best bit was after you had got it together."

"He mentioned that the adventures you had when you travelled together to Greece and India changed your lives," added Sam.

"The journey certainly made a huge impression and the experiences were certainly not ordinary. There is no more important place to us than Dryadia but we can't ignore the rest of the world. I'll tell you how I met Anaxamander. I had a job in the local health food shop. That's where I first learnt about what they call in England, alternative medicine. Anaxamander had already absorbed some of this more natural way of healing as a part of his Dryadian lifestyle. Clara his grandmother had reinforced his philosophy. Sophora had also arrived in Ceradoc about that time and he started learning from her as well.

Anaxamander often used to visit the shop and if no one was in earshot announced himself, in the best Lord of the Rings fashion, as Anaxamander son of Pericles! Soon we were inseparable. I went to Dryadia to be with him, met Clara and decided to be a Therapeutae. I had realised that there was no other place on earth that I wanted to be. I was accepted at the university course at Cantillion, made even sweeter with the knowledge that Anaxamander would start with me. But Anaxamander was restless for adventures and like many young Dryadians we decided that before we started the course we would travel overland to India, helped by some money that my parents and Anaxamander's mother had given us.

We were away the best part of a year, normally travelling by local buses. Whenever we could we slept under the stars, and in the towns and cities in cheap hostels. We meandered slowly through Europe drawn particularly to the great cultural and spiritual beacons that had featured strongly in their history. It was obviously nothing like our history but it's important to see Dryadia in context. Otherwise there is a danger of becoming insular. At that time Anaxamander, young as he was, was very much my teacher. I loved him but I was quite in awe of his knowledge and his unlimited curiosity about life and the world. His grandmother Clara had already passed onto him much of her knowledge and if he had been a little more patient with people and learned his plants a bit better he would have been a good Therapeutae.

Our first major stop was in Chartres and we paid a visit to its extraordinary cathedral. Anaxamander of course knew everything about it, even though like me, it was his first visit. I was now calling him Anaxamander the Declaimer. This was on account of his habit whenever he was excited about anything, which was quite often, of giving me a long lecture. I didn't mind as he was often mesmerising and I was eager for knowledge.

We were both bewitched by the cathedral, with its beauty and grandeur, and of course those amazing blue windows. When we were outside Anaxamander set to work like a tour guide addressing his flock.

'Did I know that Chartres, like all the great cathedrals and temples and that included the Great Moot at Cantillion, were built on mathematical principles using the power of numbers and a geometry that was shared with the Great Pyramid, Stonehenge and the Parthenon in Athens? Did I know that there was once a major Druid centre buried under the cathedral before the Druids fled to Britain taking their precious knowledge with them? In both places the Druids were destroyed by the Romans, but some of the wisest ones fled to Dryadia where they were out of reach of the legions.'

I had to confess that I didn't know any of these things.

'But did I know that the Druids taught in triads because the resonance of the number three has the energy of creation embedded in it, like a seed? And did I know that the Dryadians also taught in threes, probably because the Dryadians and the Druids got their wisdom from the same source? And would I be interested in the fact that one of those triads that we once shared with the Druids not only applied to how we live our lives, but also is a fundamental tenet of the Therapeutae? Did I realise that the words heal, holy and whole came from the same root and really meant the same thing.'

I had to say that I didn't but when he said the word Therapeutae, I wanted to hear more. But not too much because my head was reeling, and I was sure that we could both do with a cup of tea.

'All triads are short and to the point', he replied. 'Just three lines. Clara was always telling me about one of them.'

First Do No Harm

Honour The Gods

Dare To Be Brave

I later discovered that the Therapeutae have used these words for hundreds, if not thousands of years. The first one seemed obvious but I must admit that I struggled with the last two. I knew that *First do no Harm* was part of the Hippocratic oath. My Dad had told me that and I knew that Hippocrates lived in Greece more than two thousand years age. Anaxamander and I later visited the island of Cos where he taught. All the doctors in the East apparently used to swear the oath before they started practising, though I don't think they do so now."

"I don't think they could," said Sam. "The drugs they use in the East have far too many dangerous side effects. Anaxamander said he's very wary of all but the most harmless of chemicals especially when used directly on the human body or on the soil. The toxicity can then get into our food plants. We've been evolving for hundreds of thousands of years. How could our bodies adapt to a new chemical environment in a generation or two?"

"That's why the Therapeutae feel uneasy about almost all synthetic drugs both medicinal and recreational," replied Ruth. "Even if there are no immediate problems, no one knows what may happen in the long term – illnesses that could appear even years later. We prefer to work on the finer energy systems of the body. That is at a much deeper level than the bio-chemical ones. Are there any other ways that we could do harm?"

"By saying the wrong thing. You remember mum, that story you told me about the woman who walked into your health shop in England, and the doctor had told her at the hospital that there was no cure and that she was going to die."

"That was ten years previously so she obviously didn't. One of our therapists had to do a lot of work on her to get that terrible shock out of her body. Yes, we can certainly do a lot of harm with our careless words. That's why we spend time at Cantillion teaching you the gentle arts of diplomacy. Words need to be used wisely.

We must also remember that suppressing a natural discharge like a fever or a sweat with drugs can also cause huge harm. You know the old Gnostic saying – *What you don't bring forth may destroy you.* We don't want to keep old toxic rubbish in our bodies, let alone add new stuff. So, first open the dustbin and clean it out. It's not the flies that are the problem. They, or the bacteria, wouldn't be there if body and mind were clean in the first place. That's one of the first things you consider in healing – have a good spring clean to start with. So, if it is emotional toxicity that you have whether it's fear anger or grief, then express your emotions or at least acknowledge them. If you are physically toxic, then strengthen your liver and kidneys with purifying herbs and allow the poison to drain out through your bowels, your skin or any appropriate orifice. Go with the flow. Then the real healing can begin. What that really means is that you replace the old destructive energetic patterns that lie within us with loving harmonious ones. Beautiful flowers won't grow in an unweeded bed."

"What does *Honour the Gods* mean?" asked Sam. "It seems a strange saying."

"It puzzled me too at first," answered Ruth. "Anaxamander had forgotten what Clara had told him. But we worked it out together and decided that what it really meant was respecting the great forces of nature. That meant both inside us like the love and care we have for each other, and also outside in the world of nature like the lightning and the gateways in the sacred places of the earth where the serpent energy is strong. In healing we need to honour the power of our remedies, which are drawn from the quintessential energies of plants, and sometimes from the mineral and animal kingdoms as well. In the East this way of healing is called homoeopathy. The Dryadian word roughly translates as *Connecting with the power of the resonance.* Like the summer solstice celebrations in The Egg, it is another form of the sacred marriage, this time within our bodies. If you can find a remedy that has a similar vibration to that of the disease then true healing can take place. It's very hard for the doctors in the East to understand these ideas, let alone accept them."

"That leaves *Dare to be brave*," said Sam.

"That's more straight forward. It just means that you need to have enough courage to connect with your true or higher self. Learn who you really are, which is always a beautiful thing and then act it out. It takes a long time to find your own voice and not be swayed by other peoples' opinions. It also takes courage."

"That's lovely advice Mum, but we want to hear more about your travels too. Where did you go after Chartres? I'm sure you must have told Zach and me about them once but I've forgotten most of the details."

"Provence and Languedoc in the south of France. Especially in Languedoc where the Cathars lived before they were massacred in one of the crusades, on the orders of the Catholic pope of the day. Dryadia took in some of the refuges, as you know, along with the treasure, which we believe was a great crystal, now destroyed for fear of it falling into the wrong hands. We visited the castle of Montsegur perched high and lonely on its mountaintop. It was a steep climb to reach this final hiding place and refuge of the Cathars. It seemed a small place for the last few hundred of them. The castle is now roofless and desolate and terribly sad.

After weeks of being besieged the Cathars finally surrendered and walked out to meet their fate at the hands of the papal forces. They might have been spared if they had recanted their beliefs but none of them did, and the soldiers lit great fires and burned them all to death."

"At least the Cathars had the courage to be true to themselves," said Sam solemnly.

"They certainly did Sam," said Ruth. "And they honoured their Gods. In this case the Gods were the beautiful truths that their philosophy was based on. They are similar to ours, for we drink at the same fountain of universal knowledge."

"Kindness, honesty, fairness, and living simply and naturally. We learn these things when we are toddlers, Sam," added Melissa.

"Then an extraordinary thing happened. Anaxamander completely broke down. Not just a few tears but terrible sobs from a place deep inside him that neither he nor I knew existed. He trembled with both terror and grief as if the soldiers, despite the event having taken place eight hundred years ago, were murdering him before my eyes. I held him in my arms for what seemed an age before the emotion subsided and all his passion was spent. Then he slept, his head in my lap. I stroked his hair. A gentle smile of such peace appeared on his face while I looked at the mountains in the distance and the hurrying clouds above. He changed after that experience and was much quieter and contemplative. He was no longer Anaxamander the Declaimer but Anaxamander the gentle philosopher. He explained to me later what seemed obvious. He said he witnessed that terrible event as I held him. Not only had he witnessed it, he also felt every iota of the fear of being killed in such an awful way. He felt deep within him that he actually had had a life as one of those poor benighted Cathars who had suffered so much.

'Quite enough excitement for one trip,' he said later, though he and I little knew that there were plenty more strange adventures still to come. After Montsegur we had both learned the extraordinary power of emotion, another of the Gods if you like. It is one of our most important beliefs that there is nothing stronger than the power of the human heart to move or change things for good or ill.

We decided to travel to Greece. We visited all the ancient sites like the temples on the Acropolis in Athens and the oracles at Delphi and

Dodona, where Zeus was supposed to have spoken through the rustling of oak leaves. Sadly the oracles of Greece are now silent so we felt we were much better off in Dryadia where they will always help us if we are in need. Anaxamander loved the Greek sayings and as in our own oracles they were often written on the walls of their temples and academies. All of them a great help to a budding Therapeutae. I remember particularly:

All things are connected

Man is the measure of all things

Moderation in everything

Man know thyself

The Golden Rule of treating others as you yourself would want to be treated

The strangest were the Pythagorean doctrines. Pythagoras said that everything began with number, and that every number had a particular vibration and a quintessential power embedded at its core. Then it was said that Plato wouldn't teach anyone at his famous academy of philosophy unless they had first studied geometry, which was just expressing the numbers in a diagrammatic way. It wasn't until we returned to Dryadia and began our studies at Cantillion that I started making sense of these extraordinary ideas.

We sailed to the little island of Delos, a place once considered so sacred that no one was allowed to be born or die there. In the centre is a rocky hill called Mount Cynthos. It's tiny compared with Dryadia's highest mountain. But why the identical names and which came first? The Greek myths say Cynthos is the birthplace of the Sun God Apollo and that Delos is sacred to him, as is Delphi where he had his oracle. Anaxamander felt that he was sacred to us too for his name has appeared in some of our stories. Moreover scholars believe that Apollo came from the north and didn't actually originate in Greece. He was associated with the Hyperboreans who lived on a mythical island that lay beyond the north wind, often believed to be Britain though we think the Greeks were referring to Dryadia. When we learned that Apollo was the son of

Zeus, and was known as the God of Light and spiritual harmony as well as prophecy, healing and storytelling we embraced him as a true Dryadian. Just to add some icing on the cake we discovered he had been known to shape shift into that wisest of animals the dolphin and that his sacred bird was unbelievably the raven. We now felt even more sure of our Dryadian pedigree and that our ancestors were truly some of the ancient wise ones and guardians of the old knowledge.

So we had a wonderful time travelling slowly through the beautiful Greek countryside. It was spring and the wild flowers in the meadows and mountain valleys were utterly gorgeous. Nightingales sang gloriously from every thicket. So different from the dry landscape of summer. Before we left Greece, we, or rather Anaxamander had one further strange adventure. We went to the island of Crete. Partly to visit the grave of one of Anaxamander's heroes, the writer Kazantzakis. His epitaph is wise and simple. It was yet another triad.

I fear nothing

I hope for nothing

I am free

'That's how I wish to live,' he said. But as things turned out Anaxamander was shortly very lucky to be alive at all. We travelled to the centre of Crete, to Mount Ida where there is a large cave some way up. The myths tell us that this was the place where Zeus, the king of the Greek Gods, was born. Anaxamander of course believed that it was a gateway, and certainly the entrance to the cave was very imposing. You walk in some way and then it descends deep into the bowels of the mountain. It's very dark and the path down, if you can call such a rubble way a path, is very steep. We stood at the entrance with the late afternoon light streaming behind us and the darkness of Zeus' cave before us. It seemed more of a funeral parlour than a birthplace. I remember us standing there and in our young innocent way, shouting out loudly a pledge to the spirit of the earth that we would serve and protect it for the rest of our days. Another one of the Gods I suppose.

Anaxamander wanted to go further into the cave which I begged him not to. He dramatically recited another Greek saying, exclaiming:

As above, so below

Rather apt for he quickly ceased to be above, and judging by the sound of a cascade of stones followed by an odd silence, he was a lot more below than he intended. Then I heard his muffled voice. 'I'm stuck. Can you help me out?'

I was very scared. I went in as far as I could and saw a hand waving twenty feet below me. One slip and either of us could be making our peace with, not Zeus, but his deathly brother Hades. I couldn't reach him. I looked around hopelessly for a rope or long stick. It was getting dark outside. There was no one around that could help us. I went back inside the cave as far as I dared, to the edge of the abyss and looked down. There was no sign of Anaxamander. In horror, I sat down and called his name. He replied softly, but not from down below. I turned to my right and there he was sitting beside me. I could swear he wasn't there even seconds ago. I fell into his arms with relief. How did he get up without my seeing him, and without a sound? He said he had no idea. All he knew that he fell asleep for a second and woke up to find himself beside me.

'The mountain must have spat me out,' he joked. 'It didn't like the taste of me. Or it confused me with Zeus and had a kind of birth spasm.'

Better out than in!"

"Why does dad have such strange adventures?" asked Melissa. "And how did you keep your sanity? I'm terrified just hearing about them let alone sharing them."

"Your dad embraces life in all its aspects, light and dark. Most of us halt well before the buffers. He runs up to them like a bat relying on its radar to keep it away from danger. But it is rather last moment."

"What do you really think happened at Mount Ida?" asked Sam in puzzlement.

"It's a complete mystery if you think rationally. No so-called normal person would believe your version of events and might even ridicule you, or at least question your sanity. We in Dryadia are fortunate that we learn that different laws of science apply if the conditions are right, and time and space can be set aside. Somehow we entered that world but we don't really know how to explain it."

"Where did you go next?" asked Melissa.

"We spent four months travelling overland to India, timing our arrival so that we would avoid the heat of summer and the monsoon. The story of that journey is a very long tale so we will save it for another day. There is though one adventure that took place in India that is relevant to the present story. It's one that Anaxamander particularly wanted me to tell you. By the time we had reached India I had grown up fast, though I was still in my early twenties – about your age in fact. I knew without any doubt what I wanted – to be with Anaxamander and live in Dryadia and train with the wonderful Clara. I wanted to be a healer in the finest sense of the word.

As I said earlier there was once a group of people that existed in the ancient world, especially in Greece and Egypt, who were also known as Therapeutae. Neither of us was quite sure who they were or what they did but they seemed to be associated with dark underground caves and strange scary rituals, and everyone involved was sworn to secrecy.

The idea, Anaxamander thought, something that was quite new to me at the time, was that the participant underwent a particularly terrifying near-death experience. Assuming you came out of it with your brain still intact, you were kind of reborn and life thereafter became re-vitalised. Nothing was ever the same again. I felt a little nervous at seeking out such horrors and Clara and Sophora were much of the same mind. But both were curious for no such rituals existed in modern Dryadia. Anaxamander of course was very much up for it although we never found anything organised in Greece or Egypt – as if anyone would tell us if they were. Then of course we realised that we had had two terrifying experiences already – at Montsegur and on Mount Ida and we joked that we had to have a third to complete the triad. It was not until we reached Southern India that we underwent the final extraordinary experience.

We discovered an old Hindu temple not far from the sea. It was particularly sacred to the local inhabitants and very much in working use. I remember it was built in a dip in the ground with a large courtyard outside. It bustled with people and I will never forget the vivid colours of their clothes and the noisy cries of the peddlers trying to sell you everything that was ever made. We took off our shoes and went inside. There, it was even noisier. There were so many trumpets and drums and processions of people shouting out their devotions to the various gods, completely opposite to the peaceful ways of Dryadia. Around the perimeter of this inner courtyard, which was completely underground and lit by a large number of flares, were a number of doorways. They were more round than square and I remember thinking that they were so big that you could have driven a London double-decker bus through them. Suddenly we heard a great commotion coming from inside one of them, and out of the darkness a huge elephant emerged filling the whole doorway. It was bedecked in flowers and jewels and other ornaments. It was trumpeting very loudly and the echoes the noise caused within the confined area of the underground courtyard, together with the dark flickering shadows thrown by the flares, made your blood curdle. It felt extremely sinister.

Anaxamander naturally wanted to know where the elephant had come from and somehow he managed to find an English speaking saddhu who for a small fee would guide us up the tunnel, and for rather more money allow us to have an 'experience' that we would not forget for the remainder of our lives. I begged him not to accept for I had already been extremely terrified by the elephant, but he was adamant that he would go alone if necessary and I could wait for him.

I couldn't do that and that was why we found ourselves outside the temple an hour before dawn the next day, waiting for a mercenary saddhu whom we had only met for ten minutes, and whom I didn't in the least trust. I don't think I had ever yearned for the peace of Dryadia, or even England on a quiet day, so much as at that moment. To my shame I was also going off Anaxamander big-time. He was inflexible though and said such a chance would never come again.

The saddhu didn't seem quite so frightening when we met him again the following morning, and even gave me a re-assuring smile. It was still very dark and all the noise of the previous day had vanished. The spirit of Dryadia was reasserting itself. The priest led us inside and took up one of the flares. We entered the tunnel where we had seen the elephant coming out. We must have walked about a hundred yards along it in absolute silence. It would have been pitch black if we hadn't been accompanied by our torchbearer whose light cast some very eerie shadows. A dim light lay ahead. We then suddenly found ourselves breathing fresh air and we looked above our heads to see the beginnings of a new dawn. Even more surprisingly we could hear the sound of water flowing. The saddhu took us down to a gulley, which lay under a lip of over-hanging rock. We were standing at the edge of an underground river at the only place where it rose into daylight. The current was gentle but the river was quite wide – perhaps a hundred feet across. A small rowing boat lay tied up at our feet.

'It will only take two,' said the saddhu, and then he added, 'I need another twenty rupees for the fare. In fact forty rupees as there are two of you. Don't be frightened, you will be looked after. I hope you have an interesting time.'

If Anaxamander hadn't been so eager and the saddhu hadn't been so pressing I would have never stepped into that boat. I can't remember anything about getting into it. It was like a dream. I was just aware of Anaxamander rowing slowly across and helping me out the other side. There we found another underground tunnel. It was the only way out but at least it wasn't completely dark. The tunnel was extremely high, and here and there we could see fissures in the ceiling that let in just enough light for us to see our way. We seemed to be in some sort of light trance, which pushed the fear aside. I wondered whether the cakes that the saddhu had given us when we started out, had been drugged in some way. We felt strangely compelled to carry on with the journey. Somehow to turn back felt wrong, and when we turned around an unseen force seemed to propel us forward.

I don't know how long we walked for, but it seemed hours. The ground was reasonably flat and smooth and we had the feeling that the path had been well trodden in the past. Then unbelievably we heard the sound of the sea, and the roar of some very strong surf. We arrived at a sandy beach cut off by high cliffs from the rest of the coastline. There was no way out except to return the way we had come. In theory we had arrived in paradise except we had little food or fresh water. We were still in the same strange dreamy state that prevented us making any rational decisions as to what we should do. The only thing that we could do was to watch and wait.

Then we saw a boat – a very noisy speedboat that was approaching the beach at tremendous speed. There was just one man in it. He was large and bald and wore yellow-rimmed sunglasses, giving him a rather sinister effect.

'I hear you need rescuing,' he called. 'Only two hundred rupees. Special offer.'

'Bloody saddhu,' we both said together.

'In the bad old days,' the boatman said, 'you had to walk in darkness in the caves until you went mad or had beautiful visions, sometimes both at the same time. Now no longer necessary. Everything is better. You get early rescue and don't go mad. I get enough money to feed my family. Everybody happy.'

He brought his boat up to the edge of the beach and helped us in. We roared off at a speed that was quite out of rhythm with the swell of the sea. We bounced up and down as he showed off his prowess as he rapidly changed direction throwing us from one side of the boat to the other. Then he pointed ahead to a large converted fishing boat sailing across our bows about a mile away. He shouted excitedly over the roar of the engine.

'You want to see dolphins. No extra charge. They follow that boat out to the islands. Full of tourists, also looking for dolphins. We chase the big boat. It's very slow. My cousin's the captain.'

Without waiting for our answer he accelerated away and in a few minutes had caught up with the tourist boat. He started circling it at enormous speed in ever decreasing circles like a shark closing in on its prey. It was extremely dangerous. Anaxamander and I begged him to stop but he was possessed, grinning like a maniac at the tourists above him, many of them egging and cheering him on. If there were any dolphins they had fled the scene. They must have been terrified, as were we. Time and again we missed hitting the boat by a whisker specially when we cut across its bows. On about the sixth circuit we went just that little bit too close. The bigger boat clipped us. The next thing we knew we had all been thrown into the air and then back down into the sea, and were desperately trying to keep afloat. We were very lucky not to have been cut up by the ship's propellers.

The pilotless speedboat roared off into the distance, and I sincerely hoped that that devilish machine quickly found a watery grave. Thank goodness we all found our selves more above the water than below it. We were thrown lifebelts and hauled aboard. The speedboat pilot was the least shocked of the three of us. I suppose he had fallen in many times before.

He was taken to the front of the boat and to our astonishment was surrounded and feted by most of the passengers as some kind of hero. They were even organising a collection for him to replace his lost boat.

Strange are the ways of the East, as Sophora loves to say. Meanwhile at the stern of the boat we were being taken care of by some of the gentler and more thoughtful passengers. We were wrapped in blankets, someone gave us brandy, and a very kind local healer popped some pills into our mouths to 'de-shock' us as he put it. Something worked, for after about half an hour Anaxamander and myself had changed from gibbering and shivering wrecks, to recognisable human beings. Then we heard the re-starting of the ship's engines. We were going on to visit the islands that our so-called rescuer had described. Actually they were hardly bigger than huge rocks standing high above the sea. They were crowded with nesting seabirds, and we could have done with a Sam to help us with their identification.

Anaxamander and I were feeling much better. Then the dolphins returned, sometimes swimming under the ship in the same direction as us, then back and forth across us, then circling us like the speedboat, but of course with far greater skill and in complete silence. The best part was when they leaped out of the water in what seemed sheer exuberance – the absolute joy of being alive. Our small group at the back were completely entranced at their play, for what else could we call it. It was the little things too – the glitter of the sun on their watery backs, the sound of the 'blow' when they arched their bodies above the water, and their fins sailing effortlessly along as if they were not actually attached to their submerged bodies.

We felt so at one with them, with the world around us, and with the group of people that were sharing with us this truly awesome experience. It was especially wonderful for us but it was also strange when we looked at the people at the front of the boat, the ones that were worshipping at the feet of our speedboat cowboy. They saw none of what we saw. The dolphins never existed for them. They never knew our delight. Perhaps they were not even capable of it. I suppose they just hadn't developed enough awareness to appreciate a lighter way of life.

Anaxamander summed it up beautifully when we were safely back on shore that night. 'You can see why Dryadia and the East don't mix too well. Both groups choosing opposite ends of the boat enjoying completely different and barely reconcilable experiences. I would like to think that the spirit of Dryadia lies in all our hearts. It's just that some can feel it but sadly the majority can't. For the sake of the survival of humanity in the world I hope that one day the people at the front of the boat will join us at the back and learn to be at one in the magical world of the dolphins. Then they will know, as we do, that nothing else matters but feeling the joy of the moment.'

After the shock and subsequent joy of the dolphins, we felt that we had enough of travelling. We wanted to be home and that only meant Dryadia. In a way it didn't seem to be really appropriate to fly back in a noisy oil-guzzling aeroplane, but we had just enough money for the fares, so we did so. Two days later we were in a different boat, the dear old *Leaky Bucket*, and never had we felt happier.

That was the first time I had seen dolphins, but I have seen them many times since, as both of you have. The dolphins often swim into our estuary, sometimes within sight of Ceradoc when the tide is very high. Wouldn't it be nice to think that one of them was Apollo shining a bit of extra light into our lives."

"And no noisy speedboats would frighten him off," added Sam.

"I remember once," said Melissa, "that a dolphin came along side my sailing boat and rubbed its back so gently against it. I reached out to touch it, even stroked it for a few seconds. Then it rolled over on its back and I was sure it smiled at me."

PART TWO

THE HEALING OF ERITH

There remained the Fifth Element

[Known as Ether or The Quintessence]

Which the ONE kept hidden in its heart

And used for the ordering of the Universe

– PLATONIC TRADITION

CHAPTER NINETEEN

SECRETS

In the middle of Ceradoc where three green lanes converge and the gently sloping hill that acts like a spine to the village pauses to rest between the quay and the sheltering curtain of woods at its crest, lies a flat piece of verdant land no more than an acre in extent. It is as smooth as a cricket pitch and indeed acts as one in the summer months. It is fringed by great oaks although they are not as large as the ones at The Beacons or at Mount Quercus. The area is known as The Place of Unions or Armeria in the Dryadian tongue. This is the summer gathering place for the people of Ceradoc. At one end of this field is an eight-sided pavilion, which serves as the winter gathering place (doubling up as a sports changing room) when the weather is too cold or wet.

Almost all the rituals of Ceradoc are celebrated here, whether it be introducing a newborn child to the community (called the descent of the spirit) or saying goodbye to someone who has just died (the ascent of the spirit) or the union of couples who have decided to share their lives together. Every month at each full moon the Traditional Elders and any one else who wishes to be present, meet to honour nature and use the power of thought energy to assist any one in the village who needs it. Likewise, the Practical Elders also meet monthly round about the full moon to discuss the day-to-day running of the village and ensure that everything runs smoothly and efficiently.

The moon plays as important a role as the sun in the daily round of Dryadian life. Every child knows the months of the Dryadian lunar calendar. Every child looks out for the rising of the full moon in the eastern sky at sunset, and the first sliver of the new one near the setting sun in the west. Birch, Rowan, Ash, Alder, Willow, Hawthorn, Holly, Hazel, Bramble, Ivy, Water-Elder and Elder. These are Dryadia's sacred calendar trees, plus the Oak of course, which rules the solstices and sometimes has a month of its own at mid-summer. Each tree has a meaning or association and a distinct type of energy that is acknowledged by the community at the full moon gathering. For example the Alder tree honours the love that parents have for their children, and some of the seers can actually sense that kind of warm comforting feeling emanating from the tree when they stand close to it, or from holding its buds or flowers in their hands. At the full moon of the Alder month the celebration obviously centres on children and parents. The day has unsurprisingly turned into one big springtime children's party for every family in Ceradoc. Village life is punctuated by these monthly cycles, and the celebrations at The Armeria play a big part in keeping the community together. The only full moon festival that is not celebrated in Ceradoc is the mid-summer oak ritual, which of course takes place at The Beacons. This is the greatest of the full moon festivals. Nothing is written down. There are no rules or a church that tells people what to do or believe at these celebrations. People follow their instincts and do what they have always done. Sophora has often commented. 'The truth is seldom found in the institutions. The real magic lies in our hearts.'

In Dryadia couples don't get married for life but take out a kind of a lease on each other for a period of six years. Six, because in the Dryadian way of thinking it is the number that possesses the subtle energy of combining and relating to other people. Its other more visible manifestation is seen in the Dryadians' six-walled houses, where the idea is that the energy of six helps families to relate well and live happily together. When a union has run its six-year course it is automatically dissolved once provision has been made for any children. That is, unless both people wish to renew their commitment to each other in front of a Traditional Elder and their community.

Six years ago to the nearest full moon Sam and Melissa decided to share their lives together and celebrated it at The Place of Unions. After the ceremony the community did what they always did for a new couple – build them a new house or completely re-furbish an old one. During the construction work, which is done in the summer when the days are long, many able bodied villagers including children get involved and non-essential activities are suspended. It is a joyous event with a big communal feast at the end of each day, and a beautiful and well-made house ready to move into after two or three weeks.

Melissa and Sam had chosen to build a new house on a plot of land lying between her parents' house (Anaxamander and Ruth) and that of Zephyr and Amarinta, Sam's Dryadian adoptive parents. It was comfortably close to Ruth's wonderful herb garden, which Sam and Melissa had gradually become more involved in, as they trained to become Therapeutae under her guidance. Eventually they took over much of her work and often travelled around the neighbouring villages on horseback visiting the sick if there was no local healer available.

At the time of the Hawthorn full moon (the English May) in the middle of a warm afternoon with the traditional maypole standing regally awaiting its own celebration, Sam and Melissa arrived rather nervously to renew their vows to each other. Sophora herself was to conduct the ceremony in front of a few hundred onlookers. A small podium had been erected by the maypole under a canopy of hawthorn blossom and late spring flowers. After a brief introduction from Sophora, Melissa stepped forward to the front of the podium and said as generations of Ceradocians had said before her;

"I Melissa of Ceradoc daughter of Anaxamander and Ruth, have come here to this sacred place to receive your blessing on the renewal of my union with Sam because of my love for him."

Sam echoed her words.

"I Sam of Ceradoc adopted son of Zephyr and Amarinta have become before you in the month of the Hawthorn to ask your blessing on the renewal of my union with Melissa because of my love for her."

Then they held hands and chanted together in Dryadian.

"We children of Dryadia who love our country and hold its pure and ancient wisdom born of aeons in our hearts where it will ever remain, stand up in this sacred place in Ceradoc to publicly demonstrate our love and admiration for each other. We will hold fast to each other until we return here in six years time. By the sign of the Raven over the Oak Tree we promise this."

Those simple words were in essence all there was. But the 'treacle' as Sam put it was still to come. Mary was standing by Melissa's side and as was the custom, spoke eloquently about her kindness and wisdom reminding everyone that she and Pushkin had gone through a similar ceremony the previous year. Pushkin spoke up for Sam and described amongst other things the adventures they had had when they first came to Dryadia. The treacle continued to flow as Anaxamander, Sophora, Zephyr and all the rest added their sweet words of admiration, until the sun sunk in the west and the musicians struck up as a signal for dinner.

Anaxamander and Ruth had invited them for supper the next day. Zephyr and Amarinta were coming too.

"No children. Mary has offered to look after them. This is going to be a serious evening," said Melissa.

"No more accolades" groaned Sam. "Otherwise I'm going to be seriously sick."

"No, silly boy. Mum and Dad, especially Dad, want a serious down-to-earth talk with us. A sort of rite of passage, he called it. I've promised to say no more, though there's precious little more I can tell."

"So long as nobody tells me again that I'm one of the best things to enter Dryadia since the Cathars invented their version of the muffin. I hope your father was joking."

"I'm not sure he was right about the Cathars and their muffins, but you are pretty tasty, none the less!"

Dinner was simple and it was apparent that Anaxamander was eager to get started on what Melissa often called one of his 'pontifications.' Sam felt anxious. He was always nervous of 'serious chats'. When Melissa wanted one it always seemed to end up with him doing extra nappy changing duty followed by a large bunch of conciliatory flowers. However this time Melissa was agog, her eyes switching back and forth to Sam's to see how he was reacting.

Anaxamander began. "Yesterday was a momentous day, not just for you but for all of us here. Melissa has of course, in my heavily biased opinion, always been a star in the Dryadian heavens and Sam you are now absolutely a much treasured part of our family in Ceradoc, and a true Dryadian."

Sam looked down in embarrassment. 'Oh God,' he sighed inwardly. 'Treacle' in the first sentence.' But Anaxamander was laughing out loudly, and everyone was joining in.

"Sorry Sam. Melissa had told me about your aversion to honeyed words, so I couldn't resist it, even if it is true. I promise I won't do it again. Now I want to talk about something very important.

"You are now both of an age when the generation above you, that is us, needs to share certain knowledge, because it mustn't die with us. That hopefully won't happen for a very long time, but you never know. You of course both understand the system of Eldership that we have in Dryadia. Two basic sorts. The Traditional ones trained at the university at Cantillion who are spiritually orientated and guardians of our wisdom. And the Practical ones, drawn from the villages, who are good people with kind hearts and as their name describes, are responsible for more mundane affairs.

We Traditional Elders have different roles. We recognise that no one is superior to anyone else and we work very well together with the Practicals in organising the country. Because you have been to Cantillion and have lived here in Ceradoc, where the numbers of Traditional Elders are unusually high, you are particularly aware of what we do."

Melissa piped up in alarm. "You're not going to make us Elders. We're far too----."

"Too young." Her father finished her sentence. "It's not in my gift anyway to choose Elders by myself, as you know. That belongs to the Elder community overall as vacancies occur. I hope you will be one day, but few become Elders until well into their thirties when they have gained some experience of life. I believe Sophora was very young when she was made one, but that was because of her extraordinary gifts.

The Traditional Elders are a bit of a mystery to outsiders and sometimes even amongst ourselves, as there are several branches, like the Therapeutae for example. Some of us belong to more than one branch and may or may not be deeply involved in what that particular branch does. In other words we follow our vocation and if necessary can be quite secretive about what we know. The thing that we don't have a choice over is whether we have a degree of seership. Sophora tells us that this is a gift from the soul and it is really an extra level of subtle power that we possess from birth. That doesn't mean that Seers are any more important than anyone else. There should be nothing elitist about it. Nell was a gifted but un-trained Seer – that was how she managed to mesmerise others into doing her bidding, but she wasn't a very nice person.

Sophora has told me that everyone in this room has a fair dollop of this facility, especially of course Amarinta. I think I can safely say that unlike Nell we are all on the side of kindness. I don't think any of us could compare ourselves to Sophora but nevertheless, unlike most of the population, we get our hunches about things and sometimes obtain information from beyond the five material senses about stuff that we hadn't even dreamed existed. It's hard for the non-Seers to accept some of our knowledge. They don't have the inner-knowingness or the imagination to make those intuitive leaps. They can't do shortcuts. They want statistical proof of any new idea before they can climb out of their comfort box. Why I am reminding you of this is that a number of the Traditional Elders who are also Seers, possess hidden knowledge that is never officially taught, but is handed down from generation to generation, usually within families. Zephyr and Amarinta, Ruth and myself are party to this arrangement plus of course Sophora, and I can speak for a number of others in Ceradoc too. So that is why we have invited you two, because the time has come to share some of this information. You have the right credentials and we trust you to keep what we tell you completely secret."

"I've always suspected you knew more than you were letting on," exclaimed Melissa. "But I thought it was just technical stuff. Perhaps you and Sophora were playing with it at The Beacons on helicopter night."

"Well you're right in a way," admitted Anaxamander ruefully. "We were certainly sailing far too close to the wind on that occasion."

Zephyr smiled. "And we had to do a lot of covering up afterwards. We succeeded though. Elders are not normally associated with subterfuge but needs must."

"You've never shared with us how you brought thunder and lightning down into The Egg," added Sam. "Later, I asked Sophora about it and she explained the principles. Is that the sort of thing you mean?"

"Sam's like a ferret." Melissa smiled at her father. "What he doesn't get out of you, he gets out of Sophora. And because she thinks he's wonderful, which he is, she tells him. Doesn't she, Sam?"

"Sort of." Sam didn't know whether to be flattered or embarrassed.

"I know she trusts you totally," explained Anaxamander. "She agrees that you and Melissa are now ready to learn one of Dryadia's greatest secrets." He looked at Ruth. "Why don't you carry on with the story? You know it as well as I do."

"It concerns 'The Hall of Records'," she began grandly. "I learned about this extraordinary place from Anaxamander after I married him, as did Amarinta from Zephyr. The knowledge has been kept secret in about five Ceradocian families at least from the time of Alanda and Isola and probably long before that. As we are all related by blood or marriage if you go back far enough, we are in fact really part of the same big family. The knowledge is passed down the generations but only to the children that are deemed to be worthy and trustworthy enough. That is with the exception of Sophora who came from Cantillion and settled here in Ceradoc over twenty years ago. Up to that time, although we knew about The Hall of Records and roughly where it was, nobody had ever been there and its precise contents were a bit of a mystery. We were fairly sure it hadn't been visited for more than four hundred years, not since the great schism in our country. After Dryadia became united again, Isola sealed the entrance. She died shortly afterwards and hid the directions so well that no one ever managed to locate it. We knew the Hall was buried in a deep underground cave under Mount Cynthos where the moors are particularly wild and desolate, and where there are hardly any tracks, let alone roads. We had been passed down quite detailed directions, naturally all in code, and though many expeditions set out to follow them, the countryside had changed so much over the years that the entrance always eluded us.

We do know that the beginning of the journey starts on the moors at a well-known stone circle called the 'The Circle of Ancient Dreams'. We guessed that the cave contains the records of Dryadia from the earliest times and as you know from the legends, the treasure of the Cathars was once also hidden there. That was the crystal that Alanda and Isola later destroyed. We believed that the Hall was basically a library and a museum, and sometimes wondered why it was such a big secret, even in fact whether it really existed? Then along came Sophora." She looked at Amarinta. "Why don't you take it up from there? You are Sophora's protégé."

"I was fascinated by the story after I heard it from Zephyr and before the children were born I used to drag him up to the moors, and we often used to camp up there. I kept seeing visions of a track that led to the entrance but the heather was so thick that even with my insight, all the directions in the world would have been to no avail. One day we were camping on the edge of The Circle of Ancient Dreams, which as Ruth has just said is the traditional beginning of the quest. I remember us discussing Sophora. I had known her well in Cantillion and she had been my seership teacher there, and had taught me how to make sense of my visions and distinguish them from ordinary imagination. I had followed her to Ceradoc two years earlier and I carried on my apprenticeship and we grew very close. I often thought that Sophora had the power to find the Hall but as she was not related to the old Ceradocian families like Zephyr and Anaxamander, who are in fact actual descendents of Isola and Alanda, I wasn't authorised to mention it to her. Luckily I didn't need to.

When Zephyr and I climbed out of our tent the next morning, we looked across the circle and were astonished to see another tent pitched on the opposite side. We were quite sure that it wasn't there the previous evening. The morning was a bit misty but we could see a dim figure boiling up a kettle over a fire. The figure was humming and singing happily to herself. Then it got up and approached us with a steaming mug of tea in each hand. It was Sophora and she was laughing.

'You'll never hear a lark if you don't get up with them,' she said, totally ignoring Zephyr, who of course had to say they sang all day. She invited us to breakfast when we were dressed and said she would tell us everything.

Sophora had been walking the moors for a few days as we had. At first she didn't know that we were here too but felt compelled to visit the circle and stay the night. She had arrived at dusk soon after we had gone to bed. She had noticed our tent and knew she was amongst friends. She said she was on the same mission as us and had already found the entrance of an ancient cave but had not yet gone inside. She knew that it contained some very important things. Sophora had been prompted to find The Hall of Records through her inner eye and by now knew more than we did. So there was no point in keeping our knowledge secret any longer and we joined forces. She told us that we had to use the power of the full moon, which was just coming up. We also had to be aware of some energy lines in the earth that would lead us to the entrance and help us open the door. We could find these through our bare feet.

Then that very day Sophora led us to the entrance. It was hard work walking there because of the terrain. She managed to open the door, which was concealed as part of a smooth vertical face at the bottom of Mount Cynthos. You would never have guessed that it was there. It took a certain amount of experimenting on Sophora's part to persuade the door to reveal its secrets. Inside we could see the outline of a small stone room but we didn't feel it was safe to go in. Sophora then closed the cave up again and a month later, this time with the additional company of Ruth and Anaxamander, plus a lot of rope and hurricane lamps we set out again." Amarinta paused for a moment nodding at Zephyr.

"And that is quite a story," Zephyr went on. "We managed to descend into The Hall of Records without mishap. Sophora took other Elders there later, those who were already in the know, like Parmenides and Empedocles. After that there were only rare visits until about ten years ago when Sophora, Anaxamander and Empedocles extracted certain information, which eventually led to the helicopter incident. Then of course we closed it down again, but times have changed once more. We have been visiting the mountain regularly over the last year. We are about to travel there again with Sophora and with every one here in this room. And if you would like to, that includes Sam and Melissa. We would all value your input."

"I would love to," replied Sam whose mouth was open with excitement at the thought of such an adventure.

"I'm rather nervous," Melissa admitted, "but where Sam goes, I go. At least if something goes wrong we will both die together."

"No need to get over dramatic" added her mother. "If I can manage it then I know you can. There is very little danger as long as you are careful and move slowly after you have entered the cave."

"Good," said Anaxamander in a satisfied voice. "The full moon is in five days. That should give us plenty of time to get ready. We will be away three days. The first stage is to ride to the Old Lodge at the base of Mount Cynthos where we can spend the night. It's fairly spartan inside so we'll need sleeping bags. I'll explain more about the quest when we get there."

"It's interesting both your father and Amarinta used the word quest to describe the expedition," said Sam thoughtfully a few days later, as he and Melissa were making their way up the hill to the sanctuary to see if the oracle had any wise words to give them before they set off to Mount Cynthos.

"Dad's been talking a lot like that recently. He's been feeling depressed about what's been going on in the East, like the wars and the materialism and the endless environmental destruction. If you can see beyond his joviality he's just a big worrier on a global scale. My parents get the London papers sometimes. I wish they wouldn't. Dad gets all apoplectic and mum wastes energy trying to calm him down. He's like you with his super-sensitivity – takes everything to heart. He gets incensed with the East, especially with their ego driven leaders as he puts it, when they don't see things his way. Dad's right of course and maybe he thinks that whatever lies under Mount Cynthos can help him in the 'quest' to change the world – so long as any more experiments are well hidden."

The day was cloudy but there was just enough light in the sanctuary to allow a narrow beam of light to reach an inscription carved high up on one of the pillars. They had to draw two chairs up close and just managed to decipher the old Dryadian script in the semi-gloom. The oracle's advice was unusually long.

Only one creature has the power to reduce the world to the level of the gutter and the horror of absolute beastliness. And there is only one creature that has both the vision and the ability to reach towards the light, by increasing the consciousness of Erith through their thoughts and actions. That creature is called Man. The world can be moved in either direction by just a few of them, if they are powerful enough. The rest will follow. If enough right-minded people come together, thinking the right thoughts, doing the right things and acting kindly towards each other, then wonderful things will happen on Erith. It will have to happen sooner or later for it is the nature of spirit to rise, but sooner is less painful than later. Then we can be who we truly are and exist in harmony with the soul of the world. It is our choice. What way will you choose?

CHAPTER TWENTY

MOUNT CYNTHOS

It was an afternoon's ride to the lodge. They left their horses at the nearest village before walking the last two miles across uninhabited moorland. Sophora had already gone on ahead to make some preparations and would meet them at the end of the day. Supper and bed would be early, for they planned to set off soon after dawn for the next stage of their journey to The Circle of Ancient Dreams.

The track there was well trodden and the circle easy to find. It was a well-loved place and a popular picnic spot for many Dryadians, but today Sophora and her party had no wish to meet anyone else. In fact she had gone on ahead a day earlier, this time with Anaxamander and Ruth, and had left the lodge as soon there was enough light to make out the path. By the time the other four reached the circle they could see no trace of them. The only sign of life was a skylark, trilling its haunting song high above, before parachuting down a thousand feet towards its nest hidden beneath a hummock of grass. Zephyr was of course right. Skylarks did sing all day. They rested quietly sitting with their backs against the granite stones that enclosed the circle.

Unexpectedly, the faint sound of a horn floated over to them on a gentle breeze. There were three notes sounding like Do, Re, Me. Zephyr raised his spare frame and stood up. "That's Sophora's signal. Now all follow me and do exactly what I do."

He started to walk slowly around the circle in a clockwise direction and at each of the twelve stones he stopped, touched its top and hummed the three notes that they had just heard on Sophora's horn. They did this nine times. Zephyr and Amarinta had the confidence of having done the ritual several times before. Sam and Melissa were more hesitant but soon caught on. The circle was not a big one. Its diameter was no more than sixty feet and its stones no more than four feet tall. It wasn't quite circular, more elliptical, like The Egg at The Beacons. Sam knew its measurements were precise. They had to be. The numbers had to add up so the energy flowed properly. Both he and Melissa knew what was happening. They were charging up the circle like a battery, drawing the energy from the earth and from within themselves.

"Perfect," commented Zephyr when they had completed the nine rounds. "Now all of you take off your shoes. What do you feel?"

"Tingling," said Melissa and Sam almost together.

"Perfect," said Amarinta, echoing Zephyr's words." It's what we sometimes call Serpent energy. Now walk around the circle. See where the tingling is going. Does the energy line, because that's what it is, want to leave the circle? Zephyr and I want to see if you can do it by yourselves."

"Ouch," yelled Melissa. "I've got a thorn in my foot. Let me take it out first."

Sam helped her before saying, "I've found a line of tingle. It's moving out here and going this way, towards that big stone over there."

"But we can't go through all that gorse," said Melissa rubbing her toes.

"We don't need to," replied Amarinta. "Put your shoes on and remember that tingle. We will catch up with it again at that stone that Sam has just seen."

The stone was about a hundred yards away and its five foot of lichen-covered granite leaned drunkenly out of the perpendicular.

"We think it's at least five or six thousand years old", said Zephyr as Melissa sunk herself into a perfectly shaped backrest and started massaging her injured foot again.

"The stone has two names – 'The Ancient of Days' and appropriately for Melissa, 'The Resting Stone'. It heals weary backs. All the big stones and circles have names – some descriptive, some indicating inner meanings."

After ten minutes Melissa stood up and pronounced herself well, but let out a mild groan when Amarinta cried. "Shoes off everybody, it's tingle time."

They walked round the stones in widening circles until Sam cried excitedly.

"I've got it, but it's quite faint."

"That's all right," said Zephyr. Where's it going?"

In reply Sam walked along a small track that led down a slight incline towards a small clump of trees.

"I've got it too," said Melissa happily before replacing her shoes. "I'm getting the hang of this," and she and Sam raced towards the trees to look for the next stone.

Zephyr and Amarinta were content to follow at a more subdued pace for they had made this journey to the entrance many times before. It was their custom to follow the serpent line to the hidden door each time, though the way was now so familiar that they could find it with their shoes on. It was more intriguing however to track the tingle through their feet.

Melissa found the next stone amongst the copse of trees reaching up through cool fronds of bracken. "This is the nicest one as there are no prickles. It's actually a pleasure not to wear any shoes."

Amarinta explained some more. "We try and keep the undergrowth around the important stones in check, or they could easily get lost. The local shepherds do this for us, though they don't understand the purpose of the stones. Some stones are dummies without energy. They were put there to put off unwelcome seekers, not that I think we have any at the moment, not since Anaxamander persuaded the British to back off. Only us barefooted eccentrics could find the way. A good dowser though might, but of course he wouldn't know what he was looking for."

Sam and Melissa quickly located the tingle leaving the bracken, and followed the serpent energy to the edge of the wood where there was a bustling stream tumbling down to the valley below. They arrived at a prominent stone on the bank of the stream. But there they could sense no tingle or energy through their bare feet so it must have been one of the false ones. Once they realised that, it didn't take them long to find the genuine one, not very far away and half hidden by a small bush just off the track. In the end it had taken them about three hours and nine stone stops to reach their destination, a tiny stone just tall and wide enough to make a comfortable seat. The tingles were different there and as they traced the energy out with their feet they discovered no exit but a large eight pointed star, twenty foot across – an invisible diagram imprinted on the earth. Zephyr explained that the stone was simply called 'The Mark' and that the energy flowed back into the earth at that point.

It was a strange place, oddly quiet apart from the drone of insects and a few birds chattering quietly in the bushes. Zephyr guided them through thick undergrowth to a small hollow nearby. Here they were almost invisible from the outside world.

"Yet another waiting place! We'll rest here for an hour or so until we hear Sophora's horn. Then we'll go back to The Mark."

They were grateful for the cloudy day for the hollow would have been a heat trap under the mid-day sun. A cool breeze encouraged Melissa to snuggle into Sam's arms. Amarinta had the same idea with Zephyr. The murmur of bees foraging for nectar in the nearby foxgloves could easily have lulled them towards sleep, but the excitement of what was to come and the buzz of the previous night's conversation at the lodge, kept their brains on edge.

Sophora had told Sam and Melissa that all being well they would explore The Hall of Records today but first she had to remember how to unseal the entrance and didn't want to disappoint them if she had forgotten. Sam hoped that she was teasing though Sophora seldom joked.

The previous evening he found himself relating a story from his childhood. It was one that was familiar to Melissa but unknown to the others. Although a love of nature had always been embedded in his heart, it was his grandparents, who lived in a roomy but draughty house in the Weald of Kent who had taught him much of what he had learned about the natural world. Surrounded by woods and meadows, his grandfather owned a smallholding, which mainly consisted of a number of orchards. Most of the trees were big standards, which had subsequently gone out of fashion. He grew apples, pears, cherries and plums – fruit that grew particularly well in that part of the world. He also kept a flock of about a hundred free-range hens guarded by two fierce cockerels, which were not above having a savage peck out of Sam's leg if he got too close. Every year right up to the age of thirteen, his grandparents invited him to spend the summer holidays with them. He earned his keep collecting the eggs from the coops, letting the hens out in the morning and shutting them in at night. An old dog used to accompany him on his rounds, discouraging the foxes from attacking the hens and the cockerels from assaulting him. To his delight he was also appointed 'commander in chief of tree climbing' by his grandfather and because of his light frame excelled at picking the fruit from the highest branches in the orchard. Every evening his grandfather took him for a walk through an adjacent wood and to a small river that wound its way through it. He taught Sam how to recognise the tracks of fox, badger and the tiny roe deer. Sam learned where the wagtails nested on the brook and the heron's favourite fishing spot at a place where the water left the woods for the open grassland of the meadow. He looked up at the trees and discovered the nesting holes of woodpeckers and starlings and the outline of a tawny owl at the top of an old creeper covered oak, as it waited for the dusk to melt away into the coming night. Sam's visits continued for several years and these were the happiest times in his childhood. It bred within him an overwhelming love of nature but also the fear that it could be so easily be taken away from him. His grandparents were no longer young and many inroads were being made into the fields and woods around them to build rich men's country retreats. His grandfather described the process as the 'the devil's curse' for the world that he had loved for so long was being destroyed before his eyes, and what's more to no-good purpose.

Then the wood where he walked with his grandfather each evening came up for sale. Plans were approved by townspeople who lived twenty miles away. They lived in a world not of greenery but of tarmac and concrete and cared nothing for Sam's trees. Plots were laid out, access roads marked, trees felled and executive homes erected, selling on beautiful views that themselves were beginning to disappear as similar homes were built across the valley. Soon after, his grandfather died allegedly of a broken heart. His grandmother followed six months later. The smallholding was sold and the orchard chopped down, and became the way of all land that was considered ripe for development.

"How strange are the ways of the East," murmured Sophora as Sam and his audience dabbed their eyes. "Fear, greed and ignorance are at the root of all their problems. There is little freedom at local level, so the rulers don't have to account for their actions. They destroy their nest and then move on to destroy another and then move on again. Soon there will be no more nests to destroy."

"When Ruth and I lived in England," said Anaxamander, "we were invited to stay in what I must say was a beautiful house and garden on a wooded hillside in Devon. It must have been as lovely as Sam's grandparent's home. But we left after two days. We couldn't stand the noise. There was always the sound of gunshot in the woods shooting the pigeons. A tractor was flailing the hedges in the lanes around us. Another was spraying some toxic weed killer on the fields. There was a helicopter flight path overhead, and the neighbours were continually mowing their lawns, strimming their verges or chopping their trees down with chainsaws. What is it about silence and the East? They simply don't mix. It's the same with the night sky. Do you know how hard it is to see the stars? Except in the remotest areas there is always the glow of orange streetlights shutting them out. I would like to transport them to Dryadia for an hour to see the Milky Way. Then they would know real beauty and silence. Without silence you can never learn the secrets of nature or the peace of your soul. It's hopeless."

"The East, at least the majority of them, behave as if they were on drugs," said Ruth. Their senses are anesthetised to beauty and silence.

They can't feel properly or think for themselves. They need to go into rehab first."

"Hard though, if you don't think you have a problem, like alcoholics," added Zephyr. "And what's even worse, they believe that it is us Dryadians who are out of step. We inhabit different worlds and believe different things. But we are at peace with ourselves and our nest is still beautiful. Only the slightly insane would prefer to live in the East.

It wasn't long before the horn echoed around the hollow and they were back at The Mark. Before them, less than half a mile away, they could see the slopes of Mount Cynthos. Zephyr led them through a scattering of birch trees that obscured them from view before reaching a huge boulder. On the other side stood Sophora, with Anaxamander and Ruth beside her, holding a lantern and guarding a three-foot square hole at the base of the smooth rock face that lay behind. A similar sized stone that had obviously covered the empty space had been placed to one side.

Sophora raised her arms and grinned at them in gentle triumph.

"I don't think anyone could have found it let alone opened this door, by accident. It needed some crafty medicine to persuade this one to reveal its secrets. You've got to get the vibration right. I've simplified it a lot so next time it's going to be much easier. Welcome to the cave. There's room for us all. Mind your heads, you'll have to bend double to get in."

Inside it was cramped and dark. The tiny entrance only let in a little light and no one could find any internal doors or entrances. It was like being inside a small lift.

Sophora explained. "Don't be afraid. I've just done a trial run. We can't go onto the next stage until I've closed the entrance. No one then would guess that anyone could be inside. But don't worry, I've told Parmenides about our visit and he knows how to get in, now that I've broken the seal. When the door is closed it really will be dark. Much of the inside journey though will be in half-light, but it won't be frightening if we stick together. It's fine to talk. It will keep our spirits up. We will have no sense of time or space and we'll be back outside before sunset. Then we will have time to reach the hollow where we can camp for the night."

Sophora kneeled and gazed for the last time at the light outside, her arms outstretched, each touching either end of the opening. At first she looked out in silence and then emitted a low hum on two notes. It sounded like 'Ay-Oh, Ay-Oh' repeated very fast. She looked as if she was in a trance, not really in this world. The others quickly joined in and after a nod from Ruth, both Sam and Melissa added their voices to the chorus.

They felt their bodies becoming lighter and separated from their thoughts as the hum intensified. It was an exquisite feeling – like floating away on a bubble of sound. Sophora had earlier asked them to concentrate their energy on the shielding stone outside. It came into view through the entrance, moving quietly and slowly as if on oiled castors. The light inside faded as the stone propelled effortlessly by some unseen force shut it out permanently. It was pitch black. Melissa sought out Sam's hand for reassurance. The comforting world of the five senses seemed increasingly elusive. The silence was absolute and beyond reason as Sophora had stopped her humming after the stone was back in place. They were strangely not afraid, but felt almost comforted in the otherworldly cocoon of blackness.

Sophora was now on the floor with her back to them, groping amongst the ancient stones. A little light seemed to have entered the chamber. It had a bluish tinge to it and illuminated Sophora's hands as she pressed and pushed against the bottom of the wall.

"Got it," she muttered under her breath.

There was a little crunch as a slab of wall no more than three feet high turned on its axis. A stream of blue light flowed into the chamber as if the morning curtains had been drawn. Sophora crawled through the gap telling everyone to follow. When they were through she carefully swung the stone back into its original place, shutting it with a satisfying click. "Always close doors after you," she grinned. "That's done it. No going back now."

They found themselves on a small landing. Down below them were spiral steps made of stone carved through solid rock on either side. It was like being in an old castle. The walls and steps were of granite, and the embedded slips of crystal glittered in the blue half-light like fireflies at dusk. Sophora led the way climbing down very slowly for although there were hand holds on either side and above every step, the descent was steep.

"Weakest to the wall," said Anaxamander only half jesting as he clung to the hand holds particularly fiercely.

"Glad we can't see down very far," added Ruth.

Melissa could only manage a squeak in reply, holding tightly onto Sam's shoulder below her with her spare hand.

Ten minutes down they reached a small landing where they paused to rest. Melissa, and to a lesser extent Sam, were understandingly nervous. Anaxamander tried to comfort them with some hard facts. He sounded a bit like a tour guide.

"For those who haven't been here before, notice how dry the air is despite Mount Cynthos being in the wettest part of Dryadia. Its builders made sure that our path crossed no underground streams and just to make sure, you can see lumps of salt in the cavities in the walls. They will absorb any excess moisture, so we can be sure that the steps won't be slippery with algae. The temperature here is always the same, night and day, winter and summer. So it's always comfortable, like it is now, even down in The Hall of Records. Just like the constant temperature in the King's Chamber in the Great Pyramid. And to think that this was made thousands of years ago. Nobody would have any idea how to build something like this today."

Sam found himself wondering how on earth they could have done it. He once visited the Great Pyramid in Egypt on a family holiday and had been completely flabbergasted at the enormity of its construction. But this was underground and Zephyr had told them that The Hall of Records was almost as deep below as the apex of the Pyramid was high. And it was all made of granite – the hardest of all stone. He had started counting the steps. One, two, three, four hundred and they still hadn't reached the bottom. And then suddenly they did. This time, the huge cave that they found themselves standing in, seemed natural. He could just make out the rocky ceiling in the soft blue light. Anaxamander was right. The air was as dry as an old bone and he had long removed his warm sweater.

There was another puzzle. Where did the blue light come from? It was more like a mist. There seemed to be no obvious source. When he asked Sophora later, she replied that it was partly natural but the ancients had been doing a bit of tweaking, and the art of making it needed to be rediscovered. No doubt the secret was hidden somewhere in The Hall.

Sophora directed Sam and Melissa to the far end of the cave where there were some stone benches recessed into the wall. "It could take us half an hour," she said.

They watched fascinated as Sophora worked on the opposite wall humming and tapping here and there, with the four other Elders backing her up and adding their voices to hers when she called for more power.

Sophora had already explained that the famous hall lay behind the wall. Just like the entrance into the mountain above them, it would open when they had found the correct resonance.

The walls of the cave had various emblems inscribed on them like a child's doodles. The most common one was a scimitar shaped arrow pointing upwards as if it had just been released from a bow. This was the ninth letter of the Dryadian alphabet and was known as Lambda. The word was important in the Dryadian language and had many connotations. It had an obvious connection with the eleventh Greek letter of the same name. In the universal philosophy that the Dryadians had adopted, the number Nine symbolised completion and the spiritual world. Lambda was also the Dryadian name for the swift, one of the fastest of all birds, and one that had attained extreme mastery in the air. There was also the question of something called 'lambda energy' an esoteric subject that was only taught to the Cantillion educated Dryadians.

Known as leylines in the East, lambda or serpent lines were invisible lines or pulses of energy that travelled through the skin of the earth, occasionally descending into it, or rising from it, and commonly associated with springs of water. Melissa and Sam had felt its energy tingling in their bare feet as they followed the track to Mount Cynthos. At certain points in the earth the energy was intensified at what were called gateways or power points. Those who were interested in them, or who wanted to utilise the power of the earth, placed standing stones or stone circles at these places to harness that energy. Sometimes instead of stones, oak trees were used as in The Egg at The Beacons.

Many of the main gathering places of the Dryadians were situated at these sacred places. They had been there for thousands of years, although only a few Dryadians understood their original purpose. The Oracle at Sanctuary Hill was another important power point and there was a weaker one at the Armeria in Ceradoc. Many of these ancient sites were connected with each other in straight lines like a tube with the winding serpent energy pulsating within them. A well-known one linked The Beacons, Mount Cynthos and an old forest sanctuary in the far north of the country. Sam and his friends loved to plot the lambda lines and the power points on the map often with the help of Sophora and Amarinta who could sense them out like a dog sniffing out a ball. They liked to follow them across the Dryadian countryside either on foot or on horseback. Then they camped out besides the stones in the pure

Dryadian night with the heavens so clear that you could see stars that were never visible in the murky and light-polluted skies of England.

What were these lambda lines for? Sam as always had done his usual 'ferreting', long before the expedition to Mount Cynthos had been arranged.

Sophora replied. "They just are what they are. It's a natural phenomenon like fire or lightning except on a much higher vibration of energy. That's why it is so hard to detect them with ordinary instruments. But there is enormous power in these lines. They have to be used wisely. Our ancestors knew how to use them. We were experimenting gingerly with them ten years ago. Then it got too dangerous. One day we will do it again and you will be amazed at the new world that we will discover."

CHAPTER TWENTY- ONE

THE HALL OF RECORDS

Sam and Melissa remained lost in their own thoughts as Sophora directed operations to open the great door to the Hall. Sam wondered what his former friends in the East would have made of her. Anaxamander felt sure she would have been completely ridiculed. She would probably have been burnt as a witch in earlier times if she had put her head above the parapet. For who would have understood her ability to see beyond the five senses? It was so easy for the cynical and those with vested interests to whip up hysteria. These people were not truth seekers. Sam knew about the current witch-hunt in the East to destroy natural medicine, which healed the sick through the transfer of energy instead of using crude chemicals. He was aware that if you could find the correct resonance then almost anything could be healed or moved. That was the Dryadian way. Use the Eastern way of brute force, chemical drugs or ignorantly manipulate peoples' genes, then there was always the considerable danger that you could do more harm than good.

The East was facing economic collapse. They had fouled their nest seemingly beyond repair. The energy of the world beyond Dryadia's borders was far too heavy to survive in its present state. Only a catastrophe, followed by a long period of convalescence and a new way of thinking, would allow them to survive and rebuild their civilization. Much though would have to change first. For him there was no going back. He would follow the lambda way as Sophora and Anaxamander were now calling it. Sam wasn't at all sure what they meant but Sophora had told him that his mind would be much clearer after he had visited the Hall.

"The East are like children," she was in the habit of saying. "Give them too much information and it's a bit like letting toddlers play with matches. So for all our sakes the knowledge of The Hall of Records is to remain our greatest secret."

Melissa nudged Sam from his reverie and they became aware that the waiting hall had become a little lighter. Sophora had connected with the resonance. The chanting of the Elders had become louder and somehow was reverberating off the walls and ceiling. It now seemed to have a power of its own, independent of its originators. There was another noise too, grating harshly when compared with the harmonious notes that the Elders had initiated. It was a creaking sound like wood on wood. The door was opening, but not on hinges as you might expect. It was sliding upwards very slowly, under its own power and light was pouring out from beneath it. The chants ceased and the enormous door rose and disappeared into the ceiling. All was now quiet and the light so blinding that everyone had to shield their eyes.

Sophora called out. "It's all right everybody. Keep your eyes closed for a moment. I'll turn the brightness down to something more comfortable. Now open."

They opened their eyes and gasped. They were looking at the source of the blue light that had suffused their journey since they started their descent from the entrance far above. The light was alive. It pulsated, deepened here, lightened there. It swirled and spiralled. Sometimes it seemed so dense that you felt you could touch it, and then it would melt into almost invisibility. If wind had colour then that would describe it very well.

They stepped hesitatingly over the threshold. The inner walls of The Hall of Records shimmered in the ever-moving light. They were not straight. They did not rise to the ceiling, for there was no ceiling. The walls inclined inwards and culminated in a small flat surface high above the floor, no more than a foot square, which glittered and shone as bright as any chandelier. Within the three other walls there were single openings each leading to adjoining chambers.

The door to the 'Waiting Chamber' had now closed noiselessly behind them. As they looked around and above, they realised that they were not so much in a conventional hall but inside a rather large pyramid. It was empty apart from one thing. In the middle of the floor positioned exactly below the apex was a stone structure about fifteen feet high, its eight sides made from beautifully carved granite. In one of the sides were inserted steps that rose and ended in a large square platform. There was nothing placed on it and sizable as the construction was it was dwarfed by the pyramid that contained it. The platform was known as the plinth.

After everyone had climbed onto the platform and gazed in awe around the inside of the pyramid, Sophora called them down and led them into the first of the adjacent rooms, which was known as 'The Chamber of Written Records.' The chamber was simply furnished and contained only a number of stone tables both in the centre and around the perimeter of the room. On them were placed numerous leather bound books and a large number of scrolls fastened with faded ribbon.

Sophora let them look around without comment before returning them to the main hall and out into the second room, which she introduced as 'The Chamber of Artefacts.' It looked like the junk room of an old country house. Against one wall were stored a number of model houses, carts and boats and even what looked like aeroplanes. In the opposite corner was a large collection of geometrically shaped objects which all remembered from their Cantillion days as the five Platonic solids. These remarkable objects were beautifully carved in oak, stone or crystal in sizes ranging from the size of a child's hand to monsters as big as a chair. Leaning against the two other walls and much taller than a man were some extraordinary saucer shaped items broken into pieces. The most spectacular versions were three outsized models taking up most of the spare floor space each with enough room inside to accommodate at least a dozen people. There was also a peculiar collection of ancient machinery. There were no cogs or wheels or other moving parts, simply a mess of wires and what looked like circuit boards as if they had been cobbled together by the proverbial absent minded professor.

The 'Chamber of Crystals' was the name of the third and final room. One end was enclosed, and unlike the rest of The Hall of Records was dark and damp. Crystals were rooted in the ceiling and grew downwards like so many swords of Damocles while others grew up from the floor as if they were waiting for a King Arthur to pluck them out of obscurity. They ranged through the whole colour spectrum from deepest black to totally transparent. There were crystals as yellow as amber, green as emerald, and blue as sapphire. There were quartzes of pink, violet and turquoise. Their shapes were equally varied, from the octagonal to the cube, from the rhombic to the pentagonal and the completely irregular. No human mind could have imagined such variety.

"There's one tiny room left. I think you'll like this one. We can sit down and answer all your questions." Sophora grinned broadly and eased herself through the crystal garden where there was a tiny waterfall flowing into a font-like rock basin.

"So pure, you can drink it. Or wash your hands in the crystal pool. It's percolated down from the moors above. The only water that gets down here."

She swung open a stone door, which revealed a small room containing a long stone table with benches on either side. What really was amazing were the plates of sandwiches and flasks of tea that lay upon the table!

"The Water Fairy," smiled Anaxamander. "She never lets us down and nobody has ever seen her make the tea."

"That's because she made it at the Lodge. Step forward Water Fairy and take a bow." Melissa excitedly nudged her mother.

"You didn't notice me disappear when you were admiring the exhibits in The Chamber of Artefacts, explained Ruth. "That's when I turned into the Fairy. Anyway let's sit down and eat and drink up. I expect Sam and Melissa need some questions answered."

"Let me start," said Anaxamander. "The story of this place has been in our family for generations, and Sophora and Amarinta have added more through their seership. The Hall of Records is by far the oldest human created thing in Dryadia. It was actually built long before Dryadogenes and the first Dryadians. It existed before the Ice Age, when mammoths and sabre-toothed tigers roamed the frozen tundra far above our heads. So we are going back tens of thousands of years. We have no knowledge of the original builders. Possibly there may be connections with the ancient Egyptians, for you have all noticed that the main hall is designed as a pyramid, using exactly the same dimensions as The Great Pyramid of Egypt but on a smaller scale. Incidentally we have never believed that The Great Pyramid was ever designed as a burial chamber. Nor was ours. The plinth in the main hall is in exactly the same position relatively speaking (that is a third of the way up) as the so-called King's Chamber is in proportion within The Great Pyramid.

Somehow the memory of The Hall of Records found its way into the minds of the early Dryadians. It might possibly be one of the reasons why Dryadogenes came here in the first place. Nevertheless it is a great a mystery as to how it was rediscovered some six thousand years ago, and how and why it was built when men were supposed to be living in caves. Obviously some of them weren't. Anyway the early Dryadians managed to find the entrance and break the complicated codes that allowed them to come down here. They must have had their Seers too. We do know from the records that we discovered on our previous visits that they found the Hall largely empty. That was apart from the plinth that we have just climbed. The general layout of the Hall in their time seemed to have been as much as we see today. We call this place The Hall of Records, which it obviously is, but once it was used as a place of power. Its location was only known to a few for it cannot be found by the physical senses. Only a Seer as sensitive and knowledgeable as Sophora could have found it and fortunately for all of us she is a Dryadian. Sophora has told us that its potential is still immense. Partly from the point of view of the knowledge that is stored here. But also because of the extraordinary power that is hidden within its structure and in the objects that you have just seen. One day we hope the East will neither be a threat to itself or us. Then the Hall could once more be a huge force for good in the world. But not just yet. The helicopter incident saw to that.

Dryadogenes and his friends were not only wise but were well versed in the technology of the time, which believe it or not in some aspects was in advance of what we use today. They used this technology intelligently and kindly for the benefit of all. It did no harm and the power that was used was simple, sustainable and non-polluting. We know that the knowledge that the original pyramid makers had, and how they managed to build it hundreds of feet below the surface of the earth, was codified and the clues hidden for many millennia until Dryadogenes found them. He realised that our pyramid had been designed with absolute mathematical and geometrical precision. He knew that whatever the Great Pyramid in Egypt could have done, ours could do the same things too, as it was built in the same proportions.

It was certainly a powerful computer. But it was much more than that. It pulled power from itself partly because of its design, but also from the sky and the earth just as we do at The Beacons every mid-summer. In other words the pyramid can utilise the lightning from the storms that play from time to time above Mount Cynthos and even store the electricity within the mountain. The pyramid can also capture and store the power that runs through the lambda lines, a great many of which also pulsate through the mountain."

"And tingle under our feet," added Melissa.

"Exactly," answered Anaxamander. "But obviously the energy is much diluted in that form or you would have felt much more than a tingle. So Dryadogenes and his friends rediscovered this and much more too, and the knowledge was used where appropriate until Isola and Alanda shut The Hall of Records down, more than four hundred years ago."

"Anaxamander has made it sound very dramatic", said Ruth. "And so it is, but we haven't worked out a fraction of its potential yet. There's lots of low-key information as well that doesn't need to be kept secret at all. I've translated reams of information about herbs and healing ideas, some of which I knew already, but much that I didn't and some of which

I've incorporated into my practice. I've even passed some of it down to Melissa and Sam as if I had always known." She looked at her daughter's saucer sized eyes of surprise. "Tara's been down here quite a few times researching the old legends that are now being incorporated into her story telling. She was already familiar with a lot of the myths and found that many of them had changed little in hundreds of years. Parmenides too. His histories are more complete as a result of poring through those dusty old books, despite what he said. The Dryadian script hasn't changed that much over the years so our translation work wasn't too difficult as the originals are reasonably easy to understand. Bit by bit we are re-cataloguing the writings that we consider to be non contentious and are trying to make sense of the science and technology ones too, but those of course we keep to ourselves. In any case I don't think anyone that isn't a Traditional Elder could make head or tail of them, even though all the best science is supposed to be very simple. An outsider would never understand that in our technology one of the most important ingredients is the power of human consciousness, especially when a number of trained people are projecting the same thoughts in unison. This energy of passionate intention flows from the heart and is much more powerful than brain energy. It's a principle that is very important in healing."

"Thoughts need to be kind and honourable," said Sophora. Otherwise the results can become dark and heavy and not do anyone any good."

"Then lets be grateful that we are all belong to the Dryadian tradition," added Zephyr softly. "I'm sure Dryadogenes would be proud of us."

"What were those flying saucers for? I'm talking about those strange objects we saw in The Chamber of Artefacts," asked Sam.

Anaxamander answered. "In the records they are called Dryadogenes' chariots, or sometimes lambdas. We know them as lambda machines to distinguish them from the lambda lines, which we were just talking about. Chariots or lambdas appear a lot in our legends. We hear about Dryadogenes flying through the sky in his chariot. He flies around the world in it, following the paths of the swifts (or lambda lines). If he can't find any lambdas then his path is blocked. Where the swifts nest (meaning gateways to us) then his chariot can rest too. His chariot makes no sound, and sometimes emits strange lights. It can fly as fast as a swift or as slow as a leisurely butterfly or even hover like a kestrel. The chariot can disappear instantly into thin air and reappear simultaneously at the other end of the country. Sometimes the Dryadians chant before they get into the chariots or just concentrate deeply about what they are going to do. Dryadogenes has a number of these chariots because his friends fly in them too. When they are not being used they are kept in Dryadia at the bottom of a volcano. There is one story about a chariot breaking down. Dryadogenes, which is really a word for any wise ancient Dryadian, realised that a bit had fallen off and gave instructions to a friend to fly back to the volcano and fetch back a spare part. Interestingly the word for volcano in Dryadian is virtually the same as the word for pyramid, and the essence of fire is buried in both words.

Many of these words appear in our poems and stories. They are meaningless if you are not in the know but once you know the code then a very different scenario is revealed. Thanks to our exploratory trips down here we are now able to look at our legends with a completely different perspective. These early Dryadians were called Gods. They flew about in their chariots trying to civilise the wilder inhabitants of the world. They taught them the art of housekeeping and the science of agriculture. They passed on their knowledge of healing and music. Then they vanished in a flash in their chariots. No wonder they were called Gods! On some occasions they mated with the locals and stayed with them to ensure that the new knowledge was not lost. But for the most part the land of Dryadia was their home and their sanctuary. Although the Dryadians considered all the peoples of the world equal, they thought of them as being from two classes. There were the ones who didn't want to know about anything beyond their creature comforts. And there were the ones who wanted knowledge for its own sake. If their hearts were kind then they were allowed to fly with the Dryadians in their lambdas."

"The lambdas sound just like what in Britain are called UFOs", said Sam excitedly. "Bright lights, enormous speeds and sudden appearances and disappearances."

"I think you're right Sam, extraordinary as it may seem. But not these ones. They haven't been outside for hundreds of years," answered Anaxamander.

"Not even for a tiny bit of exercise on The Beacons." Melissa raised her eyebrows and looked at her father mischievously.

Anaxamander shook his head. "I will admit though we had made some baby ones."

"If we substitute the word Humans for Gods, and accept that they had an advanced knowledge of science and technology which included some rather extraordinary flying machines, we must be near the truth," said Sam. "It's fantastic."

"But true," replied Anaxamander. "We've proved it on The Beacons, though in a very small way."

"How did you power your lambdas?" asked Sam.

"As I have just explained. With the power of thought and sound, combined with lambda line or serpent energy. It's the power of concentration, which comes from the heart with as many like-minded people involved as possible. We have barely looked at the crystals and Platonic solids yet. We are sure that our ancestors used those too, to amplify the power."

"I've thought of another problem," said Melissa. "If the ancient Dryadians kept their lambda machines down here, then how did they get them out? Or if they didn't make them down here how did they get them in? We have hundreds of feet of solid rock above us and I remember Sophora telling us earlier that there was no other entrance, apart from the way we came in. You couldn't possibly get the twenty-foot machines through the tiny hole at the top, not to mention up and down that narrow spiral staircase. Unless they were all carried up in bits."

"Which they weren't." Sophora chipped in. "There is another way, but not one you would think of. I meant a physical way when I discussed the entrance with you before. We don't need exits and stairways for the lambda machines to move in and out of The Hall of Records. The machines that we have here look well worn and I'm quite sure that they have been out in the open and flown many times. There are clues in the records as to how this was done and I can see them flying in the pictures that form in my head. You know how I work. Yes, it is possible to leave and enter the pyramid with or without a lambda machine using a non-physical way of transportation. Most of the world cannot understand anything beyond the physical dimension of what we call the four elements, though even those elements are really the energy forms that lie behind matter.

We however, who have had our education at Cantillion know of a fifth element, something known to the Greeks as Ether, or as we say the Quintessence. The Quintessence is obviously linked with the energy of the number five and its related geometry. It has connections with certain spirals, certain crystals and the platonic solid known as the dodecahedron. So now you can get some understanding as to why those sorts of things are stored in the chamber. The Quintessence is not worldly. It is not a place. It is a form of energy that lies beyond the physical, but is linked with it. We experience it for example in the lambda lines and the related spirals of energy that are found when these pulses meet and enter or leave the earth. This source of power, though seldom recognised, is particularly strong at all the major sacred sites of the world, whether they be great cathedrals, healing wells or old stone circles. These are the places in the earth where it is especially possible to leave or re-enter the material world and also to find healing. The religious people in the East may associate these areas as places where miracles can happen. We call them power points or gateways. In fact it is the energy of the fifth dimension that causes these so-called miracles because it re-arranges and re-balances the patterns of life. While this happens, that same energy can allow you to rise above the forces of matter and leave the physical world. That dimension is called the Quintessence."

"And that's why when we spiral up into it and become immersed with its energy we call it the lambda way. And that's why lambda machines can suddenly appear and disappear in a flash. It's when they dematerialise and materialise into another dimension. And I remember from my Cantillion days being taught that the energy of the Quintessence was strong at birth and death and even when we have orgasms, and I'm definitely not blushing," said Melissa forcefully.

"Exactly," replied Sophora. "The energy of the Quintessence is strong in our emotional life, and in our bodies it is concentrated around the heart area. Therefore to invoke it, we need to have our feelings involved, far more than our brains. Combine the energy found in those special places of the earth where the lambda energy is concentrated, with the emotional energy of a number of people all thinking and feeling the same thing, then you have the potential for lift off into a dimension where space and time don't exist. We call the process transpiration. You are then closer to that real world of finer energy where you don't need a physical body or earthsuit to exist. See the flat area at the top of the plinth in the main hall. That's where the lambda flights began and ended."

"Wow," said Melissa. "No wonder Isola and Alanda sealed the Hall when that wicked Sastamoro nearly took over the country. I can't imagine what he might have done in the world if he had access to the lambda machines."

"And of course they destroyed the Crystal to stop that too falling into his hands", added Sam. "Which we now believe was stored here after the Cathars brought it to Dryadia."

"Other big crystals have grown to maturity down here since", said Amarinta. "The pyramid hasn't stopped operating."

"Would it be safe to restart the experiments again?" asked Sam. "Perhaps only in a small way to start with."

Sophora smiled at him. "I think we should proceed very carefully at the moment, tempting as it is."

"Maybe a small secluded hop on a cloudy night," said Sam hopefully.

Melissa giggled. "I wonder what the East would think if they could see us now, eating muffins and talking of switching dimensions. They would consider us as a bunch of self deluded fantasists."

"The ordinary people certainly would," replied Sophora. "A few of their scientists and military wouldn't though. Their attitudes are the same today as when they sent the helicopters in ten years ago. They still want power over others. Greed and fear rule their minds as they always have done. They are doing experiments into what they call the paranormal and have had enough success to encourage them to keep going. In the sub-atomic world that their scientists call Quantum Physics they readily admit that anything could happen, and the laws of Newton no longer apply. They realise that the observer's mind can influence their experiments, as of course we do. They recognise the limitations of time and space. The cleverest of them, though I hesitate to call all but a very few wise, know that the greatest secrets of life lie in the ethereal world of the Quintessence, though they will use other names for it."

"What do we do with all this knowledge, now that we have discovered it but can't really use it?" said Sam rather wistfully.

"What we have always done," replied Sophora. "Keep it safe and secret amongst the few of us who know. Watch and wait and bide our time. When the East changes and its power diminishes, which it surely will in time, then we will re-discover the art of transpirating into the Quintessence and learn the way of the lambda once more. Then we will try and help the world to lighten the burden that is rapidly destroying it."

Sophora quickly got up. "We must leave in half an hour. We need to be on our way up to the surface. We don't want to travel across the moors in the dark. I'll take you for a brief guided tour around the chambers with our newly acquired knowledge in mind."

At each stop Sophora added further information. In the Chamber of Written Records she mentioned that the oldest books were nearly five hundred years old and some were copies of copies going back to the time of the first Dryadians. Tara and Parmenides had now virtually finished copying out further editions, which they hoped would last many centuries. In The Chamber of Crystals she explained the process of seeding, growing, and in due course harvesting the crystals as if they were plants.

"The very powerful ones remain here. Occasionally we will transpirate a gentler one to the outside world. They can be useful at the 'mid-summer ceremonies'." Sophora's hands flew to her mouth and a mischievous smile flickered around her eyes. "There, I've let a little secret out."

'Gentle' thought Sam, remembering the annual dramatic events of summer at the Egg. 'If that is gentle, what might a powerful crystal do?' Sophora seemed to read his mind, as she seemed to do so often.

"Well, the main thing you need to know about crystals is that they store and amplify energy. They can attract it too as we have observed in the lightning ceremonies. The granite megaliths that our ancestors erected to mark the lambda lines in the earth are used in a similar way for they contain slivers of quartz enabling the stones to act like crystals. The power of crystals varies with their shape and colour, which affects their resonance. Size is not necessarily important. Resonance or vibration is everything. Their uses vary from healing the sick to the guidance and power systems in the lambda machines. They are also used in the transpiration process. Many of the stone or oak circles have crystals buried beneath them. They buoy up and help store sacred energy, of which there are three main sources. There is that of heaven, in the form of lightning, and that of earth, from the lambda lines and certain trees and plants. The third one is also very important, equally powerful and which many of us forget. And that is us – the unique loving and caring energy of human beings.

Sophora led them into the final chamber once more – The Chamber of Artefacts.

"Formerly this was the place where the lambda machines were built, repaired and stored. Then they were moved into the main hall and lifted onto the plinth ready for launching. I believe this happened for thousands of years right up to the time of Alanda and Isola, when the science and art of transpiration more or less ceased. After that time, this chamber became a museum or garage where the relics of the lambda age were stored."

Sophora pointed towards one of the walls. "There you can see one of the smaller machines, a two-seater that didn't need to be dismantled before being stored here. And here you can see (she pointed to another wall) is a large long distance lambda, broken into four parts." She fingered the quadrants almost lovingly, as if they were long lost friends.

"Almost everything else that you can see here apart from the big ones on the floor, are the bits and pieces and spare parts for these amazing machines. They have no engines as we know it, so they are totally silent. All the equipment that lies around you enables the lambda machines to harness the powers of nature for their propulsion and transpiration to other dimensions through quintessential energy. The equipment also aids navigation by seeking out the lambda lines and other earth grids. The machines then can find their way all over the world like their namesake, the lambda bird that can similarly find its way back to Africa. You don't want to disappear forever or get stuck between dimensions. It's not a game. The crystals and the platonic solids, amongst other things, help the pilot to lock onto the lambda lines and their associated spirals which are its main source of power, You also don't want to crash land and break your neck. Some lines only work at certain times, around the full moon for example and fail completely at eclipses. These are our branch lines. Others, the really big energy lines and there are probably more of those here in Dryadia then anywhere else in the world, operate all the year round, all of the time. These are obviously the safest and most reliable. Some of the main lines stretch all around the world. There is a big terminus here in Dryadia in the south of the country. No wonder our ancestors wanted to settle here. Ocean going stuff! You normally need big machines to follow those lines. The knowledge was learned over countless generations. When Sastamoro almost gained power, Alanda and Isola took the view that it was no longer safe to allow the machines above ground so they were hidden here. In effect the key was thrown away. Luckily we managed to find it again."

Sophora look dazed after her long speech. "I think we'd better go. Questions later when we get to the camp."

They gathered their packs and filed out into The Hall of Waiting and tried to imagine a lambda machine perched on top of the plinth before it suddenly disappeared. The closing of the main door assisted by gravity and chanting was completed within twenty minutes. Sophora left them to it while she went on ahead to open the entrance to the outside world at the top of the spiral staircase.

The light and freshness of the air overwhelmed them. They had an inkling of what a change of dimension might mean. Sophora sealed the opening into Mount Cynthos as they adjusted their minds to another world and made their way down the hill towards their tents.

THE HALL OF RECORDS

CHAPTER TWENTY-TWO

MERADOC AND THE CLOUDBERRY WARS

About three miles upstream from Viribus, the capital of the Northern Province, and on the banks of the river that flows down from the high moors of Mount Cynthos to the sea, is the small village of Meradoc. It is lost in the vast woods through which the river winds, and marks the point where the tides weakly rise and fall for the final time. Beyond it, the higher reaches of the river are no longer navigable by small boats. The village is smaller than Ceradoc, which is hidden in a bend of the river's estuary on the other side of Viribus. In no way though is Meradoc regarded as insignificant to it, and such are the traditional links between the two villages they are considered to be twin communities. No roads lead to Meradoc – only a few ancient and narrow tracks. It is usually reached by boat from Viribus when the river is full with the swelling tide, and a westerly wind is at your back. Whilst Ceradoc has a close relationship with the sea and the sandy wastes that surround it, Meradoc lying deep in the woods, seems to be sustained by the trees and the never ceasing river sounds that etch their harmonious rhythms in the hearts of all that live there.

Meradoc simply means the village that says 'Yes to Storytellers'. Along one side of the riverbank live the permanent residents, who make a living largely through woodland crafts like coppicing, charcoal burning and furniture making. There is, as in all communities, the usual sprinkling of Elders, both Traditional and Practical who ensure the smooth running of the village. During the summer months however the population is swollen by an influx of Storytellers, including musicians, dancers and clowns and all types of entertainers from all over the Northern Province. Along with their families, the Storytellers move into the empty houses that occupy the other side of the riverbank. These homes have accommodated the Storytellers for generations and although not used for much of the year, they are particularly appreciated when they are occupied for about three months after the mid-summer oak celebrations.

The purpose of this summer migration of around sixty dispensers of verbal and musical magic, plus their families, is to gather together with like-minded friends, and prepare for what is called in Dryadian 'The Great Wandering'. The origins of the annual pilgrimage of the Storytellers through the dozens of rural villages and communities in the Northern Province and in the small all-the-year-round theatre in Viribus, are lost in time. Dryadia's foremost historian, Parmenides of Ceradoc, believes that some of the stories are more than three thousand years old. The

Storytellers break into small groups and leave Meradoc for a few weeks at a time spending several days in each village before moving onto the next. Over the summer a village may play host to many troupes and as they have very little other outside entertainment, these visits are major highlights in the village year. The Storytellers stay in the village resthouse and are well fed in exchange for entertaining their hosts with a large range of adult and children's stories, both instructive and theatrical.

Tara and her husband Hermes came here regularly with their children for at least part of the summer. They were usually joined by Mary, now as an accomplished Storyteller as Tara, along with Pushkin and their two children. Normally Sam and Melissa and their young family also joined them, for they were now qualified Therapeutae and they too would travel through the villages giving healing and advice where necessary. Only a few of the villages had a resident healer and if a sick person didn't live very near Viribus then a travelling Therapeutae was much in demand. In fact Sam and Melissa were well known in the province as they had taken over much of Ruth's work. Recently though Sam's journeying had become a solitary affair, at least in the colder weather, for Melissa needed to remain at home in Ceradoc with their two little ones, Damelza and Piran.

Tara and her group had already been in Meradoc a month and had completed one tour before Sam and Melissa and the two children sailed out of Ceradoc to Viribus on a strong flowing tide. They sat in the prow clutching a child under each arm and Sam as always with binoculars glued to his eyes, was excitedly pointing out the terns skimming insects from the surface of the river, cormorants stretching out their diving wings to dry in the morning sunshine and a party of shelduck up-ending for small creatures beneath the water.

These simple pleasures brought enormous joy to Sam. He often thought that there couldn't be many inhabited places in the British Isles where such delights were just outside your backdoor. That was indeed the case everywhere in Dryadia, not just on his beautiful river. He mourned for all the people of the East where only a tiny minority could enjoy what he did. Such instant joy should be every human being's birthright and not just for the people of Dryadia. Excessive populations and over industrialisation had robbed the East of their inheritance and only a few knew what had been stolen from them.

Within an hour they were tying up at the small quay at Viribus. Another smaller boat was waiting for them, one with a shallow draught that would easily be able to navigate the upper reaches of the river above the town. It was called ironically *The Meradoc Express* – non-stop too. After Viribus the river spread its wings and lost its form over a sizable flood plain and the pilot had to carefully negotiate its passage through the dense reed beds. The boat couldn't go slow enough for Sam who, with Damelza safely clasped in his lap, was scanning the reeds through his binoculars for signs of warblers or a statuesque heron or egret. Otters had always been common here for they had never suffered the persecution and the polluted waterways that their Eastern cousins had. The river was clear and full of fish – salmon and trout were plentiful. There was never any shortage of food, and plenty for humans and animals to share.

For a mile now the river had turned into a huge marsh. The valley was wide with its wooded hills guarding it at a distance. The river's banks had become lost in the green vegetation that the river had spawned in the spring. As they sailed on, the hills began to draw in on them squeezing the water into what looked more like a river with high sandy banks, busy with colonies of sand martins visiting their nest holes and snapping up insects over the water with the accompanying swallows. The river narrowed further, tall willows and alders hemming it in, until the tops of the branches of the trees on either bank embraced each other as they sought out the ever-decreasing sunlight. The gentle current, which had its origins in the ocean more than ten miles away, was propelling them effortlessly through a watery tunnel of green and shade where the forgotten sky seemed a part of another universe. No one dared break the enchantment. Sam and Melissa had done this journey many times before but this last part of it seemed always the most magical to them. It took twenty minutes to pass through the tunnel before the trees started retreating and the sky began to break through the canopy once more. Then they were there. Meradoc's small jetty appeared quite suddenly as the river twisted hard back on itself and before them were groups of hexagonal houses hugging the hillside on either bank with an old stone bridge joining the two communities.

"Welcome to Meradoc," squealed an excited Mary, with a beaming Pushkin and their two slightly overwhelmed children in tow.

Meradoc and Ceradoc were not identical twins. One was a centre of storytelling, the other possessed more philosophers per acre than any other place in Dryadia, apart from Cantillion. Meradoc bartered the fruits of the forest, its nuts and berries and the results of its coppicing and carpentry for grain, potatoes and vegetables that grew better elsewhere.

The Storytellers, being summer visitors, did not get too involved with the day-to-day work and woodland cultivation of the residents. Their children however, who regarded their time on both banks of the river as a big holiday, basically went wild while their parents considered their adventures both in the woods and in the world of stories as an essential part of their education. The Storytellers' houses on the west bank tended to be bigger than the residents' ones on the opposite bank, as they were usually occupied by more than one family (Pushkin's Sam's and Tara's for example). The homes that overlooked the river had extensive overhanging balconies, large and secure enough to act as open-air rehearsal space. There was no conflict between the two communities and the bridge that joined them was used as much as the boat that ferried everyone back and forth to Viribus. The residents of Meradoc were both animated and entertained by the visits of the Storytellers and for their part were glad to support them during their visits with food and the daily necessities of living.

"It's like being at Cantillion all over again," said Mary, as with children safely in bed, they settled down on the balcony with the river bubbling peacefully below them. There was a lot to discuss apart from the serious work of preparing for the forthcoming storytelling season.

Pushkin and Mary had by now also visited The Hall of Records. Tara of course had been there often, acting as 'the recording angel' rescuing and copying out the precious manuscripts before they faded away into dust and the knowledge lost. Hermes often accompanied her on these visits. He was a historian and a cousin of Parmenides, and was one of the few Dryadians who had direct knowledge of the outside world for he had actually travelled around it twice in either direction bringing a breadth of vision to any debate. He was a quiet man and at first knowing he seemed to play second fiddle to Tara, but he brought stability to their relationship and she would be the first to admit that she wouldn't be the adventurous storyteller that she was without his support.

Like everyone else that had been there, their visits to Mount Cynthos had both disturbed and excited them equally. Tara and Hermes were delighted that they could at last share freely the knowledge that they had acquired several years before. The lambda lines and the idea of transpiration into different dimensions seemed fantastic and implausible to their rational minds but they could hardly deny the evidence of The Hall of Records. As Sophora once told Pushkin in a moment of doubt: 'It does seem rather unlikely that our ancestors had hidden their machines and records under Mount Cynthos just to lead their descendents astray four hundred years later.'

Meantime, across the small river that divided Meradoc's two communities a minor problem had grown into a crisis. It had brought two largely peaceful families to blows. Such a thing was rare in Dryadia for disputes were generally solved through what was called consoling, a kind of arbitration, long before they got out of hand. One of the Elders of Meradoc, Dante had come to tea and poured out his troubles, which were obviously uppermost in his mind.

"I'm at my wit's end," he said. "You know how justice works in Dryadia. A Traditional Elder who has been trained as a judge and conciliator gets the two parties together and bit-by-bit they cobble up a solution that is reasonably satisfactory to everyone and which means that they can more or less remain on speaking terms. It's all done in private, the opposite of what is done in the East. There are no barristers for the defence or prosecution, and no humiliation. Big egos may get cracked in the process but as long as the Elders can obtain understanding, no harm is done. There is no punishment as such, but wrongs have to be righted and causes removed all in a spirit of fairness and kindness.

Only in the severest cases, like extreme violence or murder, would a Dryadian be deprived of his liberty and be locked up in the Penance House in Cantillion. There are only eleven people in there at the moment, so you can see that major crime is not much of a problem."

"It's better than it was two hundred years ago when unwanted criminals were exiled and put in a small boat with three days supply of water, and told where England was," Melissa added thoughtfully.

"In my more despairing moments I almost wish that was still the case and that I could push our two protagonists, Bernard and Samson, out to sea. They are decent men at heart but at the moment they are behaving like two of the biggest and most stubborn scallywags with nothing but wood chips between their ears. I shouldn't be talking to you like this, but I really need your help."

Tara looked quizzically at Dante. "I don't see how we could. We are Storytellers and Therapeutae and some camp followers," grinning at Hermes. "We're not properly trained in consoling. None of us are even Elders yet."

"That may not matter," replied Dante. "It's what's acceptable to Bernard and Samson that counts. They've rejected my consoling, which though I say it myself, is rare. The next step is to get three consolers together to hear them. The problem is that we only have three Elders here that would be any good at it and one of them is me, another is very old and deaf, and the third is Bernard's cousin. I don't particularly want to go to Viribus in search of replacements. In fact it was Bernard who suggested that I come to see you. They both love storytelling but they told me separately that they were very devoted to Ruth when she came here as a Therapeutae, and they also have great respect for Melissa and Sam who have succeeded her and have looked after their health since then. They would be happy to be consoled by both of you with me in attendance. That would solve the problem of a shortage of Elders."

Sam looked alarmed. "We've really done nothing like this before, though we were taught all the principles when we were at the university at Cantillion."

"That will be enough," replied Dante. "You are both healers and these gentlemen are definitely in need of healing. I will console you, so you don't need to worry about protocol, not that we have much. It's just a step-by-step process to try and find understanding and a solution that is acceptable to both of them so that they can both keep their tails up in the air. It should be a common sense thing, or uncommon sense, as dear Sophora is wont to describe it. A rare thing indeed."

Dante was so relieved to obtain Sam and Melissa's agreement that he immediately took them to Bernard's house five minutes walk away from the bridge on the other side of the river. Bernard was charming, swept away by Melissa's grace and her easy smile, which as he kept saying, reminded him so much of her mother Ruth. However he was in bad shape and was nursing a bloodied nose and a black eye.

"Present from Samson," he said simply.

Samson's wife was equally angry and the two families were definitely not talking, and even worse, some of the villagers were taking sides. The Storytellers' village was unfortunately writing its own story, and an unhappy one at that.

"Right," said Dante briskly to Bernard. "We all know the rules. I will now take Sam and Melissa to see Samson and hopefully get his agreement to consolation as well. I will brief them on the situation and then we will visit both of you separately tomorrow to find common ground. If we see a solution then we will all get together later and hopefully shake hands on it."

"Give him a big punch on the nose from me first," was Bernard's parting shot.

"Have you heard of cloudberries?" asked Dante later.

"I have actually," answered Sam. "Because I've tasted them when I once visited Sweden. "They're like yellow blackberries and quite delicious. They grow wild in the forest and are very rare, so rare in fact that if you find a patch you apparently tell no one, not even your best friends. You scoff them all yourself. I was told that it brings the worst out in people because they won't share them. Like your last piece of chocolate."

"Really," replied Dante arching his bushy eyebrows in amazement. "You know half the story already then."

"But surely there are no cloudberries growing in Dryadia. The nearest ones must be in the north of England. I could just about believe there might be some on some mountain in Wales but Dryadia is surely too far south."

"You're very knowledgeable Sam, but believe it or not there are a few colonies growing here on the highest tops of the moors where the weather is wild and bleak. We think that they grow on the slopes of Mount Cynthos but very few people know for sure. One person who does know is Bernard, for one of the colonies has been a family secret for generations. A few years ago there was an exceptionally good harvest. There were so many that even Bernard and his family couldn't eat them all and he gave some of them away to a few of his best friends, me included. I was very touched as I had never tasted any before and very nice they were too. He also gave some to Samson who at that time was very close. Very kind you might think, and as sweet as the cloudberries themselves, but it has led to a heap of troubles. Now as you know," continued Dante pulling at his enormous eyebrows as he did when he was concentrating, "all land and most produce in Dryadia is shared. Meradoc is like everywhere else and the people here are as kind and generous as anywhere. Our wants are few and there is plenty of food and land to go round. There is just one exception and it really wouldn't matter a bit, just a bit of harmless eccentricity, except in this one instance of the......."

"Cloudberries," said Sam dramatically.

"Precisely. As you say Sam, it brings the worst out in people. The whereabouts of Bernard's patch was known only to him and his wife. It's only a few miles away from here so he visited it every other day to check on progress. If there are other patches around, then people are keeping very quiet about them. Nobody in fact would have known about Bernard's, if he had not been so generous in that year of plenty. The following two years harvests were poor, but last year's one was looking good again and Bernard was unwise enough to brag a little about it. He was waiting for them to ripen. At last it was time to pick them, something he had been looking forward to for weeks. The great day arrived. His previous inspection had only been two days before and he was almost salivating at the thought of bringing them home. But when he got there the whole lot had gone. Every one of them. It had rained overnight and the ground was soft. All around the bushes were footprints, belonging to some very big boots indeed. They could only have belonged to Samson, so named because he was an enormous baby, and many think he is growing still. Bernard believes that Samson followed him one day up to the moors, kept out of sight and returned to steal them the day before his final visit.

Bernard confronted Samson later in Meradoc and got a grudging admission from him that he had taken them. Samson said though that he had stumbled across the cloudberry patch by accident, having no idea that it belonged to Bernard. The result is that they no longer trust each other and don't communicate except by swopping the occasional blow or insult. A storm in a teacup, you might think, and it is, but it has divided the two families and now the only harvest is bitterness. I fear that if we cannot settle this, then someone will get more than a broken nose.

Quite a story, and one you might like to pass on one day to Tara and Mary, but I don't think they will be able to use it in their repertoire until long after Bernard and Samson are dead."

Dante took them back to see Bernard to get him to repeat his version of events in front of Sam and Melissa. It was little different to the one he had already told him.

"And how would you like it resolved, Bernard," asked Dante. "Something that just might be acceptable to Samson. So your original idea of putting him in a leaky boat and pointing it towards America is not helpful. Nor is thirty years in the Cantillion clink and throw away the key. Something more practical perhaps?"

Bernard pondered. Sam and Melissa's gentle presence was softening his heart.

"Well he can stop hitting me for a start."

"If you stop, he'll stop. I'm sure that can be arranged."

"A big, big apology."

"The problem is that Samson still denies the offence."

"Snivelling slug. Of course he followed me."

"He says he didn't. But he is, or at least was, since you have started hitting each other again, willing to apologise for eating them. He is adamant that he found them by accident and didn't know they were yours."

"I was going to make some cloudberry wine," said Bernard ruefully. "I might have even given Samson a bottle."

"You know Bernard," said Melissa brightly, "if we could find some more cloudberries, enough to make a few bottles of wine, would you then be consoled?"

"It would help a lot," replied Bernard. He was melting as Melissa worked her magic.

"But where could you possibly find any?"

"Just a thought," replied Melissa enigmatically, "just a thought."

Samson didn't melt. He wouldn't budge from his original statement that he had found the cloudberry bushes by accident. 'Well yes, perhaps he had once seen Bernard heading in that direction and of course he had known about the berries. The whole of Meradoc had, for Bernard had bragged about them in the year of plenty. But he honestly didn't know that they belonged to Bernard.'

"How do you think we could resolve it then," asked Dante.

"Three points," said Samson briskly.

"One. Stop hitting me."

"Two. Apologise to me and accept that I didn't know that they were his. Well, probably not his," he added grudgingly."

"Three. If he does the first two then I promise I will never go near his wretched patch ever again."

"Nor tell anyone where it is?"

"Fine, but he has to admit that I didn't know."

Sam and Melissa believed his story though they noticed that the possibility of the berries being Bernard's had briefly crossed Samson's mind.

"You know something," said Melissa, when she was alone with Sam later. "Bernard is not the only one with cloudberry secrets. My family has them too. My father has said that he also knows of bushes on the other side of Mount Cynthos. My mother of course knows about them too and so do I. There's a story that ours once belonged to Isola and Alanda, who are believed to be our ancestors.

My mother and I regularly visit our three patches and if you had kept your ears open instead of talking in that hollow while we were waiting for Sophora to open the door into the Hall of Records, then you might have heard my mother creeping quietly by, for one of our regular inspections. In fact my parents have a small cellar of cloudberry wine, the present batch mostly laid down in the year of plenty that Bernard was describing. We only drink it on very special occasions. You have completely forgotten that we had some on our wedding day and when we renewed our vows."

"And I thought women couldn't keep secrets," said Sam sounding a bit miffed. "You could have told me."

Melissa stroked his hair gently. "Dante mentioned that Dryadians share everything but their cloudberries. Perhaps it does bring out the worst in us. But also the best. I shall ask mum to send some bottles over, including one for us."

So the wine duly arrived and all save one bottle, presented to Bernard. He and Samson grudgingly apologised to the other and shook hands. Although it was a long time before they felt truly comfortable with each other they were at least consoled, and peace returned to their families. The 'Cloudberry Wars' were finally at an end.

CHAPTER TWENTY-THREE

STORYTELLING

Nobody had ever counted how many tales the Storytellers knew, but like the Arabian Nights the number was always considered to be one thousand and one. The repertoire though was not constant. It was believed that hardly any stories were ever totally forgotten although several were added each year, some freshly composed for the storytelling season or in recent years extracted from The Hall of Records. The Dryadian tradition was an oral one. One of the aims was to strengthen the memory, so stories were seldom written down. No one knew them all, but the very best of the Storytellers knew many hundreds by heart. The oldest stories were the spiritually orientated ones, often called the 'instructive stories'. These and the historical ones were absolutely never altered, not by even a word as they carried within them the Dryadian philosophy and traditions. The ancient knowledge could therefore never be forgotten. The other stories were known as 'entertainments' and were often a riot of pure theatre, humour and improvisation. In these the Storytellers would let themselves go, playing to the audience as the mood took them. In their summer tours they carried both traditions with them, with another set aimed at the children.

The art of storytelling was minimalist. They used few props and rarely any scenery, but plenty of hats and cloaks, masks and sticks and perhaps music – just enough to excite the imagination, something that the Dryadians believed to be of extreme importance. The power of the story was in the telling and the vivid mime that accompanied it. After the Storytellers had finished rehearsing, and before they set off on tour, they refined their acts in front of the villagers of Meradoc and their children. Many of the entertainments had their Eastern counterparts, but forests and ravens unsurprisingly featured more strongly than beggars and wicked stepmothers.

The first afternoon was given over to entertaining the children but in the evening Tara and Mary, and Hermes in a non-demanding supportive role, were to open the adult season with an old story of the 'instructive' type. Hermes had been born in Meradoc and just happened to be a relative of Bernard who had promised a bottle of Cloudberry wine to the act that pleased him most, an irony that was not lost on Melissa. Their story was an old favourite called *The White Ravens beyond the Dreagle*. Being an 'instructive' tale the narrator had to stick to the age-old form of words. But the accompanying mime had no such restrictions and the two supporting actors with their array of cloaks and feathers and ravens' masks, not to mention some strange bassoon like contraptions which when blown produced a remarkable impression of a raven croaking, added a lot of life and colour to the age-old story. Tara was the narrator and stood between Mary and Hermes who were clothed in their raven outfits. As she related this ancient tale the two ravens nodded wisely when in agreement; bowed their heads if in supplication; or flapped their wings in anger or excitement. Sometimes they flounced their cloaks and stretched out their arms in a convincing interpretation of flight or blew deep croaks on their bassoons.

Long ago before Dryadogenes came to this land, when the great forest of Dreagle did not end at the Drangle but stretched far in to the East, the black ravens reigned supreme in our country. No humans lived here then, and the nearest ones lived hundreds of miles away on the forest's edge. Of course animals lived in our woods and moors and along the riverbanks, and they lived as they always did, existing according to the rules of nature, neither good nor bad, just the way it is and always has been. Sometimes of course they changed their appearance slightly to adapt to different conditions, like growing thicker coats if the weather cooled or lighter ones when it warmed.

The beaks of birds might lengthen over the generations to probe deeper into the mud if the climate became wetter, or move nearer the water if it became drier. But animals and their kind are animals, wonderful of course in their way but always animals. Erith could change them but they did not have the power to change Erith.

Ravens are strong birds, intelligent and curious, and able to fly long distances. There are few places in the world where they are not found .Our ancient Dryadian Ravens though were different. Some of them, you will remember, had made contact with Dryadogenes and his friends in the far south. Recognising their wisdom they invited them to settle here in what later became to be known as Dryadia. The ravens knew that while animals did not have the power to lighten their higher nature, humans did. The ravens had great hopes of Dryadogenes and his kindred, for as they put it they were on the side of 'The Great Ravens of Erith.' After Dryadogenes and his tribe had settled here, the Dryadian ravens decided to send ambassadors of their kind to all parts of the globe to obtain knowledge of what other humans were up to. For they had heard that their numbers were growing after a great comet had half destroyed the earth, and they were beginning to put the forests to the axe. The ravens knew that Dryadia was safe for the time being, especially since Dryadogenes had settled here, but just to be sure they encouraged the jays and squirrels to bury acorns further and further afield until the forest of Dreagle extended far beyond the Drangle, and its area was more than twenty times the size it is now.

The ambassador ravens were away six months and most returned in a pitiful condition with heads hung low. Their sleek feathers no longer shone in the sunshine. Their plumage had become dull and matted like an old gardening coat used on rainy, muddy days. Another peculiar thing was that their feathers were no longer all black. White feathers were appearing in their plumage like white hairs in the head of a middle-aged human. With some of the ravens almost a third of their feathers were white. I understand the language of the ravens (continued Tara). They tell me that they have lived amongst the habitations of men. They have not liked what they have seen and heard. The numbers of these men are expanding far too fast, for they cannot control themselves. They are like rats or mice when there is an absence of foxes or cats to catch them. These men have an insatiable desire for land and are destroying the forests to obtain it. The forest of Dreagle is shrinking as a result. Men look upon the woods as an enemy, something to be conquered and felled. They have lost their love for the trees and the earth on which they grow.. They think that they can live without them, but they are mistaken. They don't realise that Erith will become sick without the trees, as we ourselves are becoming sick. Men have forgotten that they are equals. The stronger dominate the weaker while they have the strength, until they in turn are overcome. It is like the stag that rules his harem casting out the weaker males. It is acceptable for animals to live by tooth and claw for that is their way but we expect finer things from humans, if Erith is to evolve. Men have also forgotten to live simply. They want gold and furs. They want to hunt, even when they have plenty of food. They plunder their neighbours' land in search of slaves and women. They are building large ugly cities, dry and dusty because they have no trees. These men are violent and do not speak the truth for they have never been taught to.

There are some good men and women amongst them for all hearts are pure at birth, and a few of them have not lost their connection with the light. But most of these are weak, and are afraid to speak their truth in front of their rulers. They are unable to blossom as they might, for they spend too much energy in merely surviving. The ravens like these kind of humans. They would like to teach them a better way of living, and not to live like the beasts. First though they would have to be removed from the harem.

If only men could smell the dreadful stink of their own fear, greed and ignorance, as the ravens can, then they might change their ways. At the moment it seems impossible. It seems that most men have to loose their innocence in the gutter before they have the desire to regain it.

The ravens felt polluted while they were living amongst these men for they had never experienced such heaviness before. Their feathers started falling out and if they grew back they became white and reminded them of the stains that had been imprinted on Erith. When the ravens returned to Dryadia they told their friends that these men should never be allowed to live in the land of the ravens. They managed to breathe into the dreams of all men whose thoughts were heavy, a memory of a haunted bewitched land called Dryadia that if entered would destroy them.

The years healed the ambassador ravens and their plumage became black again. Dryadogenes reminded them that not all humans had dark thoughts and that Dryadians should act as watchers for humanity, and reach out through their dreams to those who thought like them. Then they would be helped to know the difference between living like earthbound beasts, or becoming truly human and seeing the wonder in the stars. So when we hear the ravens croak, think not that you only hear the sound of a great bird but let it remind you of your true destiny. Consider that black is not only the colour of darkness but that of your own spirit when it makes itself known to you through your slumbers. Remember in truth that our spirits are really as light and free as a raven as it soars and tumbles over the woods and moors of Dryadia. Remember it is good that we never forget the difference that our own brief lives can make to the world if they are lived in balance, peace and harmony.

The tale of *The White Ravens* was one of a number of 'instructive' stories that opened the evenings of the storytelling season. Their purpose was to remind the Dryadians of their inner life; how to nurture it, even though it meant that they had to isolate themselves from the materialistic influences of the East. There was never more than one of these stories in an evening, and then both storytellers and the audience were free to enjoy themselves with the 'entertainments.'

These were stories of the forests and the wonderful, but sometimes dangerous and mythical animals that lived there. There were tales of wizards and witches and elves who lived beneath the earth. Strange foundlings reappeared hundreds of years later after being kidnapped by aliens or reared by bears. The storytellers now let their hair down improvising outrageously and abandoning any pretence of a script. The accent was on a mixture of mock horror, humour and plenty of music where appropriate. It was pure theatre and the storytellers enjoyed themselves as much as the audience. The first night at Meradoc was a great success.

There was a small village on the north coast of Dryadia lying between the woods of the forest of Dreagle and the sea. Tara and her team had hired two covered wagons, and planned to make a leisurely two-day journey to this community where their next storytelling session would begin. Progress was at little more than walking pace and the adults often strolled behind, leaving the children in the wagons. There were few people on the road and all were excited at the thought of camping on the beach under the stars at the end of the day. Very little wind came off the sea that night and when the children were settled and the fire was burning warmly, the conversation turned as it often did, to lambdas, the Quintessence and The Hall of Records.

Their new experiences had shed more light on a strange incident that had happened to Anaxamander about two years ago. Although most people in Ceradoc knew about it in a general sort of way, for basically Anaxamander had fallen off a ladder while cleaning an upstairs window and injured his ankle, few realised how extraordinary the fall actually was. Pushkin of course had a theory and wanted to relate the story once more but Mary butted in excitedly and said not unkindly, "Oh, let Melissa tell it. She was actually there and we'll be here all night if you start pontificating."

"Then it's a good thing that Dad's not telling his own story for he knows only a part of it, and on his day he can easily out pontificate Pushkin," replied Melissa. "Well, as you know Dad was cleaning a window about fifteen feet up, standing rather stupidly on almost the top rung of the ladder and holding onto the window ledge with one hand and wiping the pane with the other. Mum was holding the ladder, telling him to be careful and he kept saying he was perfectly safe. I was watching the scene from the middle of the lawn no more than ten yards away from the house. Dad certainly looked well balanced up there, though I must say it did seem somewhat precarious. So far, so good. Then mum shrieked and Dad lost his grip on the ladder without disturbing it. I watched in absolute horror as he toppled backwards but it was as if he was in slow motion. Dad told me later that he had suddenly gone unconscious and that's why he fell and then remembered no more. What's interesting is that he had never fainted like that before, or indeed since. Dad later described it as like the lights being suddenly turned out. I expected him to fall like a stone probably on top of my mother who of course was directly below him. He didn't. The ladder didn't move an inch, and nor did my utterly astonished and petrified mother. My father didn't crumple or buckle but fell backwards with his arms in front of him, away from the wall. It was as if he was flying. I watched him turn on his side in mid-air and he flew in a circle facing away from me like a banking seagull, for far longer and further than humanly possible, over my mother's head, and then towards the lawn and me.

He was completely unconscious and totally relaxed. He didn't seem to be there. I was just watching an Anaxamander costume floating around me in slow motion. Dad was weightless. He seemed to have no mass, only his clothes wafting through the air. Time didn't seem to exist. I've no idea how long it all lasted. It could have been an hour but it was probably seconds. Then he landed in front of me at my feet, on his back. It was incredibly graceful. It reminded me of a magpie flopping to earth. Both my mum and I seemed to be in a trance as we watched. All three of us seemed to be existing in a bubble. It was only when he had landed that we realised the gravity of the situation.

My mum and I screamed his name as we peered at his body. He seemed so at peace. We thought he was dead. Then he opened his eyes, looking dazed after a very deep sleep. He wasn't in any pain apart from a bruised ankle. It seemed incredible that he wasn't paralysed or even killed especially as he had fallen flat on his back and head. We let my father lie there for five minutes and gave him arnica for the shock. We were all amazed to find that apart from his ankle he wasn't bruised or cut in the slightest way. Then we helped him to a chair, and after a cup of tea he gradually returned to normal.

Dad felt he had had a vision while he was so deeply unconscious. He felt his body had been hovering over a mountaintop and was watching a group of people having a meeting below. The landscape was dry and scrubby, definitely not in Dryadia, but more Mediterranean. Moreover he felt the people were Cathars, which puts the place in what is now the south of France. He felt part of those people. They were kind, almost

Dryadian-like, and very concerned about something. They were under threat and were discussing what should be done, because something terrible was about to happen. They knew that there was little hope and were resigned to dying."

"Explain again what Anaxamander made of it all." asked Mary.

"Well you know Dad. He wanted a little time to mull it over. Eventually he said it was a past life experience about seven hundred years ago, when he was a Cathar. He already had had an emotional experience about the Cathars when he and mum had visited Montsegur more than thirty years ago. It was at the end of the papal crusade, whose main purpose was to destroy the Cathars and their religion. Dad felt he was a 'parfait', which was the name for their priests, and if captured, which was virtually certain, he like all of them would be burned to death by the soldiers. Some Cathars escaped and came to Dryadia and settled here around about that time. He had talked to Sophora about the vision and she felt that it was genuine and added that a past life could usually only be accessed if it was relevant to the present one. In other words it was a warning about our own times and there was probably a connection between the end of the Cathars and what was going on in the world now. He thought he was given a date in his vision but was not sure he had got it absolutely right and felt it was better that he should keep it to himself."

"My theory," said Pushkin, getting a word in edgeways at last, "was that Anaxamander somehow transpirated into the Quintessence where time and mass don't exist and you find yourself in another dimension. Not rocket science, but lambda science. He's often talked about having that ethereal gateway in his garden, which could be slipped through if the conditions were right."

"Then the normal laws of science wouldn't apply," added Sam. "Anaxamander certainly had no mass or weight after he fell which would account for Melissa seeing him float effortlessly around the garden, and land on his back without major injury. And both Ruth and Melissa described it as happening in slow motion like being in a timeless bubble. Anaxamander in a sense left the earth via the fifth dimension and returned in the same way. All without a lambda machine, chanting or crystals. The only question that remains is how he did it, and how it can be done again consciously. No wonder everyone is fascinated by what lies under the Hall of Records."

"Mum is keeping a very careful eye on Dad now", said Melissa. "He's certainly not allowed to clean upstairs windows anymore. But the incident has certainly not dampened his enthusiasm in learning more."

"So the lambda quest goes on," said Sam. "We can't stop now."

CHAPTER TWENTY-FOUR

THE ROAD NORTH

The storytelling expedition made a late start on the second day, and decided to set up camp in the late afternoon for they didn't want to arrive at their destination after dark. When they had settled down, two men travelling the same way approached them. They announced that they were coastguards who regularly patrolled this stretch of the coast and they were in a hurry, because unlike the Storytellers, they wanted to get home before dusk. In fact both parties knew each other slightly for although the coastguards lived in Linaria the most northerly village in Dryadia, which was where the Storytellers were heading, Ceradoc was the place where their patrol finished. This was where they stayed the night before turning around and starting the two-day journey back to Linaria again. All the coastal villages contributed towards the coastguards' upkeep and indeed provided the manpower for the teams, which rotated every fortnight, so they didn't need to be away from their villages too long. This was a good example of how the Dryadian system of community service worked, serving in lieu of taxation.

"We don't want to alarm you," said one of them. "But a motorised dinghy landed not far from here yesterday. The boat is still moored on the beach so its crew have obviously gone walkabout. No need to worry. It's not unusual for people from England to try their luck in the summer. They normally leave the same day but this lot are obviously camping out somewhere. We've never known any of them to be violent and they usually run if they see us. If we catch them we escort them back to their boat and send them packing. Unless the weather is bad. Then we are a bit kinder. They usually come for the adventure. Thankfully, the English authorities do try their best to put them off, but unfortunately for us those irresponsible adventure guides encourage them to sail here, as of course they can only reach Dryadia by boat."

The other man went on. "The English try to scare them, saying we are all riddled with measles and that they might die if they get too close to us."

"That's a bit like our old stories when we put it about that the forest of Dreagle was full of devils and witches so that the Easterners would be frightened enough to leave us alone", replied Tara.

"That story won't wash now sadly, but fear of catching measles often does," said the coastguard. "It's so funny to see them put on their masks when they see us approaching them. I haven't seen any of them drop dead yet, but it does encourage an early departure! But this lot should have gone by now. We always worry they will set the forest on fire."

"Well we must be going," said the first man. "My tummy's rumbling and I want my supper. If you see those Easterners, just breathe over them. That will do the trick. We will probably see you on the morning patrol coming back. We've disabled their boat so no doubt we will confront them tomorrow."

"Look," demanded Sam as they were walking behind the wagon on the last two hours to Linaria the next morning. The previous night had felt blissfully peaceful under the Dryadian sky. Mary had commented that it felt as if they all had been 'plugged into the celestial mains'. They stopped suddenly when Sam spoke and Melissa's eyes followed his outstretched arm until she saw what he saw – two people crawling on their bellies at the edge of the forest some two hundred yards away. They were so engrossed in whatever they were doing and so low down in the undergrowth that it appeared that they were either trying to conceal themselves, or were completely oblivious to the two wagons on the ridge above them.

"They must be the two men that the coastguards were talking about," said Melissa. "Quick Sam, get your binoculars out." But Sam already had, and at the same time the men must have spotted the flash of the sun on his lens for they were now lying motionless on the ground. They couldn't though deceive Sam's sharp bird watching eyes, which could almost spot a sparrow at that range.

"What are they doing now," cried Melissa in a squeaky whisker.

"Staying very still. They're wearing camouflage gear. They definitely don't want to be seen by anybody."

"Certainly not locals then. They would have waved. Should we approach them?"

By now the wagons in front of them had stopped. Pushkin had jumped out and Sam could see that he was talking to the two coastguards who were now on the southern part of their journey back towards Ceradoc. Sam and Melissa sighed with relief and ran quickly towards them.

"I've got them," exclaimed the elder of the two coastguards peering through an ancient spyglass that Sam thought would have probably been old when Dryadia signed the peace treaty with England more than two hundred years ago. "They look very shifty. What in Alanda's name could they be doing? Most of our illegal visitors don't linger – they just want to add Dryadia to their 'places I have been to list'. They seem to be looking for something. We had better go down to the forest and haul them in, but this needs a proper investigation and our English is not totally fluent. Some of you are from the East. Perhaps one or two of you might come as an interpreter and act as an extra guard in case we need one. I'm sure there's no danger."

"I'll go", volunteered Pushkin.

"And me," trumped Sam.

"I'll guard the wagons and the children," said Hermes. We need someone strong!"

"My hero," said Mary smiling at Pushkin.

"So brave," murmured Melissa, squeezing Sam's hand and looking at him with what seemed slightly overdone admiration.

The two trespassers did not run. They had hoped that their cover would hold but when the coastguards told them to reveal themselves, they stood up looking sheepish and not a little scared. One of them had mud all over his face and a floppy hat half over his eyes. Both Sam and Pushkin felt they had seen him somewhere before. Around them was their half-taken down tent, surrounded by a couple of trowels and various plastic packets and bags. It appeared that they were collecting plants and soil samples, and when the coastguards turned out their rucksacks more bottles and specimens tumbled out, as well as various documents and books

"Right," said one of them in his grandest English. "Follow me to the road where that wagon is. We need to talk."

"Names?" demanded the senior coastguard.

"Tom," said one.

"Steve," mumbled the one with the muddy face.

Mary stepped forward and looked directly into his eyes.

"I know you. Most of us here know you. You're not Steve. At least you were not called that when you were last in Dryadia and you left in disgrace. You're Stephano aren't you and you were banned for life from this country after what you did."

"Nobody told me," replied Stephano, the familiar jauntiness rapidly returning. "I was born here. Nobody can take away my right to be here."

"There have been two exceptions to that rule in out country's history so far as I know. One is Sastamoro and the other is you. Both of you betrayed Dryadia and were responsible for harming a number of your fellow countrymen."

"A bit rich coming from you Pushkin. You weren't even born here. You're not exactly a proper Dryadian."

"I'm a Dryadian in spirit like Sam and Mary here and that's all that matters. In any case our citizenship was formalised at the 'Great Moot' in front of all the Elders," replied Pushkin angrily.

"Which was the same place where it was proclaimed that you were no longer a Dryadian. You are no longer welcome here. And I am Dryadian born, not that it matters." Tara joined in, surprising herself with her fury.

"All right Tom and Stephano," said the older coastguard. "First I need to declare an interest. It was my brother who was one of the shepherds who was taken away with Anaxamander by the helicopters at The Beacons. What do you have to say to that, Mr Stephano? He was cruelly treated. He took a long time to get over it, as it has me, though I will still try to treat you fairly"

"Very good of you I'm sure, but it was nothing to do with me," replied Stephano. "It was the Americans, as you know only too well."

"You were part of the conspiracy, I've no doubt. But more importantly what are you doing here in Dryadia?"

"Just a little plant collecting as you can see. We got swept ashore by the wind. Then the weather changed and we thought we might stay a night or two and do a bit of botanising along the shore."

"You don't know any thing about plants," said a shocked Sam, who had been quiet up to now. "You used to mock me about my interest in nature and say that shops and casinos were far more important than trees."

"A man can change, Sam," said Stephano trying to conceal a smirk. "I'm sure you will agree that we all see the light eventually."

Melissa had been looking through the various specimens in Stephano and Tom's bags. "Why are you collecting these particular plants and these soil samples? And I can see you've got specimens from further down the coast too, because some seldom grow round here. This is not the first place that you've put ashore. How could these be of interest to you? They are not particularly rare."

"Well, we were told to – I mean me and Tom just wanted to find out what grew here. It's in the interests of science. It's not documented."

"It is by us," replied Melissa. "Why should you think that whatever grows here should be any different from what grows in England. It's after all less than twenty miles away."

You know, if you had approached one of the Therapeutae or one of our botanical experts we would have willingly shared our knowledge with you. We would have even sent you specimens if you had asked. There's nothing particularly secret about your plants, judging by your collection."

"We just wanted to check," said a worried looking Tom.

Sam and Melissa walked down the track a little way from the visitors taking the senior coastguard with them. "I hope they won't run away," said Melissa anxiously, "but there's something we need to discuss privately. The specimens are not really that interesting to an experienced botanist. Some of them are healing plants, others not. They are collected at random, with no particular thought behind it. In other words they know very little about the world of plants."

"In other words," echoed Sam vehemently, "Stephano is lying through his teeth. A leopard cannot change its spots. Stephano knows as much about nature as I know about espionage, which is what I suspect he is about at the moment. Moreover, there are some very interesting things in their bags. I'm sure that it's permissible to rummage through our prisoners' possessions."

Melissa had been sorting through them and had laid them in neat piles on the ground. Various receipts and bankcards confirmed their identities and addresses. The most interesting document was a letter addressed to Stephano from a large British company, a well-known conglomerate with substantial interests in the leisure industry. The letter stated that it enclosed a cheque for five hundred pounds against his forthcoming trip to Dryadia with a similar sum to be paid after he returned, if the information received was satisfactory. Another letter set out his itinerary and pinpointed the places for his 'research'. They all happened to be on the remote northern coast of Dryadia, an area famous for both its beautiful scenery and magnificent sandy beaches.

"So, what do you make of it all?" said the coastguard looking perplexed.

"I'm as puzzled as you are," answered Sam. "Obviously they've been sent here. We know that Stephano used to work for the British secret services when he was at the university. That was a long time ago, and I don't think the British government have much interest in us now, especially since Anaxamander signed the last treaty at the time of.." His voice tailed off. He didn't want to draw attention to his own self-imposed exile with Nell in front of Melissa.

"I think the plants are a decoy in case they got caught. It is just possible that someone might be interested in slight divergences in certain species, as the forest has separated our two countries for thousands of years. But I doubt it somehow. Only a very pernickety botanist could be excited about such a thing. I suppose a drug company might be interested in patenting a deviant herb if one was found, but again I don't think so. This letter is from a commercial company. Someone wants to make money out of Dryadia, but not from our plant life. So what could they be after?"

"Then let's put the question to Stephano and Tom," said Melissa.

Tom did know a little about plants but it really was a little. He was an old acquaintance of Stephano's and because the boat belonged to him and he was a competent sailor, he had been persuaded by Stephano to make the journey to Dryadia. Otherwise he seemed an innocent party. Stephano for his part stonewalled, and was unwilling to give much away. When confronted with the letter, he said that he had taken it at face value that the company wanted the plants, and not realising that he had been banished from Dryadia for life, he didn't feel he had been doing anything wrong. Stephano stood up to his grilling well and wouldn't budge from his story. Finally the Dryadians realised that they were not going to get anymore out of him and with the coastguards' assent they handed back their belongings, apart from the incriminating letter.

"Evidence," smiled Sam sardonically.

As Stephano was replacing the things in his rucksack a mobile phone fell out of his pocket. Melissa quickly scooped it up and handed it to the coastguards just before Stephano noticed he had dropped it.

"Give it back," he said abruptly. "It's private. It doesn't work in Dryadia anyway. There's no signal".

"Don't these things take pictures," said Pushkin. My nephew was explaining how they worked when I was last in England."

The coastguard handed it to him and Pushkin was soon scrolling through hundreds of pictures of the Dryadian coastline.

Pushkin handed the mobile phone to the others. The pictures were taken at many sites and from many angles and concentrated on Dryadia's best beaches, the ones that had been highlighted in Stephano's itinerary. It seemed that every square yard of sandy beach had been photographed.

"You've even got the estuary, and look you've got pictures of Ceradoc as well. You must have been in Dryadia for weeks. How on Erith did you manage not to get caught before?" Melissa felt outraged, probably fuelled by memories of Sam's relationship with Nell. She still laid much of the blame at Stephano's door. "You're still a spy, aren't you Stephano. Sam was right. A leopard cannot change its spots."

"Admiring my holiday snaps? Good aren't they. You've got an overactive imagination. You should get out of your herb garden more."

Melissa lunged at him and Sam for the first time in his life had to restrain her.

"I think we will remove this problem from your life," said the coastguard, taking Stephano firmly by the arm. We will inform the Elders and no doubt a stiff letter will be sent to England. Meantime we will escort these so-called gentlemen, minus their camera, to their boat. Have a safe journey to Linaria, and happy storytelling. I wonder if this one will be added to your list one day."

Mary felt she would like the last word and shouted after them as they walked away with the coastguards. "So sorry you won't get the other five hundred pounds. And don't forget the incubation period for measles is about two weeks."

The party spent about two weeks in Linaria and the surrounding villages. While Sam and Melissa involved themselves in healing and just as importantly giving advice on how to keep well, Tara and Mary and two of the locals did the rounds of storytelling accompanied by Pushkin and Hermes, or their faithful 'bag carriers' as Pushkin put it.

The senior Traditional Elder in Linaria, a wise and vigorous middle-aged woman called Lola, came to see them on their day off. The coastguards had already told her about Stephano and Tom's expedition but she was never the less very keen to know more about the Storytellers' own observations.

"I'm afraid the coastguards are making more light of it than is wise," Lola commented after the six of them had finished relating their adventures. "They may not know the full story. We do indeed have a fair number of illegal visitors in the summer months when the sea is calm. As you know it only takes an hour for a motorboat to reach here from

England. We do not have as many illegals though, compared with our southern coast. They depart from the big English city on the other side of the Drangle and are becoming a bit of a nuisance. Our northern coast is rockier but once they have steered their way round the forest there are still a number of secluded coves where they can land.

We do not worry so much about a few of them trespassing for we can easily forgive their adventurous spirit. Much more worrying is what they bring with them and their contacts with our youth. Alcohol, cigarettes, drugs even, not to mention their loud music and general rowdiness. People from the East would no doubt think us old fashioned to think like this, but they have their ways and we have ours. The main thing is that we don't want our young people corrupted by them. We don't like the ways of the East, but we have to admit that they are very seductive. We warn them of course, but what young person wants to be told what to do. It's a small issue at the moment but it's getting worse and we are all concerned. We're putting extra teams of coastguards on patrol in the summer, and the forest rangers are checking on the tracks through the Dreagle more regularly. I doubt any Easterners would find their way through, but you never know.

One thing you might be interested in, at least Melissa and Sam might be, if they are wearing their Therapeutae hats; these Eastern youngsters are not as well as they ought to be. They have lots of colds and coughs and general aching, a bit like flu. They are always having big flu scares in the East as you know. They frighten themselves rigid about it. We obviously don't want to catch their flu though I remember you have always told us that Dryadians are probably too healthy to be troubled by it."

"I really don't think we should worry," said Sam. "I've heard of a few possible cases in Cantillion. They've all been mild, and of course we don't suppress any resulting fever or sweat with drugs. Toxins need to be allowed to come out naturally. I came from the East, so I know how aggressively the government acts so they don't get caught out. Then the media fans the flames by publishing all the resulting fear and chaos for the sake of a good story. Sometimes I think the main cause of most illnesses is fear. Thank goodness that is not the Dryadian way of doing things. It makes me think of our herb garden back in Ceradoc. The herbs are like the Dryadians trying to promote harmony and doing our bit to heal the world. They wouldn't flourish though, if we didn't weed out the vigorous grasses that would take over if we weren't always on our guard."

"Just like the Easterners I think," said Lola with only the faintest of smiles.

The storytelling season was ending. The two wagons were on their way back to Ceradoc. As they were putting up their tents on their final evening, the sun was setting over the ocean, a blood red ball of flame dipping slowly towards the horizon. A raven flew over them, so low that they could hear the whooshing of its wings accompanying its unmistakable croak. As it flew towards the sun it started flying higher in the sky, soaring in great circles silhouetted against the fading light. Another raven joined it, and then another, until there were now six of them, so high that they were no bigger than dots in the sky.

With wings half closed, they started to tumble and dive towards the sea as only ravens can, not because they had to but because they wanted to, in the sure joy of being alive and living unfettered lives. Sam and Melissa often talked of that day and wistfully wondered if the ravens, the mythological protectors of Dryadia, would someday symbolically extend their influence eastwards. Then perhaps the East might discover a more harmonious way of living and not need to invade Dryadia's tiny coves with pocketfuls of drugs and the sound of heavy metal. They could create a Dryadia of their own in their own country.

CHAPTER TWENTY-FIVE

THE GATHERING OF THE ELDERS

Dark shadows flickered through the brains of the Traditional Elders of Dryadia. Lola had informed all of them about Stephano's illegal landing on the north coast, which had prompted a number of others to report similar visits on other stretches of the shoreline. It was nothing new of course but numbers were increasing at too fast a rate. More contacts were being made with the locals, who were becoming highly curious about the Eastern lifestyle, especially about the electronic gadgetry the visitors brought with them, even if Dryadia did not have the infrastructure to make most of it work. The problem was just about manageable at the moment. Some of the Practical Elders didn't even see it as a difficulty, although almost all the Traditional Elders took the opposite view. The visit of the Delegation and the two invasions had not been forgotten, and they had learned that the East was never to be underestimated.

There were more legal visitors now. Apart from regular intakes of students studying at the University of Cantillion, there were supervised adventure holidays for children in the wild Dryadian countryside, or working vacations with the horses on the farms. Nature lovers, artists and lovers of storytelling were welcomed in small numbers. Dryadians wanted to demonstrate to the East that it was possible to live both harmoniously and comfortably. Visas were still hard to obtain though, as Dryadia did not want to be swamped by visitors. The Elders hoped that some of their traditions would percolate through, even though they now believed that the East was far too industrialised and overpopulated to change, without first undergoing some kind of cataclysm. It would be like trying to steer the Titanic round the looming iceberg. Nevertheless the Dryadians had agreed to share their knowledge and traditions wherever possible. That excluded their scientific knowledge of course. That was safely buried under Mount Cynthos.

The Elders decided to call a major moot in Cantillion to discuss these issues once again. Every community would send at least two representatives, including one Traditional and one Practical Elder. As the building was very large it was hoped that many more Dryadians would attend in the spirit of true democracy. The Principal Dryad who was elected annually by their fellow Elders chaired the moot. It was important to have the skill of keeping tight order, as the gathering was so large. Dryadia had no executive or elected president in the political sense. Power lay in the villages and in the ancient Dryadian philosophy, as interpreted by the Traditional Elders whenever their advice was needed.

It was the turn of the Northern Province to provide this year's Principal Dryad. Amarinta had been selected at the previous year's moot to be, what was called in Dryadian – 'The Shepherd of the Way.' Less pompously the position was known as 'The Sheepdog', which meant that everyone else were called 'The Sheep'! (It sounds much nicer in Dryadian). Amarinta's job was to guide the rest of the moot to a consensual agreement. It was a bit like consoling but on a much larger scale. It would take a while and three days had been set aside for the moot. It was a true democracy, quite cumbersome and long-winded in a way. But it worked.

The decision making process was based on the old Dryadian principle of 'last man or woman standing' which basically meant that only when no one was left on their feet with anything constructive to add or objection to raise, would the meeting adjourn. Amarinta would then sum up and highlight the alternatives that lay before them. The moot then entered what they called the 'Great Silence'. There, guided by eternal Dryadian principles, they searched their hearts to find agreement.

There might have to be compromises on the details, but it was important that no one should be left feeling that their voice hadn't been heard, or end up being upset by the outcome. This way of Dryadian government was the complete opposite of the 'winner takes all' or 'arm-twisting by the strongest' which was the custom of every country in the East.

About three months before the moot was due to be held, and not long after Stephano had been deported back to England, two foreign letters were sent to the senior Dryad. They were deemed to be so important that they were copied to every Elder in the land and through them circulated to every community. One was from a major British cancer charity wanting to do some controlled drug trials back in England on some of the medicines used by the Therapeutae. Sam and Melissa noticed that many of the herbs mentioned were the same ones that had been collected by Stephano. The letter seemed pointless since the plants were freely available on both sides of the Drangle. A reply went back to the company stating that they could do what they liked but the Dryadians preferred not to get involved. They explained that the philosophy behind their two countries' forms of healing was too far apart, and indeed the chronic degenerative diseases of the East tended to be rare or non-existent in Dryadia anyway. The Therapeutae felt the letter was a decoy, perhaps in order to justify Stephano's activities.

The second letter was taken a lot more seriously and it was decided to make its contents the focus of the moot's agenda and to have a full debate about it. In the final month of the year, appropriately named after the Elder tree, the Elders of Dryadia left their villages and towns. On foot, horseback, wagons and bicycles they journeyed through the peaceful leafy lanes that converged on the *Great Moot of Cantillion*. All the inns were full and many local Cantillions had offered up their spare rooms to the visitors. *The Leaky Bucket* lay quietly at anchor. It would not sail again until the moot was over. The students at the university had returned to their homes for the winter solstice celebrations, save a few who would attend the moot as observers. A great sense of anticipation seemed to hang over Cantillion in the crisp winter air. The contents of the letter weighed heavily on each Elder's heart.

There had already been many conversations about the letter between most of the Elders, and Sophora herself (by common consent the wisest person in Dryadia) who was determined to get deeply involved. She had talked at length to Sam, Mary and Pushkin, particularly valuing their opinion because of their Eastern origins. All three would attend the moot. There was almost complete agreement between the Traditional Elders. There would probably be more division between the Practical Elders. Since they had not been Cantillion educated and therefore not well trained in the traditional wisdom, they might be more inclined to think in a short term way. A consensus was required and this needed understanding.

It was a full house. The contents of the letter had seen to that. As was the custom the Elders sat in silence for ten minutes before Amarinta rose to open the moot. She got straight to the point, her words ringing clearly round the magnificent amphitheatre, long famed for its acoustics. The purpose of the meeting, as everybody already knew, was to discuss Dryadia's relationship with the East and in particular the contents of the now notorious letter. The challenge was to not only ensure that the Dryadian principles were adhered to, but that any decision should leave everyone in the moot reasonably happy about the outcome. For there was no point in winning if it left a legacy of bitterness and resentment. The

Traditional Elders would not compromise on their principles of what they called The Great Dryadian Tradition but gaining understanding between opposing arguments was just as important.

Amarinta reminded them of the three traditional questions that they were always asked when they arrived at a fork in the road and were tempted to follow an unfamiliar path.

Firstly, would the proposed action be detrimental to the 'nest' as the Dryadians called their countryside?

Did it reduce or enhance the bond of kindness that drew all Dryadians together?

And thirdly was it 'heavy', meaning did it drag people down towards a more materialistic way of living?

The Dryadians had asked such questions many times of themselves over the last two or three hundred years especially when it concerned new inventions or their relationship with the East. In effect that had meant the rejection of almost all heavy and electronic industries, and the imposition of an isolationist policy with their neighbours and the whole global economy. However the Dryadians liked their comforts as well as anyone and if technology served them lightly and well and caused no harm, then all well and good.

Amarinta paused and waved a letter above her head.

"Now you have all read this, I expect. I will summarise it for you. It has been sent to us by one of the biggest development corporations in the world and it has more money in its coffers than most of the smaller countries on the planet. It is American owned, though this letter has been written by its British subsidiary. Hundreds of international businesses have shares in this mother company. They have unlimited funds and I have been informed that they are very belligerent and their policy is that what they want is what they get. That makes them a formidable enemy and they will try and spread a lot of fear amongst us. They are already putting a lot of pressure on us through their follow up letters. They are promising a lot of material benefits, which will be very appealing to our young people in particular. The letter has been obviously written by lawyers. The details are not easy to understand and are there, I imagine, to make us feel out of our depth. Anaxamander of Ceradoc who used to run our consulate in England has very kindly translated the letter into Dryadian and has summarised the main points for me. It is those that I now want to read to you.

The writers of this letter have identified a large stretch of our northern coastline, which they wish to acquire so that they can create an enormous holiday resort for the people of the East. It extends six miles on either side of the beautiful Tamara estuary on which Ceradoc and Viribus stands. Some of the best beaches in Dryadia are contained within this area. Many of them are called surfing beaches. Surfing is a major sport in the East and people travel all over the world in search of gigantic waves like ours. They stand on small plastic boards and ride the waves that roll in from the Atlantic to the shore. There is nothing wrong about this and I am told that it's very exciting. Some of our young people have discovered this sport and enjoy it very much. It is only when thousands of surfers get together and need places to stay and require the heavy infrastructure that is needed to support them, that there is trouble. Every year small parties of illegals arrive on our beaches to surf on the waves and our coastguards are kept busy chasing them off. We wouldn't even particularly mind if their numbers remained small. The coastguards often turn a blind eye if they behave themselves. What we are less happy about is when they contact our youngsters and teach them the more dubious activities of the East. I'm afraid that there have even been fights between the two parties. There is no easy solution to this problem except to contain it. In fact speaking generally, that is what we have always done in our relationships with the East. It's a bit easier than it was, as the British now accept us for who we are, or at least they say they do.

Now this letter offers us a second solution. At least for a while until the next demand is made. It tells us, that along this part of our coastline and up to a mile of hinterland, we have one of the greatest tourist resources in Europe. They inform us that they would like to exploit it for our mutual benefit. They appreciate that our country is not for sale and that land in any case cannot be bought or sold.

There is a suggestion that we may be a little backward here, for they tell us that we are the only country in the world that has this custom. They insist that they have no desire to change the Dryadian way of life for which they have the greatest respect. So this is their proposal.

It is that we give them a one hundred and twenty year lease on this coastline so that they can turn it into one of the greatest holiday and surfing resorts in the world. It would be entirely self-sufficient being serviced from outside, by air and sea. They would provide roads, hotels, flats, houses, restaurants and places of entertainment. Reservoirs and sewage treatment plants and an airport and heliport would also be built. If we wished they would create a perimeter wall around the whole site so that it would be entirely self-contained. On the other hand there could be thousands of jobs available for Dryadians during the five-year construction period and very many thereafter when the project is up and running. They say that this would be one of the most exciting enterprises ever seen in Europe. It would cost us nothing except to give up some under-used and sparsely populated land. They are offering us twenty million pounds a year rent, enough money as they say, to completely modernise our country. We would want for nothing."

Amarinta sat down, before jumping up again to add.

"Before I open it to the floor would every one who would like to speak, please stand up?" About half the Elders rose.

Amarinta smiled and remarked that she had written to the corporation saying they would send a reply a month after the solstice, after they had discussed it at the moot. But since there were so many wishing to discuss the subject, she wished she had said a year.

Most of the Traditional Elders were on the apoplectic side.

"We've been here before. Remember the delegation."

"What about the invasions. We can never trust the East."

"A betrayal of all we stand before, all we believe in."

"Six thousand years of sacred tradition up in smoke."

"We can't measure the value of land, it belongs to nature."

"Wholesale destruction!"

"Horrible Intrusion!"

"Act of violence."

"Unthinkable!"

"Materialism will triumph over the spirit."

"We all know that meaningful human contact and love for each other and our country is far superior to money and possessions."

"Like everybody else, we Dryadians need to feel secure and know we belong."

For hours they vented their spleens.

Amarinta was not surprised at their passion. It would have been extraordinary if there had been anything else. These Traditional Elders loved their country, its spirituality and its way of life as much as they loved their own families. The blood of Dryadogenes flowed strongly through all of them.

The Practical Elders as expected were more divided.

"We should think it through. There may be benefits."

"If we can't beat them we should consider joining them," referring to the constant flow of illegal visitors.

"The world is too strong for us now. We can't oppose them forever."

"We will have walled them off. We'd never notice them."

But other Practical Elders were against the idea.

"What would we do with all that money? We don't have banks."

"We don't really need anything. The kids would just get spoiled with all that wealth."

"They are our beaches. Where will we go for a swim or a sail?"

These Elders were not called Practical for nothing. But they were still very human. Some of them could be seduced by wealth and grandiose ideas just as Sastamoro and his friends were, more than four hundred years ago. Most of them respected the spirit of Dryadia but unlike the Traditionals it wasn't embedded in their hearts.

Zephyr then spoke eloquently about the wildlife of the coastline. He described the ravens and peregrines that nested on the cliffs in inaccessible places and survived because few people visited them; he told them of the amazing migration of the wading birds that used the shorelines to forage, stopping off on their long journey between the Arctic and Africa; the offshore islands where the seals bred in autumn; the guillemots, and puffins that also bred on the islands and cliff faces; and the dolphins that visited Dryadia in summer. Would we dare risk losing all this? For that is what will happen when the motorboats, helicopters and tens of thousands of people move in.

It took two days for almost everyone to have their say with only Sophora and Anaxamander scheduled for the following morning. Each session ended in 'The Great Silence' with Amarinta always reminding them that their thoughts should be guided by the three great Dryadian principles: the purity of the nest, the harmony of the people and the need to proceed with lightness.

That evening all of the Ceradocians, apart from Anaxamander and Sophora who were preparing their speeches, met for supper.

"Nobody mentioned that the wall would come right up to the edge of Ceradoc," said Melissa. "We wouldn't be able to sail down the estuary. We would be cut off from the sea. It would destroy the village and we would have to live somewhere else."

"We won't let it happen," said Zephyr. "Don't forget the Traditionals have a veto."

"All the Practicals know that and most of them accept the situation," agreed Amarinta. "After all I'm a Traditional and they know what I think and they don't complain, so far as I know. But our way of deciding is through agreement. If we don't agree then the corporation will have another go in a few months and we will have to have another moot. And then another, if we still don't agree and then another. So it will go on until we're all worn out with it all and then maybe we will give in through sheer exhaustion and frustration."

"At least the Practicals see you as fair and that you let everyone have their say. That must help our cause," said Zephyr, smiling at his wife with approval. "And unlike the East everything is in the open. We all know what's happening."

"Melissa and I mingled with some of the Practicals. They didn't really know us so they spoke freely. They are definitely split. Their hearts are good but too many of them see golden ducats swimming in front of their eyes and are wondering how they should best spend them in the East," said Sam, his voice shaking with emotion.

"Then Sophora and Anaxamander must pull out all the stops tomorrow," said Mary. "They can do it if anyone can. Everyone respects them and who can resist Sophora when she's in full flow and at her best?"

Sam's dreams were disturbed that night. He was desperately worried and Melissa said that he cried out several times in the night. Dryadia was his life, every sacred bit of it. He was unable to imagine that some of this precious jewel might cease to exist. He could no more accept surrendering the coastline to the East then cutting off one of his fingers. He knew this area well. Zephyr had taught him much about the birds that lived there and about the small creatures that inhabited the dark world of the rock pools. Melissa and the children often accompanied him on his walks along the shoreline and they all swam there in summer.

His dreams were full of ravens flying low along the beaches or high above the cliff tops.

More bizarrely, a large black cat smiled benignly down on him from the bottom of the bed punctuating his dreams. It reminded him of Anaxamander's old cat, also called Sam. The feline Sam mouthed the words:

"If you let this happen you will all need your heads examined. Only a complete ignoramus would even entertain the idea. Have courage Sam."

Melissa was calmer – she barely had known anything else apart from a few childhood years at the consulate in England with her father. Her utmost faith in Dryadia's future soothed some of Sam's fears in the night.

The next day's session began with Amarinta again asking of the moot who would still like to accept the corporation's proposition and who felt strongly enough about it to speak up. About fifty Practicals stood up. You could tell them by their red scarves; the Traditionals wore blue.

"Then we still have a lot of work to do," said Amarinta simply.

One by one the Practicals aired their views and concerns. Some of them were suggestions or compromises, like renting out a small section of beach just to obtain a bit of useful currency. Amarinta had to remind them that international institutions didn't do small. Other Practicals had their imaginations set on fire.

"Just think how we could help the world with all that money. We could have Dryadian embassies in every country. How much easier would it be to spread our philosophy with the Dryadian flag flying high in every capital city. We could be great diplomats for peace settling disputes in every continent. Everyone would respect us. We would no longer be grouped with the third world."

Others were more down to earth.

"We need a new boat. *The Leaky Bucket* won't last forever."

"What about a proper radio station.? It will bring us closer together."

"We could send out children to England for a proper education."

"Decent tractors. Do we really have to have all those horses? With all that money we could afford the oil."

The list went on as the few left standing got more and more excited. Sam was reminded of the small mindedness of the developers who destroyed his grandparents' smallholding shattering their dreams and breaking their hearts. He thought of death and city streets without greenery. It reminded him how easy it was for beastliness to make a takeover bid for our hearts. The Practicals spoke for another hour and the moot became heavy with the frustrations of the Traditionals. The opposing Practicals were definitely in a minority but they made up for it by the vehemence of a strong willed few.

When they were finished, Amarinta called on Anaxamander to speak. He was not to be outdone. He told them of his years in England. He described the extremes of wealth and poverty and the lack of true democracy for ordinary people. He spoke of the materialism and the ignorance that allowed a cloud of heavy negativity to hide those things that Dryadians held so dear. He described the ugliness and noise of most of their cities, the polluted air that is not fit to breathe, and the larger beach resorts where the buildings are so tall that they block out the sun and the views of the sea. He told stories of drunkenness and drug taking, the gambling and disorderly behaviour that takes people over when individual spirits are trampled by the excitement of the mob.

"Worst of all," he went on, "are the people who exploit these situations, like I suspect, the leaders behind this corporation. They don't care if lives are ruined. They don't care if most of the earth is no longer green. Do you want a land without a soul, and be like these people who have forgotten they have one? Do you really agree that these sad greedy people should have a foothold in our beloved country? And don't think it will stop there.

Next they will look at our other beaches, then our estuaries and rivers and our forests and mountains. They are like locusts and will want more. They will never stop."

Dryadians do not normally applaud at moots, but the stirring in their hearts after Anaxamander's moving words was almost palpable. Some of the Practicals stood up to modify their views or even to withdraw altogether. They were beginning to see the dangers. But a small rump, which wanted to accept the corporation's proposal, still 'remained standing.' The united consensus that was necessary for Amarinta to send a resounding NO back to the corporation was still out of reach. But one important person had not yet spoken, and that was Sophora. Virtually all the Elders of Dryadia, both Traditionals and Practicals knew her at least a little, and through her remarkable seership she had comforted and advised many of them in their personal lives.

All were wondering what she would say. Sophora had presence – there was no doubt of that. Even if people didn't understand or agree with her they were more often or not transfixed by her measured words and her air of authority.

"I won't keep you long," Sophora began, "for much of what I wanted to talk about, has already been said by my fellow Elders. You can rest assured that I wholeheartedly oppose any invasion of Dryadia's coastline or countryside or any weakening of our sacred traditions. As I am sometimes reminded by some of my friends who have lived in the East, the word development is a euphemism for the destruction of nature. Never forget we are part of nature. What we do to our nest we do to ourselves. The proposal is heavy, very heavy indeed. The journey towards heaviness is a journey into a sticky bog from which we may never extricate ourselves. As Anaxamander has just explained the developers are greedy and ignorant with no interest in a gentler way of life, let alone Dryadia's unique pathway towards a lighter way of being. They are motivated only by money. If we allow this part of our beautiful countryside to be destroyed then we have sown the seeds of our own destruction. Whether a wall that separates the proposed resort from the rest of Dryadia is built or not, our more vulnerable countrymen and women will be drawn deep into the materialism of the East. It will produce a poison that will bind us to the earth instead of allowing us to lightly dance upon it.

Dryadia began as an experiment more than six thousand years ago by some of the wisest people who have ever lived on this planet. It is an extraordinary miracle that it has survived intact to this day and it has evolved successfully ever since. Usually such societies eventually collapse either from the belligerence of those from the outside or the inflated egos and ignorance of its inhabitants. It is not that men are born bad. It is rather that they are weak and lack true knowledge of the heart. In Dryadia we have no such excuse. The knowledge has been part of us for a long time and there are many wise men and women who live here today who are able to remind us of what we need to know.

I have long seen Dryadia as a beacon in a dying world. We have a society here that can survive climate change, oil depletion, overpopulation, financial collapse, disease and famine. That is because our culture and population is sustainable and based on sound principles and doesn't draw heavily on the capital of the earth. There is no reason that if left to its own devices Dryadia could be as vibrant and happy in six thousand years time as it is today or as it was six thousand years ago. It is not that things never have to change. It is that change works best when we act within the rhythms of Erith and those of our higher natures.

It is not sensible to invite the East to steal a bit of Dryadia so that they can destroy it. Rather it should be that we teach the best of them so that they can try and save some of their own world. We have made a beginning in encouraging a small number to study at our university. Others come for working holidays on our farms or study our extraordinary wild life. We welcome these visitors but have to keep numbers small so that we can assimilate them and not be overwhelmed.

Rather than inviting the unworthy to appropriate our coastline it would be better that we visit the East, give talks, write articles and explain our Dryadian life to their wise ones. For unless they change and adopt at least some of our ideas they will destroy themselves. It will probably affect us too and that day will probably not be long away. It may already be too late. The ships are overloaded and they are running out of fuel and water and there are only a few lifeboats. Dryadia is one of the lifeboats of the world. We can keep the knowledge alive. We can continue to be the watchers and keepers of a better future. But to do this we need to keep ourselves reasonably isolated from the East, and wait patiently for the tide to change.

Our future is an affair of the heart. We have to feel deeply with all our emotional being if we want to make our wishes come true. That is where truth lies, not in the development corporations or in the machinations of banks. Nor in any institution for that matter.

We have a saying, don't we? 'That nothing matters unless you want it to matter.' Well this matters very much to me. I ask you from my heart to reject this offer and keep faith with our Dryadian experiment."

With that Sophora sat down. There was a deep silence. All were moved and stunned by her words. No one rose to speak despite Amarinta's pleading.

"We will go once more into 'The Great Silence'. Search in your highest being for the way forward. In one hour we will confer again."

Except that after an hour nobody wanted to speak. Almost everyone at the moot knew Sophora was right. Anyone who still had doubts preferred to keep them to themselves. No one was 'left standing.' All were agreed that Dryadia should remain as it was. Dryadia had won its most important battle, the battle for its soul.

The next day the Elders of Ceradoc and their families streamed towards the beach at the mouth of the estuary to celebrate their victory. This was one of the beaches that the corporation had wanted for their own. Now it was forever Dryadian. Zephyr and Sam led small parties along the shoreline small pointing out the small sea creatures and birds that could have disappeared if the decision had gone the other way. Others built a huge bonfire from driftwood. It was said that the flames could be seen from The Beacons many miles away. Smaller fires were lit to keep out the cold and heat up the food that they had brought with them.

They stayed until the sun set over the ocean and then walked back to Ceradoc with a bright moon shining across the water. The air seemed warmer. Perhaps there was not going to be a frost that night after all.

CHAPTER TWENTY-SIX

A VISIT FROM THE EAST

'The Greatest Moot', as it was long remembered, was a turning point in the history of modern Dryadia. Six years had passed since that day. The country was as united as it had ever been especially after Sophora's stirring speech. There was a new pride about being Dryadian and a greater understanding about its purpose and its unique heritage. There were always a few dissenters of course, and those who yearned for the ways of the East were allowed to settle there by agreement with the British government and an equivalent number of Easterners were allowed to make their homes in Dryadia, if they were sufficiently Dryadian in spirit. Britain and Dryadia had found a new respect for each other even if they disagreed on a majority of fundamental issues. They no longer wished to fall out. Britain had come look to upon Dryadia as an extraordinary social experiment, increasingly fascinated by its culture. They now wished the country well, even to the point of protecting it from outside interference. The secret services had long lost interest and even the medical profession had stopped being neurotic about Dryadia harbouring dangerous diseases. Some doctors were secretly impressed by their neighbour's excellent health and the simple and effective remedies used by the Therapeutae.

All was not well in the East though. Unlike Dryadia they were losing their self-belief. Oil production, on which they were so dependent, had peaked and had become increasingly expensive. There was constant talk of rationing. As the world's climate heated up and rainfall patterns became unpredictable, food and water shortages appeared in some countries. Many economies began to wobble and even that great taboo over-population was being taken seriously, although nobody knew what to do about it. In short, governments in the East were learning that their life-style could not be sustained for much longer although they also realised that it would be political suicide to try and persuade people to take a substantial cut in their standard of living. They therefore kept their concerns largely to themselves.

The Dryadians wanted to help, because they realised only too well that everyone lived on the same planet. The East were not so proud that they didn't want to listen, even though they felt paralysed at the thought of action. The Dryadians continued to open their doors and organised summer schools in Cantillion for the Easterners. The courses were always oversubscribed and included seminars on natural philosophy, healing, storytelling and a particular favourite one – *The Dryadian Way of Life: a successful experiment in sustainable and contented living.*

The British had even given the Dryadians a new *Leaky Bucket*, admittedly a second hand boat but perfectly serviceable and usefully bigger than the old one, which unfortunately was beginning to live up to its name.

It was now more than twenty years since the original three students from the East - Sam, Mary and Pushkin had arrived in Dryadia. They had prospered and grown wise and were known as Traditional Elders in Waiting and would become such, as vacancies arose. There was no rush. Eldership was hard work and life experience was essential. To quote Tara who had recently been appointed one. "Being an Elder is like being married – to the community. So enjoy your single carefree life as long as you can."

Pushkin was truly contented. Married to Mary with two children, they lived in Ceradoc near the meetinghouse and the big walled garden. Pushkin had discovered a passion for gardening especially for vegetable and fruit growing, a world of which he knew nothing when he lived in England.

He had even learned to plough and found great peace walking behind two farm horses in the barley fields that lay just above the village. He still shared his love of history with Parmenides and they were now engrossed in *The Complete History of Dryadia* which was about a hundred times longer than the previous edition. It was now supplemented by Sophora and Amarinta's far-seeing, and previously un-translated documents that they had discovered in the Hall of Records. Nothing like this had been attempted before and Pushkin said it was going to be his life's work.

"You'd better live to a hundred and twenty then," said Mary when she realised that after five year's work he'd barely got beyond the Romans.

Yet another passion was studying the lambda lines, one that he shared with Sam. Together they had explored large areas of Dryadia and had made a considerable number of visits to the Hall of Records for additional information. They felt they were almost ready to do some experiments to reactivate the lines as Sophora and her friends had attempted when he first came to Dryadia. However Sophora always urged great caution.

"Remember the Beast that lives in the East," she used to say.

Mary too had blossomed and like Pushkin and Sam had not the slightest wish to ever leave Dryadia. Helped by her strong bonds with Tara and her musical talents she had grown to be a formidable Storyteller. The Northern Province's summer tour was still the highlight of the year but there were also autumn and winter shows in Viribus, which she helped organise. Mary extended her repertoire by drawing on the stories of Wales and England. She never stopped reminding her fellow Dryadians how fortunate they were not to live in the East and hammed up many horror tales that had originated from over the border. Domestic quarrels and ghost stories were her speciality but she told them with such good humour that her audience were seldom scared for long. Irony was Mary's middle name.

Sam was probably the most natural Dryadian of them all. The product of an unhappy childhood, and half traumatised by the loss of his grandparents and their idyllic smallholding, the 'Beast in the East' had hurt him more than anyone. Here at last his sensitive nature had found refuge while in England, as Sophora put it, he had been like a canary midst a flock of sparrows that never stopped pecking at him. In Dryadia, surrounded by like-minded friends he had grown into his true self. He had had the best of teachers both in Ceradoc and at the university of Cantillion. The icing on the cake was of course Melissa who after his disastrous relationship with Nell had loved him enough to pick him up and restore his self-respect. Their marriage was an unusually deep one and was truly more than the sum of its parts. They had had two children, worked together as Therapeutae and had developed an unpretentious spiritual awareness that was almost on a par with Anaxamander and Ruth. Sam claimed that he was going to write three books before he died; one on healing and on healing plants with Melissa and Ruth; one on Dryadia's natural history with Zephyr; and one on the world of the lambda with Pushkin and Anaxamander.

"Take a look at this," exclaimed Anaxamander over the breakfast table, pushing a letter across the table towards his wife. "Wearing your English hat what do you think?"

Ruth read the three-page document carefully. "Where did you get this? It's been around a bit – dated three weeks ago."

"It's a copy of course. Sophora gave it to me this morning. And she got it from old Alfred in the Southern Province who is of course the current

'Shepherd of the Moot' this year. See, it's addressed to him from the British Government. A nice polite and respectful letter, not like the old days."

"I don't think I really understand my ex-country men. Twenty years ago they were invading us and scorning us. Now they are virtually asking for help. What are those lines that Gandhi wrote that you are always quoting?"

"First they ignore you. Then they laugh at you. Then they fight you. Then you win.

Well there aren't exactly any winners, but they do want some kind of conference."

"About fifty years too late," replied Ruth. "After all the misery they put us through. What did Sophora say?"

"Much the same as you. And she added that she sensed London was worried, very worried about what's happening in the world. The Americans and the Europeans are panicking as well. They see that they cannot go on as they have been. And they can also see that with our way of life Dryadia can carry on indefinitely. The only problem we share is that of climate change and even that I reckon we will adjust to. The British say they want to understand us more and pick our brains."

"As if they haven't done that enough already." Ruth had long lost patience with the East.

"I can't forget the many years of ridicule we have been subject to and the scorn that the British medical establishment, together with sections of their cynical press, have hurled across the border at the Therapeutae and our energy medicine philosophy for that matter. To think we give much of our waking hours to help the sick with no reward, except the joy of restoring health to those who ask for it. If the East really wants to change, they have to adjust their sets and think in a different way. There is no point in picking and mixing. They have to see the whole picture. That's how we run our country."

"Sophora thinks we should meet up with them none the less. These mandarins move slowly though. First, as the letter says, they want to meet us informally. Then they go back and report. Then another lot will come over to have a proper conference. It will drive us all mad. Our lives are so simple that we can tell them everything they need to know in two or three days, and that should include time for some nice long lunches."

"So what happens now," asked Ruth?

"We ought really to discuss it at the moot but as it's not the mooting season and it's all very friendly and informal, Sophora proposed that we initially invite the mandarins to Ceradoc for a few days. We'll inform all the Elders in the country that we are going to do this and keep them posted. No one should really object as no decisions are going to be made."

"Did you see on the last page that twelve of them want to come? Where in Erith's name shall we put them?"

"The resthouse has six rooms. They will just have to share. That will please them! They will have to travel here in the *Leaky Bucket*. We've forbidden them their helicopters. That will please them even more though the new boat is more comfortable."

"Don't worry about them," responded Ruth. "I expect they will be drawing lots to come here. It must be quite a change from New York or Moscow."

'The twelve men in suits' as the Ceradocians initially started calling them, even though four of them were women, duly arrived.

"No, the voyage in the latest version of *The Leaky Bucket* was not nearly as bad as they had feared. Yes, they had enjoyed their stay in the Cantillion resthouse, and the subsequent carriage ride and boat journey across Dryadia."

Feeling that their grey suits were rather at odds when compared with the Dryadians' colourful clothes they quickly asked their hosts if they would mind if they could slip into something more 'casual'.

In fact once the British civil servants had divested themselves of their uniforms they also largely dropped their Mandarin-speak. Both parties soon sensed that the other side was not particularly threatening and even quite humorous and they found they actually began to enjoy each other's company.

The name of their leader was Sir Horace Bassett who surprisingly turned out not to be in the slightest bit pompous. To Zephyr and Sam's delight he was also rather keen on bird watching. It was decided that the Dryadian side would also consist of twelve Ceradocian Elders including Sam, Mary and Pushkin because of their British connections, even if they were still only Elders-in waiting.

"Call me Horace," said their relaxed leader. "I shall open the batting. We are merely a reconnaissance expedition, as you know. First of all I want to make a formal apology on behalf of the British Government for the various military and commercial invasions over most of this century I am sad to say. A question of the right hand not knowing what the left was doing. Not thinking things through. That sort of thing. I hope our gift of your new boat will show you how sorry we are. And Zephyr, perhaps you could point out those ringed plovers' nests you were talking about. Very rare in England. Ha-ha! Then I'll know you'll be on the way towards forgiving us."

"Horace of London, you and your friends are very welcome in Dryadia and here in Ceradoc." Anaxamander was trying very hard, and not entirely succeeding, in trying not to mimic Horace's clipped English accent. "You've told us a little of the purpose of your visit and we are assuming that you want to know more about Dryadia and how it works, and to see if we can help you."

"And see if we can help you too," answered Horace benignly. "I hope it will be a two way process. So let me explain myself. I won't beat about the bush. You know as well as I do that the earth and a great swathe of its population is in trouble. It's actually worse than we predicted three or four years ago and generally many of our scientists think we've got past the tipping point, past the point of no return in many areas. CO2 levels are out of control, and world governments have done little to stop them. Methane may follow suit. The Arctic ice cap will have melted by the end of the century and Greenland and Antarctica will follow. Sea levels will eventually rise by at least fifty feet and a lot of seaside cities will disappear under water. Already there are great storms and drought where there shouldn't be, and colder winters and hotter summers. The climate is topsy-turvy and we are worried that climatic pressures on certain countries will result in violence, even major wars. To make matters worse, oil is getting very expensive as world demand now exceeds supply. Almost every country apart from Dryadia is totally dependent on it not only for fuel but also for chemicals and other resources. We will probably run out altogether in about thirty years, and unless our scientists can come up with some pretty amazing discoveries then it all looks rather bleak for the human race, except for you of course. Global warming though will affect even you eventually. Much of this might not matter if the world's population wasn't so big. But governments don't want to talk about it probably because they don't know what to do about it and it's such a political hot potato. There are too many mouths to feed, clothe and house and all the rest. We call it 'The perfect storm' though it beats me what's perfect about it."

Horace looked quite pale as he spoke. His delegation, even though they were learning nothing new, watched his face with rapt attention and with more than a little alarm.

"So, what are you doing about it?" Sophora said in a surprisingly calm voice.

"Well of course officially we are trying to reduce CO2 emissions, some countries more than others. We're working hard in trying to discover greener and more sustainable fuels but I'm afraid it's a drop in the ocean. Unfortunately there are so many vested interests. Commercial big business is making so much money out of the present situation that they want the party to last forever. They think tomorrow will never come. We went through all this some ten years ago but people have forgotten. Consumers, who of course are also voters, are not interested in having their standard of living cut. Not to mention of course that no politician who wants to stay in power dare tell them that it will soon be closing time.

Our little department and the scientists who advise us try and buck the trend of denial, but until recently ministers listened but were reluctant to act. Now at last the penny has dropped and the powers that be are getting nervous, even scared. The prime minister, although he doesn't really know what to do, is at least setting up little initiatives like this one."

"In my opinion, it's all a little too late," replied Sophora. "The rise in greenhouse gases are certainly making the situation a great deal worse but we also mustn't forget the earth's thermostat is always adjusting so that it can keep itself in balance. To that end the earth is now having a kind of fever. This will continue until it reaches a temperature that suits it, at least for the moment. In a thousand years it may need to change again. Unfortunately the earth doesn't consider human needs. It acts for itself. Humans also have fevers or sweats for entirely selfish yet beneficial reasons. Many people don't know that about five thousand years ago both our countries were quite a bit warmer than they are today. Humans lived very comfortably in the far north, as in the Orkney and Shetland islands, and you can still see the stone circles that they built at the time. Later, they largely abandoned these places because the weather cooled. It's a natural cycle, something that you can't fight. Nature always wins. It is far, far stronger than we are. Industrial emissions are certainly like throwing petrol on the fire and therefore a very bad idea and you should stop it but you can't stop the tides. It must be equally obvious to you that a finite earth cannot sustain its huge population much longer, especially as the oil that you depend on so much, will soon be gone."

Horace had no notion of Sophora's seership and even the Elders found it difficult to distinguish between what everyone already knew and her visions of the future.

"So, you think there's no hope for us?"

"For most of you, probably. I know it's a terrible thing to say but I suspect disease will cull you first. You're so crowded and stressed and have nowhere to run. You're like battery chickens. One day a new mutation of a disease will run riot through your population and kill a lot of you, as your immune systems won't be able to cope. You already see this in nature. Remember what happened to the elm trees or the red squirrels. I'm amazed that this hasn't happened already with all the drugs you put into your bodies and the chemicals you spray onto your soil and food."

Horace stared hard back at Sophora. "It's interesting what you're saying about infectious diseases. There are far more of them at least in Britain then there were a few years ago. I don't mean just the flu' epidemics which the press keep making such a fuss about. What we have tried to keep quiet about, not that we're having much success, is the increasing rise in the incidence of measles. It's a new strain. Not the one that we used to accuse Dryadia of passing onto us in the bad old days. This one is different, more virulent than the old one. There have even been a few fatalities. It's a state secret but the immunizations no longer work properly even though we're giving more of them. Antibiotics are now very much a bit of a hit and miss affair. Chronic diseases too, especially those of the nervous system and certain cancers, are increasing faster and our hospitals can't always cope. Fertility rates also seem to be down, both in men and women. Most scientists say our drugs are perfectly safe but who knows really? Our medical people are worried but say they will manage, as they always have in the past. We work hard to keep our concerns away from the media and avoid hysteria and hyped up panics like the bird flu and the swine flu of many years ago."

"Well, it does sound a bit grim, the way you tell it," replied Anaxamander. I sympathise with the East as we call you but how do you think we can help you?"

"We would like to make some observations during the short time we are here, on the way you run your lives and your country. Show us how you live so well barely using any fossil fuels, and keeping your beautiful forests intact. How do you all keep so well without modern drugs? How are you so well fed and clothed on next to nothing?

How do you have such a vibrant and cultured society without any crime, or for that matter virtually no government? That will help us a lot."

"We will of course help you all we can. It's our nature to share knowledge," replied Sophora. "There are no protected commercial secrets here. We don't want a starving angry world living on our doorstep. Your world though is very sick and it's going to have to contract very quickly in order to survive. And I can't see that happening without a great deal of pain."

The meeting went on all day. As was the Dryadian custom all the Dryadians present had their say and Sophora insisted that all the British delegates speak up as well, from Horace to Bethany the young woman who took notes and who would have made them all tea if the Dryadians hadn't been so hospitable. The London party included a number of scientists, notably a doctor, an agriculturalist and an environmentalist who was eager to measure Dryadia's carbon footprint. They wanted to study in particular Dryadia's medicine and their farming right down to measuring the methane that their cows farted!

The following day the British settled down to their various tasks. Door to door interviews were carried out to find out more about the Dryadians' green credentials. Unsurprisingly their carbon footprint was virtually non-existent. The doctor had long discussions with Ruth, Melissa and Sam about their healing methods and found great difficulty in understanding their 'energy imbalance within' philosophy of disease. His medicine was much more interested in chemicals and genes, with dangerous bacteria and viruses seen as the enemy. He asked to be shown over the nearest hospital and was flabbergasted to be told that there were none in Dryadia and that there was no need. He was told that everyone was nursed by their loved ones in the peace of their own home with regular visits from the Therapeutae if needed. The medicine used was the energy of nature both in the remedies of the countryside and what they called 'the power of intention' which came from the ' heart of the healer.' It's really just love.

The doctor was bewildered. "But how can I measure that?"

"Use your imagination and your powers of observation," answered Ruth. "You'll soon see that people get better in the quickest possible way using simple methods without doing them any harm."

"And what about births and deaths? Where do they happen?"

"Same principles. Almost all at home. Lots of love and least stress. We don't have many problems in our exits and entrances."

The agriculturalist scratched his head at both the quality and quantity of their oats, rye, wheat and barley, grown without any artificial fertilizers or pesticides.

"The secret is in rotation and dung," he was told. "We accept that yields are greater in the East and that food is cheap there, although we would consider much of it wasn't real food. You substitute chemicals for goodness. No wonder you have so much degenerative disease."

At the end of the day Zephyr and Sam shepherded Horace to a patch of shingle on the edge of the Tamara estuary where a small colony of black and white wading birds known as ringed plovers had their nests. They were more like hollows amongst the stones, the eggs so well camouflaged that they were very easy to step on them unless you were extremely careful. Horace had already commented on the density of Dryadian bird life not only on the estuary but also in the woods, fields and hedgerows that surrounded Ceradoc.

"At least twice, perhaps three times, as many birds as in England. Nor have I heard dawn choruses like yours, not since I was a tiny child."

"Farm like us, be kind to your insects and you could hear them again," replied Sam.

Horace was not a stupid man and he had done his homework. Nor was he a cynic and he was clearly impressed at what he had seen in Dryadia.

"It's just so beautiful," he kept saying. "No poverty. No great wealth. No crime. No rulers to speak of. No stress. All those birds. One thing puzzles me though. Where's the aggression channelled? You have no politicians or generals. No competitive bankers in their thousand foot towers or ambitious lawyers fighting each other in court. There isn't any non-stop sport. Your chaps must have as much testosterone as ours. Where do they put it all?"

"Oh, you mean the big egos. Some of them put their heads above the parapet a few years ago when you tried to buy our land. Yes we have big egos too but we don't nurture them. It's the lower part of our nature, the beastly bit. They make an appearance when we start fighting like animals. The problem can apply to a greater or lesser extent in all men and if it gets out of hand is very destructive."

Zephyr paused. "The difference between our countries is that you encourage the beast unless it is overtly criminal while we acknowledge it but try and steer it in safer directions. For the young we organise our huge annual endurance race and other adventure sports as well as the normal football and cricket at weekends. Most of us work on the land alongside our parents as soon as we leave school and often before. We are encouraged from an early age to take responsibility for our actions, and those of our children until they are old enough. We have to put right the harm we have done. That is the price of freedom. If we can't agree on what should be done then we call in the Traditional Elders to help us. As big egos are not allowed to be Elders, they tend to be trusted."

"Dryadia seems to work, I have to say," commented Horace.

"It certainly works," replied Zephyr. "That doesn't mean we haven't had our wobbles and our history tells us that there have been times when we have nearly lost it. We are as human as you are. The traditions and the wisdom of the Traditional Elders keeps this particular country upright. Then we see that the enemy within is really just a tiny dragon that only comes up to our knees!"

"Do you have an enemy without," asked Horace?

"Well it's officially your government although that's never been our wish. Now perhaps we don't have one since you have sought out our friendship, though we have to say it's hard to be over friendly with anyone who's not on the side of nature."

Later that evening Mary and Pushkin, with their two small children tagging along behind, were on their customary walk through the large walled garden where Pushkin had a number of plots. It was their turn to close the various gates that led into the garden from the outside world. Not against human thieves for they barely existed in Dryadia. The problem was wild animals – rabbits and deer which could strip a lettuce bed overnight; foxes and badgers who wouldn't be able to resist the chickens; or even the wild pigs and their ploughing matches. Cats were of course allowed in to keep the rats and mice down to reasonable levels.

As they were ambling around the garden Pushkin was enthusiastically informing Mary what he had done that day and Mary was rehearsing her latest story on him, pausing only to shout at the children to keep out of the ponds – all at the same time.

"You can't possibly be listening to me as well," complained Pushkin.

"Yes I am, dear. The lettuces and radishes are coming up really well, the cherries are doing a treat, and you have weeded so hard that your back is hurting. Women don't have to listen – they just absorb."

They heard quiet footsteps and saw a young woman quickly trying to catch up with them. She was dressed in jeans and a dazzling lime green hooded top, so completely different from the more flowing clothes and natural dyes of the Dryadians. It was Bethany, the youngest member of the British group, looking happy yet with a hint of anxiety etched on her forehead. After admiring Pushkin's embryo apricots carefully threaded in long espaliers against the south wall, and chatting politely to the children, she suddenly blurted out.

"You know, I've just spent the happiest three days of my life. Not just because Dryadia's so beautiful but also because it's so peaceful and quiet. No planes or cars or canned music. Do you know almost all of us want to come and live here? They were so cynical at first, especially the scientists and the doctor. Their attitude changed almost overnight. They can't believe how healthy you are, how vital the land is, and we're beginning to feel really healthy too, just after three days. It must be all that home grown food. We've never tasted anything like it. The scientists are going to tell you that you are as green as green can be and much healthier than we are, not that you don't know that all ready. But you know how they work. Nothing is true unless it can be proved in a laboratory using double blind tests and incomprehensible statistics and all that stuff. No room for common sense. They're nevertheless impressed at what they have observed here. Your carbon footprint doesn't seem to exist. Even your cows fart less apparently, but maybe they're smaller than ours. It's wonderful to see how we have all lightened up. None of us will be able to 'Sir' Horace again. He hasn't told you everything though. The situation is worse than he has said. The future does look bleak. Horace was joking this morning that we should all apply for political asylum, if we didn't have to leave our families behind. I don't have a family though and I'm only twenty-two and this is the best place I've ever been too. I don't need to live in London. I hardly need any of my possessions. I realise you don't have much but I can see that you have everything you need. I know that you both moved here from Britain, as well as Sam and Ruth, and you were allowed to stay. I don't know if you're the right people to talk to, but do you think I could apply for political asylum? And would there be any possibility for my boyfriend as well. He loves nature and I'm sure he would be very happy here."

Mary at last collected her thoughts. "I'm sure you'll be allowed to stay if you can impress Anaxamander. We did, many years ago. Don't tell all your friends though or we'll get swamped. Sophora always said that the East would eventually rise in love with Dryadia. Many will I expect, and maybe for the wrong reasons for it's hard work and we can't take everybody. Far better that the countries of the East make a Dryadia of their own."

It turned out that Bethany's boyfriend, appropriately named Green, was one of the British party and he had already drawn attention to himself through the number of questions he kept asking, mainly of a practical nature. Most of the Dryadians had been buttonholed by him at one time or another. He had learned that Ceradoc's water flowed from a spring at the top of the village near the walled garden and was channelled to each house through underground conduits made from elm wood, which didn't rot when waterlogged. Each home had stone cisterns to store the water, with small electric pumps attached to bring it into the house. Wood burning stoves provided hot water and heating, although the well-insulated houses almost kept themselves warm. Green was fascinated by Ceradoc's watermills, some on the small yet fast flowing river that flowed from the spring down to the estuary, and one on the estuary itself driven by the tides. All Ceradoc's power was generated from these mills whether it was the small amount of electricity needed for their homes, or more directly for threshing, sawing wood or grinding grains to make flour.

A week had passed and the conference had finished. Bethany and Green had been granted a trial visa for later in the year, and the British team were ready to leave for London. They had thoroughly enjoyed themselves and would report favourably to their superiors. Horace though had told them privately that the Dryadians shouldn't hold their breath as to what might happen next. Bureaucracy is a frustrating thing.

"They're probably too far gone anyway," said Sophora bluntly.

"There's one other thing," Bethany whispered to Mary as they were saying their goodbyes. "One of our scientists was telling us yesterday. Even Horace didn't know this one. The agricultural companies are playing around with genetically modified crops far more than they're letting on. In some places it's got out of control and some sort of blight has not only got into our grains but into the countryside at large. No pesticide can get rid of it. Plants are being poisoned and are withering in the ground. Our bees are disappearing. We suspect the toxicity is endemic in our bodies. Nobody knows quite what to do and the few who understand the situation are very frightened. That's probably why we are getting sicker. Governments are burying their heads in the sand if they know anything at all. The scientists are now of the opinion that our biggest problems are disease and the lack of water in some areas. The soils are becoming increasingly toxic and dry and it's making us ill."

Mary and Pushkin decided to walk to the sanctuary and consult the oracle. To their delight they discovered Sam and Melissa were already there with the intention of doing much the same thing.

"Are our bees alright?" asked Mary of Sam and Melissa since she knew they had a number of hives in their garden.

"Never been better," she replied. "I can speak for Ruth and Amarinta's as well. Our bees never cross the Drangle as far as I know, so they don't get infected. The purity of our soil and flowers keeps both them and us well."

"Have you heard of super-measles? Bethany was telling us, amongst other things, that the East was getting rather worried about it. There have been a few deaths, some in the adult population, Horace has played it down but he doesn't know much about it. They are immunising like mad but it's not working very well and their doctors are at a loss how best to play it."

Melissa looked at Mary thoughtfully. "I had heard a rumour from one of my pen friends in the East. She said it wouldn't be so bad if they didn't use so many drugs and that so many people's immune systems were weak in the first place. She suspected that scientists were mucking about with plant genes and that was affecting peoples' bodies."

"That's exactly what Bethany was saying." Pushkin nodded his head in agreement.

"We should be alright on that score," said Sam. "Dryadian measles is what it always has been – nothing to worry about so long as it's treated right. I often wondered if a more virulent strain would make a come back in the East. It could wipe out the weakest of them as they have little natural protection left. We don't need to be worried here though. The greatest defence against all diseases is to stay healthy in the first place and have peace of mind and heart, as most of us have."

"My mother doesn't seem to be worried and her healing memory goes back more than forty years now," added Melissa. "I asked Sophora her opinion as well. She was her normal calm self. She said we would be fine and just to do what we always do. But when I asked her to make a prophecy about the East health-wise she said she thought that it was more than probable that they had a very rocky road ahead of them."

"Let's consult the oracle and see if it will comfort us or not", said Pushkin suddenly.

"Then let's ask two very precise questions," said Melissa. "Firstly, what's going to happen to the East? Secondly what's going to happen to us?"

Mary looked at her in admiration. "You couldn't get much more succinct than that."

There was plenty of sunshine pouring down into the cupola that afternoon, but it was not directed at the pillars.

"The East?" they called in unison, and concentrated their thoughts on Pushkin as he made the now familiar adjustments to the blinds and mirrors so that he could focus a narrow beam of light downwards towards the semi-darkness where the pillars stood.

He climbed down the staircase and peered at the place high up on one of the pillars where the beam danced and then remained still. His ancient Dryadian was perfect now but he spoke in English.

As you sow, you shall reap.

"Pretty succinct," he commented.

High above him came another call, "And Dryadia?"

This time Sam adjusted the blinds and mirrors while his companions focused their thoughts on him, the question bearer for his adopted country. This time the beam seemed to be aimed at a point just to the right of Pushkin's head and he saw almost immediately the curling Dryadian script depicting a raven flying above the sun. He started in surprise for the oracle rarely gave its answers pictorially. But not quite, for underneath was written:

Much in little.

A VISIT FROM THE EAST

CHAPTER TWENTY-SEVEN

NEMESIS

The Atlantic winds grew fresher as summer lost itself in the cooler days of autumn. Three years had passed since Horace had led his team into Dryadia. As was feared his report to the British government was largely buried and no further formal approaches were made from London. Ruth's herb garden was beginning to look bedraggled as the sun's energy weakened in the colder air, but the healing work of the Therapeutae continued as it always did. They had long talks about the declining health and environmental problems of the East, now appearing to be in freefall, and were relieved that Dryadia continued to stay healthy.

Following Sophora's advice to take Dryadia to the East, various groups of Therapeutae, Natural Philosophers and Storytellers made short tours of English towns. They discovered in their audiences a hunger for knowledge and a way of life that their brains had long forgotten, although dim memories still seemed to resonate in their hearts. The meetings were always sold out and well received wherever they went. Dryadia now rode high in the opinions of the open-minded, although as always, the cynical and the un-imaginative continued to scoff. Solutions for them had to be high-tech and sophisticated if they were to be worthy of consideration. The Dryadians' simple common sense approaches to problems were, well, just too simple.

Bethany and Green had long completed their probationary period in Dryadia and had been allowed to settle there. They continued to commute to England to do a little part time work in Horace Basset's department, and with the consent of both parties acted as informal ambassadors. Green was actually a distant relation of Horace and despite having had no formal education, but having a photographic memory, was the only person in his department who could regularly beat Horace at chess. Green's almost super human powers of recall had drawn him to the attention of the British secret service. He had had an interview with the ageless Mr B and even had lunch with Stephano. The murky depths of espionage though were not much of a temptation, and his extraordinary intelligence and genial nature found a ready home when Horace managed to second him to his department in London. It was there he met Bethany. Bethany's sister Miranda, a nurse in one of the major London hospitals, had suffered super-measles particularly badly despite being considered an expert in its treatment. Bethany had persuaded the Elders to accept her and some of their family and they too had settled in Ceradoc. Through these un-official contacts Dryadia continued to be well informed about events across the Drangle.

The prices of grains and oil were especially high and there was real poverty in isolated parts of the British countryside and in the poorer parts of the towns and cities. Prolonged droughts alternating with un-seasonal torrential rain and floods were an increasing worry. A substantial part of the population had been further weakened by the genetic experiments on food plants, and some of these rogue species had become established in the wild. The insect and animal population had crashed as a result. Acute diseases like the infamous super-measles and other infections were rampant in a population that was rapidly losing its natural immunity. Hospitals had closed their doors to almost all new patients and the sick had to cope as best they could. In fact people were safer outside the hospitals for most antibiotics no longer worked and the hospitals had become reservoirs of infection. It was not only Britain that was under siege – there was hardly any part of the world, apart from the most isolated areas, that had not been affected.

The Therapeutae were often asked about acute diseases in their lectures and why the Dryadians seemed to have a natural protection: indeed the audience seldom wanted to talk about anything else. Then they noticed a number of dark suited gentlemen standing at the back of their meetings taking notes. Shortly afterwards the Chief Medical Officer of the UK forbade them to talk any further on the subject on the grounds that they were giving false hope to sufferers and that only conventionally qualified doctors should be allowed to treat infectious diseases. The Therapeutae were once more demonised and subsequently they were banned from giving any more lectures across the Drangle.

The East once more put Dryadia into quarantine and *The Leaky Bucket* sailed largely empty. Several hundred British people had been stranded in Dryadia and not surprisingly chose to stay and were allowed to bring in their dependents. Horace and his family were amongst them. The telephone line to England remained open and as Dryadia did not want to abandon the East, regular newsletters were sent across and distributed by a band of friendly sympathisers. The Dryadians were willing to take a reasonable amount of refugees on a temporary basis until the situation improved. After *The Leaky Bucket* was forbidden to dock at the English port, small numbers of Easterners crossed the Drangle to meet the Forest Guardians. They were then led along the maze of tracks through the Forest of Dreagle and across the moors to Cantillion.

The Dryadians continued to help by sending 'thought bubbles' to the East on a daily basis. To protect their own country the Traditional Elders did what they had always done which was to meet up every day in small groups at sunrise and sunset, and in the silence of their hearts spread a veil of energy over and around Dryadia to keep it strong. The Elders had calculated that they only needed about five hundred participators throughout the country at any one time to provide 'full power'. As there were about two thousand Traditionals in all, this particular type of human energy was seldom in short supply. The energy of the Seers and the Therapeutae was particularly potent, although a majority of the Traditionals possessed this great healing gift of the soul. The energy was particularly strong at the full moon and at the various power points or gateways in the earth.

Meantime the situation in the East was dire. At least a hundred thousand British people had now died in the epidemics, and many more were wasting away from the chronic diseases caused by the poisoned soils. The pattern was repeated all over the world.

"It will burn itself out eventually," claimed the Chief Medical Officer more in hope than knowledge. "That's if our scientists don't discover some new wonder drugs first."

The Dryadians took a different line. One of the Therapeutaes' favourite sayings was –

Flies are only attracted to a dirty dustbin. If you want them to go away, you first need to clean out the dustbin.

The Therapeutae offered their help again, but it was again firmly declined by the British authorities. For a while *The Leaky Bucket* acted as an offshore clinic with several more set up on the Dryadian side of the River Drangle. The results were extremely encouraging but the British medical authorities were unable to accept that Dryadian medicine could work. This was perhaps from a question of pride as much as anything, and guards were placed on their shoreline to prevent people leaving the country. In the East, governments became increasingly authoritarian as hungry mobs roamed the streets and law and order began to crumble. People were growing weak from both the lack of food and its poor quality. The birth rate started to tumble as fertility plummeted, not only from biological reasons but also because people had no faith in the future.

Prolonged droughts and floods in all the wrong places continued to make food shortages even worse. There was a succession of extremely large earthquakes and tsunamis all over the world, which caused enormous destruction. The earth itself was in turmoil and the Dryadians believed that its natural cycles had been affected and exacerbated by the irresponsible behaviour and negativity of the people of the East.

One big worry was whether the hundreds of nuclear power stations scattered throughout the world were being managed properly by the increasingly limited numbers of operators. There were constant radiation scares. Nuclear reactors could be shut down but the spent radioactive fuel rods needed to be kept cool for generations to avoid serious contamination. Some were on the verge of meltdown.

Small wars were fought in every continent not just over the rapidly decreasing oil reserves, but also for food and water. As the infrastructure of countries broke down and jobs became a luxury, the beast in man surfaced and a bloody desire for survival took precedence over everything else.

The Dryadians watched and waited. They wanted to preserve two things: themselves obviously and their priceless knowledge. Their self-sufficiency had paid off. Their large water cisterns and cool protective forests had largely insulated them from the new unstable climatic conditions. Two more years passed. The East weakened further and became increasingly silent. Hardly anyone approached the Drangle now. Neither world knew what was going on in the other. Dryadia's fishing boats no longer saw any other ships at sea, nor aeroplanes overhead for that matter. There was no oil to power *The Leaky Bucket* and it remained tied up at Trigonia. The Forest Guardians reported that an uncomfortable quiet reigned on the other side of the Drangle. They said it could be their imagination but they had hardly heard a bird sing from the English shore for months, even though it was springtime.

The Traditional Elders had taken great care to keep their knowledge safe. Their great oral tradition ensured that that most of their teaching was learned by heart so it could never be forgotten. The Storytellers, most of whom were Traditional Elders, also had the key to wisdom and anything that needed to be kept secret was encrypted within their stories. Knowledge was always available to those who had a real need to know, so long as their intentions were honourable. It was always hidden from the faintly curious and the self-centred. The greatest scientific secrets though were still safely locked away in The Hall of Records under Mount Cynthos.

However The Hall of Records was not the only hidden place in Dryadia where secrets were stored. There were also what was known as 'The Repositories'. Originally there were believed to have been thirteen of them, one for each of the twelve provinces, plus Cantillion. Most were lost or had decayed over the years. The Cantillion one was safe as it was part of the university, and was well used by the Elders there. A second was concealed in the far west of the country where sea and moor met, but no one had yet managed to locate the sealed entrance. The third one was in the Northern Province and lost deep in the Forest of Dreagle. Only Sophora, Anaxamander and their fellow Elders had visited it. It was so well hidden that it could only be found with the help of the Forest Guardians.

Sam, Melissa, Pushkin, Mary, Tara and Hermes had never been there. In view of the terrible situation in the East and the fact that they had by now all been made Traditional Elders, Anaxamander felt that an expedition should be arranged so that the knowledge could be passed down to the new generation. Anaxamander explained. "The Repositories are store houses, safe from damp and excessive heat, where the blueprints and practical necessities of civilized living are kept. They are there as a reminder to future generations if Dryadia ceases to be.

Information will be available to what is left of mankind if it falls so low that it doesn't have the knowledge to raise itself up again. Any visitor who finds the repository merely has to look around him."

He and Ruth would act as guides but only to the forest edge where a Forest Guardian would take all of them the rest of the way. The repository had long been known as 'Dryadogenes Lair' as there was a tradition that one of the many Dryadogenes that had been known to exist in Dryadia's history, had founded it.

Magnus the Forest Guardian was tall and athletic and quietly spoken. In fact he didn't speak very much at all. He was a well-educated man, a Practical Elder, who lived in one of the villages at the edge of the forest. He earned his living through coppicing chestnut and burning charcoal, when he wasn't patrolling the forest. He was at the head of about twenty other Forest Guardians, an old and much respected Dryadian profession. Zephyr was a good friend of his and both being lovers of wild life they used to visit each other several times a year for a change of scene. Sam in particular already knew him well from those regular visits.

Magnus had arranged to meet them an hour after sunrise at their campsite on the edge of the forest. Dryadians did not wear watches, so time was regarded as the spaces between sunrise, noon and sunset. Sundials were therefore more useful than clocks. Dryadians though had a fondness for chiming grandfather clocks especially if they had lots of additional dials that told them things like the state of the tides and the moon. Most meetinghouses had such clocks but they always had to be synchronised with the sun, which was considered to be the true conductor of the orchestra.

"All light and well, Magnus," asked Anaxamander shaking his hand warmly.

"Light and well," came the reply. "At least on our side of the river. Across the Drangle it's a different story. Not much activity, but when we do see anyone they're like shrunken wraiths. Eaten away on the inside by the look of them. I used to worry that they would cross the river and force themselves through the Dreagle. They carried axes and guns and you wouldn't want to get near them. Not any more. They haven't the strength. Sometimes we carry sacks of bread through the forest, grab a boat – we've got several hidden away – and throw them loaves across the water when we get close to their shoreline. They fight for them like squabbling starlings. I hope the food helps but it doesn't seem much to give. They look as if they have been poisoned. The few of them that we do see nowadays look yellow, and their eyes seem haunted as if they were no longer human."

Sam had never heard Magnus talk so much. "They really are poisoned," he answered. "Their soil and crops as well. Far too many chemicals. We call it toxic overload. From the way you describe them their livers are giving up on them. It's bad news."

"Let's get going," replied Magnus. "Such talk is depressing There's not much we can do about it now. I don't think any of you have ever been to Dryadogenes' lair except Anaxamander and Ruth."

"We've been a few times," said Ruth. "But we haven't a clue how to get there."

"That's good," grinned Magnus. "If you don't remember, then there's little chance anyone else will. It's safer that way. Now follow me. It's a very confusing path so don't lag behind or you'll never be seen again. Then you will be food for wild cats." He grinned again, but kindly this time when he saw Melissa and Mary's anxious faces.

There was no apparent path into the forest. Magnus inched himself around an enormous hollow oak tree, its trunk seemingly sculpted into fantastic carvings of goblins and witches trying to escape from out of the deeply fissured bark. On the other side of the tree daylight turned into semi-darkness. Magnus quietly picked up a trail that was virtually invisible to the others. No one talked. It felt like sacrilege to raise your voice above a whisper.

The silence was intense. Once or twice they heard the chatter of a squirrel, or the alarm call of a blackbird warning the forest of their coming, but there was little else. The track twisted and curved, turning back on itself, sometimes dividing into two or losing itself in the bracken. Magnus seldom wavered, just hesitating occasionally when he seemed to sniff the air like a spaniel seeking out a scent. Despite what he had said earlier he often looked back to count the shapes following him through the gloom. Now and then the track opened up into a glade where fallen trees had slashed open a gap in the dense canopy above. The sunlight was welcome not only to the travellers but also to the pink campions and willow herb that raised themselves to greet the light after their long dormancy in the undergrowth. Here the Dryadians paused to drink their tea and eat their barley cakes. They sat on on the fallen giants marvelling at the peace that lay in these lost places of the forest, and allowed the sun to penetrate every cell of their being.

The journey seemed a lot more than the two hours that Magnus had estimated, but then they had spent a lot of time in the glade. Suddenly without warning they were blinking in the light, for the forest ended and they saw in front of them a narrow oval-shaped strip of grassy land, kept short by rabbits. Apart from the narrow exits from the forest at either end, a five-foot high wall half covered in ivy surrounded the whole area. The opposing walls curved gently towards each other almost touching at either end like a pair of open lips. Indeed the other name for Dryadogenes' lair was simply 'The Kiss.' Magnus led the party through the hundred yards of 'The Kiss' towards the trees at the other end and down a slope into a small depression hidden from view by a circle of mature oaks. In the middle was an exquisite octagonal building made of a pinkish stone. The colour contrasted strongly with its bright blue shutters that were closed tightly against the elements.

Anaxamander had explained that great care had been taken in its construction so that the interior always remained dry and cool. Magnus and his friends maintained the building, which included repainting it every few years. There was one entrance that stood at the top of eight steep steps. Suddenly Mary squealed as she saw two skulls covered in moss on either side of the door on the highest step.

"Good afternoon Mr and Mrs Dryadogenes," smiled Tara, placing a comforting arm around Mary's shoulder.

"If they were that old they would have crumbled years ago," said Pushkin before he realised that Tara was pulling their legs.

"Not if they had been enchanted," said Mary adding to his confusion.

"What's the story Anaxamander?" Sam asked, trying to be serious.

"Nobody knows. They've been here at least a hundred years. One story is that they are all that remains of two lovers from the East. They tried to find their way through the forest, got lost and sadly died here, appropriately enough at The Kiss. The Forest Guardians are supposed to have found their intertwined skeletons many years later and placed their skulls at the top of the steps to frighten off unwanted intruders."

"That's the tale that's passed down through my family," said Magnus. "Tara is right though. We really do call them Mr and Mrs Dryadogenes. It's his lair after all."

Sam pushed at the door. "Locked. I wonder where the keys are."

"You need to ask Mr and Mrs Dryadogenes," answered Ruth.

Sam carefully lifted the skulls to find only spiders and dead leaves. Melissa's sharp eyes though saw a thin wooden tube barely protruding through each mouth and containing the two keys needed.

"No point in taking a lot of trouble to hide them," said Magnus. "It's finding the lair in the first place that's the challenge."

Inside, a small amount of light from the cupola penetrated the gloom on the ground floor. It wasn't though until they threw open all the shutters allowing both light and fresh air into the musty interior that they became aware of a number of rooms spread over the two floors. On each door was inscribed a small picture which indicated the contents of the room: a sheaf of barley; a covered wagon; a bucket of overflowing seeds; a woman telling a story to a child with a man playing a piano; a typical Dryadian house in the course of instruction. More bizarrely, the upstairs doors each had a skull and crossbones painted on them.

"All things that we would like to preserve for our descendants if our civilisation disappeared. It would help us, or more likely I suppose the East, to start again after a catastrophe like this one," said Anaxamander. "Look around. Lots of models of our farm machinery, transportation and house building, even if it is very low-tech. There is a seed bank here and information about agricultural rotations. Some of our stories and music are here too. Each room is crammed full of portfolios and exhibits like a pharaoh's tomb. You can look it either as a time capsule or an interesting museum. There's nothing here though that would be useful to those with ill intent."

Upstairs it was quite different. The skull and cross bones pointed to a different world. The rooms were heavy and dull. There was nothing of Dryadia in them. The objects were from the East: models or photos of guns and tanks and other weapons of warfare; aeroplanes and enormous cars and boats; computers and televisions; many sacks and bottles of chemicals with the formulae written on them; pictures of sick people and plants lying withered beside them; treeless city landscapes of tower blocks and tarmaced roads crowded with cars and trucks surrounded by smoky fumes

Anaxamander smiled grimly. "All the things that we'd like our descendants to avoid. The desires and the addictions of the East. My father started these rooms more than fifty years ago. Then later every time I went to England I came back with a little horror story, and brought it here. It's a warning how not to run the world if you want to be happy and well."

Anaxamander rummaged around in his rucksack and drew out a small photo album.

"More high-tech images from the East for our chamber of horrors. All those enormous machines. They cut people off from nature, and it's not good for either our physical or mental health." He placed the album on the table in one of the Skull and Crossbones rooms where Melissa and Ruth were carefully tidying.

Ruth had brought more seeds for the Barley sheaf room, and Tara more stories, which she had recorded on Anaxamander's old tape machine at his suggestion.

"I think the Moot has moved on since they banned these tape recorders from Dryadia," smiled Pushkin as he extracted a few chapters of the latest history from his bag. "Only three hundred years left to write!"

They spent about two hours in the repository and while they were there gave it a good spring clean. Magnus had told them that that no one had been inside for six months since Sophora and one of the Elders from another village had made a visit.

"Ready," said Anaxamander after he had ushered them out and returned the keys to the mouths of the grinning skulls. "Now I have a suggestion, which I've already discussed with Magnus. Instead of camping here we could go on to our next port of call and spend the night there. It will really surprise you and it's only an hour away. There's a stream of pure water and a comfortable place to sleep. Interested?"

"We will if you can," answered Melissa thinking of her father's slightly lame leg.

"See how the forest climbs up over there," said Anaxamander pointing along The Kiss towards the top of a wooded hill about two miles away. "It marks the centre of the Forest of Dreagle. On a clear day, if you have binoculars, you can see the sea in both directions. It's a very remote place, one that is hardly ever visited. It's called 'The Tower of the Ravens.'"

"I have a vague recollection that was where Dryadogenes went to consult the wisest of the ravens. I often wondered though whether it really existed," exclaimed Tara.

"That's the place," replied Magnus. "And the ravens still nest there to this day."

The walk was not as bad as they feared. They followed an 'animal highway' as Magnus put it which ran alongside a small river that flowed down from the top of the ravens' hill. As they walked, Mary told a burlesque story about Dryadogenes' love life and the resulting twelve children he had fathered through each of his twelve wives.

"To think that Pushkin won't put it in his history," she added.

Pushkin smiled, gritting his teeth. He was not going to rise to all of Mary's wind-ups.

Melissa nudged Mary. "But it's really good. I've not heard that one before."

"Of course you haven't, my darling. I've just made it all up. Good, huh. I'll include it in the repertoire for next year – in the entertainments part. The not to be taken very seriously bit. Pushkin gets very cross when I tease him about including these sort of stories into the history or instructive sections. As if I would. I do love to see him frown though," and she affectionately squeezed his arm.

CHAPTER TWENTY-EIGHT

THE TOWER OF THE RAVENS

"Another Egg," exclaimed Sam. "What enormous oaks." He started counting them. "Fourteen of them, just like at The Beacons. But the 'eggy' bit seems smaller. Look how smooth the grass is. I suppose the rabbits keep it short as they do at the lair."

They had reached the top of the hill with Dryadogenes' lair a couple of miles behind them. From the summit they dropped down fifteen feet or so into a large dip, where the oaks had been arranged in the familiar ellipse enclosing a smooth sward of grass.

"It's exactly half the size of the Egg at The Beacons," said Anaxamander. "The geometry is very important as you all know. The rabbits may help keep the turf short but it grows slowly anyway as the oak canopy shuts out a lot of the light."

"It's amazing," said Melissa, after gazing in wonder at what lay before her. "It feels much lonelier than our Egg though. I suppose that's because there are no rituals here."

"It's not been used for generations," answered Magnus.

"I think I can hear a stream bubbling away," said Hermes, "but where's the resthouse you were talking about?"

"That's my next trick," replied Anaxamander. He walked across the circle and retrieved a long billhook that had been lying against one of the oaks. He raised it high against the trunk and managed to hook it into a loop of rope that was hanging down from the branches. He pulled it down, and along with it fell a rope ladder loosely wrapped in a tarpaulin sheath. He tugged at the ladder to ensure it was firm.

"I'll go first. If it can bear my weight then the rest of you are safe." With that he carefully climbed up towards the leafy branches before disappearing into the canopy.

"Wonderful. Perfectly safe," cried an invisible voice, "Now, the rest of you."

One by one they left the safety of the ground until they were all standing on a small oak platform virtually invisible from the ground. Three sides were open to the canopy; the fourth was the wooden wall of a concealed cabin.

"The resthouse," exclaimed Anaxamander throwing out his arms dramatically like a conductor about to begin a great symphony. He opened the door. Once they were inside, they realised that they were standing in the hall of a typical hexagonal house in miniature, with the doors of five rooms leading off it. There was a major difference though

– the branches of the oak tree were sticking out of the walls and roof at odd angles, as befitted all good tree houses.

"Four primitive bedrooms and an eating room," said Ruth. "There's just enough space for all of us. Oak tree houses are bigger than you think. Facilities are in the forest and washing is in the stream. Hope you've all got good bladders. Cooking is on the ground floor at the bottom of the ladder."

"What about Magnus?" asked Melissa solicitously. "We don't have enough bedrooms, if you can call them that." She looked at the simple slatted beds without any mattresses.

"Magnus likes to sleep under the stars when ever he can," replied her mother. "You don't need to worry about him. He's brought his sleeping bag, as we all have, and if you look in those cupboards over there you'll find some roll-up mattresses and pillows. We have to keep them locked up to prevent damp."

"What a night. I've never slept so deeply," said Sam the next morning over their breakfast of fried eggs and wild mushrooms that were growing conveniently nearby. "I heard an owl hoot and knew nothing more until it was well past sunrise. What a place. I've always wanted to live in a tree house and when I do, I sleep through it!"

"You missed all the animals that were in the glade last night too," commented Magnus. "I managed to keep awake for about ten minutes and I had already counted three badgers, a couple of roe deer and a fox, before I nodded off."

"I wonder how old this tree house is," said Pushkin. "It's extraordinarily well built."

"We like to think that it's as strong as the tree itself. I suppose it could be hundreds of years old though no doubt it's had a few repairs in its time. The legend is that it was made for followers of Alanda and Isola so they had a safe place to live during the civil war. But who knows? Not many people come here nowadays. Well, very few know about it, let alone be able to find, it, without the Guardians' help. Sophora likes to come here now and then, usually alone. I leave her for a few days before collecting her. She says it's the only place where she can disappear and find peace and quiet. I don't know what she does here but she certainly has plenty of colour in her face when I return."

"I can't hear any ravens. I thought this place was called Raven Hill." Sam was reminded of the purpose of the visit.

Anaxamander looked up from his breakfast. "That's our next surprise. We're not quite there yet, though it's only a short walk away. It's a strangely invisible place – always seems to be hidden from view. You can't see it from Dryadogenes' lair, or from here. If you've nearly finished then we can set off soon. It's only across the stream. Even I can show you the way."

The stream was more the size of a small river, about fifteen feet wide. Anaxamander had warned them that there was no bridge within miles and that they had to use some small flat stepping stones to reach the other side.

"Go slowly. The stones are slippery, and the water is extremely cold." Sam was the last to go across and almost the first to fall in. He stopped half way, mesmerised by the river's eddies and currents and by a pair of dippers walking under water, one of the few birds that can do so. He stood entranced until Melissa's cries brought him back to his five senses causing him to almost lose his balance. Then he too at last stumbled over to the further bank without any more mishaps. Once they had dried off their shoes, Magnus led them up a steep track from the riverbank that was half concealed by bracken. High above the river another much wider path followed the fast flowing water below them. They walked upstream along the forest path for some five minutes until the trees started thinning. At the top of a rise they stopped at what seemed to be the edge of a flooded crater.

In the middle, was a large sixty-foot high ivy-covered tower, surrounded by a moat. A narrow bridge connected it to the mainland. Across the bridge there was an opening into the tower, and the outline of a spiral staircase could be seen rising up on the inside. The lower walls of the tower were jagged and rough like a grey plug of rock and seemed natural enough. Further up though, the walls were smoother and were constructed in granite blocks right up to the crenallated roof.

"It's safe," said Magnus, "but I'll lead you up." A minute later after climbing two spirals round the building everyone was standing safely in a small rounded empty room with a flat paved floor, and two large cracks in the walls which served as windows.

"The Tower of the Ravens," announced Anaxamander with his usual dramatic flourish. "They still nest on the top."

Once everyone's eyes had got used to the gloom inside and stared out over the magnificent views of the forest all around them, Magnus excused himself and left the floor to an unusually excited Pushkin. He beckoned everyone to the window and unfolded his map, and placed a prismatic compass on the window ledge.

"The tower is definitely on the Lambda line that goes to Mount Cynthos, The Beacons and beyond to Southern Dryadia and towards the Atlantic. It goes into England if you trace it the other way. This place must be important or the tower wouldn't have been built here."

"You're absolutely right, Pushkin," replied Anaxamander. "The tower is very important indeed, or at least it was, and I like to believe that it will be so in the future. That is why we've brought you all here. Times are changing. We believe that it's nearly safe to re-start the experiments that we began over twenty-five years ago. I don't think we'll get any more visitors arriving by helicopter. The East is now too far gone and besides, we believe their spy satellites have virtually stopped transmitting."

"What's the purpose of The Tower of the Ravens?" asked Tara.

"You almost know already," replied Anaxamander. "See if you can work the rest out for yourself. There are plenty of clues if you look around you."

Sam had been gazing out at the forest, transfixed by five ravens tumbling down over the forest, probably from the top of the tower. 'A quintessence of ravens,' he thought. 'Could there be meaning behind that observation? Five is the energy associated with exits and entrances; with the Fibonacci series; with strong emotions; and moving in a spiral sort of way rather than the slow plodding rhythm of the energy of four, which is how the physical three-dimensional world normally worked. His mind was in overdrive with new ideas when he felt a tug at his hand and Melissa drew him towards the others standing in the middle of the room where Anaxamander was conducting a lively debate.

"Indeed," he boomed, his voice echoing around the chamber. "And as Tara and Hermes have just reported, the two rooms above including the open one on the roof are almost identical to this one. What do you make of that?"

"We're working on it, Great Maestro," answered Tara. "We need time to think."

"Come over here," interrupted Melissa from where she was standing by the window. "I've discovered some drawings on the walls. They're quite faint. The sunlight is illuminating them now. There are touches of colour here and there, but it's all very faded. I can make out some spirals, in fact lots of them. I've seen similar ones drawn on rocks by the sea. Dad once said they were like maps of the serpent energy rising through a gateway from inside the earth."

Hermes was examining another set of drawings on the other side of the window.

"Five discs all in a line. The first one on the left is almost invisible. Then the other four get increasingly more defined. The last one is the most deeply engraved and then if I'm not being too imaginative, I can see two little stick men sitting on top of it."

"I've found the reverse," exclaimed Mary excitedly. "Five discs in a row, but this time the most well defined is on the left with your two little men sitting on them, and the other four discs gradually fading away."

"And over here," said Pushkin not to be outdone. It's astonishing. There are engravings of the five platonic solids – the dodecahedron in the middle surrounded by the other four. What are they for? I remember that there were models of them in the Hall of Records."

"I've found something too," added Tara. "Heavens, that really is the right word. It's a star map. Unmistakable! Orion's Belt, Sirius, The Pleiades." She lifted her hands upwards to the top of the circular map. "Even a non-astronomer like me can see that this is The Great Bear and The Pole Star. This place must be a kind of observatory. Did they have telescopes thousands of years ago, Anaxamander?"

"I guess so," he replied. "Even though they were supposed to have been invented only five hundred years ago. Extraordinary construction isn't it, built of solid granite. Very hard and very heavy. Amazing how they got those blocks up here and built a perfectly circular building, exactly aligned, as we know with Mount Cynthos and The Beacons. Can you remember any more etchings on the walls, Ruth? You've been very quiet."

"I wanted them to find them by themselves. They seem to be doing very well. But come and look at these by the doorway."

"It looks like a lot of starbursts radiating outwards, with triple circles on some of the lines," said Sam. "What do they mean?"

"Look very carefully round the perimeter. There's a very faint higgledy line. Follow it and see what it reveals."

Melissa saw it first. "It's the Dryadian coastline. It's a map of Dryadia. A very strange map. What do all the stars mean?"

"Got it," cried out Sam. "I'm quite sure it's a lambda map. Look, here's Mount Cynthos with I think three circles round it except there are two more faint ones – so five in all. Here's the Tower of the Ravens – five circles round that too. The same at The Beacons and The Repository at Cantillion. Lots more places all over Dryadia, mostly with three circles. I suppose they are the less powerful gateways. The map seems to mark all the lambda pathways in Dryadia. All our work has been done for us, Pushkin. We've been wasting our time all these years, charting those serpent lines."

Pushkin though was beaming with satisfaction. "Well it proves that we didn't get anything wrong. We've obviously located all the important ones in the country and I think all of the smaller ones in the north. The map confirms that we were right and we can have confidence in our work."

"Sophora came here some time ago and scanned the map in her extraordinary sensitive way", said Anaxamander. "She told us that she felt it was completely genuine and that the information it revealed was absolutely correct. She also felt that the people who actually used the tower were the same ones who made the map. Sophora thought that the tower hadn't actually been in use for hundreds of years. Since then it has only been occasionally visited by people like us who come to stare and wonder at it all."

Anaxamander then guided them up the steep spiral staircase to the room above. This was similar to the first one, perfectly round but with far fewer drawings on the walls. Yet another similar space lay above the second one, but this had no ceiling and had been deliberately left open to the skies, though protected by the high circular wall. The view from the summit confirmed that the canopy of the surrounding trees was at a similar height to the top of the tower, making it virtually invisible from prying eyes until you stood close by the drawbridge. The Tower of the Ravens was designed to be concealed at ground level and could really only be seen from above.

"The Americans paid a visit here unfortunately. They must have let a few men down by helicopter. Obviously they didn't find anything but they left an awful mess behind them – bottles, cans and cigarette ends. Magnus and his family spent a lot of time clearing it all up and burying it in the woods. If archaeologists excavate that hole in a thousand years time they will say that we were conquered or corrupted by the East. They will also consider Dryadia as an inferior and primitive civilization since we leave so few artefacts. Such are the ways of men and the so-called experts."

"But Dryadia will still be here in a thousand years time," said Sam emphatically.

"Of course we will Sam," replied Anaxamander, so long as we don't forget our principles."

The Tower of the Ravens was well cared for by the Forest Guardians despite it looking like an ivy-clad ruin from the outside. The inner rooms were kept clear of debris and the droppings of the ravens and jackdaws that nested in the rocky crags adjacent to the top of the tower. Their nests consisted of mighty structures of twigs accumulated over many years. A pair of ravens sat serenely on top of one of them with a colony of raucous jackdaws burrowing beneath. The ravens kept a close eye on the Dryadians but showed little fear, for like almost all wild creatures in Dryadia they were cherished and had never been persecuted. Moreover as everyone knew, ravens, at least in the myths, were considered as wise as men. Although the Forest Guardians had long looked after the tower they had no idea of its purpose.

"It's always been here," Magnus had told them. "Nobody knows its history. There is a story that Dryadogenes used it as a watchtower and sometimes the ravens used to give him rides on their backs. He must have been a very small man though or the ravens have shrunk a lot since those days!"

There was a light wind and the Dryadians, apart from Magnus who had gone back down below, sat snugly under the parapet walls in a reverie of soul searching as to the original purpose of the tower. Anaxamander and Ruth in partnership with Sophora had already worked much of it out many years before but wanted the others to find out for themselves using their inner wisdom or intuition. The ravens croaked occasionally and the jackdaws chattered continuously. Otherwise there was complete silence.

"I've just remembered," said Mary suddenly. "There is a story about the Raven's Tower in our repertoire. It's seldom told now but I think it goes something like this. Correct me if I'm wrong Tara. Your memory goes back further than mine."

With the blessings of the ravens, Dryadogenes and all his tribe settled in Dryadia and prospered. They did not live with the ravens but built their homes and villages in the river valleys where clear water streamed down from the moors to the sea. The ravens lived where they always had – on the sea cliffs, on the wild mountains and the wisest of them on remote towers, where Dryadogenes often flew in a blink of an eye to learn their wisdom. He never went alone but always took two companions when he attended the Parliament of the Ravens. In those earliest of times Dryadia was much bigger than it was today and there were Raven Towers all over the British islands. But the peoples of the East lost their respect for the ravens and their precious knowledge, and the towers fell into disuse and crumbled into the earth. The wisest ravens retreated back into Dryadia and the knowledge of the towers was forgotten by all but a few.

"Then it's obvious," said Sam excitedly. "Flying in the blink of an eye; wisdom; three people to keep the knowledge; spiral maps; lambda machines appearing and disappearing; three smooth round floors on this tower at least, though we don't know about the other towers. This place must have been a staging post for lambda machines, where they landed and departed and spread the Dryadian message." Sam looked at Anaxamander almost beseechingly for approval.

"Am I right?"

"I believe you are correct. There is just one other problem we have to surmount before we can confirm what you say. Any idea what that might be?"

Tara got it first. "I can see that lambdas can land on the roof of the tower but what about the two lower rooms. The windows are tiny and the spiral staircase tortuous. No lambda could get through those thick walls in one piece."

"Except that they did," said Pushkin, "but not in material form. Remember the clues are on the walls – those queues of five lambdas fading away into invisibility or rematerialising out of the ether."

"Of course," said Sam thinking of the five ravens spiralling outside the tower earlier. The quintessence, the energy of five. The energy of the spiral that moves us in and out of the physical dimension. Transpiration that's the name of the game. That's how they did it. No mass, no time, no space, just absolute lightness and invisibility. The same way they got the lambdas in and out of the Hall of Records under Mount Cynthos. Find the right vibration and the lambdas can appear, disappear and move effortlessly to the other end of the country. Brilliant, but I've no idea how they did it."

"The knowledge has long been believed to have been lost, but it has almost been rediscovered," said Anaxamander. "Remember our experiments at The Beacons, which we shut down quickly after the helicopters came. We were getting very close to solving that problem though only in a small way."

"And it's now all buried under Mount Cynthos," said Pushkin.

Anaxamander nodded. "Of course, The Hall of Records is the safest place in the country. You all remember the old lambdas there in various stages of undress!"

"Are you now dressing them all up, so they can travel the lambda lines again?"

"Yes, Hermes." Anaxamander seemed pleased with the way they had worked it out."

"Starting with The Beacons, Mount Cynthos and the Tower of the Ravens branch line," exclaimed Tara.

"Yes", said Anaxamander again. "Though I would prefer to call it a short stretch of the main line, as you will see if you look at the diagrams on the wall again.

These are two of Dryadia's greatest secrets. Firstly the knowledge of the lambdas and how to fly them along the serpent lines. The second one is the knowledge of the Quintessence, and how to transpirate effortlessly through it without being concerned about the world of mass, space and time. We are telling you all this because the East is collapsing fast and it's now time that Dryadia comes into its own. We now nearly have the knowledge to open the line between The Beacons and Mount Cynthos and here. I have to say that just coming here today and thinking about that possibility has brought it a little nearer."

"When will that be?" asked Pushkin.

"Not quite yet, but I think very soon. We just have to ensure it's safe."

"When the East's satellites have stopped working, presumably," said Hermes.

"We're almost sure they have," replied Anaxamander. "They're fading fast. A lot of the experts in the East who keep them going are sadly dead or are too frail to service them. We suspect none of them will be working in a few months time and the East's armed forces will be too busy worrying about their own survival to think about us. My brother Empedocles thinks he's almost worked out the technology and Sophora is helping with the short cuts in her inimitable way. Other teams in Dryadia are also about to do some experiments but we are making sure that the knowledge is being kept secret within the Traditional Eldership. Sophora has led several parties of Elders from other provinces to the Hall of Records. As the East dies we hope our knowledge will ensure the world doesn't enter another stone age."

"We'd like to be there when you do the lambda flying experiments," said Sam excitedly while Pushkin and Hermes nodded in agreement.

"Us girls want to be there too," said Melissa. "So long as I or my Sam can keep our feet safely on the ground and don't have to be pilots."

"Don't worry," Sam said consolingly. "You can't crash if you're in the quintessence, and you can make me barley cakes for the journey."

"Don't be silly Sam", added Mary. "How can you eat them when you don't have a proper body? They will transpirate with you and you will have to save them for later."

CHAPTER TWENTY-NINE

AFTER THE FALL

The situation in the East went from bad to worse. It was thought that the population of Europe had shrunk by at least three quarters. No one knew what was going on elsewhere in the world. The experiments in genetic engineering had got so out of hand that the resulting alterations in DNA had weakened people's survival systems – so much so that they were unable to offer much resistance to those infectious diseases that would normally be thrown off easily. None of the Eastern scientists could put their finger on exactly what had gone wrong – it was probably a combination of factors – but they certainly didn't know how to put it right. The majority of people suffered from extreme lethargy and weakness and could barely look after each other or themselves. The periodic epidemics of influenza and super-measles had become almost a blessing, bringing to a quick end the suffering of the old and the sick. The state of the nuclear power stations continued to be a constant worry. No one knew how many had melted down and how much lethal radiation had been released.

Order had long broken down, especially in the towns and cities. There was much looting and robbing by starving mobs. There was no longer any oil. The East had been totally addicted to it and their civilisation was unable to manage without it. A world without oil meant a world without modern transport. It also meant a world without plastic, fertilisers, drugs, computers and television. Only a handful of people were still well enough to maintain the sophisticated technology that had been developed over the last hundred years. In an age of specialism few knew how to look after themselves properly. The developed world now resembled the un-developed one. Buildings started to crumble. Roads started disintegrating as frost and weeds began to uproot the tarmac. In a few years they would cease to exist. The East was lying belly up and dying. Its civilization had been built on quicksand defying the laws of nature and could not be sustained. It seemed unlikely that many people would be left alive much longer.

The Leaky Bucket had been regularly sailing as far as the mouth of the Drangle to see what signs of life lay on the other side. Sailing was the right word for there was now no oil to power its engine. At one time the people of the East used to signal frantically from the shore but the boat dared not land in case the Dryadians were attacked or kidnapped. After several years of pestilence the East had gone quiet. No one waved from the shore anymore. The TV and radio stations, the phones and internet no longer functioned. No doubt in places there were isolated pockets of men living like wild beasts, foraging and farming in a small kind of way in order to scrape a basic living. Few though would be aware of their neighbours if they lived beyond walking distance. In four terrible years mankind had plummeted four hundred years back, to a time where the most important thing was just to survive.

Except for Dryadia. They were not susceptible to the problems of the East. They had not tampered with the genes of plants or animals or those in their own bodies. Nor had they dosed themselves or the soil with dangerous chemicals. They remained healthy. They lived in a country that could support them indefinitely. They possessed a wisdom that would always guide them with hope for the future and provide a safe anchorage in times of trouble.

Since the days of the original Dryadogenes, the Traditional Elders had called themselves *The Watchers of the World* and *The Keepers of the Sacred Wisdom*. These names were only known to themselves and were not used from any sense of arrogance. Only if mankind sunk so low into almost unredeemable brutishness was it envisaged that Dryadia would rise to its original calling. A special moot had been summoned. It was agreed that as soon as it was safe and practical and ways had been found to transport them safely and quickly, some of the Elders would travel to the East.

There, they would offer help to anyone who needed it. Anaxamander and Ruth had recently visited the oracle at the sanctuary and asked how they should engage with the East. Asked two questions: about timing and the likely outcome of any proposed expeditions, the oracle replied:

The only moment that exists is the one that you are in.

True healing only can take place when the broken pieces come together again.

"Let's take that as a yes, then," said Anaxamander when he addressed the moot later.

"And that means no hanging about either." He restated how Dryadogenes had come north to The Land of the Ravens thousands of years ago for the same purpose as well as seeking sanctuary for future Dryadians. He added that the lambda experiments in transpiration and opening the serpent lines were going well, at least on paper, and that the practicalities should be sorted out soon. Sophora also spoke strongly in favour of a lambda powered mercy mission to the East. For the first time since Alanda and Isola's time the descendants of Dryadogenes became excited at the prospect of reactivating their original mission.

"What happens now?" asked Melissa of her father after they arrived home and she and Sam were having some cabin talk with him and Ruth.

"I've already talked to Sophora, as you know, and she has agreed that we can go full steam ahead on the experiments but that she will keep a very careful eye on them. We will especially need to manage the safety angle as we are entering the unknown territory of the quintessence. Once we start leaving and entering the physical world where the material laws that govern space, mass and time no longer apply, we obviously need to be careful. We're planning a big journey soon – to the Hall of Records. We want all the Ceradoc Traditionals to come, including both of you of course. The lambdas are going to fly again. No one is watching us from the sky anymore. Almost all of our equipment and notes are still under Mount Cynthos where we already are doing a lot of initial preparation. Empedocles has been going there regularly and nobody is a greater technician than he, as you know. He's trained up a number of Elders that he can trust, and between them they are constructing some lambdas that at least in theory should be able to both transpirate and fly."

"When are we going?" asked Melissa glancing anxiously at Sam, who was looking just too over excited in her opinion. She preferred the calm of the herb garden and she preferred Sam there too.

"Next week I hope, before winter sets in. We'll be grateful for the constant temperature under the mountain. Please don't worry." Anaxamander smiled reassuringly at his daughter.

"Sophora will use her seership aided and abetted by Amarinta of course to psychically check every step of the way before we go ahead."

"But nobody has been into the Quintessence for hundreds of years"

"You forget I did at least partially, when I flew off the ladder, and I suppose in my adventure on Mount Ida as well, although I have to admit that I didn't know quite know how I did it. I suspect many others have had similar experiences. Knowledge has to progress. Life perishes if it doesn't keep moving and changing, even if it is slowly. Don't worry any of you. It's not our intention that anyone gets remotely hurt in our quintessential experiments."

The winter that year was very cold. Global warming seemed to have been put on hold. A thick frost lay on the ground for weeks on end, even during the day, and the tracks that led over the moors to Mount Cynthos were invisible under several feet of snow. The expedition had to be deferred.

Meantime the Dryadians were glad that their barns were full of grain and potatoes, and enough vegetables and bottled fruit put aside to see them and their animals through to spring. The Elders of Ceradoc however were not idle. The Storytellers had memorised much of the information that they had seen under The Hall of Records and had continuous discussions with the others on the best way to fly a lambda. All were practising their chanting and thought projections. They had even succeeded in making a paper plate rise a few inches above Ruth's kitchen table!

All the two thousand or so Traditional Elders in the country now knew about the lambda way and the great plan to fly east as soon as the technology had been worked out. Some of the more steadfast of the Practicals had also been enrolled in the project to help make the new machines. Not just in Ceradoc, but also in Cantillion and in every province, the Elders were coming together to ensure that the new lambda way was going to work.

At last the great cold melted and a surprisingly early spring arrived in Dryadia. The woods and hedge banks were covered in violets followed by the golden yellow magic of gorse, primroses, celandine and wild daffodils. Sophora and Anaxamander finally fixed a day to lead the expedition to Mount Cynthos. About twenty Traditional Elders of Ceradoc would take part. It took the best part of a day to ride the fifteen miles through the freshly green meadows and woods of the Northern Province to the resthouse on the lower slopes of Mount Cynthos where the bleaker moors began. They left their horses in one of the lower villages and for the final hour they walked single file along a track hemmed in by thickets of gorse and sloe. The countryside became increasingly wilder as it changed into open moorland until at last they reached the rest house where the guardian had a hot meal roasting in the oven.

They awoke to a sea fog rolling in from the Atlantic coast. It muffled the sounds and sights of spring wrapping damp compresses round their necks.

"We can still go," said Sophora seeing everybody's disappointment. "We've done the journey often enough. We'll be fine if we go carefully and I'm sure the sun is bound to break through eventually."

They set off, again in single file. The morning mists swirled around them. They saw imaginary faces in the few trees that managed to lead solitary lives amongst the jumble of stones and marshy bog. Then at last streams of sunlight and warmth managed to penetrate the mist and they saw looming ahead of them, as if to greet them, a large fifteen-foot hunk of granite decorated with slivers of quartz, glinting in the sun as if they had just been newly minted. They all smiled. The Ancient of Days was like an old and much loved friend. This stone marked the place where they had for many years picked up the serpent line that wound its sinuous way to the hidden opening at the bottom of Mount Cynthos. All the Elders had done this journey so often that they no longer needed to take their shoes off to detect and follow the tingle of the serpent's vibration. They all knew by heart the positions of the various standing stones that acted as signposts and stimulators of the lambda line energy.

The sun had melted the last of the mist as they approached the familiar fifty-foot high wall of granite at the bottom of Mount Cynthos. Somewhere within this vertical face of smooth stone was the entrance to The Hall of Records. There was not the faintest sign of any cracks and the opening was completely concealed as if it was the result of a piece of invisible mending. Sophora had invited Sam and Melissa to see if they could open it without her help, as they had assisted her before often enough. They positioned themselves at either end of the wall of stone and walked slowly towards each other. Each had one hand hovering over the granite face trying to pick up an almost imperceptible tingle. They met in the middle where Melissa felt the vibration was beginning to weaken. Then she walked five paces back with Sam following.

"This is where it's strongest," she said looking at Sophora for approval. "This must be the top of the opening. Melissa and Sam then started tracing their fingers downwards, following the subtlest of murmurs within the granite until they felt they had located the edges of the still invisible opening. It was hardly more than three feet square. With one voice they started mimicking the thin sound of the murmur – that thread of vibration that was somehow concealed in the stone face. Every Elder's hand stretched out to touch the entrance of the still closed door. The granite seemed to murmur back in close harmony.

Everyone raised their voices to join in with those of Sam and Melissa. The effect was hypnotic. It seemed funny too. Mary looked at everyone's strained and serious faces and smiled as she realised how ridiculous they would seem to an outsider. She glanced at Tara who winked back at her. Tara then passed her smile onto Melissa who immediately infected Anaxamander. Before long they forgot their chanting, although they kept their fingers on the stone face, and began to roar with laughter. Even Pushkin couldn't keep a straight face. Then their laughter stopped quite suddenly as a slab of stone powered silently it seemed by human energy alone, pushed outwards and then sideways. A dark hole, like an absent tooth, appeared in the smooth base of Mount Cynthos. Even Sophora looked a little taken back.

"The opening has never appeared as quickly as that before," she commented.

"It felt as if we were going through butter," added Ruth. "What happened?"

Sophora smiled. "It was the laughter. It came from the heart, from the quintessential you, if you like, and it lightened us up. We were more serious than we needed to be and the energy around us was a getting a little too heavy."

"So we need more levity to levitate," grinned Sam.

"That's clever," said Melissa. "We need to be lighter in future."

"Then lift off will be easier. We must tell our lambda machines." Anaxamander started to roar with mirth again shaking his great frame as he did so.

As a new round of infectious giggles started again, they crammed themselves through the entrance into the little room beyond. Melissa stretched her arms across the lintel as they uttered the closing chant through muffled laughter. The stone closed almost immediately shutting out the daylight. But they still laughed on while Sam got down on his knees groping to find the lever that opened the inner door onto the stone staircase that led down through the misty blue light to The Hall of Records. The Elders felt so light that they felt they could have floated through the rock but Sophora assured them that they still needed to take great care of their bodies.

As they gathered in The Hall of Waiting Sam and Melissa began rubbing hidden spots on the large door that guarded the three chambers that held the records. Sophora had already briefed them. "The door will speak to you. It will tell you what to do if you listen to its vibrations. It's the exactly the same principle that you used previously when the outside entrance was revealed to you and we got beneath the mountain's skin. Now, first you need to dim the lights. Then more power will be available to raise the door. Once you have found how to do that, by finding the right place to press, you can then begin to find out how to release the nine locks to the door. They have to be opened in the right order. The place with the most intense vibration will be the first one, and so on. At each spot press with heart and mind engaged and trace a circle clockwise around it. When it approves of what you have done it will stop humming. You will then have undone one of the locks. At the second lock you press and trace two circles around it. At the third point, three circles and so on. If you get it wrong you'll have to start all over again. Try and work together and combine your energy. It's a good idea to hum as you work as it calms the brain and you won't get too intense. Otherwise we'll have to start laughing again! Remember that the energy of our hearts and our unconscious is more powerful than that of matter."

The whole procedure took about half an hour of diligent searching until Melissa undid the ninth lock. The great door rose into the ceiling and the blue light inside almost blinded them until Sam managed to dim it further. Sophora had promised that she would teach all the Ceradoc Elders how to open the doors but they would only respond to those whose intentions were honourable and those whom she had 'introduced.' Moreover there always had to be three people present for the doors to open. At the moment only about half the Traditional Elders of Ceradoc knew the induction procedure, including Sophora herself who had worked it out psychically in the first place. It was her intention to pass the knowledge onto the next generation throughout Dryadia as there were so many wise ones now living in the country. In this way the Hall of Records would be protected from unauthorised entry but enough trusted Elders would possess the knowledge to ensure that it would not be lost again.

The Elders found the main hall as they remembered it, apart from the platform on top of the plinth. On it was the circular shape of a lambda machine about ten-foot in diameter. Perched rather cheekily on top of it was a tiny version of its parent, no more than the size of a large dinner plate.

"Not the ones in the museum," explained Sophora pointing to the adjoining Hall of Artefacts. "These are new. We managed to co-opt two Traditional Elders from the west of Dryadia who were skilled in metalwork to make these modern ones based on the original models. The large one is actually a two-seater though one day we will make them a lot bigger than that. The mini version is to play with and might accommodate a bumblebee. All we need to do now is to finish making the machinery and fit it into the lambdas."

She then led them to a small room adjacent to The Hall of Artefacts that had been turned into what looked like a blacksmith's forge. However there was no sign of fire or any hint of iron or steel. There were just strips of copper and tin bent into spirals and wrapped around crystals of varying shapes and colours. They lay amidst the skeleton of yet another partially constructed lambda. In another corner of the room were a number of three dimensional shapes including some beautifully crafted dodecahedrons made from oak embedded with small slivers of sparkling crystal.

"How do you bend the metal into these extraordinary shapes?" asked Sam examining the exquisite workmanship. "There doesn't seem to be any heat available or tools to work with. And why isn't there any iron?"

"In exactly the same way that those psychics in the East bent their keys," replied Sophora.

"With the power of the focused mind and heart. Sometimes we add sound and sometimes laughter to lighten the heart, as you now know. We had to make those sheets small enough to carry them down here in the first place. That's our only very minor problem. We don't use any iron because we don't want the earth's magnetic fields to upset the lambdas."

Pushkin poked around the simple machinery, if you could call anything machinery that had no moving parts or any apparent power source. He was fascinated by its ingenuity.

"Who built this and does it work?" he asked of Sophora.

"Two more of our Natural Philosophers, ones with a scientific bent including our very own Empedocles here." Sophora turned to him and invited him to continue.

"All the original details and designs of the lambdas were stored here, including some very old complete ones as you have seen. Some of you have already made translations from the old records but as they were encrypted they may not have made much sense, unless you had the key and knew what you were looking for. The first prototypes we made were large, complex and clumsy looking. They had no chance of flying.

These latest ones are much more promising. They are smaller and lighter and we believe that we are getting closer to something that can use ethereal energy, which will enable us to transpirate between dimensions. It's called the power of the quintessence, as you all know only too well by now. Then the lambdas will be able to leave the Hall of Records in one piece."

"How can we be sure that they will fly out safely? You know how worried I get about these things," said Melissa.

Anaxamander looked kindly at his daughter. No longer young, though with most of his strength still intact, he still took a keen interest in all the new developments in Dryadia.

"There's no need to worry, the first experiments won't involve humans. We already know that we can move objects short distances. We did that at The Beacons nearly thirty years ago and we've been recently repeating those experiments, though only here within the safety of Mount Cynthos, apart from the mini experiment on Ruth's kitchen table.

They are beginning to work and we're getting better at them. We've managed to raise the lambdas and will soon connect them to the lambda energy in the earth, both up and along. It's a bit like making a helicopter rise and then travel forward but using the power of nature instead of a petrol engine. The main problem is to sustain the energy. We've made the large lambda on the plinth rise twice, though only by a few feet. When we've learned to speed up the vibration a lot more we'll do much better."

"And then crash against the ceiling." It was Mary's turn to feel nervous as she looked up at the steeply sloping sides of the pyramid above and then back at Anaxamander

"Well you would if you stayed in the physical dimension. We don't intend to do an Icarus and fall back to earth and break our necks. We need to leave the material world first, loosing mass and visibility as we do so. The particularly strong energy that spirals up through Mount Cynthos will help us, and remember it's as strong here as anywhere else in the country. Add human power and lambda machine power then we should be all right. We're nearly there. It's all been done on earth before, in a similar way. How do you think they built this extraordinary place or the Great Pyramid in Egypt? It wasn't through the labour of a hundred thousand slaves toiling away for a hundred years as the history books of the East tell us. That's impossible. And how did Dryadogenes fly so quickly around the world? The lambda way is the only way to do it, in our opinion."

"Why don't we do a little experiment today?" asked Sam enthusiastically.

"I'm not sure," answered Sophora. "We've not quite mastered using full power at the moment. It will be easier at the full moon in a couple weeks. I don't think we can yet de-materialise the lambda in absolute safely, which is why we are only operating within the hall. She looked around at their disappointed faces. Our next step was to transpirate the small lambda through the quintessence and out through the walls of the pyramid to The Beacons. We had thought of transpiring a daisy to start with, then maybe a spider. We're not quite ready yet for a human volunteer – might even be one myself one day. What do you think, Empedocles? Could we do a less demanding experiment?"

"I don't see why we couldn't raise the little lambda by a few feet. We have the power of twenty people here. We've done it before, as you said earlier. Let's go and bring it down from the plinth – there's not enough room for us all to stand safely on it." Empedocles fetched a round table and placed it at the bottom of the plinth. He carefully put the little lambda on it. Everyone gathered around as close as they could.

"We'll try and lift it by sound energy," said Sophora. She started humming – a curious otherworldly tune with five different but closely related notes. The others joined in and the little lambda started to tremble as it began to resonate with the human sounds. When the lambda seemed to connect with its own power it started to hum back and spin like a spinning top. Sophora smiled and beckoned them all into silence. For five minutes the lambda hummed away under its own steam causing the four walls of the pyramid to resonate with it, in a kind of celestial harmony. The Elders caught the magic of the lightness and intense bliss of it all as they watched the lambda changing into a shimmering saucer of light. Its humming gradually increased in pitch until it became inaudible. Then it rose slowly, and hovered above their heads until the humming restarted and the lambda gently returned to its place on the table.

Anaxamander looked on in amazement. "We've never had it so high before. That must have been all of ten feet. Such a strange feeling too. I felt I was a part of the lambda – almost inside it, looking down on our bodies as if they were separate from us. I felt a great oneness with the universe. Indeed I felt I was the universe." He smiled broadly at everyone's faces. They understood and smiled back. They all now knew what it was like to cross the border into the strange land of the quintessence.

The news from the East was heartbreaking. Whenever the wind and weather was favourable The *Leaky Bucket* sailed across the mouth of the Drangle towards England. It anchored about four hundred yards from the great city, which it often used to visit, even three years ago. They saw little activity. Green as a relative recent newcomer to Dryadia and having an adventurous spirit had often volunteered to be dropped ashore in his old country to find out what was going on. He had now stopped this activity after having been dramatically chased by starving vagabonds. He was only saved through his shipmates coming close to shore and throwing loaves of bread at his potential captors in order to distract them. They made a quick getaway.

No one knew what was happening in the hinterland of Britain, but it was believed that only a tiny fraction of the population had survived the catastrophe. The Dryadians would have liked to help but their own numbers were small and the dying embers of Britain still uncomfortably hot. They would not enter Britain until they could develop their lambda machine technology so that they could safely fly in and out. They would only land and make contact with survivors if they were completely peaceful. Those were the simple instructions decided by the moot. Nothing would happen though until the lambdas could fly, and enter and leave the physical world at will.

AFTER THE FALL

CHAPTER THIRTY

FLYING LESSONS

One summer day at the time of the full moon Anaxamander and Ruth invited all the Ceradoc Elders and their families to a lunchtime picnic at The Beacons. Only Sophora, Empedocles and his wife Oceania declined, saying they would be otherwise busy on that day. Anaxamander had asked them to all meet at the old sundial there, which had been a favourite gathering point for centuries. They needed to have finished eating no later than three hours after noon and ready to join together in a small period of silence at that time. When their plates were clear, Anaxamander invited them to be quiet and to everyone's surprise started humming the familiar jerky five-note tune that they all remembered from their experiences under Mount Cynthos. Involuntarily they all joined in, and an ethereal dizzy, though not unpleasant feeling, gradually enveloped them.

No more than a few minutes later Anaxamander beckoned them to fall silent but the humming didn't quite stop. The five repeated notes continued but not through human mouths. They seemed to be emitted from an invisible source above their heads. All looked up and thirty feet above the sundial they became aware of a kind of disturbance in the air. It looked like an imperceptible wispy spiral of wind, like the merest flutter of a breeze. For a minute it hovered there, at the edge of their vision, until the apparition started dropping slowly down, the humming fading away as it did so. Then with a strange plop like air escaping from a balloon, it landed in the middle of the sundial. There before them emerging from the ether into the material world was the small lambda that they had last seen under Mount Cynthos. It was slightly warm and shimmered gently in the afternoon sun. Anaxamander stepped forward and pressed the red button on its summit. The lid flew open and he drew out a piece of paper. He read it aloud.

"With love from Sophora, Empedocles and Oceania. Three hours after noon at The Hall of Records."

Anaxamander beamed and smiled, as only he could, like seven laughing Buddhas all rolled into one. "Mass negative. Time negative. Visibility negative. Speed and controllability ultimate. Success perfect. We could not have asked for more. Now lets do another experiment. Can life be sustained within the lambda? Our hunch is – that it can. Now, can anyone find me a daisy? We'll see if we can fly it back to Sophora."

Melissa quickly found one and said: "It's a particularly appropriate flower. The daisy is a herb for bruising and shock, not to mention jet lag. I'm very glad and relieved to hear that you don't want an animal".

"Perhaps later on," replied Anaxamander enigmatically. "Now I agreed with Sophora that I would return the lambda and the daisy to her at precisely three and a quarter hours after noon, Dryadian sun time."

He pulled a large pocket watch out of his jacket. It had been in his family for generations and he was very proud of it though he seldom had a use for it nowadays. "Synchronised with Sophora's. Only seven minutes to go."

He carefully placed the daisy in the little container at the top of the lambda, moved a lever on a dial to a position marked Mount Cynthos and closed the lid. Finally he pressed the red button on its roof. Anaxamander smiled and half closed his eyes. He hummed that same five-note riff that Sophora had shown them previously. They all joined in for a few minutes before Anaxamander signalled them to stop. In the silence that followed, the lambda seemed to almost tremble with excitement like a dog that was about to be thrown a stick. It shimmered and began to spin, humming back the familiar tune before it started melting away.

It rose and hovered some way above their heads, shaking a little in its twilight world before turning slowly as it sought out the lambda line of energy that it needed. Then suddenly it vanished, so fast that no one could tell which direction it had taken.

"If all goes well then Sophora is sending it back in fifteen minutes. Instant feedback. You can get that in the Quintessence."

"Amazing," said Zephyr. "The power of the imagination, the power of the serpent energy and the ingenious lambda machinery. You know one day when we truly believe in our power and use it honourably we might be able to manage without the last two elements. What a beautiful world we could create."

"Last night I virtually did just that, though it wasn't beautiful." added Amarinta. "I visited Australia in my dreams. It was so real. I must have taken a lot of my consciousness with me. I saw that the devastation was just as bad as in Europe. Worse really, as there has hardly been any rain. Very little is growing there."

"It once seemed," said Ruth, "that we used to have three choices in how to live: like beasts , like the East or like Dryadians. Now we have re-discovered the lambda way, we're going to have a fourth one where we may be able to refine and spiritualise our bodies and truly live lightly upon the earth. But we would be still be part of it and care for it.

Seers like Amarinta and Sophora can almost add a fifth way and lead a conscious life while they sleep and barely need a body."

"We need a physical body to live properly in the world," replied Amarinta. "Otherwise how can we help Erith, and each other, to evolve? I like my earthsuit. It likes barley cakes too much for me to surrender it lightly!"

Anaxamander laughed. "It's the lambda way for us then. The lighter we are, with or without barley cakes, then the lighter Erith will become, the greater our consciousness and then the possibilities will be limitless. We have to keep the courage of our convictions. It's going to take us a while though."

"This lifetime?" asked Melissa.

"Maybe next," smiled her father.

The lambda was not long in returning. Did they detect a touch a of eagerness in its demeanour as it settled on the sundial after its return? Perhaps a tiny wiggle of its red button as if it was a puppy returning a ball? When Anaxamander opened the lid he retrieved the daisy looking as fresh as ever. There was another container too, which contained a sizable spider. A note from Sophora was attached asking them to find it a fly and release it. It certainly seemed no worse for its adventure when Sam placed it gently into the nearest gorse bush and it scuttled off.

"Now for the final experiment of the day." Anaxamander took out of his pocket a small box. It squeaked for it contained a tiny mouse. Melissa and Mary looked horrified. This seemed a step too far.

"Don't worry," said Anaxamander. "Squeaky will come to no harm, I'm sure. He'll be back here in fifteen minutes."

While they were waiting for the lambda's return Pushkin started talking about the next step. He knew, as they all did, that the much larger experimental lambda was nearing completion. Although not quite full size it was as big as a very large dining room table and could obviously carry something much bigger than a mouse. He looked at Mary mischievously.

"What about Darwin?"

Mary recoiled in horror, as did Tara, for they both possessed identical twin brother cats called Darwin, and they were forever discussing which of the two were the most intelligent.

Both Darwins were famed for their snootiness and Mary and Tara were convinced that they regularly had serious philosophical conversations under the garden fence at night, especially at the full moon!

"Never Darwin," they said, almost together.

"But he would be the first cat to transpirate," said Pushkin.

"What you don't realise, Pushkin," said Hermes is that the Darwin that is not selected for the journey will never talk to the Darwin that is, ever again. Such is their mutual jealously."

"Our Darwins are far too wise and superior for such capers," replied Tara. "What about one of Anaxamander's cats?"

It was Anaxamander's turn to look alarmed. "Listen, our cats are called Hubris and Nemesis. With names like those they wouldn't stand a chance. I'm sure we can find a stray one that no one is over attached to. We know now that it won't be in any danger."

Their conversation was broken by the sound of a gentle hum from above their heads. The lambda had returned exactly on time. After Anaxamander had opened it there was a squeak and he promptly dived into his pocket for a lump of cheese.

The tragedy of the East weighed heavily on the Dryadian soul. For those like Sam, Mary and Pushkin who were born and brought up there before moving to Dryadia it was especially painful. They had to accept that almost all their families and friends, the ones whom they hadn't managed to persuade to join them in Dryadia, were dead. Letters had stopped arriving a few years ago and although they suspected that there were still pockets of survivors it seemed statistically unlikely that anyone they once knew were amongst them. The small volume of trade that had once existed between Dryadia and Britain had also long ceased. Dryadia was self-sufficient not just because it wanted to but because it now had to. The new situation made little difference to their standard of living and they continued to manage their lives as well as before. Nevertheless an air of melancholy hung over their land. Countries need extensions of themselves in the same way as humans. The Dryadians missed their big neighbour. They may not have talked much but they still liked to know that they were there. The Dryadians felt orphaned and alone in the world, as indeed it seemed they were.

The lambda experiments were coming on well. A simple bit of equipment enabled the lambda to lock on to any available energy in the serpent lines on the earth's surface and warn the pilot if it started straying. This was essential for if the lambda lost its power source then it could crash to earth. The device also located the gateways, the entrances and exits to and from the quintessence. In these places the subtle energy of the earth indicated potential landing and taking off points. Once discovered, all this information was memorised and stored in the machine like a computer's hard drive.

The Dryadians believed that something similar was built subtly into a bird's beak. It enabled it to lock onto an invisible grid system that covered the earth. That's how swallows managed to navigate to Africa and back, even to the place where they were born. Even more amazing were the cuckoos that did the same thing completely alone, not even having had guidance about the journey from any other cuckoo. The answers, the Dryadians felt, were so often to be found in nature.

Quintessential energy, the fifth element, didn't really belong to the physical world, and if you wanted to leave the material dimension you needed to understand it. The lambda's journey started at the gateways where serpent energy spiralled upwards like a spring of water. It was not certain where the spirals ended or whether they just petered out. The Dryadians wondered whether the stronger ones extended well into the earth's atmosphere or beyond, perhaps linking up with wormholes, as the East sometimes called them.

Then it would be possible to travel ethereally through space to distant star systems, without having to be confined to the mass, time and spatial dimensions of the physical world. In theory these huge distances could be travelled as effortlessly as a squeaky mouse transpirating between Mount Cynthos and The Beacons.

Dryadian technology however had now evolved beyond transporting and transpirating squeaky mice. Much to Tara and Mary's relief, no cats had been requisitioned but the new dinner table sized lambda had carried rabbits without mishap not only from Mount Cynthos to The Beacons but also to The Tower of The Ravens and to most of the spiral energy points that lay all over Dryadia. The Dryadians now knew the locations of all the major serpent lines and gateways in their country where a constant energy supply was available. Once they had extended that knowledge across the Drangle they could safely direct the lambdas on short journeys into England.

Nearly a year had passed since the first mini-lambda flew. Every experimental flight since had been a success. The first full size lambda was now sitting on the plinth in The Hall of Records and ready to fly with its first human test pilot. Everyone was confident that nothing would go wrong as the technology was identical to that used in the prototypes. Sophora had offered to be the first pilot and she would take her dog Phaedra with her. Anaxamander and the other Elders were appalled at her idea. Where would Dryadia be without its greatest seer if there were any mishap? She was nearly eighty now, although she was as active as ever, and there were still no sign of any wrinkles on her face. They gave in when Sophora assured them that she had more or less completed the journey already when they weren't looking.

"Just a round trip to The Beacons without stopping. It was easy," she said. "Phaedra could have almost done it by herself. When you fly a lambda on your own, you don't need anyone to help you. The power of sound and a deep belief in an unlimited imagination – that was all I needed. The lambda was already programmed to transpirate and find the serpent energy. With all that to hand, you just enjoy the journey."

All the Elders and villagers of Ceradoc as well as those from the surrounding villages had been invited to The Beacons to witness the first official human flight in a lambda. The Oak Summer rituals had taken place only the day before, so everyone was there anyway, having as usual slept overnight in the Egg. The energy felt particularly potent and everyone that was present felt an inner heightened state of awareness and excitement.

Sophora had been unusually late for the Oak ceremony. She had arrived with Anaxamander and Ruth, all three with strange smirks on their faces. Amarinta sensed straight away what had happened. She whispered to Zephyr:

"I bet Sophora has just arrived by lambda straight from The Hall of Records. She landed in the stone circle, I'm sure. I think Ruth and Anaxamander helped her to hide the lambda in the undergrowth. It's quite light to move. That's why they look so dishevelled and have those guilty smiles on their faces. Sophora wanted to do a dress rehearsal before tomorrow's main event."

The ancient records had revealed that both the stone circle at The Beacons and the Egg had been major lambda landing places in the past and were therefore also gateways, as all the Ceradoc Elders knew by now. After breakfast the revellers were asked to remain in the Egg. At noon they were asked to watch the alter stone as they had done yesterday, when they had seen the lightning flash and the subsequent fire.

At mid-day when the sun was at its zenith, the lightest of hums was heard high above the trees hovering almost directly above the alter stone. It seemed to be emitted from a shimmering mirage that would have been invisible had the sun not been so bright. The lambda dropped very slowly, gaining visibility as it did so. With a final plopping sound it landed gently beside the charred remains of yesterday's fire. Its roof flipped back. There was a loud bark, and Phaedra jumped out followed by a triumphant and beaming Sophora.

A new Dryadian industry had been born. Within a year, a dozen full sized lambdas had been constructed, both two and four-seaters. Many pilots had been trained up. Virtually every able-bodied Elder, recruited from both the Traditional and Practical families, had had a ride. The only rule was that one of the crew needed to be a Traditional Elder as only they had received the training in mind control that was so important. It also meant that powerful knowledge that could create havoc if used unwisely, was kept safe in the possession of a few wise people. The walls of The Tower of the Ravens had now been successfully breached by the lambdas without any physical evidence that they had done so. Three lambdas had nestled safely together within its confines, one on each floor. Lambdas had now visited and landed safely at all the major Dryadian gateways usually marked by a stone or oak circle or a flat piece of ground at the top of a hill. All the main lines into England had been identified, along with the appropriate gateways, and dummy runs had been flown deep into the East.

There were two ways of operating the lambda system. The first was to transpirate into the ethereal dimension after takeoff and remain there until landing at a pre-planned gateway. The lambda was invisible throughout the entire journey. Journey times were virtually nil and the lambda's occupants were more or less un-aware of what was going on as they remained in a dream like state. The other way was to remain in the physical state when flying along the lambda lines and only entering the quintessence if needed for invisible landings and take-offs. Both the lambda machines (their equipment by now highly miniaturised) and the lines were regarded as so reliable that once in the air it was like flying on automatic pilot.

It wasn't long before the pilots had located all the main lines across Britain as well as some promising branch ones. As they flew the lambdas any information on newly discovered gateways found on the serpent lines was immediately transferred and stored not only in the brain of the lambda used on that particular mission, but to all the other lambdas simultaneously. They discovered that the most powerful lines and gateways were in their own country and tended to thin out the further east they travelled. They therefore planned their first landings across the Dryadian border, but initially no further than about sixty miles over the Drangle. As more machines were completed each Dryadian province was allocated an area of England to explore, and if conditions were favourable on the ground, to land. Once an area had been mapped the lambda pilots chose to fly visibly along the lines about two thousand feet or more above the slumbering countryside. This was high enough not to alarm any survivors especially as the lambdas made no sound. As they were so quiet they attracted little attention unless anyone happened to be looking up at the time. The height was also low enough for the crew to get a good idea what was happening on the ground. To help them in this they could vary the lambdas' speeds from a walking pace, or even hovering, to travelling at several hundred miles an hour when the earth energy was particularly strong. If the energy of a line sunk too low (this was only in the branch lines,) then warning bells would ring in the cabin and the lambda would automatically turn round to find a safer path through the sky. Some of these minor lines could only generate enough power when the sun was high; others were governed by the phases of the moon; a few just petered out like an English country lane. The most bizarre one that they found was actually moderated by the orbit of the planet Venus. The great adventure towards the East was under way.

CHAPTER THIRTY-ONE

MAKING CONTACT

The Dryadians soon discovered that there were a number of small colonies of survivors in England – at least there were in the mile or more wide corridors that embraced the lambda lines. They felt certain there were many more colonies that were not so accessible. If they felt reasonably sure that the inhabitants were not aggressive, the lambdas flew slowly and low over their villages, deliberately drawing attention to themselves but not daring to land until they felt completely safe. Communities of course had to be near, but not too near a gateway for a successful landing to be attempted. Sometimes encouragingly the local people waved at them, whilst a few sunk to their knees raising their heads beseechingly as if some long lost God had at last remembered their existence, and had come to rescue them from their misery. There were a few cows and sheep in the fields but only small areas were being ploughed by men with makeshift wooden implements. The lack of oil had put paid to the tractors and heavy horses had not been bred for more than sixty years. They also seemed to have lost the knowledge of using iron – the lack of fuel and expertise both playing their part. The arts and crafts of old England that had been developed over centuries had been almost completely forgotten during an age of intense specialisation, urbanisation and un-sustainability. The people of the East were well on their way back to the Stone Age.

The Dryadians of the Northern Province had identified three gateways in their allocated area in southwest England. All were situated on high ground, on or near tops of sizable hills with good all round views from every angle. At first they concentrated on just one of them and the lambdas landed only briefly, ensuring firstly that no one was near. They were of course watched, and as the lambdas deliberately landed almost every day to gain the confidence of the local people, they soon noticed that a small group of children used to await their arrival at the bottom of the hill. Neither party got too close to the other. To ensure their protection every lambda was now equipped with loud thunder flashes, which if necessary would go off harmlessly but extremely loudly just before they made their escape into invisibility. It wasn't too long before the Dryadians were spending an hour or two outside their machines and exploring the surrounding area, but always leaving someone guarding the lambda in case they needed to make a quick get-away. At the end of their visits they always left small gifts of friendship, usually barley cakes, bread or warm clothes for the children, half way down the hill.

Sophora took a special interest in this particular community and felt that the time had come to speak to the children. Sam, Pushkin and Mary (who were of course English by origin) and a rather nervous Melissa were to accompany her. After flying around the hill a few times at various heights making sure that no one had set up an ambush, the Dryadians landed uneventfully. Three little girls, no more than eight or nine years old, were waiting patiently for them at the bottom of the hill. Pushkin and Sam stayed by the lambda and the three women slowly wandered down the hill until they were within about twenty yards of the children. Sophora raised her right hand in greeting, the age-old sign of peace. The sun was behind the three Dryadians and the children saw them like visiting angels shimmering against the strong light. The children stood their ground looking tense and ready to run if it became necessary.

"Hello," Sophora said simply speaking in English.

"Hello," mumbled the girls shyly in return.

"Do you like barley cakes? We've brought you some."

"We liked the ones you left us last time. They were all raspberry."

"These are raspberry too and blueberry."

"Do you live down there?" Sophora pointed to the village further down the hill.

"Yes. But we're hungry. We don't get enough to eat. Dad says it will be better in the summer when he's got the harvest in."

The girls were not well clothed and it was not a warm day. Their coats were worn and patched, and often re-patched in whatever materials came to hand. Somebody was looking after them though – their hair shone and their faces were clean, but there was a gaunt look about them. They definitely looked as if they didn't have enough to eat.

"Do you live in the sky?" asked the second girl. "Like God and his angels. My mum is an angel now and my brother and uncle."

"Sort of," replied Sophora. At this stage she didn't wish to reveal that they were from Dryadia even if the children may well not have heard of it before. "What's the name of the place you live?"

"Temple Leigh. We only live in a part of it though. My sister and me and our little cousin here are in one of the houses. She pointed to the youngest of the children, who had been quiet up to now. And my dad of course. And our aunty – she's our dad's sister. They look after us."

"What happened to the rest of the village? It looks quite big."

"All overgrown now. We only use twelve of the houses. Most of us died or ran away when I was a baby and I'm nearly nine now. My dad called it the Great Pestilence –there were so many people who lived here who got sick and died. The twelve families are the only ones left."

The oldest of the three girls was eager to talk. She was friendly though unused to strangers. Soon Dryadians and children were sitting down together munching barley cakes. They learned that no more than fifty people scratched a subsistence living in Temple Leigh, through growing what they could and scavenging the rest. There were about half a dozen other children in the village and some attempt was being made to give them a bit of an education. They seldom saw anyone from outside their community and they believed that there were no more than two or three similar settlements within a day's walk of their own village. The villagers didn't seem to be at all aggressive according to the children who were obviously treated kindly by the adults. Nobody was likely to hurt the Dryadians or their lambda. In fact the adults were more frightened of them. All the villagers were aware of the flights and they were already known as 'The Raven People' because of the insignia painted on the lambdas. The children announced their names as Linda, Tracy and Caroline and told them if they came again they would bring some of the other children, especially if they brought some more food.

The Dryadians spent over an hour talking to the children and felt that Temple Leigh was a reasonably safe place to become their first foothold in the East.

"Are you sure you will come again?" asked Tracy as they were preparing to leave.

"In three days time, but only bring your friends. There's no need to tell the grown-ups just yet."

"They know already. They would be too scared to come close. They say you are ghosts, or God or the Devil."

"What do you think?" said Mary gently.

"We think you're very nice, especially if you bring us those scrummy cakes."

"You know what," said Sophora gazing at them intently. "Why don't you make a list of all the things you need? Essential things. Not televisions or mobile phones if you've ever heard of them. But things that would be really useful. You could ask your families too. You can show the list to us next time. We really want to help you."

It was a poignant moment, this first meeting with the East for many years, and it was considered a great success. "Considering what they've been through," said Sophora later, "they've picked themselves up remarkably well. They've not descended into as much beastliness as I once feared they might. We must help them all we can, especially the children. They won't carry so much grief."

Within a few months the Dryadians had made contact with a dozen small communities in the far southwest of England. The meetings were almost all initially with children who in any case were more likely to wander further from their homes in search of adventure. Later the women started to appear and generally the Dryadians found them more receptive than the men. No one was allowed anywhere near the lambdas and the loud and devastatingly bright thunder flashes had to be used only once to keep some overly curious little boys away. Overall their meetings were peaceful, the natives being far too weak and far too grateful for the Dryadian gifts to want to cause any trouble.

Sometimes the Dryadians used their un-manned mini lambdas, known as marimbas. They incorporated a clever device that opened the hatch automatically on landing. Inside was something a bit like a jack-in-a-box that propelled the Dryadians' gifts out of the machine before it closed again and flew away. Before winter set in the Dryadians were in communication with virtually all the southwest communities, even those that were up the branch lines. It was possible though that there were some people still lost in the larger towns, which were difficult to reach. But they guessed that most people had fled to the countryside where they could grow their food more easily.

Only two problems sometimes held up the rapid expansion of the Dryadians. One was the security angle. Despite taking great precautions one lambda had been ambushed and its four passengers taken prisoner. Fortunately every lambda was in constant silent communication with its base back in Dryadia, as well as all the other operational lambdas, in case anything amiss happened. On that one occasion a lambda was immediately dispatched to investigate. It hovered above the captors and loosened a number of thunder flashes. They quickly fled leaving the Dryadians behind. Fortunately the prisoners had not been harmed nor the lambda damaged, and they managed to fly off safely. It was a close thing though, and no lambdas visited that place for quite a time.

Another problem was that of excessive veneration. Some communities, especially if they had had a religious background, treated them like gods. Sophora warned them that this might happen for in her far seeing memory she could see that this had occurred in the past. More than a few ancient so-called gods had merely been space travellers, much as the Dryadians were now. Most of these old Gods were not divine beings at all, but just ordinary people with some advanced technology. Some of them might have been wise like the Dryadians with the well being of others at heart. Most though were not, and often were hardly any more than glorified pirates of the sky. They were no better than the people on the ground, whom they sought to dominate, rob and enslave.

The Dryadians were creating a new world. Originally they had not sought to do this but now there seemed to be no choice. In their hearts they knew that this was their destiny if the earth fell into too low a state. The Elders felt that it was inevitable that the catastrophe had happened, although they felt broken hearted at all the human suffering it had caused. They realised that the world deserved a rest from the heavy thoughts and actions of men. The earth was like a field that needed a fallow period after becoming exhausted from a long time of continuous cropping. They knew that the earth would have been unable to carry its enormous population much longer. Too many people had regarded it not as a living entity but merely as a source of material wealth.

The Dryadians now took a delight in its greening as trees invaded the cities, and clear and sparkling rivers found their own way to the sea through moors and valleys that had not been so alive for half a millennium. They wanted to do every thing in their power to ensure that the earth would never suffer like that again. They did not necessarily want everyone to live as they did but they knew that their principles were spiritually sound and naturally based. The principles worked well so long as big egos, with thoughts of fear and greed fostered by ignorance, did not get in the way. The Dryadians wished to teach the remnants of the East how to move towards a sustainable and harmonious future. They started with simple gifts of food, before teaching the essential ingredients of living a civilized but simple life. They reminded them of the arts and crafts that they had virtually forgotten. With their permission, volunteers from Dryadia came to live amongst them to consolidate what they had learned. When they were ready they were taught the perennial wisdom that is the birthright of all men. The Dryadians had considered inviting some of them into Dryadia where they could be taught there but eventually they thought that it would be better if their country remained a secret to all but a few like-minded students. Dryadia would still continue to be a land apart.

Meanwhile the Dryadians were continuing to develop their lambdas. They experimented with different materials. There were even wooden lambdas made from oak, ash or yew. The equipment was becoming increasingly sophisticated in what it could achieve but never lost the simplicity of its original design. Outsiders could never replicate a working lambda because they would not be able to understand how important the role of human energy played in their operation. Nor would they understand how to harness the energy of the lambda lines. The Dryadian philosophy was that the best inventions were very simple, as were the best ideas. The most difficult bit was the first step. They were totally fascinated by the power of the serpent or lambda lines that they now realised enveloped the world. The possibilities of exploration seemed limitless. The gateways also offered undreamed adventures into other dimensions, although they were treading carefully, for this was unknown territory and perhaps dangerous ground. They wondered how far up into the atmosphere the spirals stretched. Would they even be able to fly the lambdas into space one day? The Dryadians were beginning to realise that there was no good reason why they shouldn't.

Within a year the lambdas were operating and making contact a hundred miles away from their borders, almost half way across England. Moreover they were regularly flying over most of Britain being limited only where the earth energy was weak or non-existent. They had reached Scotland and even crossed over the sea to Ireland, where in some places the lines seemed to be very strong. If they flew high enough and used binoculars they reckoned that there were very few areas they hadn't covered. The human situation was the same all over the country. They had estimated that there were no more than a hundred thousand survivors living in about a thousand communities. Even those numbers were in decline, as the Easterners discovered they lived better if they amalgamated their smaller settlements. The Dryadians actively encouraged this especially as it made their rescue and teaching efforts more manageable. It still meant that each Dryadian province would eventually be trying to oversee almost a hundred settlements a piece – a Herculean task. The emphasis was on helping each community help itself. Lambda visits were usually arranged on a monthly basis although a Dryadian often took up temporary residence to speed the process up. Unfortunately there were not enough Elders to go round, so tasks were allocated to Cantillion graduates and even to existing students in their vacations. Where ever possible, local people were taught to teach others and so spread the newly acquired knowledge to other villages nearby.

The Dryadians had discovered a very powerful energy line that stretched from the west of Ireland through Dryadia and across the sea into France. From there it went on through Italy, Greece and the Aegean to the Levant. There were many significant gateways along the line, many marked by old castles and monasteries. The lambdas made many journeys along this line both physically, and ethereally when they wanted to move fast. When their confidence grew they decided to follow it further. Could it be that this line stretched around the world? Lambdas made searching flights in the physical dimension to half way across Europe, and even to the west coast of North America where they found a further series of gateways. They reported the same devastation that they had found in Europe. They felt reasonably sure that the two ends of the line joined up and fantasised that there might be a convenient gateway on an idyllic island in the middle of the Pacific Ocean. A perfect Dryadian outpost in the sunshine and hopefully once they had summoned up the courage to make the journey, it would be reasonably easy to reach!

Although many of the Elders were teaching and travelling in the East, Dryadia was so stable and at peace with itself that domestic life carried on in much the same way that it always had. The Elders were only too aware that with the collapse of the East, there was no longer any opposing force for it to push against. There was a vacuum. The Dryadians hoped that they could overcome this problem by rising to the fresh challenges in the East and through exploring the world in their lambdas. They were under no illusions of the difficulties involved. It had taken thousands of years to bring Dryadia to the state that it now was. They had never forgotten that it had almost imploded four hundred years ago when it lost faith in its own principles before Alanda and Isola rescued them from their own folly.

Half the British communities now had semi-resident Dryadians in their midst or at least very regular lambda visits. The most aware were offered places at the university of Cantillion on their three-year course. Then they could return to the East, taking their new knowledge with them. The local people remained largely in awe of the Dryadians and there was little conflict. The task would take generations but the Dryadians believed that everyone was born with a pure heart and if they were continuously reminded of their inner wisdom then men would become truly human.

Sam and Melissa were now much respected as Traditional Elders as well as being leading Therapeutae. They had recently paid another of their regular visits to the oracle at Sanctuary Hill. They went in search of guidance that summed up the new lambda way and the surrender of the traditional Dryadian insularity.

If you ignore what is within you, then you may find yourself without.

All the provinces were putting a lot of energy into lambda exploration. The Northern Province was still very much in the forefront led by the Elders of Ceradoc, who largely dominated the long distance flights, not that it was in any sense a competition. They of course had had a head start because of Sophora's wisdom and the knowledge they had obtained from The Hall of Records. Entry to the hall was still only open to a few, mainly to those whom Sophora had personally vetted, although she was delegating much of her work to the younger Elders who were rapidly rising in wisdom.

Sophora had long been wondering whether there were other isolated groups of wise people around who had survived the catastrophe. It was possible that some of them had a Dryadian heritage. If there were, then she was eager to find them.

The ancient knowledge though could never be entirely lost. It existed eternally in the great energy field that enveloped the earth. Exceptionally sensitive seers like Sophora could tap into this field at will if necessary. The oracles also were a source of the traditional wisdom. The stories extracted from the Hall of Records seemed to confirm that there were, or at least had been, other groups of Dryadians scattered around the world, although it seemed that Dryadia had been the biggest. The oracle was hinting at the same thing and at the next moot it was agreed that the next stage of the lambda way was to seek out any like-minded communities that might be still living quietly in secluded corners of the world.

CHAPTER THIRTY-TWO

TO THE ENDS OF THE EARTH

If there were such a Dryadian colony existing outside Dryadia, Sophora sensed that it was probably lost somewhere deep in the Himalayas, inaccessible to outsiders and far away from civilisation. Unlike Dryadia, such a place had never been described let alone visited, although there were a number of legends around, which mentioned Shangri-La type lost valleys. However, nobody knew quite where any of them were. Sophora could see such a place in her mind's eye but unfortunately was not sure of its location or how to get there She thought that it might not be on a major lambda line, more on an obscure tributary. She was sending thought forms in the hope that the community did exist and in some way might be able to reply. Sophora though believed that they had no wish to be found for when she felt she was getting near them, she got the impression that they were immersing themselves in their own defensive thought forms. It felt like a foggy wet blanket.

After many months of trying Sophora felt that the protective blanket was becoming less dense than it was, and that someone was aware of her presence. However the only faint acknowledgment that she picked up was that the recipients, whoever they were, needed to be convinced that the Dryadians' intentions were honourable and peaceful.

"It's very important to pitch the question absolutely right," said Pushkin for about the third time as he and the three others consulted the oratory as to the whereabouts of any hidden Dryadias. "If it's precise then we are more likely to get a good answer. If you ask vaguely than it will answer vaguely."

"How about," said Mary, "tell us your exact position with relevant latitudes and longitudes. You can't get any more precise than that."

Sam and Melissa laughed but Pushkin was upset. He liked to be taken seriously in such matters. Before he saw the twinkle in Mary's eye, he retorted: "It's subtle, the answers really come from inside us. It's unlikely that anyone would have programmed the oracle with such measurements specially if they want to remain hidden. You're a poet. Put the question in poetic language."

"Oh dearest Pushkin. You should know by now that you can't be precise and a poet."

"Why not ask first," said Sam thoughtfully, "if they wish to be found and having digested Sophora's thoughts, would they like to communicate with us?"

"That's very polite Sam," said Melissa smiling at him admiringly. "That is of course what we'll do first. Let's all concentrate on that question together for a minute and see if the oracle approves of our request?"

Mary climbed down the ladder and read a small part of the illuminated pillar.

Like seeks like and can do no other

Dryadogenes' children should seek each other

"That sounds encouraging," Pushkin shouted back.

"And it's a sort of poem," replied Mary trying to sound conciliatory.

After Mary rejoined them they tried hard to work out the next question.

"Well it looks as if at least they are considering about communicating with us just as Sophora thought," said Sam. "I know why don't we simply ask: How can we best find each other? That's straightforward enough. The oracle will hopefully give us a straight answer. Let's all project that thought."

When they had finished, Sam readjusted the shutters and curtains and Melissa followed the newly created beam of light that ended in a dance high up on one of the pillars. She needed to stand on a chair to read it.

"My, this is a long one," she called out.

In the earliest days, Dryadogenes' children were scattered all over the world, spreading the divine wisdom and finding safe havens for themselves. All the colonies were in communication with each other by way of a great web using the lambdas, and following the serpent lines and spiral gateways of the world. The most important centre of the communication hub was in Arabia.

"Well, that's precision for you," said Mary.

"Arabia is enormous. Do you know just how big it is?" commented Pushkin.

"I do O wise one. We only need to locate the gateways though. And doesn't the big line that goes all the way round the world go right through Arabia?"

The four of them were sitting around the table in Melissa's kitchen. Maps and books were scattered amongst the teacups. In their midst was a large globe with a number of lengths of coloured string drawn tightly around it. Sam placed his finger on the red one and traced its path from a point at the most southerly place in Dryadia, the site of a spectacular rocky mound three hundred feet high and almost entirely surrounded by sea. It was known as Dryad's Leap. There were many legends about the rock mainly concerning Dryadogenes. This was his first landing place in Dryadia after the ravens brought him here. It was also the last place that he saw when he left Dryadia to travel round the world. It was said that his tears of grief filled a large lake that lay nearby. It was also, the Elders had discovered, the site of a particularly powerful gateway, only rivalled by that of Mount Cynthos and The Egg at The Beacons.

"What do we know about the gateways of Arabia?" asked Pushkin. "Sam and I have never travelled anywhere near. Too long, too hot and too dusty."

Sam and Pushkin were keen lambda travellers and often made journeys together.

"Sophora and Anaxamander did an ethereal journey once and she managed to retain enough consciousness to make some notes about it afterwards. In fact I have a copy here."

He rummaged through a file on the table. "Good thing I'm organised."

He grinned and pulled out a large piece of paper. On it, superimposed on a long strip of a map of the world that confined itself to a thirty-mile corridor that linked Dryadia and Arabia, were marked the major gateways on the route.

It wasn't just one straight line that had been drawn in the middle of the corridor. Within it, Sophora had also marked in fine ink, two lines winding in and out of each other, like a caduceus or a strip of DNA. Wherever the lines crossed, usually on or near the centre of the corridor, there were gateways, which Sophora had delineated with big circles. She regarded the two lines as male and female, or straight and curved energy, as she put it. There was a slight difference in the feel of their energies. To highly sensitive seers like her, the male one seemed direct and purposeful, the female gentler and more sinuous.

Where they met, and there might be many miles between meetings, it was if they had mated and the resulting combined energy then vanished into the ground. Renewed and reinvigorated, a spiral of energy reappeared, rising from a sibling gateway nearby. The energies then separated again and both lines proceeded with their journeys along the corridor. These gateways marked the places where power was available to allow the lambdas to land and take off. They pored over the precious map all wondering which one of the three Arabian gateways marked, was the one that was presumably referred to by the oracle.

"Let's look at Dryad's Leap in the south of Dryadia. Sophora says that six major lambda lines meet here. It's like one of the railway junctions that used to exist in England. As we know, the line that we are interested in right now goes to Arabia one way and America the other. Another one crosses England and probably travels to Scandinavia. The other two are Dryadian branch lines, one of which joins up with The Beacons."

Pushkin continued. "Now look at what Sophora says about the three Arabian gateways. The northern one has three exits. The first is the continuation of the one we will be travelling on. Another goes towards India and there's one that seems weak and insignificant. The middle one had no tributaries that she can detect. The most southerly Arabian one is quite near the coast and you then have a choice of continuing your journey in five possible directions. All go across the sea except the one that travels to India, but probably not in quite the same direction as the line at the first gateway. We won't know which one to take until we get there. I don't suppose by any chance you're free tomorrow, Sam? We could do a reconnaissance expedition."

Mary and Melissa glared at them.

"It's not a bird watching trip, Sam," cried Melissa. Lambda trips to England are one thing, even France and Italy, but you've never travelled so far before."

"Let some of the younger ones do these long journeys," added Mary. "Like Amarinta's nephew Ponchus who lives in Cantillion. He was on the first trip to America. He's only twenty-five and already an experienced pilot. That's nearly thirty years younger than you, Pushkin. You're far too precious to me to lose."

"And Sam to me", echoed Melissa. "We're not letting you go."

"Boys need adventures," complained Sam.

"Boys do," answered Melissa. "But not middle-aged men. Mary and I are not letting you fly so far away."

"Then we'll have to send our children."

"I don't think so. They're far too young."

"Only a few years younger than Ponchus."

"I've got an idea," said Pushkin thoughtfully. "All the lambdas have at least four seats now. All of us have at least travelled into England many times both physically and ethereally. We all know it's safe. The journey to the Himalayas and back won't take more than a week. Why don't we all go together? Then no one will worry about anyone else."

Mary and Melissa looked appalled at the idea, before Mary weakened.

"It could be a lot of fun, like travelling to Dryadia from England for the first time all those years ago. And now we're going to look for a new Dryadia in the Himalayas and if we find it, Dryadia won't be alone in the world anymore." She smiled and continued:

"Now what am I going to wear?"

"All right I'll come too. I certainly don't want Sam to go without me," said Melissa. "Have you thought of one thing though? Those terrible nuclear power stations. There are hundreds in the world and we all know that most of them are in melt down. The earth is becoming a very dangerous place. We've already make sure that none of us land within twenty miles of the British ones and one of them is horribly close to Dryadia.

Do we know whether there are any power stations on the line to Arabia or in India or anywhere near the Himalayas for that matter?"

"We've thought of that," answered Pushkin. "We've got another map of the world showing them all. Sophora and Amarinta have psyched into most of them as to how lethal they are. We believe there is only one really dangerous one on the line, on the northern coast of France. We certainly won't be stopping there and we can fly over it ethereally if necessary, where we know we will be safe. That's the only one that we could be in danger from. We know that there are none in the Himalayas. Reactors tend to be built near the sea for cooling purposes. The people of the East were completely insane over nuclear power. They ignored the fact that global warning is causing the sea to rise and that will flood the reactors eventually. They even built some on earthquake fault lines. There was also no long-term strategy or technology for storing nuclear waste. Their attitude was that everything would be all right in the end because future generations would sort it out. Three generations have passed since the first reactors started working and hardly anything was sorted out. Then came the catastrophe so now no one will deal with all that toxic waste – ever! If only Dryadogenes and his friends had left some instructions for us under Mount Cynthos on how to deal with the problem. So it's left to us Dryadians, a totally innocent party, to work around this horror story and the radiation that will be dangerous for hundreds of thousands of years to come. It makes me very angry."

It was a sobering thought if not a new one. Mary brought them back to their senses by reminding them of what the oracle once declared when they were feeling depressed.

Low spirits sink. High spirits fly.

It took a week to prepare for the journey, rather more than the optimistic whole day that Pushkin and Sam had at first thought. Initially they had planned to fly from The Beacons to Dryads Leap and catch the eastbound lambda there. But as it was the anniversary of their original journey to Ceradoc from Cantillion and as the weather was good they decided to make that original journey in reverse over-land, and then spend an extra day travelling in the southern part of Dryadia to Dryads Leap. It would be a kind of pilgrimage for them in honour of their first visit and as Mary said rather flippantly:

"If we don't return, then our last thoughts will be of our final Dryadian journey."

"Of course we'll be back," replied Melissa. "We can't leave our children as orphans. I hope they won't miss us too much."

Most of Ceradoc saw them off as they sailed away from its tiny jetty across the estuary on the first stage of their journey towards Viribus.

The plan was to transpirate straight away at Dryads Leap and then travel invisibly along the great eastern lambda line to the first gateway in Arabia that they had already identified as having a tributary line heading towards India. They then would materialise into the physical world and take stock. The lambdas were much more sophisticated than the early ones. The chanting and humming that were once necessary for taking off could be created by the machines themselves although the pilots still needed powerful thought forms to find the correct resonance. They had first been introduced to these techniques at the university at Cantillion, and had practised them ever since. Dematerialisation could now be made at the throw of a switch at any time during the flight. They could disappear at will – a good safety feature too if ever they felt threatened. A pre-programmed device chose in advance the gateway the lambda should materialise at. All the gateways were numbered and the information locked into all the lambdas' brains.

The number of Dryads Leap was one. The number of the first gateway they would reach in Arabia was twenty-four and the relevant switch had to be pressed twenty-four times. This was done before take-off and they would recover consciousness just as they landed in Arabia. Get the number wrong and they would wake up somewhere else.

Take-off was uneventful. Pushkin and Sam were the pilots. Mary and Melissa sat behind them half frozen in fear – they had not flown ethereally before. For a few minutes they sat in silence concentrating with all their being until Sam told them all to lighten up a bit. Mary giggled and made a silly joke. The lambda shuddered and murmured in response. Sam and Pushkin pressed a few switches including the vital one that needed to be pressed twenty-four times. The four explorers felt their bodies evaporate into jelly and their brains drift into unconsciousness and then they remembered very little more.

"I suppose we counted right," said Sam as he looked out of the lambda's window at the hot shimmering sand outside. "I'll turn on the lambda gateway finder. Yes it says twenty-four. Ladies and gentlemen, we have just landed safely at Arabia's northern gateway. I hope you all enjoyed the journey."

Mary giggled. "I had some lovely dreams, about Dryadogenes I think. He said the journey would be better later on! How long did it take us?"

"About two minutes," murmured Pushkin.

"Bit early for lunch," said Mary. "What shall we do now?"

"Let's work out our options," answered Pushkin in his deliberate way. "Sophora said there were three exits that she could see. Let's see what the lambda direction finder says, now that we are here."

He twisted a green switch and looked at the dial and peered at it for few seconds. "Good, it confirms Sophora's ideas. There are just three exits. The round-the-world one that we are already on and which eventually will go out to sea when it has finished with Arabia. There's the weak one, which we will give a miss of course. And a powerful one that points to India. But is it this one or the other Indian one at the third Arabian gateway?"

"If we take this Indian line, how do we know which gateway to land at?" asked Mary. "And how do we know where the gateways are anyway? We are in completely uncharted territory."

"I was asking Sam about that yesterday. He said that Empedocles had incorporated another idea that he had found in The Hall of Records. It was something to do with bees at which point I lost him." Melissa looked at Sam in puzzlement.

"Well you know how bees wiggle their bottoms and point them towards a supply of nectar to help their fellow bees find the appropriate flowers. And I believe that the number of wiggles indicates how far away the blossoms are."

"I remember Mum telling us that when Zach and I were children. I'm afraid we used to mimic the bees in our garden when we were trying to find something. I don't see the connection though – but I have just seen a switch with a bee on it."

"Otherwise known as a gateway finder," answered Sam. "As always it's all to do with numbers. The energy of five moves us in and out of the quintessence. The energy of six as we all learned at Cantillion is the energy of combining and relating and also limiting. That means reaching out towards something outside us and knowing when to stop. The gateways are like sources of nectar and the lambda can find them up to more than a thousand miles away until it is limited by the curvature of the earth. Clever creatures, bees. We could learn a lot from them. They even build six sided cells like our houses. It's the energy of six that prevents us spiralling out of control."

Pushkin directed the lambda through ninety degrees until it locked onto the Indian line. The machine hummed contentedly. Then he pushed the bee switch, and the lambda started gently nodding up and down.

"Heavens," said Mary, "it's doing a bee dance."

"That's the easy part," replied Pushkin.

"Now what we have to is to do is to send a beam of lambda light down this corridor towards India." He pressed another button and the lambda became absolutely still, frozen in space. A screen displayed a succession of rising numbers before stopping at 1440.

"That means 240. We have to divide all numbers by six as we are using the energy of six. That means that the first gateway is 240 miles away and its position is now programmed into the whole lambda system." He pressed the bee button again and the screen ran on until it stopped at 2940. "Divide by six. The second gateway is 490 miles from here, and the information is now all saved into its little bee brain."

All the time Sam had his map on his knees plotting out the distances with a ruler and pencil. "The first gateway is probably near Baghdad, perhaps close to ancient Babylon. The second one is in Iran, not far from Isfahan. That's another very old and holy city."

Pushkin pressed the bee button again allowing the lambda light to penetrate even more deeply along the energy corridor. The lambda was humming particularly vigorously which meant that it was locked onto a very strong energy line indeed. The screen stopped at 6066 – 1011 miles away.

"That's in Afghanistan – just over the border," calculated Sam. "It's definitely on track for the Himalayas."

"I don't think the light will shine any further from here," replied Pushkin. "We'll have to travel to that third gateway in Afghanistan to see any further ahead. I vote that we programme the lambda and wake up in what is probably another desert. If we travel ethereally we'll be there in a flash."

They landed in a desert, rockier and bleaker than the one that they had just left in Arabia. Sam opened the hatch and the four of them clambered out. The sun was fierce and there was definitely no shade where they might have the hoped-for lunch. The most interesting thing about their landing place was that the lambda was encircled by a number of flattened and unobtrusive stones obviously man-made and marking the gateway that presumably was in Afghanistan, 1011 miles away from their last stopping off point.

"I don't like it here one little bit", grimaced Melissa.

"The circle is interesting though," said Pushkin thoughtfully. "I wonder when it was last used. It could have been hundreds or even thousands years of ago. Perhaps there was rain then and there wasn't a desert. There's certainly not much here now."

They climbed back into the lambda cheered by the deep croak of a pair of ravens flying low overhead. They would travel on. There was nothing to keep them in this barren world.

"The line is still very strong," said Pushkin happily. "Let's shine the lambda light along it and see if we can find some more gateways."

"Preferably ones that are a bit more hospitable," added Mary hopefully.

Pushkin started pushing the various switches including the bee one, which caused the lambda to quiver as it shone its ethereal torch up to a thousand miles eastwards in search of the next gateways. Sam plotted the co-ordinates on his map (they had forgotten the lambda could do that job for them when they were in Arabia) and hoped fervently that they were getting near the foothills of the Himalayas.

"34 degrees north, 75 minutes east. The lambda doesn't calculate seconds for some reason. Where's that roughly, Sam?"

"Kashmir," Sam replied excitedly. "Quite high up but hopefully not freezing, probably not too far from a big lake. Lots of birds no doubt."

"And wolves and bears," said Melissa. "We'll need to be careful. I hope someone remembered to check the thunder flashes."

"We'll soon find out," answered Sam, as Pushkin started preparing for take off into the quintessence. With a slight tremor the lambda melted away as if it had never been and re-appeared almost instantaneously hovering over a small green island in a vast lake surrounded by mountains. It wasn't quiet. The screeching from hundreds of noisy parakeets saw to that.

The parakeets woke them at dawn and allowed them no more sleep. As they unzipped their sleeping bags the sun rose dramatically between two snowy mountains across the lake. Once they had accustomed their eyes to the growing light they realised that they were not alone and were being intensely studied. A troupe of curious monkeys had almost encircled them and were sitting motionless on their haunches like dozens of furry statues.

"I hope they're not hungry," said Mary anxiously.

Sam laughed. "I'm sure they are as vegetarian as any of us. Walk towards them and I think you'll find they are more nervous than you are."

"Why don't you?" retorted Mary

Sam got up and walked slowly towards the nearest monkey who then inched away backwards from him at the same speed.

"I only think they want to share our breakfast," said Melissa as she fetched down supplies from the lambda. "The problem is that we may all have similar tastes."

The monkeys kept watching. They seem to have emerged from the small forest that covered the central area of the island. The lambda had landed on a small ridge, which looked down on both woods and water. From their perch they could see that the island was no more than a few hundred yards across and so was unlikely to harbour either humans or dangerous animals. The island was one of many that studded the enormous lake, all wooded, like emeralds in a sea of sapphire.

Snow-capped mountains ringed the horizon east, north and west. Only in the south, which they guessed looked towards the plains of India, were the hills lower and less dramatic.

Breakfast over; they set off together to explore the island. There were plenty of paths through the forest possibly made by the monkeys themselves who were following them excitedly at a safe distance. Melissa had made the fatal mistake of throwing them the leftovers. The island was certainly unpopulated by humans but they were not sure whether that had always been the case. Who brought the monkeys here, in the first place? The shores of the lake were at least two miles away. Surely monkeys couldn't swim that far. Pushkin remembered that the animals were sacred to the Hindus and wondered if they had been brought here and whether there was a lost temple somewhere on the island. Possibly it was thousands of years of years old and long buried under the forest creepers. Lambda gateways often shared places with ancient sites of worship, which was not surprising as both schools of thought were attempting to link up with the same energy connection, although for different reasons. Sam was scanning the far shores with the lambda telescope. There were no signs of life. Had Asia been affected by the catastrophe, as much as the rest of the world or was this just an uninhabited area?

They returned to the lambda from a different direction and Mary suddenly had a thought that the huge mostly overgrown forty foot rock that they had landed by, was perhaps not as natural as it first seemed. The monkeys enjoyed clambering over it and chattering at them from its pinnacle. They noticed that on the other side hidden from view was a favourite monkey path spiralling up to the top. It was stepped and built into the wall of the mound and although crumbling and half reclaimed by the jungle, it was not too hard to climb.

The steps led up to a smooth platform, invisible from below and smoothed out from the rock like a children's' playground, largely kept clear by the continuous games of the monkeys. Around its perimeter were eight statues standing like caryatids in a Greek temple. It slowly became apparent that the platform was octagonal with a statue at each of its eight corners. The torsos of the figures were clad in simple robes as if they were from Greece. They definitely were not Indian or from any where in the Himalayas so far as any of them were aware. The heads were a puzzle – they weren't human at all. They were birdlike with exceptionally large beaks. The four of them looked at each other in awe. There was no doubting it – these statues all had raven heads.

"Are there ravens this far east?" Pushkin asked of Sam.

"I did some research just before we came. They are probably getting towards the end of their range, but yes, there are ravens in the Himalayas."

On the far side of the platform there was an old octagonal building, still roofed but in a wretched state. It had not obviously been visited for some time. An opening in one of the walls beckoned them into a scene of chaos. It was now a home for undomesticated monkeys who had destroyed most of the furnishings. Tables, chairs and carpets lay mouldering on the floor in the last stages of decay. Windows gaped open like holes in ancient jaws. The wall showed faint outlines of writing, all sharpness and colour long gone, but there was no doubt about their significance. There were ravens in flight, their wing tips splayed and massive beaks open as they croaked. They were tumbling and diving through the sky. Others were nesting on the tops of giant trees or rocky outcrops. There were raven men standing on mountaintops lifting their eyes towards the heavens. In other places were depicted elliptic orbs some still with flakes of silver or gold paint still sticking to them. These orbs, like the eyes of Horus, appeared to be flying at every possible angle, some etched deeply, others in outline as they faded away. They were similar to the engravings on the walls of the Tower of the Ravens in Dryadia. There could be no doubt what they represented.

Pushkin scratched his head in amazement. "They must be a thousand years old, as ours are, or at least created from folk memories. There's no way they could be recent surely. It would be like finding humans on another planet."

"We mustn't be so arrogant to think that other descendants of Dryadogenes didn't have the knowledge to fly lambdas in the same way we do," said Mary.

"The spy satellites would have picked them up if they had flown recently unless they made them as invisible as their country. And if they are clever enough to hide a country from prying eyes, then flying a lambda should be a doddle in comparison," added Sam.

"I think we should go on now," said Melissa when they had examined every inch of the temple. "We won't find anything more here and we need to make contact with our country cousins if of course they are still around. I hope they survived the catastrophe."

The lambda rose gently in the air over what was now marked on Sam's map as the Island of the Ravens even if he had not spotted any of the avian kind. They had decided to fly the next stage of their journey in the physical dimension so that they could keep a sharp eye on what was going on at ground level. Lambdas made no noise and if they flew reasonably high they probably wouldn't be seen. Inside the lambda, only the slightest tremor and murmur of the machinery, which had barely any moving parts, gave any clue that they weren't watching a beautiful travel film on the foothills of the Himalayas. There were villages below with small populations but they passed over virtually unnoticed. It seemed that the catastrophe had not been so severe in the wilder parts of Asia where perhaps they had not been exposed to the diseases of Europe and America and practised a much greater degree of self-reliance.

There was a change of plan. They could not risk landing amongst strangers who might not turn out to be friendly. Pushkin and Sam felt the lambda should travel to the next gateway about three hundred miles east from The Island of Ravens. The lambda had informed them that the energy was very strong there. Pushkin took the lambda up to a thousand feet and pressed the bee button. The craft started turning slowly and twitched a little like a cat sniffing for scents wafting in on the breeze.

The cockpit instruments were very simple. Just a joystick to control speed and direction and five switches in different colours each etched with a distinct design – a bee, a raven (manually controlled flight), a swift drawn like the letter lambda (take-off and landing), a dodecahedron (transpiration into the quintessence) and a caduceus with two serpents twining around one another (locking onto the serpent lines). Above each switch was a small screen linked to the lambda's brain. Anaxamander used to joke that the lambda was much more intelligent than its pilot – it could virtually fly itself so long as it could connect with both human energy and serpent energy. When you understood this energy and knew how to use it, as the four of them did, flying was a simple affair, but as Anaxamander often said, it takes a long time to learn to be simple.

As the lambda was looking for the most suitable energy corridor, wavy reddish brown lines were appearing on one of the screens. A close reading of the lines showed the best path to follow and the best landing place. There were a few weak lines emanating from the place the lambda was hovering over but the one that they had locked onto ever since they had left Arabia still seemed the best, so they agreed that they would keep following it. The next gateway seemed to be in southern Tibet not far from the Nepalese border and about three hundred miles away. They would continue to travel in the physical dimension so they could observe the countryside beneath them and the increasingly high mountains around them.

As they neared the next gateway there was an explosion of light on one of the screens that indicated they were connecting with its spiral even though they were about twenty-five miles away from its centre, flying at a height of twelve thousand feet. Moreover another light was warning them that they would be crashing into a mountainside unless they took special care. Pushkin pressed the raven switch, which basically made the lambda think like a raven and fly slowly and carefully around the mountain, which towered above them. The air outside was thin and bitterly cold, and there was a danger that they would lose consciousness. The gateway indication light was now flashing so brightly that it was beginning to hurt their eyes.

Pushkin looked at the others anxiously. "The strongest gateway we have ever come across. Where on Erith are we?"

"Sam was looking at his map. "I know exactly where we are. We are nearing Mount Kailas. It is sacred to both Hindus and Buddhists and no one is allowed to climb it, let alone land on it."

He was interrupted by Melissa's scream. Then in a strange trance-like voice she spoke: "We're going to crash. Pushkin. It's an emergency. If you want us to stay alive then pull the quintessence switch now."

CHAPTER THIRTY-THREE

DRYADJANI

Sam and Pushkin, and now Mary and Melissa, had transpirated in and out of the quintessence on several occasions and were slowly learning to maintain a semi-conscious connection with the physical world when they weren't in it. At first they were in such a deeply unconscious state, they remembered nothing of their travels. Now it was more like being in a light dream. They were just about aware of the lambda and each other and could occasionally communicate telepathically. They could imagine moving the appropriate switches although they wouldn't actually have had the physical strength to do so. Sometimes they felt that they were floating above their bodies (or earth suits as the Dryadians often called them) but feeling a strange detachment from the physical world.

This was what was happening as the lambda got caught up in the enormous spiral of energy around Mount Kailas. They no longer had any power to leave the ethereal to return to the physical world or to reach out and connect to another gateway. The process of connecting was called hexing as the energy of the number six was used. The energy of seven lay beyond. Its power instigated the beginning of a new cycle. It was no coincidence that the musical octave was also based on the number seven. This number was also the energy of communication in all its many aspects, and in learning to use its power the Dryadians had found it was possible to connect with people and places far away from where they actually were. As if confirming it, they were hearing Sophora's soothing voice deep inside their brains and it seemed too that in return she was responding to the power of their own silent thoughts. A kind of ethereal telegraph was operating.

Their destiny was out of their control. Unseen forces had taken over, but whether they had good intentions or not towards the Dryadians were not clear. The lambda was presumably still programmed to dock at the gateway somewhere on Mount Kailas. As it was being tossed around the mountain like a piece of driftwood at the bottom of a waterfall, they heard strange sounds penetrating their dreams. They sensed in a hazy way that it was coming down the lambda line from the place they were heading to. It sounded like three deep croaks, a second or so apart repeating again and again. Nine sets in all.

Then they returned to the physical world. The lambda was hovering above a mountaintop in a swirling blizzard. It was impossible to see more than a few feet away from its windows and it was far too dangerous to get out. The lambda repeatedly tried to touch down before bouncing up again. They felt that they could all be ripped to pieces at any moment. The lambda though seemed determined to land. None of them had been so terrified in their lives, all the more so because there was nothing that they could do about it. Pushkin made several attempts to press the quintessence switch but the lambda refused to respond. Then the problem was taken out of their hands. The atmosphere inside the lambda was turning a pale pink, a sign that they were after all about to transpirate but through the will of something or somebody else.

Immediately their fears dropped away and they felt cocooned in an ocean of peace. They thought they could hear Sophora again over the fury of the storm outside, now softening in its intensity. They could see nothing but snow flurries outside the lambda's portholes. They could hear the croaks of the ravens again, mingling with Sophora's voice. There was another voice too, one that was unfamiliar to them. It started as a whisper. Then as it gathered power they knew it was male and speaking with authority. The physical world started fading away. They could no longer see their bodies, the lambda or the violence of the snow and the wind on the mountain.

The last thing they heard before they merged into oblivion was the sound of the mysterious male voice, calming and protective:

"Be at peace, dear children of Dryadogenes. You have nothing to fear. We will call you when we are ready."

The Dryadians remembered hardly anything of their adventures in the darkness nor how long they had been away, or where they had gone to, if anywhere – only foggy dreams slipping in and out of their brains. The mountain seemed to have been angry with them – it had been caught unawares for no one had visited its summit for thousands of years. Pilgrims never climbed it. Mount Kailas was sacred to the Gods. The croaks of ravens repeatedly flew into their unconscious brains. The ravens said that they had flown from all the corners of the earth to greet them, yet paradoxically the sound seemed to emanate from inside the Dryadians' own heads. There was a feeling of accomplishment but also that of failure at the final moment – being defeated by the overwhelming powers of nature caused by getting too close to the mountain uninvited, as Icarus had once flown too close to the sun. Yet comfortingly, that voice from outside had said they were under his protection.

The lambda had landed on a small patch of flattened rock covered in about a foot of snow. It was at the top of Mount Kailas, perhaps very close to where they were buffeted by the blizzard previously. This was a fully formed mountain, not just a peak on a ridge. There were astonishing views of snow-covered ranges, their slopes on fire with the strong morning sun. The intense light illuminated deep rocky valleys on all four sides. They could not guess how long they had been away but since that time the storms had passed, and the winds had dropped completely away under a clear blue sky. Far below them they could see with earthly eyes once again, for they were in their physical bodies, groups of pilgrims slowly perambulating clockwise around the mountain's base, like a disjointed serpent.

The Dryadians felt like pilgrims themselves. The mountain's rage had vanished. They knew that they were now welcome even though it could be for only a short time. A band of serenity separated them from the turmoil of the storms like the rest between two heartbeats. The mountain had breathed in, paused, and allowed them to experience its very soul. The four of them climbed out of the lambda gasping in the thin air and extreme cold. They knew they could stand only a few minutes of this. No one could survive long without a considerable period of steady acclimatisation or some very strong magic indeed. They were like gnats on the face of a giant. No one spoke. No one could speak in the presence of such wonder. With a great effort the Dryadians clambered back into the lambda and managed to close the hatch before it started to ice up. Quickly they pulled the quintessence switch and returned to an invisible and lighter world, which knew no cold or suffering. They rose unseen within the great spiral of energy that enclosed the mountain until it weakened and the lambda was released from its power and started being drawn eastwards by some invisible force along the serpent's path. The force was irresistible like a boat being propelled along a fast flowing river. The Dryadians were powerless to oppose it and fortunately were in too much of a dream state to feel any fear. They would have known, if they had been conscious, that any human powers that tried to fight the forces of nature would always eventually be overcome by them. When the Dryadians returned to the physical realms, with no idea as to how long they had been absent, they observed a very different landscape to that of Mount Kailas. They looked out of the windows and saw blue skies above them and benign mountains and dense green forests around them, stretching to the horizon in every direction. Immediately below the lambda though was a grey mist extending many miles out towards the peripheral forests. The mist seemed strange. A dense fog, like a spongy blanket, would describe it better. It was if a giant had placed a hand on a freshly painted picture and simply obliterated it. It didn't seem quite natural.

The lambda was still under automatic pilot directed from outside and was ignoring every attempt of Pushkin and Sam to regain control.

"Oh, come on bird brain," Pushkin kept saying in frustration as Mary kept a restraining hand on his shoulder.

"We have to trust who or whatever has brought us here," said Sam. "It's obviously highly intelligent and it must have our interests at heart, or we would have all been left to perish on the top of Mount Kailas."

He looked at the lambda's screens again and could see that it was very much locked on to a spiral of energy that was presumably emanating from the gateway that lay beneath the fog. "I think we're stacking," he said hopefully. "It's just like the way planes used to encircle airports when they were queuing up to land."

"Except that I can't see any other lambdas queuing around us," replied Pushkin. "But I do get a funny feeling that the lambda is waiting for something."

"Clearance for landing," said Melissa cheerfully.

After about ten minutes the lambda stopped its circling and remained completely stationary at around five thousand feet. Then it started descending, dropping very slowly towards the dense fog below.

"You know," exclaimed Mary suddenly, "I do believe it's beginning to clear."

The fog certainly didn't seem quite as opaque as before. Moreover the forest that surrounded it appeared to be moving inwards. The mist was melting away from the perimeter. After a few minutes another world started coming into focus through the rapidly evaporating clouds. The lambda was about to land in a long valley surrounded by steep wooded cliffs with high mountains far beyond. A river ran through the middle of the valley and on either side of it was a fertile countryside of green fields and woods. There were small villages linked by narrow tracks and everywhere, they could see small groups of people staring and waving and walking towards a raised mound that lay within a stone circle. The lambda manoeuvred itself with gentle precision towards the centre of the mound and floated down to land amongst the welcoming crowd.

"Did you notice their houses?" exclaimed Sam excitedly. "They were hexagonal."

Willing hands helped them out of the lambda. Children were touching their clothes curiously, their faces lit up by big grins until their parents pulled them away. They chattered away in a language that was obviously unknown to the Dryadians yet there were words that seemed strangely familiar, like a dialect that was just out of reach. Their clothes were not like the traditional Indian garb or the flowing costume of Tibet or other Himalayan peoples. There seemed to be some Grecian influence in their well cut and practical robes. A tall man in a blue tunic approached them holding up his hand in blessing while the welcoming party moved respectably out of his way.

"Welcome to Dryadjani. My name is Helion, and this place is called Mala. We have been expecting you for a little while now."

To their amazement he spoke in fluent English which he later explained was due to having had a formal education of sorts, two years being as much as he could stand, at an old English school in Darjeeling in the Himalayan foothills in India.

"I am familiar with both the ways of the East and the West but the way of the Dryadjani is much nicer. Sophora and I have made contact at last and she has explained the purpose of your journey. I'm glad we knew of your progress before you found yourselves at Mount Kailas, otherwise you would have been very lucky to be still alive. Now you need to eat and rest and then we can have a long discussion. We have prepared quite a feast for you and everybody is eager to meet you.

We seldom have visitors and generally we have no wish to be found. You though are the exception, and although Dryadia makes an appearance in our histories, it wasn't until very recently that we realised that you still existed."

Helion was an imposing man in late middle age with long greying hair tumbling almost down to his shoulders. He spoke softly but intensely. As with Sophora you were compelled to listen. Nevertheless his eyes shone and twinkled and he regularly broke into a giggly laugh whenever anything amused him, which was quite often. It seemed quite an inquisition as he shot question after question at the Dryadians. After nearly two hours he had drunk his full on their travels and their life in Dryadia. Now and then Helion broke into his local language to translate their words to his fellow countrymen and women, the Elders of Mala, who didn't have his fluency in English and were listening patiently as they sat beside him. The Dryadians were not absolutely sure what they should be revealing to someone who after all was a complete stranger, but oddly he seemed to know half their story already. Helion's warm humour, and the fact he seemed to have exchanged a lot of information with Sophora previously through some kind of telepathic contact, did a lot to ease their concerns. He also seemed to have known about their adventures on Mount Kailas without any prompting. The Dryadians were now aware that the great forces of nature that had rescued them had actually emanated from Dryadjani.

Helion wanted to know all about the Dryadians' political structure, their Storytellers and the Therapeutae. It appeared that the Dryadjani had something similar. It was like talking to the British mandarins all over again except that the Dryadjani were totally receptive. The university at Cantillion fascinated him for there was none in Dryadjani and the universal education that they both shared was taught in small groups. The Dryadjani unbelievably even had a tree calendar though different trees were obviously used. Their measurements were also based around the traditional foot, which was regarded as particularly sacred as it had a profound relationship with the earth's circumference around the equator, not that the Dryadians didn't already know this. All this information fascinated Helion and his companions in equal measure. They absorbed it so well that if they were at Cantillion there would be no doubt that they would be top of the class. They were of course particularly interested in the lambdas and how they worked and how they were controlled, but for the moment didn't volunteer as to whether they had any themselves.

The Dryadjani climate was a delight as befitted a country that lay partially in the tropics but was situated just high enough up in the hills to take the edge off the heat. They lived in a long sloping river valley about fifteen miles wide, and a hundred miles long from north to south, with enormous waterfalls at either end. The one in the north dropped dramatically from wooded mountains of rhododendrons and magnolias while the southern falls plunged out of the country through an almost impenetrable tropical forest. The river descended through about three thousand feet from beginning to end in its course through the country. It was therefore a river of mixed character, bustling along as it dropped through narrow rapids, and moving slowly in a stately way when it flowed through flatter countryside. The Dryadjani River acted as the lifeblood of the country and though it was only navigable in parts owing to its turbulence around its many smaller falls, there were many bridges uniting both halves of the country. The climate was cooler in the north, but in the tropical south where Mala was situated it was almost always warm enough to eat outside. The climatic variations were already obvious to the Dryadians when they examined the fruit on the table. They included cherries, walnuts and apricots from the far north; apples and plums from the fertile orchards that lay along side the river a little further south of the northern falls; and mangos and bananas that grew happily around Mala in the markedly warmer south. Rice too was cultivated in the south and barley and wheat in the north.

The valley was largely fertile through its length, although like Dryadia, half its area was left uncultivated and left as forest or wilderness. About a hundred thousand people lived in the country, in villages of varying sizes at about the same density as in Dryadia, which was roughly twice its size. There were no settlements that were large enough to be called towns. As in Dryadia, the people lived simply but comfortably, turning their back on modern technology and largely working on, or close to the land.

The waterfalls, the thick forests and the steep cliffs that enclosed the valley on the eastern and western sides meant that Dryadjani was almost unknown to the countries around them. It was only when men learned to fly over a century ago, that the Dryadjani realised that for the first time in their history they were vulnerable from above. That was when they perfected the creation of thought forms that could effectively obliterate their country from unwelcome eyes.

Helion explained that they had a history almost as twice as long as the Dryadians although they obviously were descended from common ancestors. He led them into the local meetinghouse where the Dryadians noticed with astonishment that the walls were covered in an ancient flowing script that was almost identical to the Dryadian sanctuary writing. Although the pronunciation of the spoken language had changed a lot they could read the written one with ease.

They had a similar form of Eldership to the Dryadians, both of the traditional and practical kind, which had been passed down through the generations. As there was no university, the wisest of the Elders educated the younger ones through a form of apprenticeship. The Dryadjani philosophy was almost identical to that of Dryadia for both communities had drunk from the same stream that Dryadogenes had drunk from long ago. There was almost no communication with the outside world. Like the Dryadians they had worked out that isolation was absolutely vital if their way of life was to survive.

Some of the Elders like Helion had travelled outside the country especially to India and Tibet to gain information beyond their borders and bring back ideas and a little trade that might be useful to them. Strangely enough no outsider had ever mentioned Dryadia to them. Unlike the Dryadians they had never been warlike for they never had needed to defend themselves, nor had there ever been any civil conflict. The living was relatively easy due to the benign climate and fertile soils, although that didn't mean that people didn't have to work hard. The result was a good natured and gentle population. However there was no stagnation. The Elders ensured that everyone was stretched intellectually and physically so that boredom and complacency didn't set in. They also made sure that all were treated equally and no one had too much or too little. That meant too that every one had access to the opportunities and knowledge that suited them. But as in Dryadia some knowledge, notably of the scientific kind, was only known to the wisest of the Elders. Excess energy was often channelled into their art. The walls of their meetinghouses were riots of colour – landscapes, people and abstract paintings and of course the scripts of wisdom. As Helion told them the purpose of art, and music too for that matter, has at its best a single purpose – to raise the spirits and the consciousness of the people who connect with it and help them discover whom at heart, they truly are.

The Dryadians were flabbergasted at how advanced technologically the Dryadjani civilisation was. They thought that they were being clever in dematerialising a lambda and travelling half way across the world in another dimension. But to conceal a whole country from outsiders was truly remarkable. Although the Dryadjani were not particularly forthcoming on the subject it seemed obvious that their knowledge of lambda science was profound for they were not at all fazed about the Dryadians' arrival, and indeed were expecting them.

They had not only sent raven croaks down the lambda lines to greet them and rescued them from the terrors of Mount Kailas but had taken over the controls of the lambda from more than a thousand miles away and safely guided them into their country.

The Dryadians were not too upset at the lack of information given on Dryadjani science. It seemed that Helion was still sizing them up. And of course if the boot was on the other foot and the Dryadjani were visiting Dryadia they wouldn't be offering guided tours to The Hall of Records. They wondered though if the Dryadjani still travelled. They certainly did once as the Island of Ravens in Kashmir had revealed, but did they now? They were certainly aware of the catastrophe in the rest of the world and hinted that they were not ignoring it. They were very interested in the lambda rescue missions in England. The Dryadians got the impression that if they were not already exploring the world around them then they might be soon preparing to do so.

The four travellers had spent seven days in Dryadjani and had barely ventured out of the confines of Mala. They were concerned about their families and it was agreed that they would return home and come back soon. Helion particularly wanted them to bring Sophora with them. He had sent word that they were all safe and well (He didn't explain how) and that they would soon be on their way home. However they were concerned about the journey and Mary in particular wondered whether their return would be like the famous fairytale where a hundred years had passed like moments, and no one would be able recognise them when they got back. Then the Storytellers would have a new story.

"We will answer all your questions in due course," said Helion as the Dryadians were saying their goodbyes. "We hope there is nothing to fear and if there is, we will do our best to make it lighter. At the moment we need more information of the outside world, and decide if it is safe. What you have told us already is extremely helpful, but we the people of Dryadjani still have a lot of work to do. So go now and be with your families and friends. We think you will return sooner than you think. We are enormously grateful for your visit. Like you we have discovered that we can no longer live apart from the world. We will work together to do our best for it. We have made some adjustments to the lambda line network. There is now a direct line between our two countries." Helion smiled benignly at them. "And we have made sure that it will by-pass Mount Kailas."

They climbed into the lambda moved to tears by the smiles and waves of their new friends. The lambda rose into the air above the shining green landscape of Dryadjani and quickly melted away into the ether. They knew very little more until they became aware of their lambda sinking down on a familiar hilltop overlooking the estuary near Ceradoc. "Sanctuary Hill is an occasional gateway for special occasions," Sophora told them later. They looked out of the window to a sea of familiar and welcoming faces. To their great relief all of them looked exactly the same age as when they left!

CHAPTER THIRTY-FOUR

MINDS THROUGH THE ETHER

Sophora, Anaxamander and all the Traditional Elders of Ceradoc not to mention most of their families, of whom many were Elders in waiting, wanted to hear every word. They were sitting at the top of Sophora's house in her cupola with all-round views of the village and the estuary. The dramatic news of the lambda's journey had now spread around the whole of Dryadia and it was considered so important that a special moot had been arranged at Cantillion at the next full moon to fill everybody in.

"We can't wait that long or we'll cry with impatience," said Sophora. "We'll have a mini-moot here in Ceradoc first so that we can share our knowledge. I too have a lot to tell you."

No one took their eyes off Sam, Pushkin, Mary and Melissa as they described their travels at length. Mary being the only Storyteller in the expedition described the Mount Kailas episode with such a dramatic flourish that she had to be slightly restrained by Pushkin to avoid over exaggerating it.

"Are you sure that the Dryadjani rescued you?" asked Anaxamander. "That's some pretty awesome technology if they did"

"They must have done," replied Sam. "We heard the ravens croaking and Helion's calming voice, though we didn't know it was him at the time. Then finally we woke up above that extraordinary cloud that was hiding Dryadjani."

"Are we ever going to be able to do that sort of thing, Empedocles," asked Anaxamander of his brother?"

"Well, we obviously can't hide a whole country yet, but I imagine they hid it in a thought form rather than etherealising it. But we can transpirate lambdas and humans so in theory we should be able to do it with bits of land eventually. I've heard of yogis fogging up your film if they didn't want their photograph taken. All with the power of their minds. Hopefully the Dryadjani will teach us how to do it one day. I wish we had known that trick when the English were trying to invade us. It would have saved us a lot of trouble. The piloting of your lambda by remote control from Dryadjani does interest me though. We're getting near to doing that, as we'll explain later."

"Yet they said they had no lambdas," said Ruth.

"They didn't actually say that, Mum," answered Melissa. "They just didn't give a straight answer. They gave the impression that they weren't flying at the moment, probably because they didn't need them. We know they had them once because there are drawings of them on the temple walls on the Island of Ravens. They understood our lambda very quickly, though we didn't give anyone a spin round the country. I've got the feeling that they've got a few tucked away in their own Hall of Records and now that we've gone, I expect they're going to dust them down rather quickly."

"Dryadjani is absolute paradise," said Mary changing the subject. "They've really looked after the country as we have, but the climate is much warmer, semi-tropical when we were there, so you can live out of doors most of the time. They told us that the winters in the north can sometimes be quite cool though. There can even be a bit of snow there, where it is quite high up. We've been asked to visit there next time. And the food. All vegetarian and there's such variety, especially the fruit. You never tasted pineapples and papayas like it. Much as I love my country, I might be tempted to apply for dietary asylum unless Pushkin builds an extra hot greenhouse in the walled garden!"

"It would be easier to fly them in by lambda," replied Pushkin. "It's possible."

"Absolutely probable, added Empedocles. "As Anaxamander likes to say, "In the quintessence the seemingly impossible becomes possible. Anyway, remember how Squeaky flew unaided between Mount Cynthos and The Beacons."

"Pushkin, you must repeat what you were telling me earlier about Dryadjani's early days. It looks as if we're going to have to include yet another few chapters to our history." Parmenides ignored Oceania and Mary's groans that it would be another hundred years before it would be finished.

"Helion told us that they have records that go back further than ours, to at least ten thousand years ago when they first came to Dryadjani. We were all descended from a group of people known as the Dryas. That was even before Dryadogenes. The Dryas were wanderers and their mission was to keep the planet pure and civilise people whenever they were behaving like animals. Sounds familiar doesn't it! The Dryas claimed that they came from the stars and didn't originate from Erith and had completed similar missions on other planets before they came here. Thousands of years ago as we know, most of the people on Erith were wiped out when an enormous comet hit the earth and there was a great flood. Most of the Dryas escaped because they managed to predict when and where the comet was going to land. Some moved to higher ground. Some even managed to transpirate themselves at the critical point. The flood forced them to split up. One group settled in the Dryadjani valley and Helion admitted to us that they probably travelled there originally by lambda. Much later, another group led by Dryadogenes founded Dryadia. There were probably other groups too. Like us, they preferred to live apart from other people both to preserve their philosophy and because they found most of the world coarse and belligerent."

"I wonder if he thinks any of the other Dryas groups are still living in the world or are they all extinct?" asked Anaxamander.

"Helion feels probably that there is no one else." said Sam. "But then they had not heard of us until quite recently, or we of them. We are both elusive tribes. He told us that their records stated that there were many Dryas around tens of thousands of years ago, before the flood. They settled all over the world. Too many of them lived in small groups and got overwhelmed by the people they were trying to help. They forgot their principles and became beastly and disappeared. Only the very large groups like the Dryadjani and the Dryadians could survive with their culture intact because they chose to live separately."

"In the former East they called us racist for our separatist philosophy," added Sophora. "They misunderstood us. It was a question of survival. We've always welcomed like-minded people whatever their race or background. Quite a few of us here are incomers. New blood is good for us. It's rejuvenating. But if you want to live our sort of life and then help others with our thinking, then you have to live apart."

"I wanted to ask you Sam all about their bird and animal life. I suppose we had better leave it for later or we will send every one to sleep." Zephyr smiled at his old friend. His eyes were not as good as they were and he relied more than he did on Sam's observations.

"I have another question though having listened intently to your remarkable adventures and the equably remarkable Dryadjani. They are obviously quite extraordinary and their science in some areas is rather more advanced than ours. On the face of it they are our soul mates and it is wonderful to think that we are no longer alone in the world. It's tempting, very tempting, to share everything with them but my question is, to put it bluntly, can we be absolutely sure we can trust them?"

"I've got good feelings about them when I start sensing them in my mind's eye. I would like to know though what Sophora thinks." Amarinta smiled at her fellow seer.

"I'm going to answer that by telling you of a little adventure that I had when you were away, which I have already shared with Anaxamander and Ruth and with Sam and Melissa's children.

Hopefully, it may come as a surprise to you all as I swore Piran and Damelza to secrecy in order not to spoil the effect today. Mary and Tara may have some rivals in the story telling department. If they would like to begin and tell the story of our travels then I will tell you of its conclusion and whether I believe we can trust the Dryadjani or not."

Damelza was the older of the two and had just finished the course at Cantillion and had all her mother's liveliness and good nature. Piran was still at the university and although he was nowhere as shy as Sam had been at his age, he had inherited his modesty and seriousness.

Damelza began: "Our story starts strangely enough in our grandparents' garden just outside Anaxamander's cabin. You will all remember that he believes that there is a gateway there. It's not a big one but strong enough to have once spiralled him around the garden. He has refused naturally to do it again and show us how it is done!"

She grinned mischievously at her grandfather. "But he and Uncle Empedocles have been doing experiments and have discovered that the gateway is a lot more powerful at the new moon when it is conjunct with Venus at sunset. Why this is so, nobody is sure. It's just the way it is as grandfather puts it. So they found one of those mini-lambdas that were used to propel Squeaky around the countryside long ago and started a lambda service for spiders between the cabin, Sanctuary Hill and The Beacons, which just happens to be linked by a serpent line. That poor spider – the number of times he went in and out of the quintessence! I shudder at what shape of web he is spinning now, or whether he can still spin at all. Empedocles has made flying a lot simpler since he invented that portable lambda keyboard, which feels a bit like summoning up ghosts at will in a haunted house. I'm exaggerating of course to make a good story. I bet the Dryadjani had a similar machine, which took control over your lambda at Mount Kailas. Then one day Empedocles summoned up a full-scale lambda that was parked at The Beacons. He didn't tell Anaxamander who got the shock of his life when it materialised in front of him in his garden. Empedocles then whisked it back to Sanctuary Hill where he had his command post at the oracle, got in, and then reappeared at the cabin still in the physical dimension. Ruth was quite cross as the lambda blocked the beeline to her hives but must have forgiven him as I came across him ten minutes later in her kitchen tucking into freshly cooked muffins."

Damelza paused and looked at Piran, who took up the story: "News got around fast. Sophora came to the cabin and was telling us that she had had rather an amazing idea. She said that she was picking up what we now know was Helion's voice, informing us that you were all safe, which was quite a relief to us I promise you. The messages though were not always clear, and she had this inner prompting that things would be much clearer if she went to The Hall of Records for inspiration.

Anaxamander and Ruth offered to go with her and she suggested that Damelza and I should go too as we had only been there once before. Sophora said she felt her old bones were a bit too rickety to ride and walk there, so why didn't we all go there by lambda through the quintessence and make a deft landing on the plinth. If Empedocles didn't mind he could direct the lambda straight to Mount Cynthos. It's strange that this was all happening about the same time that you were being rescued by the Dryadjani at Mount Kailas. So the five us clambered into the lambda in Anaxamander and Ruth's garden to take advantage of the new moon and the Venus conjunction. Empedocles waved us goodbye and we saw him directing our path with his amazing invention that looks very similar to a lambda control panel.

We still had to visualise take off and our proposed destination. We used the power of our minds and hearts as we were taught at university which Anaxamander and so many of you never let us forget. We younger ones have found these techniques quite difficult so Damelza and I were grateful for the support of the others.

I doubt whether we would be quite strong enough yet to fly the lambda without them. I can see now why we keep this lambda knowledge safe and glad it's so difficult to use. We remember our teachers' words; 'No levitation without levity. No lift-off without lightness of being. No illumination without imagination. No awareness without concentration.' All rather hard to do at the same time. Anyway we managed with Empedocles' help and in a blink of a raven's eye we found ourselves on the plinth in the pyramid under Mount Cynthos. Then Sophora took us to the Crystal Chamber and then a lot of things happened which I only half understand. I am sure that Sophora can explain it better."

"Thank you both of you. I'm thinking that I'm only beginning to understand myself. I mentioned to you earlier that while you were away

I felt Helion was trying to break into my dreams and was consequently reassured that you were all safe. Communication was muggy though. That foggy cloud of theirs never seems to go away. Then I had this moment of revelation and I knew I had to go to The Hall of Records and in particular to The Chamber of Crystals. What started focusing strongly in my mind was that one of the original reasons for the building of The Hall of Records was that it was to be a giant communications centre. I'd had a vague idea that it might be such for quite a while but never could properly develop it. I already knew that the pyramids of Egypt, especially the Great Pyramid, were used for that purpose. They were certainly not burial chambers as archaeologists used to think. I also could see with my mind's eye that the Great Pyramid was unable to operate as the casing and the mini-pyramid capstone that graced its summit had been removed. Without them the pyramid was not complete. When I thought about it I got the feeling that this was not the case with our pyramid. Although of course they are not visible from the inside, the casing and capstone are still there. Our pyramid, as it was originally built, is therefore complete. I also felt that while the original equipment within the Great Pyramid had long been removed that was not so with ours.

In short we had a working pyramid, probably the only one in the world. If my theory is correct then we could utilise the unique geometry of the pyramid, its crystals and other bits and pieces that are still there, and make contact with the Dryadjani or indeed any other people in the world who might have the right apparatus, and who wish to be contacted. It also may be possible to reach out beyond the earth, the solar system and even to the furthest ends of our galaxy or further still. If we use the equipment correctly then we are not bound any longer by the restraints of the physical world. Of course we already do that in the lambdas, using the energy of five as well as the finer energy of six of combining or limiting, what we call hexing. There is also the energy of seven, which as you know commands the world of cycles and communication.

I believe that the Dryadjani are masters of using this type of energy. I don't believe that the Dryadjani use their lambdas very much now. Not because they can't but because they really don't need to. They don't need to travel in their physical bodies anymore because they can do it in their minds. I was interested why the Dryadjani asked very few questions about our countryside and our villages. In fact they didn't have to because once they had made the initial contact they could see Dryadia for themselves.

That is why we went back to explore The Hall of Records because if we could understand some of the things that are stored there, that we haven't really looked at before, then we can do what the Dryadjani do.

In the Crystal Chamber, as you already know, there is a wide selection of colours in the crystals. There are ones that look like rubies, emeralds, rose quartz, amethysts and sapphires. We breed them in the crystal garden round the pool. It was the amethysts and blue sapphires that I was particularly interested in as they are connected with the energy of seven and eight respectively. Eight as you know is aligned with the higher wisdom and preserving it for all time. We gathered a number of the amethysts that were lying around as well as some rather strange looking wooden helmets that were studded with our homegrown sapphires.

I didn't feel that the Crystal Chamber was the best place for our experiments, and I was drawn to the most powerful point in The Hall. This was on the plinth where our lambda was now parked. We returned to the lambda with our finds and got in. Putting aside the helmets for the moment I was prompted to arrange the amethysts in two rows, nose to tail as in two parallel waves, like the old symbol for Aquarius. The sign is also the traditional sign for communication, one line representing transmitting, the other receiving or listening. I could see with my inner eye that the crystals shimmered and sparkled a thousand times more intensely together, than individually. We sat in the lambda between the two rows of amethysts and all focused our minds in our lambda kind of way in making contact with Helion. We didn't wait long. Helion's voice started playing in all our heads, clearly and strongly. The fog had gone. What was more, we could see his face. All of us – even though I was the only one there who was naturally clairvoyant. Even more wonderful was that we could see the place where he was talking from – the table, a cup of tea and the tree behind him. What was particularly interesting was that he was sitting under a wooden contraption like a canopy. It had no walls. Only the struts defined its shape. He was sitting under the skeletal outline of a pyramid. We couldn't talk or see long. It was hurting our heads. Helion told us that it gets better with practice. I hope so. One thing we agreed before we went. Within the next month or so, once we have held the moot at Cantillion, we have been invited to send a large party of us Ceradocian Traditional Elders to Dryadjani by lambda on the new direct line from Sanctuary Hill. We will explore Dryadjani at our leisure and have a joint moot with our new friends.

One more thing. We were asking ourselves whether we could trust the Dryadjani. Are we about to fall into a terrible trap? Do the Dryadjani wish us harm? Have they become corrupted over their ten thousand years of isolation and lost the purity of the higher wisdom that we hold so dear? We now put on our helmets. They're like truth bubbles. The sapphires arranged inside them in the way that they are, help us discern what is pure, honourable and true. We meditated on Dryadia and the feelings within us were almost blissful. We focussed on other beautiful things like our families, some of our best poetry and our way of healing. The result was the same. Then we sent our thoughts to the Dryadjani. We felt their thoughts returning to us. The feeling was exquisite. Yes, I assure you, we can trust the Dryadjani."

CHAPTER THIRTY-FIVE

A LIGHT IN THE DEPTHS

The latest sixty-seater lambda, with enough room for all Ceradoc's Traditional Elders and their families, was ready and parked on Sanctuary Hill just outside the oracle. It was within walking distance of the village. The six banks of ten seats were arranged in a semi-circle like an amphitheatre, over looking the small cockpit. Comfort was not a priority for the journey to Dryadjani would be completed almost as soon as it had begun. The plan was firstly to make a short flight to The Beacons and land amongst the oak trees in the Egg. The departure time was planned for the day after the summer festival so that the whole community could see them off. The days of complete secrecy were over. Sophora had explained the purpose of the mission to all those who had witnessed the lightning rituals and said that one day many of them would also be able to visit Dryadjani just as they were about to do.

The hatch was closed and the Dryadians that had been left behind at The Beacons watched the giant machine tremble and shimmer as it slowly rose, its high-pitched hum dying away as it gained height. Then it suddenly vanished as it lost its attachment to the physical world and was absorbed into an infinite ethereal one. The lambda's passengers knew little of the journey, once Empedocles had flicked the transpiration switch. They had no idea how long they had remained in the dreamy sleep of oblivion. They just knew that at the end of their journey, they awoke to find themselves hovering above the grey amorphous cloud that they were all expecting. They had no control of the lambda. It was locked into an energy spiral directed from a powerful gateway far below them.

After ten minutes the cloud started losing its density. It seemed little more than a morning mist melting away in the sun. But instead of clearing from its edges towards the centre as it did before, it held its complete form. A few lines started appearing in outline like a child's simple drawing and it was quickly apparent that a smiley face was being traced out on the cloud. On its forehead were inscribed a few words of Dryadjani. All the Dryadians could read it easily, for the scripts of both countries were very similar.

Welcome to Dryadjani. We have missed you

Soon the mist completely melted away and the lambda floated gently downwards towards the small mound that lay on the edge of the great river that flowed from the mountains of Tibet to the plains of India.

Helion and hundreds of Dryadjani greeted them warmly and garlands of flowers soon graced every Dryadian neck. Dryadjani's ten thousand years of isolation from the world had ended in the best way it could. The Dryadians were billeted in two large rest houses on either side of the river. A large wooden and rope bridge, a hundred feet across, linked the two banks and swayed gently over the bubbling torrent of water that flowed below it.

"Much safer than it looks," said Helion as he saw the concern on some of the Dryadians' faces. "If you can fly half way across the world in a lambda, this crossing should be a piece of cake." It was an idiom he must have picked up from his Indian education.

With practice the bridge could be quickly crossed, so long as you didn't look down and held tightly onto the ever-swaying ropes that acted as handrails. They were slightly comforted by the safety net that stretched across the river a few yards downstream. Helion assured them it was seldom if ever needed.

The River Dryadjani was the lifeblood of the country. The paired villages, united by the horizontal rope ladder across the river, appeared every mile or two through much of its course. Only in the sparsely uninhabited north of the country, where the river plunged vertically downwards in an enormous waterfall of frothy foam straight out of the Himalayas, was it too wide and too turbulent to be successfully bridged. The river was also known as 'The Water of Life' because the Dryadjani considered that much of their exceptional health and the richness of their soils were due to the properties and minerals contained in their river. There were many natural, and some artificially constructed tributaries, flowing through the country so that both water and fertility reached every corner of it – essential as most of the rains only fell in late summer. Like the Nile, the river never failed them. You could dig down to six foot in some places and still find the rich black earth that fed the abundance of crops and trees that sustained the Dryadjani. Their diet was similar to the Dryadians in that it was mostly vegetarian, with some fish caught from the river, but with more rice than other grains, and a much greater variety of fruit. Dryadjani was well forested. Trees were considered sacred and there had to be compelling reasons for cutting any of them down. They grew much taller than they did in Dryadia, due to the bright sunshine and the fertile soils. The highest of them could reach three hundred feet. Some of them had been planted in circles or ellipses mimicking the Dryadians' Egg, and marked the gateways.

The great trees were also important to the Dryadjani for another reason – tree houses. The Dryadians had their few like the one near The Tower of the Ravens but the Dryadjani had made their construction into an art form. The tree houses were built very high, as much as a hundred feet up from the ground. Some were so large that they spread across several trees, providing living space for scores of people. Local people often migrated to them in the hot summer months to sleep. The tree houses were also used as schools for the children and meeting places for the Elders. Wooden spiral staircases enveloped some of the bigger trees so that access was easy and simple. The only problem was keeping the monkeys out, so unguarded food had to be locked away. As Dryadjani was largely flat until you reached its borders and the country narrow, there were magnificent views from the tree houses across the countryside to the densely forested cliffs and mountains that protected them from the outside world.

Helion and his fellow Elders were much more open on this second visit. They wanted to reciprocate the knowledge that the Dryadians had already shared with them. It was decided that a moot would be held in a fortnight with both parties present. Meantime Helion would like to take them to visit the caves of the north where their records were kept and studied – the Dryadjani equivalent of Mount Cynthos.

The Dryadians were asked to gather at dawn at one of the gateway tree houses. There was plenty of room and a hundred people could probably be fitted in, so Helion had brought some of his Elders as well. The floor was covered in oriental carpets on which lay a number of comfortable cushions. As it was not the rainy season the roof had been removed, but there was plenty of shade provided by the tree canopy. Sturdy wooden railings protected people from falling over the edge and it was interesting to note that the floor had eight sides.

"Eight sides because it's here that we learn and teach," explained Helion. "Our journey to the northern waterfall starts here in this very room because, as you have already guessed, a gateway lies beneath us. We won't actually need a lambda today although we do have some stored in the caves we're going to visit. We'll do something different. Believe it or not we are going to travel to the north by flying carpet!"

"Not the one we're sitting on?" asked Mary incredulously.

"The very same," answered Helion. "Just as in the Arabian Nights. An awful lot of knowledge is hidden in our fairy stories, as you are very aware. Knowledge is a funny thing. The way is circular. It's always being found and lost, and then found again.

We're going to the furthest end of our country, and then even further. As we are flying we will avoid the secret paths in the mountains and forests that are impossible for the uninvited visitor to find. When we reach the end of our journey you will learn about our extraordinary history, some of which we happen to share. We Elders often go to the caves for short periods to find peace and quiet away from the bustle of the valley. Now let's begin our journey. There are about sixty of us. Will some of you take each one of the eight corners of the carpet you are sitting on, and roll it inwards so there is just enough room for all of us to sit on it in a huddle? The spiral energy is very strong here and actually rises high enough to escape the earth's gravitational pull. You can see how effortless space travel might be. In some other places the energy spirals downwards into the earth and shortly we will be arriving at such a gateway. So are you ready? If you are nervous you could of course walk. But it would take you about four days following the course of the river, which I must say, is incomparably beautiful. Today though, I think we will use the lambda way."

The Dryadians took their cue from the Dryadjani and closed their eyes and sat in silence. They were aware only of the rustling of the leaves around them and the distant chattering of monkeys. The quiet was broken by the sound of a drum – single beats at first, followed by more complex rhythms containing five beats to a bar. Then more drums joined in followed by some flutes. It was strangely hypnotic. The sound seemed to come from somewhere below them but spoke of far away places. Helion and his colleagues sat bolt upright on their cushions, closed eyes raised towards the sky. The world seemed to shimmer and the carpet closed tightly around them creating an unbroken circular wall. They looked as if they were sitting within a woollen saucer. Then the sound died away and like a candle being snuffed out they all drifted away into the realms of the unconscious ether.

They awoke still sitting on their cushions while the carpet had rolled itself out again to its natural flattened state. They were not in the same place though. They were sitting in a tree house but it was not the same tree and the countryside around them was different. In the distance they could hear the continuous sound of water.

Helion spoke: "As you have noticed, you have just been transpirated from Mala to Neopol by flying carpet. For short journeys like this you don't need a lambda. A carpet will do just as well if you know the technique. The basic principles are just the same. If you listen, you can hear the waterfall. It's not very far away."

Neopol was the most northern village in Dryadjani about half a mile away from the waterfall, where the river entered the country in a wild torrent of energy sweeping all before it down to the calmer reaches below. The noise would have been deafening if they had been much closer. Dryadjani's most northerly point was shaped like a narrow horseshoe around the waterfall. Above it were steep forested slopes honeycombed with caves, reached by barely defined tracks sunk in the dense greenery.

To the Dryadians' delight they were to live and sleep in the huge tree house that they had just landed in. It spread across at least ten trees and a labyrinth of walkways connected the various rooms. As Helion showed them around he started to explain about the caves they were about to visit.

"There are the accessible and the inaccessible ones. The accessible ones are only accessible in the sense that they can be reached by a long hard scramble up the cliffs around the waterfall. These ones are not so interesting and are largely empty. The dampness of the air does not make for good storage and material things quickly disintegrate. There is one that is high up and right behind the waterfall where there are wonderful views through the spray, which we will visit. It is no longer accessible so we will use one of our few working lambdas, as we don't want to ruin our carpets!

I mentioned the inaccessible caves. Inaccessible, because there are no physical paths into them. They could never be found in the normal way. For they lie deep underground or within the mountain itself. Even better concealed than your Hall of Records. Their whereabouts, even their very existence, is only known by our senior Elders. However we have decided to share it with you. The caves are very old. Perhaps millions of years old, which is supposed to be longer than man has existed on the planet. I assure you that humans have been around much longer than you think. These caves can only be reached by lambdas travelling ethereally. But we have to use gateways where the spiral energy can be reversed – where it can be directed downwards into the earth as well as upwards. There are not many places where this can be done. The waterfall cave area is one of them. Down below the mountain that lies behind the waterfall, people once lived and made comfortable homes for themselves. Fresh air was pumped down from the surface through tiny crannies in the rock. Light and power was created from the electricity, which was produced from lightning that was stored within the mountain itself. Water also percolated from the surface so they could grow their own food. Most of the caves though are very dry and warm. Documents can be preserved there for almost ever. Here is our own Hall of Records with our history and indeed the world's history. Inside are our museums containing objects that we have used over the ages including our old lambdas. There is even a cave that includes the remains of terrible weapons that were once actually used and we hope will never be used again. Much worse than nuclear bombs. You can't imagine the horror that men once created in the name of war. But most of what you will see is beautiful and fascinating which we would like to share with you."

"It must be rather like our pyramid under Mount Cynthos," said Sam.

"There are great similarities though we don't have a pyramid and so far as I know there was not a community of people living under your mountain. The people that lived under ours were not Dryadjani but even older. They made contact with us in our early days and eventually trusted us enough to pass down their knowledge, which was in danger of being lost as they knew that they were beginning to die out. The records were originally theirs and therefore far older than we can conceive."

The next day Helion led the party to a large circular mound five minutes walk from the tree house. Upon it was an extremely large orange lambda not dis-similar to the Dryadian ones, although the internal layout seemed quite strange.

"One of our few air-worthy ones at the moment", said Helion. "We use this lambda mainly to ride the spiral energy both up and down, though it's quite happy travelling cross-country too. It's made many journeys down through the rock into the caves. It has also risen high above the atmosphere of the earth, and is capable of space travel as once men did frequently. We understand the lambda way in the same way as you do. Like you we can travel much faster than the speed of light once we have locked on to the serpent lines. There is no judder and we can be equally comfortable cruising above the treetops at a slow speed, as we would be in the ether."

Unexpectedly Helion and his friends first directed the lambda southwards following the river, until it disappeared over the unmarked border into dense jungle.

"Literally a bird's eye view of the river. A little treat for you. You will be interested to know that the river is a major migratory highway for many birds. You should see the spring and autumn flight of the cranes. You would have to be dull of mind not to be impressed by those magnificent birds."

When the Dryadians had drunk their full of the landscape in its many shades of green unspoiled by any industry more advanced than a water mill, Helion turned the lambda towards the north, flicked a switch and the lambda vanished from view.

It re-materialised in a large cave five hundred feet above the ground behind the huge waterfall at the other end of the country. The force and roar of the water was enormous, and they looked out over a large parapet that had been built to prevent accidents, through a curtain of swirling mists and myriad rainbows down to the valley far below. All of Dryadjani seemed to be laid out before them.

Helion explained that because of a rock fall this cave could now only be reached by lambda. The Dryadjani stored some of their lambdas in the adjacent caves behind. As the Dryadians wandered through the caves they counted about a dozen working lambdas varying from single seaters to two large space versions one of which they had just arrived in. The smallest ones were known as ferry lambdas and could be summoned empty from the caves, as a shepherd might call his dog. Empedocles had invented something similar back in Dryadia. In this way no lambda was exposed on open ground for longer than necessary.

After an hour's exploring Helion got them back into the big lambda, which had been moved into another cave. He explained that it was a bit like moving a train onto another track. The new position connected with the downward spiral that linked it with the inaccessible caves that were hidden many hundreds of feet below.

"Ready?" he announced.

They sat back, and came-to in an enormous cavern. It seemed gloomy but you could see well enough, once you had got used to it. The light possessed hints of many flickering and shimmering colours.

"This is our version of your crystal cave," smiled Helion. "We seed, grow and harvest them here. This cave is one of my favourites."

He beckoned them to the entrance that beamed pink quartz at them. Rivers of crystal seemed to flow up and down the damp walls like water on a roof. Another cave contained sapphires of darkest blue, which glittered like small flowers on dewy grass. The topaz cave shone as if was buried sunshine and the ruby one looked like dragon's eyes in the dark. The amethyst cave drew the Dryadians in as if it wanted to communicate with them. Not only did each cave have a peculiar beauty of its own, but each seemed to have a kind of unique personality and power of its own as well. The energies were not isolated though. All were connected. From the sapphire cave steps led up to an upper gallery where the walls glittered with pure seams of gold. Beneath them they heard the sound of an underground river, which had walls rather than banks and on which threads of silver were etched as if they had been created by a thousand snails.

Helion explained that apart from being exquisitely beautiful all the crystals and minerals were used in their technology. This was mainly in creating, amplifying and directing fine light energy rather than being used in a physical way. He was delighted to hear that the Dryadians were doing the same thing. He doubted though whether they possessed crystals in such profusion.

"Each type of quartz or mineral has a different vibration or energy emanating from its geometry as well as its colour. We use them in the lambdas and in healing the sick as well. We have learned how to alter the disharmonious patterns that lie behind all disease into something more balanced and vibrant. I would like to say that we change the patterns from destructive ones into loving ones. You can do this with thought forms too. That stops you getting ill. We inherited a lot of this knowledge from the original inhabitants of this valley though most of them then lived underground, in fact in these very caves. Some of their genes still live on in the Dryadjani to this day. There was some interbreeding many thousands of years ago.

I think some of you are wondering why you keep getting drawn back to the amethyst cave. It's no accident. Sophora has already explained how she talked to me from Mount Cynthos using the power of the amethyst. Amethyst energy encourages the facility of transmitting human thoughts and speech, however far apart people are. We work out of time and space. I have a feeling that someone wants to talk to us right now. So lets go into the cave and watch and wait patiently. You are going to have a bit of a surprise."

The Dryadians were speechless. They had no questions for it was hard to connect this new world with their own. They waited quietly for five minutes comforted by Helion's benevolence and self-assurance. Then they suddenly heard a slight cough behind them as someone was trying to attract their attention. Two people were sitting in a recess of the cave smiling gently at them. They were small in stature – a middle-aged couple dressed in orange robes like Tibetan lamas. Their pallor had an un-earthly greenish-yellow tinge as if their skin had never really seen the light of day.

Helion spoke to them in English.

"Hello, Leisha and Gidron. Where did you spring from?"

The two lamas, if that is what they were, didn't exactly answer back in English but it sounded English inside the Dryadians' heads. It seemed as if secret interpreters had transplanted themselves silently within their brains. There was no sound and Leisha and Gidron didn't move their lips but their meaning was quite clear:

"Same place as we always spring from," answered Gidron firmly. The two looked alike but he was obviously the male side of the partnership.

"And very nice to see you again and all your friends," added Leisha. "It's been a long time since we travelled to Dryadia. I always thought you should explore under Mount Cynthos. We thought it was a most interesting place, but of course we never touched a thing. Those are your old records of course. Not as old as the ones here and even these ones are not as old as the ones at home. We need to explain things. We travel by lambda as you do. That's how we originally found Dryadia. We've just now arrived here in this cave and dematerialised our lambda. We don't actually need to. It's just force of habit. Sometimes we go exploring on the surface. The locals see the lights on our lambdas. They think we are spirits or ghosts. But we are physical beings as they are but with a lot more knowledge. They get scared of us. That suits us. Their fear keeps them away though we would never hurt them. We're only foraging. Bit boring living on algae however well we cook it. Helion and the other Dryadjani Elders know about us and our lives under the earth's surface. Our ancestors have been friends for thousands of years."

The eyes of the Dryadians were on stalks. Helion and his fellow Dryadjani were looking at them with great amusement. Each Dryadian face was etched with one question.

"Who are these people?"

Helion explained. "Our friends are sub-terraineans as they have indicated. They are very wise and have the most advanced science in the world so far as I know. Their ancestors taught us a lot once when they lived here. Later they moved deep into Tibet but still lived under ground. They only come up to forage as they say and to observe conditions on the surface. They too of course are appalled by the catastrophe. They realise that things are desperate on the surface and they want to use their know-how to try and help us all."

Gidron continued. "We are the last of our line and the Dryadjani are our last remaining contact with the surface. We used to be many and were scattered all under the earth in every continent. We used to mingle with our friends above, if they wished us no harm. The memories of our contacts are in your stories and folk tales. Ever heard of little green men? They were us, not Martians. Ever heard of the fairies stealing your babies? That was probably us too when we wanted fresh blood, to breed from, not to eat. Not that I'm proud of the people who did it.

Ever heard stories of humans disappearing and turning up one hundred years later unchanged? Well you know there's no time in the ether. So surface people who found us by chance and stayed too long within our vibration, didn't age.

Some of our tribes are very primitive, even mad. That's because they have become too isolated and in-bred. Some of us are very wise and have the most advanced technology imaginable. We are now much reduced in numbers. The underground nuclear explosions killed a great many of us. Very sad and quite unforgivable. The perpetrators were murderers. It was genocide. Now we keep ourselves to ourselves even more than ever. But we are aware of the state of the world. We want to help.

One thing we are doing is cooling down your nuclear reactors. They are burning out of control, as there is no one left to manage them. We take the heat and radiation into the quintessence and change its structure before returning it back to the physical state. We are having some success. Otherwise the world will soon be half uninhabitable. I shudder at the ignorance and craziness of the men who allowed this terrible and pointless invention to happen. It's happened all before, you know – millions of years ago. That's why we fled underground, to escape the terrible radiation and destruction. We know all the secret caves of Erith. We will show you some of them. Then you will know that we are speaking the truth, even if you couldn't imagine it."

"Can't get lost," cried Helion as they climbed into the lambda. All the Tibetan caves that we know about are programmed in. Gidron and Leisha have gone on ahead. They'll meet us there. At one time we were very worried that the Chinese nuclear explosions had destroyed them but we were lucky. Close your eyes and we will be there in a tick."

In a few minutes Leisha and Gidron were leading the party into a small cave they called the library. The air was exceedingly dry and pleasantly warm.

"The same temperature as your Hall of Records", exclaimed Helion.

Most of the books were on parchment scrolls that were attached to something similar to Tibetan prayer wheels.

"Nothing rots here," said Leisha. "Not even your bodies, should you die here? Some of these scrolls are more than one hundred thousand years old. They are written in a strange script but luckily we can decipher it. You wouldn't believe how long humans have lived on this planet. Millions of years we think. Just as there have been many extinctions with the animals like the dinosaurs and the mammoths over millions of years, it has been the same with humans even if fossil evidence is difficult to find. Comets, meteorites, floods and climate change have all helped to wipe humans out from time to time.

There have been wars too, terrible wars, using nuclear weapons and most terrifying of all, harnessing the direct power of the sun to scald the earth and burn much of its life to death. We see some of the results today in some of our deserts, even now still bereft of most life. And if we hadn't had the recent catastrophe, we would have almost done exactly the same thing again. Let's consider ourselves fortunate that despite what has happened, most of the earth is still intact even if the population has been decimated. At least we have another chance to change human thinking and create a lighter world."

"Come and see," said Gidron. "We will show you the cave next door." He guided them down the short corridor and ushered everyone through the entrance. Here they saw piles of old machinery cut into fragments so they could be squashed into the room. Some looked like the parts of gigantic flamethrowers, jagged and black with the remnants of fire and ash still embedded in them.

"Horrible old weapons. They've been used too and taken from the battlefield and put here as a lesson to mankind that they must never be made or used again."

He pointed towards a heap of old boxes, stuffed with wires, circuit boards and broken glass. "Old computers. Don't think they are a modern invention. The first visitors to earth had them and most of them were not very nice people – more like pirates wanting to plunder our lovely planet. Computers never did much good. They stifled our imagination and we lost our memories. They allowed people to expand too fast. Things got faster and faster until nature couldn't cope. Our brains are our best computers. The artificial ones are not necessary for our happiness. That's the main thing, isn't it Helion. To find happiness, and feel connected to our souls and with Erith. And learning to live in harmony with the companions that are sharing our earthly life. What more do we want? Simple, isn't it.

Do you find it difficult to believe that the first humans on our planet came from the stars? We weren't descended from the great apes as was thought, although man-like beings were beginning to make an appearance. They're all extinct now. The first people who visited Erith used their lambdas to find us. The best of them were wonderful and wanted to make, what was already one of the most beautiful planets in the galaxy, a paradise. They half succeeded. Most other visitors were robbers. They were greedy for the earth's minerals and from their genetic experiments they created a race of slaves with barely any brains. Don't think that genetic engineering is a new idea. Millions of these zombies worked in the mines. When they had no more use for them they exterminated them with those terrible weapons. The world was almost destroyed several times over as invaders fought each other for power over the earth. Only some escaped. Some fled underground like our ancestors did. Others lived on the tops of mountains to escape the floods. When will we ever learn? It would have been the same again this time, except that nature got there first. Now we have a few hundred years to recover. We hope. It's important that you children of Dryadogenes spread the word. Inject some reason and kindness into the minds of the survivors as well as your knowledge. But not the lambdas. Keep them secret. Too dangerous for ordinary people.

Don't think all the space people who settled Erith were bad. Some of the best were the Sirians and the Serpent people. They wanted to educate the primitive earthlings. They wanted to raise them out of beastliness so they could be proper humans and behave humanely. Their wisdom spread to the ancient Egyptians, the Sumerians, the Indians, the Hyperboreans, which was another name for the early Dryadians. All of that history is kept safe in this cave. There are other hidden places as well, which contain this knowledge so it can never be forgotten. There are no space visitors now. We are sometimes confused with them when we come up in our lambdas to forage but we come from below not above. After the Sirians and the Serpent people, other planets discovered the earth. They only wanted to exploit it. They didn't care for its beauty or for the welfare of the creation. The Sirians and their friends withdrew. They were not interested in confrontation or warfare. Their names were still honoured in some nations' histories especially that of Egypt. And don't we say 'as wise as a serpent'. The snake in The Garden of Eden was not evil. The story got twisted.

Did you know that the Sirians were known as 'The Gardeners' of the galaxy? They were creators, not destroyers. They didn't steal. They wanted to make our world even more beautiful. This is what we must do now. Become Erith's gardeners. Restore the earth to its original splendour. It's becoming old and tired after the way it has been treated. We need to heal it. Never underestimate the power of humans to heal the earth. It doesn't need us to survive but we can soothe its pain, which we created in the first place. And like a good gardener we can embellish it and make it more glorious still. We can make it our responsibility and make the earth sing again. No one will rescue us. We will have to do everything ourselves. What a challenge though. What a joy to work with the creation instead of against it.

We can choose to be lighter beings and the result will be that we will grow into happier ones. We have all the wisdom within ourselves to make that happen already – all of us. We have nothing else to teach you. Most of the knowledge that is stored in this cave is already planted in your hearts. I am so glad that we have met."

The conversations with the Tibetan sub-terraineans and the visit to their caves, and indeed the whole Dryadjani experience, had made a deep impression on the Dryadians. Never would they, or the Dryadjani who thought likewise, feel isolated again amidst the ignorance of the world. Although Sophora had mentioned it many times before, this confrontation with the world's terrible and violent past and the weapons of destruction that had actually been used in overwhelming genocide, made the Dryadians even more determined to do their bit to help raise the world's consciousness. Then it would be impossible for such things to happen again.

Over the next few years there was a constant exchange of peoples between the two countries until all the Elders of both kinds, and some villagers as well if they were interested, were familiar with both lands. The work in spreading the universal knowledge that both Dryadians and Dryadjani had lived by for thousands of years to all communities of the world continued. It speeded up enormously and exponentially after it was reckoned that over one percent of the world's population had taken this simple wisdom to their hearts. That number was considered the tipping point. After that the knowledge snowballed and the world started taking responsibility for its own actions, resulting in true freedom and happiness. People were becoming quintessentially Dryadian in spirit, even if they didn't recognise the word. But no country needed to sacrifice its own culture if was not harming the earth or other people.

The sub-terraineans were also playing their part. Although there were not many of them they came up to the surface more often, and continued with their work of calming down the nuclear hot spots. There were also places where plant and animal mutations had got out of hand due to radiation and genetic experiments. These problems would probably only be solved over centuries but at least the sub-terraineans had ensured that they were not getting any worse.

We have reached the year 2035 in the old Eastern calendar. The world has changed out of all recognition since the catastrophe. There is stability although the sea levels are rising. That is less of a problem now as small populations can move quickly. We have peace at last. We have learned not to forget our history – so we won't be doomed to repeat it. Nor will the world forget the wisdom that Dryadia has kept safe for so long. We will do our best to ensure that the light won't go out again. We believe that we now have hope for the future.

CHAPTER THIRTY-SIX

EPILOGUE

I am growing old now, although not so old that I can't still ride across Dryadia in a day and lambda travel to Dryadjani in an instant. I have to confess that I wrote Dryadia partly for my own enjoyment. But I also wanted to record my own story and the momentous events through which I have lived. One day Pushkin might even include it in yet another edition of 'The History'.

The year is now 6300 and it is the number of years that have passed since Dryadogenes reputedly founded our country. In the old Eastern calendar we are in the year 2052. Over fifty years ago Mary, Pushkin and I stepped off *The Leaky Bucket* and became Dryadia's first students from the East and apart from Ruth the first to attend the university course at Cantillion. It was an education that existed nowhere else in the world at the time. That first interview with Anaxamander changed our lives forever and although we did occasionally visit our childhood homes in the East we could no more return there anymore than an escaped prisoner could return to his jail. Our hearts were immersed in love with the Dryadian wisdom and the Dryadian way of life. This was not only because we became a part of it but also because it touched a door in our hearts that had long been ready to embrace the vibrant spirituality that Dryadia had to offer. Later we came to the view that this door existed in all peoples' hearts, whether they had heard of Dryadia or not. We believed that our simple way of living, based on equality, honesty and kindness, was one of the best ways to open it.

I am told that one of the reasons for writing an epilogue is to inform the reader of the fate of the story's main characters. My generation now provides the senior Traditional Eldership. Almost all our old teachers who were still alive when we discovered Dryadjani some twenty years ago are no more. Only Ruth, beloved matriarch that she is, lives on still pottering around her herb garden whenever the weather is fine. Anaxamander left us only recently and typical of him made a dramatic exit as he described the extraordinary light that drew him away from us, and the spirits of the already departed that waved him on. We all owe him a huge debt for his unforgettable exuberance that could light the darkest path in the forest. Gentle Zephyr and Amarinta, who took me into their home and became my adoptive parents, are also gone. Amarinta illustrated his 'Natural history of Dryadia' and I got involved with the writing of it too. Amarinta also drew psychically some of the pictures for Parmenides' History. Both she and Sophora managed to draw on their powers of clairvoyance to reveal some of the events of the past. Parmenides actually managed to finish the History before he died although he couldn't have managed without Pushkin's help. That leaves Sophora, Dryadia's greatest spiritual leader and seer since the days of Alanda and Isola. She formed a happy friendship with Helion much to everyone's joy and surprise and they regularly commuted between their two countries until their strength faded. We all wondered how we would manage without her wisdom but she taught us so well that her passing was relatively seamless. That is how it should be and it is to her eternal credit that it happened in the way it did.

All our generation are well, even though we are all in our seventies. Our children and grandchildren have all stayed near us in Ceradoc. There is a special friendship between our two, Piran and Damelza, and Mary and Pushkin's children Tolstoy, Emma and Sarah and their spouses, all of whom are now Traditional Elders.

Melissa and I are still working, healing and teaching. Mary and Tara have never stopped telling stories and Pushkin and Hermes are still writing and philosophising. Gradually our children and their generation are trying on our shoes and we are all pleased as to how well they fit. Dryadia has not changed much internally and we still like to think it remains a fountain of wisdom and an example of harmonious living. Ceradoc is no longer pre-eminent in this and I am glad to say that there are an equal number of wise Traditional Elders in all the thirteen provinces. Our country is now much more open to the outside world as it is no longer threatened. East and West are coming together and new little Dryadias are coming into being all over the world.

As expected the earth has grown warmer and sea levels have risen by several feet. Here in Ceradoc we have abandoned some of our houses close to the shoreline and re-built higher up. There is no longer any summer ice in the Arctic and the Greenland and Antarctic icecaps are melting as fast as ever. Our Dryadian summers are definitely a little warmer but are still very comfortable. Our winters, though normally mild, are still capable of giving us some intense freezing snaps or monsoon type rains from time to time. Then perhaps they always did. Other parts of the world are not so fortunate. In Europe people are moving north to escape the extreme heat of the Mediterranean summer. Fortunately there is now plenty of room.

It is wonderful to see the greening of Britain and Northern Europe as the trees swallow up the old ugly industrial landscape. Almost all the old roads, including the motorways have reverted to green lanes, if they are visible at all, and many of the old villages seem un-connected with each other. It is sad to see them and the old English country towns and cathedral cities crumbling away. We have noticed though that almost all the inhabitants that once lived in those industrialised bloated cities have moved away out of the ugliness into more rural settings so we hope that some of the old beautiful places will be saved and re-claimed. It is said that even the tallest skyscraper will collapse after a few hundred years. Let us hope that people will realise they will be more content when they build to human scale.

Oil is hard to extract since the expertise has gone. Very little is used now, and I think generally the world is happier without it. The industrial and chemical age is over. The world has slipped back four hundred years but without the poverty, ignorance or inequality. The animal and bird life of Britain is now as rich as that of Dryadia, as the main predator, man is so diminished in numbers. Most people no longer see nature as the enemy and pollution and chemical sprays are a thing of the past. The standard of living in the East is now as good as ours and we like to think that they are as happy as us too. Our way of the lambda seems to have paid off, although we keep the knowledge of the machines and how we fly them to ourselves. We do share the rest of our knowledge though and have set up many Cantillion type universities all over the world. The East can teach themselves now but we maintain contact, as we like to know what is going on.

We are still learning ourselves of course. The Dryadjani taught us how to use thought forms to make protective clouds. We have extended that idea to occasionally putting clouds around people or communities if they might wish others harm. It is like building a mental barrier against toxic thoughts before they become activated. We have extended our knowledge of lambda travel through further exploration in The Hall of Records. The Dryadjani have helped us and our science is now on a par with theirs. We are completely convinced that the power of the human mind and the universal forces of nature are limitless and utterly awesome. These powers have been used destructively in the past and if Dryadia has any purpose, then it is to ensure that to the best of our ability they will only be used wisely and kindly in the future. We want our world and the people who live on it to be light and loving, not heavy and violent. If we have succeeded in helping to change the hearts and thinking of the world and raise its consciousness we will be well pleased.

We, that is Melissa, Mary and Pushkin, Tara and Hermes and our age group, don't travel much now. We old dears are content in finding happiness in the slow rhythms of nature and the gentle rounds of family and village life. For the young it is different, as it always has been, where ever in the world they live. They need adventures, excitement and fresh challenges that channel their exuberance and latent creativity. In Dryadia of course we still have our annual race over the countryside by foot, horseback and water for those who want it. Most youngsters and in fact people of all ages participate, as it is a lot of fun and graded in difficulty. Others need more, and want unknown frontiers to explore. No one thankfully goes to war anymore; few are attracted by the excitement of a life of crime; and you can be on the other side of the world in a moment thanks to lambda travel. We do encourage young people though to put a pack on their back and travel overland to Dryadjani – just for the thrill of it. It can take six months and there are plenty of resthouses on the way. If they don't want to come back the hard way we can always send a lambda to pick them up.

Something else excites them, indeed excites us all. Ever since the Dryadjani explained about the gateways in the atmosphere and beyond, and how they linked up with the serpent lines that crossed space, we have wanted to see it all for ourselves. At first we Elders resisted the idea because we were not sure how easy it was to return to Erith. Eventually we held a moot to debate the matter. We agreed that since space travel was highly feasible, and that it had almost certainly taken place thousands of years ago on lambdas that were almost identical to those that we use today, we would go ahead. However we would proceed slowly and carefully. No lives were to be lost.

One of our imaginative grandsons Dryadogenes, although we call him Drodgy for short, has rigged up a small model of the earth in a sheltered part of his garden. From it extends many wires, and every now and then he has tied ribbons on to them, which he tells us mark gateways in space. I'm not at all sure how accurate it is but he tells us that he knows what he is doing and he is fairly sure that he has mapped a path to the moon although he is not yet sure about the return journey! It will be safer once the route and the gateways have been programmed into the lambda system. We had learned to do this before we went to Dryadjani, but I suspect quintessential space travel may be a bit more difficult than going round the world. But I do believe it is possible. The Sub-terraineans, the Dryadjani and our own dear Sophora, all insisted that our ancestors, who looked very like us apparently, originated from the stars or rather from planets that were not unlike our own. These planets are many light years away from Erith and therefore too far away to reach by ordinary means. So we are left to the obvious conclusion that space people arrived on their lambdas and that their technology was good enough to find us. We have now re-discovered the lambda way and if our forebears found us then we should be able to find them, or rather their descendants, wherever they may have come from.

Well it's happening already. Once the Elders at the moot had given the go-ahead, there was no stopping our potential explorers, and our Drodgy is amongst them. He has apprenticed himself to Tolstoy, Mary and Pushkin's eldest, and one of the leaders of this new revolution. Tolstoy confirms Drodgy's ideas and that at the very least lunar travel will soon be imminent.

The trouble about space travel as compared with earth travel is that obviously you cannot get out at the gateways to explore. Each gateway has to be located and tested from within the lambda itself just as we did when we travelled to Dryadjani. Even then we needed some assistance from the Dryadjani. That won't be available outside the confines of the earth although we think we can put some form of quintessential safety harness around the craft to ensure it stays on course and doesn't get lost in space. There are no limits to the power of the mind and heart, either in our thinking or found in our experiences so far. We can even draw oxygen, warmth and food from the ether and materialise them in the lambdas.

Our needs are packaged in thought bubbles and opened as necessary. We can also easily communicate with our friends back on Erith while we are away. Gradually we are turning these space gateways into invisible resthouses where we can stop, rematerialise and recuperate from the journey. We have created similar ethereal places on earth such as along the overland journey to Dryadjani. There are many of these bubbles available for the weary traveller along the road and they are never more than a day's ride apart. Our old proverb that wherever there is a Dryadian a barley cake cannot be far away has proved its worth in a way we would never have dreamed of thirty years ago.

We ask Drodgy where it's all going to end up and he says Venus and Sirius, both heavenly bodies that have strong traditions in our history. Impossible to reach of course through traditional means – Venus is too hot and Sirius too far away and not even in our galaxy. But our lambda way means that anything is possible. Our technicians are now building giant machines for these journeys and nothing can contain Drodgy's excitement. Being happy cultivating our garden, as Melissa and I do, is not for the likes of him.

We are now able to use the invisibility techniques that we learned from the Dryadjani. Although we have no need to hide our country under a cloud, the idea can be useful in concealing the lambdas from prying eyes. Melissa and I have a strange feeling that Drodgy sometimes hides one of the smaller lambdas (the only one he is allowed to pilot at the moment) at the bottom of our garden when he is too lazy to return it to its base on Sanctuary Hill. He is able do this, thanks to the development of fine instruments which have located a small gateway near the house. It is though only operative every fourth week around the time of the full moon.

We trust him and his friends. If we didn't there would be no chance of him becoming a Traditional Elder one-day. For now he is allowed his occasional indiscretions. He is only nineteen – about the same age that I was when I came to Dryadia for the first time. At the moment he is trying to impress his girlfriend Avena, who happens to be Mary and Pushkin's granddaughter and Tolstoy's niece. Tolstoy has located a gateway over 100.000 miles away about half way to the moon. He has already visited it along with Drodgy and Avena and a few others. The complete journey has just been programmed into the lambda system and therefore should be perfectly safe. It is proposed that all the Traditional Elders of Ceradoc set off next month in one of our biggest lambdas to have a picnic of all things at this gateway, and view the earth from space. The date is significant for it marks the anniversary of the Ceradoc Elders' first visit to Dryadjani. Many of the current Elders including Melissa and myself were part of that unforgettable journey of discovery. Melissa is not so keen on the new adventure. She was always a nervous traveller. She's coming round though. She says, as she occasionally does, that at least the whole family and all our friends will die together!

The great day has arrived. We're going to fly to the moon or at least half way. We will fly from The Sanctuary on Kantala Hill, a gateway for special occasions as we say, at the next full moon. Tolstoy says he has just done another trial run. Everything went perfectly although there were only a few of them on board. This next time there will be as many as sixty of us and a few of us are getting a bit doddery and there are small children too. What an education for them. Everyone wants to see the world from space. We'll see Dryadia too if it's not too cloudy. There's no wavering now. The bubbles are secure and the barley cakes packed or at least etherealised. The first part of the journey is simple – just a short walk winding our way up to The Sanctuary. The serpent energy spiralling up out of the gateway is extremely strong. Quintessentially strong, as Anaxamander used to say.

We are up at dawn. There are so many of us that we are must look like a serpent ourselves as we wend our way around and up the sacred hill towards the oracle. We decide not to tempt fate and consult it, but to trust the life force whatever it decides. We are all very quiet and thoughtful although on edge with excitement. Will we come back safely? Tolstoy obviously assures us that we will, but he has yet to make a complete stop in space on any of his previous journeys. It feels like a migration to the Promised Land.

Our lambda has recently been built, designed especially for space travel. It is a magnificent machine, sixty feet across and our biggest ever. It looks like an upturned coracle, its silver and pinkish green livery gleaming bright in the morning sunshine. It is elliptical and crowned with a flattened cupola. Fourteen small portholes are spread equally around its perimeter. It reminds me of the fourteen oak trees that enclose The Egg. The lambda looks light, frail even, and already seems not quite in the physical world. I wonder how we are all going to fit in as we troop through a door that opens upwards and outwards, rising silently like a gull's wing. The cabin is a surprise and is warm and inviting. It's walled in pine and the sixty or so seats are arranged in an oval around the two pilots' seats with their dials and instruments. It feels like a theatre in the round except that the passengers can also see out through the windows and by a trick of mirrors the ground below.

Tolstoy closes the door and takes his seat. Drodgy is allowed to sit beside him and pretend to be the co-pilot but is not allowed to touch anything except in the direst emergency. Tolstoy assures us that Drodgy would be able to cope well if such an event arose. We fall quiet and enter the deep silence that breathes through the whole universe. An overwhelming lightness of being enters our bodies and minds. We feel at one with our very souls and wait expectantly to loose ourselves in the quintessence. Out of the silence emerges the familiar hum. The hum moves up and down the scale as it seeks out the resonance of the spiral energy rising from the earth beneath our feet. It has a rhythm too – that familiar five time. We find ourselves humming along in the swelling chorus of sound while the lambda vibrates gently in unison. Then we watch Tolstoy flick the transpiration switch and we suddenly loose consciousness and are no longer aware of the physical world.

We awake to the sound of Drodgy and Avena calling our names softly as they walk around the cabin. It reminds me of the prince kissing the Sleeping Beauty back to life. How did they wake before us? I suppose it's because some of us older ones live in a semi-dream state anyway! Tolstoy stands up and with mock formality and a twinkle in his eye, announces:

"Ladies and Gentlemen. We are now positioned about one thousand miles above the earth's surface. Don't worry about what you learned at school that there was no warmth or oxygen. We've conjured up plenty of both from the infinite ether. Now look through the portholes and you will clearly see the curvature of the earth. Look more closely still and you will see our beloved Dryadia, like a green horn stretching out into the blue sea. There are no clouds. It must be as sunny as we left it this morning."

Tolstoy carries on in the same vein for a few more minutes. He is quite a wordsmith and so wasn't called Tolstoy for nothing. But he was right. We had never seen anything so unbelievably glorious. We must have spent an hour, gazing in rapture at this wonderful spinning globe that we know as Erith, and described in our histories as the most beautiful planet in the galaxy. Then Tolstoy sent us back to our seats for the second part of our journey.

After a period of quintessential oblivion we were awakened again by Avena and Drodgy's gentle voices. It's so nice to see the harmony that lies between them. We are now 100,000 miles from the earth and nearly half way to the moon. Through the inky blackness of space Erith shines blue, green and white.

It is so pure and beautiful, now it is free from the human tyrants who almost destroyed it and only saved by the catastrophe that destroyed them first. Looking the other way we see the moon shining in its own reflected glory, much bigger than we see it from earth. In this oasis of space the lambda hangs with its precious cargo of humans like a spider suspended in the centre of its web.

Time had lost all importance as we sit with our barley cakes and tea. We talk about our old friends thinking how much Sophora and Anaxamander and the others would have enjoyed it. Many of us older ones will not do this journey again. But we look around at our children and grandchildren with pride, and know that the spirit of Dryadia and the restored spirit of Erith flow strongly through their hearts. They will use their wisdom wisely. The beast in man will find it hard to rise up again if people like them are around. We all hope so, for we may not get another chance. Meantime Erith has time to convalesce and recover.

Our reveries and the excitement of our trip into space are interrupted by Tolstoy's strong voice. "We need to be back on Erith well before dark," he exclaimed. "Don't forget we've got to walk back to Ceradoc before the light fails."

It is a matter of moments before we are in and out of the quintessence and hovering above The Sanctuary. Tolstoy allows Drodgy to take the controls and guide the lambda to the ground and show off his landing skills to Avena. We are home at last. An hour later as the sun is setting over the western ocean we are recounting to Ruth, who had been too old to travel, the story of the day's incredible adventures.

"What bliss," she said. "You don't need to go into space to find it though. While you were away a robin flew into the kitchen. I held out my hand with a few crumbs and it sat on my finger. And do you know, he sang to me. A song especially for me."

33806873R00270

Made in the USA
Charleston, SC
24 September 2014